THE
FORGING
OF EVE

M.J. LINEHAM

First published in Great Britain in 2024 by
TIGER LILY PUBLISHING COMPANY
71-75 Shelton Street, London, WC2H 9JQ
www.tigerlilypublishing.co.uk

Paperback ISBN: 978-1-0686509-0-1
Ebook ISBN: 978-1-0686509-1-8

1

A CIP catalogue record for this title is available from the British Library.

Cover Designed by Fantastical Ink

Printed in the UK.

To Fong, my other half and greatest supporter.
To my grandparents, who always said I'd find my way.
To Amanda, my dear friend and first reader.
To Zoe and Shannon, for their time and trust in me,.
And to you, for journeying with Eve.

THE
FORGING
OF EVE

M.J. LINEHAM

Chapter One

In the land of Evergaune, peace reigned and Presence—
an organic, naturally formed magic—bettered the daily
lives of people. The age of s had passed, leaving those
who used to fight Evergaune's wars to become normal
civilians working new trades – teaching, crafting,
cooking, and more to help Evergaune and its various
cities and towns prosper. With the war behind them,
people have been enjoying this time of peace.

Eve worked as a bartender, serving customers and
keeping them in check when things got rowdy. With so
many former s struggling to follow a path outside of
fighting, there were regular outbursts of violence on
most nights, frustration and anger coming in waves as
people drank more and more. Tonight was another one
of those nights, and another brawl broke out, forcing
Eve to abandon her conversation with another customer
at the counter. She pinched the bridge of her nose and
sighed. If only they could hold their drink as well as they
cause a scene.

This was tonight's second fight and Eve was not
impressed. Tearing the two men apart, Eve quickly threw
them through the tavern's doors and onto the street.

"Oi!", a muffled shout cried out as one man spat dirt
from his mouth, having fallen face first onto the floor.

"Watch it!", shouted the other, the fight between the two men forgotten.

"If you're going to keep causing trouble, then you're not welcome here any longer!"

Irritated, Eve closed the doors behind her and warned the tavern against any further incidents, "if you're here for a bad idea of a good time, then go get your fix elsewhere, or you'll have me to answer to."

Walking back behind the bar, Eve left her warning lingering in the air, falling widely on deaf ears. Being a daily occurrence, only those close-by to the incident bothered to bat an eyelid at it.

Huffing to herself, Eve resumed cleaning glasses when someone barged through the tavern doors, almost knocking them clean from their hinges, causing some of the guests by the doors to spill their drinks. in shock.

"I see someone here doesn't know who they're messin' with."

Eve felt her eye twitch.

The man stomped through the crowd to Eve, pushing patrons out of his way, to where Eve stood cleaning the glasses, only her eyes raised towards him.

"Wanna explain to me the sorry state of my friends outside?"

She gently placed the glass down, not breaking eye contact.

"I didn't do anything. Your friend had too much to drink and picked a fight, and I tossed him out of here when it became clear that he wasn't going to cool off."

"Really, lady, you threw him out?" He sneered. Eve ignored his jibe.

"I don't tolerate threats or violence in this tavern, so please leave."

"What, lady, do you think you can make me leave?" He jeered again, smirking. Some watched with grins on their faces, whilst others averted their eyes and sipped from their drinks. A ripple of tension could be felt from table to table.

The brutish man spat inside the glass Eve had recently finished cleaning.

She sighed and slammed her fistcleaning cloth on the counter, walking around the bar and pulling herself up to his eye level, looking directly into the man's eyes. The man did not move from his spot, but he drew his head back, his smug smirk growing ever larger.

"I could brush off your insistence on calling me 'lady', but it's time for you to leave."

This time, everybody in the tavern was silent, in mixed anticipation and nerves as to what would happen next.

Eve grabbed the man's forearm and roughly steered him toward the tavern's doors.

"Hold up, I don't take someone hurting one of my men lightly, and you need to pay." He snatched Eve by her forearm, looking down at her.

Enough was enough. Eve activated her Presence. The familiar sensation of summoning fire warmed her, the bright flame not causing her to break a sweat. Condensation on nearby tankards broke into a streaming flow. The stamping of feet and yelling could be heard as some people ran for the door. The roaring and clapping of hands soared as those who remained grew excited. Those closer to the action wiped their arms across their foreheads from the heat. She scorched the man's forearm, causing him to utter a roar of pain, and he delivered a swift punch to Eve's stomach in retaliation.

Groaning lightly, Eve weathered the blow and quickly moved her hand to the man's shoulder to keep him in place, then used her free hand to lay a Flame-infused punch to his chest. With a yell, he barrelled out of the tavern doors, the doors finally swinging clean off their hinges to join him.

Eve winced and rubbed her neck. That would be coming out of her pay. Again.

Huffing to herself, Eve returned behind the counter to clean the once again dirty glass, as the rest of the patrons went back to enjoying their evenings, a breeze from the open doors shifting through the tavern.

This was just another night in Thorne's Tavern.

Eve rarely slept well, so it was no surprise to her when she woke up the next morning feeling unrested. Shielding her eyes from the intruding sunlight, and with a soft sigh, Eve shut off her alarm and got out of bed.

As a retired , Eve had chosen a life far from normalcy and was used to many things that would tire someone who had not vigorously trained their mind and body for the past decade. Though s were no longer needed, she tirelessly made the effort as a mercenary to keep her body in shape, and her mind sharp, proving to be a force to be reckoned with in this new era.

Retired s were still called into action every now and then, but not for war, and not as s. Instead, they were mercenaries, tasked with various missions ranging from escorting a person of interest, fighting off opportunistic bandits, and culling the surrounding forests to ensure that wolves – and other animals – do not make their way into residential towns and villages, such as Fallwood, where Eve resided. Sometimes, they could be out on a mission that could have lasted several days, even weeks, or required them to relocate permanently.

Today's mission was short and simple. It was Eve's turn to brave the Fool's Woods. As the quest to venture into Fool's Woods had not had any takers, she'd accepted it before it could grow into a problem.

Eve's battle gear consisted of her trusty scythe and dragon pistol, long, dark-brown boots, a plain-white t-shirt, a dark-green chest-length jacket, and black leather trousers with a brown leather satchel for her outdoor necessities. Eve had always enjoyed darker, earthy colours, which complimented her snow-white hair.

A scythe was not a common weapon among s, but for Eve, it fit her fighting style perfectly. Many disliked how long and unwieldy it could be when compared to more traditional weapons such as a swords or axes, but the long, curved blade meant that she could attack multiple opponents at once, whilst the length of the metal pole allowed her to keep enemies at bay, and when she had finished using it, it could be folded away, neat and compactly by her waist.

Fool's Woods was aptly named - unless you were competent and skilled at combat, then most wildlife would make short work of you. Even the environments were deadly, such as the vegetables you picked or the plants you brushed across. Understanding the threats of Fool's Wood was vital to survival.

Wolves had been getting dangerously close to Fallwood recently, and so former s were being sent into the woods often. Back in wartime, Eve was a well-regarded , but she retired shortly before s were no longer needed, having already taken up the path of being a mercenary. She was not present for the catalyst in ending the war, the fall of her homeland, Irone, which pushed the powers that be to set stricter punishments when conflicts arise. Be it out of fear or contentment, war quickly ended, but s lived to fight. Eve never had a stake in the war, but she wished to keep those close to her safe, and she became a revered who could hold her own against almost any threat, and so Eve was able to wipe out the pack of encroaching wolves without little trouble. It was easy work, but she struggled to say she enjoyed it. She turned away from the dead pack of wolves, their bodies strewn about in-between the densely packed trees.

Nature's creatures rarely posed a threat during wartime, mostly because they were actively and often hunted so s could camp peacefully, or they were killed for sustenance. They could simply have been caught in the crossfire, and eventually animals realised that they had to stay away from humans as they posed a threat that they could not possibly overcome. With the war's end, however, these animals began to reclaim forests and the like for their own, and quickly grew in numbers.

Eve was not entirely content with her daily life, but she had accepted that tedium also brings peace. However, old habits die hard, and Eve could not change who she was, leading to her being at Fallwood in an attempt to protect its inhabitants who have never experienced war on the front lines.

After arriving back at Fallwood, the sun hanging low in the sky, Eve was met with jeering.

One man yelled, "there she is! There's that bitch that scorched me!"

Eve was not unfamiliar with the taunts of men, especially the drunkards and thugs who visited Thorne's Tavern, and so she ignored it, not sparing them a glance as she passed.

"Look at me when I'm talking to you!"

"Yeah, or you'll regret it!" One man shook his fist, and Eve rolled her eyes.

The provocations from the man and his friends were tiring, and soon she was out of earshot, and they were out of mind.

After working another night at the tavern, Eve managed to doze off at home with another regular day, much like all the others, put behind her.

The smell of smoke and sounds of screaming broke the calm of the night, and Eve's heightened senses told her that something bad was happening, instantly setting her on high alert as she bolted out of bed.

Being wise against rushing, Eve equipped all that she might need and headed to the centre of Fallwood in her battle gear. She was shocked to see Thorne's Tavern, alight with flame, indistinguishable from the building that it was only a few hours ago.

A booming laugh came from one of the group. "Burn it to the ground!" A group of men shouted in delight as they threw wood onto the raging inferno, the fire casting long and distorted shadows reflecting the demons that Eve could see.

It was those bloody brutes again.

Eve stormed over to confront them. She might not have been overly fond of the place, but it, and its people, did not deserve this.

"Hey!" Eve's yell did not startle the men, "what do you think you're doing?!"

One man clapped his hands together as he threw more wood at the wreck, "here she is, the wretch! I told you that burning down her dear tavern would work a treat!" The men laughed loudly, their raucous roars echoing in the night.

Eve glanced again at the wreckage. It was unsalvageable. A concoction of anger, hate and grief twisted her stomach.

The wreckage and scared screams as people began seeing the destruction were enough for her to take immediate action, rather than trying to diffuse the situation in another way. Dashing forward, her combat scythe still packed away by her waist, Eve grabbed the closest man, and with a throw propelled by an explosive, controlled burst of her Presence, Flame, launched him down the street. His cry was cut short, his impact with a thick, wooden column knocking him unconscious.

"I just want to do my job in peace," Eve shouted with desperation in her voice, now regretting having come to Fallwood at all, "why is that so hard to understand?!" Her pleas fell on deaf ears, a tinge of guilt tightening a knot in her stomach.

"You'll be joining this tavern—and whoever is in it— real soon, Evie." The men threw more wood to fuel the fire and turned towards her. They charged at her with their fists raised, and Eve countered each of them with ease, their attacks were sloppy, showing her that the tavern only fell simply because it could not defend itself.

"God, I hate it when people call me Evie, you arsehole!"

Eve drew her dragon pistol and a handful of hollow pellets. She squeezed them in her hand, her Flame burned bright, then she popped them into the gun. She fired the pellets, now infused with Flame, at the remaining three men. They exploded on contact, causing the men to yelp in anguish as they hurried to put the small flames out.

"That's enough," said one man, frantic, "I'm not sure we can take her!"

"If you're scared, then you're useless!" A second man unleashed his Presence and swiftly killed his "friend" with a bolt of lightning, Spark, direct from his hand.

This act of brutality shocked Eve, "you monster, don't you dare treat lives so lightly!" Eve unsheathed her scythe, the roaring fire illuminating its sharp blade.

"Oh ho, here we go," taunted the man, "I've always wanted to face off against the legendary Evie!"

Shaking off her annoyance at being called Evie, Eve dashed toward the large man.

"Today's your unlucky day then," Eve pulled her scythe back, "because the likes of you stand no chance!"

She swung her weapon forward and up from the ground, summoning a controlled wave of Flame directly at her opponent. The man took the full brunt of the Flame and attempted to quell the growing fire quickly spreading across his body, his cries muffled as the Flame consumed him.

Eve grimaced and looked away from the man's suffering.

The man continued rolling in the grass and frantically patting himself down, but it was already too late for him to recover. His last remaining ally ran off during the battle.

Eve began walking away when the man weakly spoke to her, "there are people out there who really want you dead, Evie, you know that?" She did know that. If this man knew, then it was no secret.

"But who? Who is it that wants me dead?" Many may have wanted her dead, but there were not many who could make it happen, and fewer who could convince someone to take on the fool's errand in their place. Whoever put this man to the task must have known that it would end in their failure, and sent in him and his group ill-prepared.

"Who could say..." His laughter grew faint, interspersed with several dry coughs, until it stopped completely with one last raspy breath.

"Damn it..." Eve shook her head and retracted her scythe.

After a brief, wistful look at the smouldering remains of the tavern, Eve returned home to collect her belongings, her mind made up. She could not stay here any longer.

Shortly after gathering her small number of possessions, Eve left hoping not to see anybody, not wanting to see the guilty faces that her being at Fallwood had brought. She avoided the main street and trod light steps behind a row of houses, all mostly vacated as the townspeople gathered outside, talking about what transpired. She snuck by unnoticed, breathing a sigh of relief as she left through the entrance to town.

"Are you leaving us, Eve?" Eve stopped, having not seen a slightly older woman cradling her child on the side of the path. The child was fast asleep in her arms.

"Yes, Renee, I don't want to bring any more trouble to Fallwood." She looked back at town, the smoke still billowing thickly.

The woman nodded, not offering any argument like Eve was expecting. "I wanted to get this one away from the smoke." She stroked the child's head. "But know that you always have a home back here, okay?"

She lightly took the hand of her infant son and softly waved it in Eve's direction. "This one will miss you too, you know?"

Eve felt her eyes prickling. "I know. I'll miss him too. Tell him to eat his vegetables, okay?"

The mother laughed, "will do. Take care of yourself, Eve."

"You too, Renee."

Eve turned and walked away without looking back.

Leaving Fallwood behind, Eve journeyed toward the neighbouring city of Thous in the hope that maybe, just maybe, she would not get into trouble there. With Thous a few days away by foot, and only a minute number of rations brought from Fallwood, Eve knew that she'd have to hunt for sustenance as she journeyed through Fool's Woods once more.

Trudging her way through Fool's Woods, the first rays of sunlight beginning to break through the thicket, Eve thought about the relatively peaceful life she had once again been forced to leave behind. She thought about the kind-hearted owner of Thorne's Tavern and its sometimes-odd clientele, the market stall owners, the people who wished her well and to return home safe as she set off on missions. What twisted luck.

Brushing aside tangled low-hanging branches, and crushing leaves and twigs underfoot, Eve trekked through the dark overgrowth of Fool's Woods. It was easy to become lost or fall victim to the claustrophobic nature of the close-knit trees, and easier still to be surprised by any of the wood's dangerous wildlife. As Eve had recently been through to slay some wolves though, there were far less dangers now than there would have been had she not.

Chapter Two

Eve had been travelling for two and a half days. She should have been able to reach Thous in no more than twenty-four hours. The hooting of owls and chirping of insects had been her only company, and she had all but run out of the few rations she had brought. The food she could manage without, but the water was a different problem, but then, she heard it. The subtle trickling of a stream not too far from the path where she walked. A few minutes later in the direction of the running water, she reached a clearing. It sat in a faint, golden glow, the greenery bathing in the warmth of the sun. Sitting by a jagged stump with a relieved sigh, Eve was able to rest.

She let out a heavy sigh and looked towards the sky. This would be as good of a spot than any to sleep tonight.

Eve searched the surrounding area of the clearing, both for threat and for food, and came across a deer lying down in a nearby brush. It's body was twitching.

Taking gentler steps as she approached the deer, she noticed it was fatally wounded. Its rear legs were broken beyond repair, its body entangled in vines and dirt. Fool's Woods was not fit for any living creature.

"I'm sorry, little one…" Kneeling down next to the whimpering deer, Eve gently stroked its small head as she rested it in her hand, its breathing beginning to relax as she did so. Knowing that she would be unable to do anything for it other than put it to rest, Eve landed a swift blow to the young deer's head with her small hunting knife, using her free hand.

Its breathing, once rapid, ceased in seconds.

Eve began guiltily carving the deer for its meat, and fur, knowing that she might be able to sell it when she arrived in Thous, especially with no guaranteed work when she got there. She stood and patted the dirt from her legs. She was a few feet away when she stopped and looked back at the brush where she left the deer. She walked back and started to dig a hole for the small animal. With the deer buried, she slapped her hands together, ridding herself of the excess dirt.

"Thanks," said Eve, staring down at the makeshift grave for the deer, a mound of unsettled dirt and moss.

Eve returned to her clearing for the evening and lit a campfire to cook the deer meat over. Twisting and turning, Eve stared at the meat, her chin in her hand, waiting for the food to be ready.

As the campfire continued to crackle after Eve had eaten, she found herself alone with her thoughts. So little went right, every time.

Tossing more wood onto the campfire, Eve recalled fond memories of Fallwood. She might have run into her fair share of problems there, but it had treated her well—for the most part, at least. The residents were generally nice to her, but her being there put them all in danger. They did not care for Eve's past and, relying on their kindness, Eve thought that, maybe, she would not have to care about her past either. Were they frightened of her? Were they glad she had left?

Staring at the stars in the night sky, Eve sighed before returning her gaze to the fire, prodding at the flames to keep them burning.

"It's only forward from here, hey, Eve?" Eve said to herself, her hollow laugh blending with the crackling firewood.

*

The sun broke in a new dawn, sunlight dripping from the leaves above. Eve checked herself over to ensure all her valuables were on her person, and then she set out for Thous, hoping that she might be able to settle there for a while. Perhaps even for good.

Several hours later she could see the outline of Thous from a distance, its large stone walls loomed high into the sky, and its thick steel gates towered and denied access to anyone without permission. Some of the tips of the taller buildings could be seen, weathered and tired when compared to the nearly pristine walls. She approached the flat, wide, cobbled bridge and took her first steps into what could be her new home, and Eve was filled with a sense of forlorn hope.

They say good comes to those who wait, but did that apply to all people equally? Was it only for the traditionally good? Was time enough to make up for any wrongdoing? Taking a deep breath, Eve approached the guards standing at each side of the gate.

"Good morning," she smiled at both guards in turn, "will you allow me passage into Thous?"

The guards looked Eve over with raised eyebrows, suspicion clear upon their features. With a sneer, one guard spoke, "That depends. What good will you be for Thous?"

"I'm a skilled former , and I'm more than able to earn my keep," Eve placed a hand on her folded scythe, "maybe you'd care to test my skills out for yourselves?"

Their eyes widened as her intention dawned on their faces, the guards quickly signalled for the gatekeeper above to lift the gate.

"Thank you."

Having made her way into Thous with little issue, and with so little belongings to find an immediate home for, Eve wandered around soaking in the sights. She rarely allowed herself to relax, and when she did, she questioned if she had the right to do so. Sometimes the scenery flooded her mind with nothing but peaceful serenity, and she was grateful for it. As a , she learnt to appreciate any given moment of downtime, and appreciate the beauty around her. At any point it could be her last time to do so.

The hustle and bustle of the local marketplace, came alive each day at sunrise and was replaced by vibrant nightlife in the evening, with peddlers trying to pawn off illegal goods down the shadier alleyways, and hopefuls hoping for a little more than a potent potion to add to their inventory prowling the streets. Right now, the scent of fresh, warm bread, flowers, and paper and ink filled Eve's nostrils, causing her muscles to loosen up in Thous' ordinary main street as she soaked it all in.

After peering at each of the colourful stalls and wondering what she would like to pick up once she landed herself a job, Eve took to the market board to search for any job vacancies. While she was a skilled bartender, she preferred playing to her strengths as a former . It generally paid better, too.

There were several jobs along the lines of being an assistant at stalls and stores, or tutoring students, but the one that caught Eve's attention was for a local mercenary group known as the Marauders of Light. Eve found the name to be a little tacky, but it was enough to satiate her interest. The notice stated that the group's leader, a woman known as Scarlett, also ran the Marauder's stalls, and to seek her out if you wanted to know more about it.

"Scarlett, huh." Eve made a mental note of the name and took off, hoping she wouldn't be hard to find.

Back among the stalls, Eve's eyes were drawn to a woman - more specifically her deep red hair - who was leaning over the front of her stall, attempting to grab the attention of potential customers. The owner makes eye contact with Eve and breaks out into a huge smile, "hello, looking for something to eat?" Her smile was dazzling.

"Ah, no, thank you, I'm actually looking for someone."

"Maybe I can help?" The woman throws a thumb over her shoulder, "over food?"

Eve groaned, but her stomach betrayed her with an audible rumble. "Sure, food sounds good."

Swiftly walking over to the stall, it was impossible to not note the deep red of the woman's long hair, tied into a ponytail down her back. It perfectly matched her equally intense eyes.

"I'm Scarlett, and I don't think I've seen you 'round here before."

Eve's eyes widened, amazed that Scarlett found her instead. "You're actually the person I'm looking for, I heard you've got work available?" Eve took a seat at one of the three stools available, and asked for a mixed vegetable skewer.

Scarlett glanced over as she prepared Eve's food, "done mercenary work before?"

As Eve was about to respond, Scarlett cut her off, "never mind, you don't see someone with a scythe very often."

Despite her scythe being folded and packed away, Scarlett managed to spot exactly what it was.

"Well, that's more like it." Scarlett grinned and walked around the front of the stall. "It's hard to find good help 'round here." She handed a skewer over to Eve before continuing, "we take on missions to cull the numbers of the growing wildlife, bandits, etcetera, so that they don't attack travellers and citizens, as well as use the meat to sell here at the stall. You could say that there's a fair bit of money coming through the group, but I wouldn't think about making off with it." Scarlett smiled again, but the glint in her eye betrayed the good nature of her tone.

Not fazed by her threat, Eve continued, "I'm in. When can I get to work?"

"Not so fast, Eve." Scarlett pulled a clean knife out from underneath the counter, and laid out a white cloth over an empty part of the stall. "I like to play a game with people first, before taking them on."

"A game?" Eve eyed the knife, a faint memory tugging at the back of her mind.

"Have you played 'finger grips' before?"

The memory slipped away from Eve. "No, I've not heard of that before."

"Okay, it's easy, lay your hand down here," Eve did as she said, and Scarlett did the same, their hands intertwined just enough for their fingertips to be side by side. "Easy does it, but now for the hard part. We're both going to take turns with this here knife, and we're going to stab it as fast as we can in the gaps between our fingers."

Eve frowned, "it was called 'finger tips' when I was a child, but we used a stick instead."

Scarlett laughed, "we're in the big leagues now, so are you in?"

Eve nodded, and Scarlett flipped the knife and held the handle out, "then you're first. 30 seconds and you're done."

With a deep breath, Eve began slotting the knife in the gaps, counting the numbers down in her head. The environment around her faded to silence, and her heartbeat filled her ears.

"Very good, not a scratch on me." The time was up, and Eve flipped the knife back to Scarlett, and they played again.

"Ouch! How embarrassing…" Scarlett managed to cut her index finger toward the end. "Well, I found out what I wanted to."

Eve asked if Scarlett was okay, which Scarlett assured that she was, before she asked what she meant.

"In doing that, I know I can trust you. Most people simply say no and leave, and fewer do it with the hands left intact."

"I see. So what's ne–" Eve was cut off by a booming and jovial voice.

"Again, Scarlett? Why don't you pick a game you're good at?" The man was short but muscular, his arms bare and endowed with a bushy brown beard.

"Oh, get off it, Barron. You know I enjoy it." She sucked on the side of her finger where she injured it, before wrapping it in the cloth they were using. "This is Barron, who is next on shift. He's a mean cook, but come with me, I don't think my heart could take it if you tried his cooking so soon after my own." She laughed and waved to Barron, who was tying an apron around his back.

"Good to meet ya, uh…" He squinted, and Scarlett introduced Eve. They shook hands, "I look forward to working with ya."

"Likewise." Eve smiled.

They walked down the path and past the stalls. There was no break in the noise as they moved from one crowded place to another. "I guess you look like you can handle yourself, after all." Scarlett said, again with a wide grin. They stopped at the doors of a large building, its large brown doors swung back and forth constantly. "This here is Willkeep's Tavern, come here later tonight. That's where the group meets to go over upcoming missions and distribute tasks. We'll have something for you there."

Thanking her for the opportunity, Eve bid Scarlett goodbye and went off in search of a local inn.

Chapter Three

Eve looked out from her inn's bedroom window, the last remnants of the sun's rays trickling across the neighbouring rooftops. It was getting dark out by the time Eve left the inn for Willkeep's Tavern. Of course, she did not leave any of her belongings behind, leaving her room looking as if it was never occupied at all. She thought back to just a few days earlier, and the thought of losing her only worldly possessions to a fire was one she did not want to chance.

The clinking of tankards and the general ambience of the tavern spilled out onto the street, with groups of people hanging around the entrance, laughing and stumbling around. Eve bristled, and she was briefly transported back to Thorne's Tavern and the thought of it in a smouldering wreck. She drove those thoughts from her head and started to make her way through the crowd. Eve was almost through the open doors when someone sloppily grasped her shoulder.

"What does a pretty face like you want in a place like this, huh?" His words slurred as he giggled drunkenly.

As Eve opened her mouth to respond, a voice shouted from inside, "she's with us!"

The man immediately removed his hand and scrambled to apologise.

Taken aback by how quickly the man sobered up, Eve nodded and followed the voice to the back of the room, leaving the man looking on high alert outside.

Tables all around Eve were filled with laughter. People played cards cards and talked while further drinking themselves into a stupor. Scarlett's team appeared by far the most sober group present, although they were not without their own drinks in hand.

"And here she is now," announced Scarlett, waving a hand towards Eve, "our next hopeful to ask after our merry band!"

Eve was still unsure about joining the group, but she understood that making an effort with them off of the battlefield could be almost as important as the relationship when on it.

"It's a pleasure to meet you all," making eye contact with the several members dotted around the cracked, stained wooden table, Eve made quick mental notes of their appearances, "you can call me Eve."

Scarlett stood to shake Eve's hand and to introduce her to the others. "Drake here is my second-in- command, although we're such a small group that rank doesn't carry too much meaning to us." Drake wore a proud expression as he stepped up to shake hands with Eve, and with a quick "pleased to make your acquaintance", and then he sat back among the group, hand resting on the hilt of his sword. The scars crossing his rugged yet handsome sun-kissed features told stories of the past battles he'd seen, complimenting his muscular build along with his brown hair, cropped short to keep out of his face. Eve was not sure if she felt he was arrogant or confident, but did not have much time to think on it as the next member of the team was up.

Continuing on, Scarlett next introduced the short and stout Barron with his fiery, bright orange hair, giant axe and brown leather armour. He was immediately welcoming and familiar with her, and Eve could not help but feel taken in as if the man's joy and loudness was terribly infectious. He took her by the hand and shook hard twice, and she returned it in kind. Barron laughed and Eve grinned. "Hang around long enough, and maybe I'll treat you to a meal as the team's cook!"

Next was Clarissa, boasting wavy, waist-length black hair, a bottle green dress and a plain matching poncho that mimicked her eyes, brown boots, and a pair of shiny silver daggers at her sides. "It's a pleasure to meet you, Eve." Her hand felt soft as their hands made contact, and Clarissa gave one, gentle shake before letting go. She did not give Eve much to go off, but the way she shook hands indicated to Eve that she might be a gentle soul.

Finally, Eve was introduced to Scarlett's sister, Amie, who bore similarly deep-red hair—although she kept hers cut slightly shorter with tips that ended in curls—pale features, and a rapier at her waist as her chosen weapon. As she approached, she asked if Eve was "more of a handshake or a hug sort of girl", to which Eve responded with the former. Amie enthusiastically grabbed her hand but barely made any movement, and it stayed that way until she let go. She beamed at Eve. Eve was not sure how best to handle someone so jubilant, but noted that she came across as softer and bubbly when compared to her spunky and straight-forward sibling.

Maybe things here won't be so bad, Eve thought to herself, pleased that the group was smaller than she had expected. Faces from her previous guild pop up in her mind, and she felt some comfort in knowing that this guild was similar in number.

Having divided up the work between them, Eve found herself paired with Scarlett on a mission to slay a werewolf which had taken unwanted residence in a nearby forest, along with countless lives. None of the team had come up against them before, but the few former s who lived to tell the tale of their encounters were deeply shaken and did not dare set foot into Ember

Woods again. Many had been reported as having returned covered in slashes and deep gouges, shaken by their experience and unable to adequately describe the fear set deep within them, so Eve turned in for the night to ensure she was rested for tomorrow. She bid them all goodnight and left for the inn.

The Marauders of Light watched as the door closed behind her, and Barron spoke up first, "she seems nice."

"I thought she seemed quite quiet." Responded Clarissa, and Drake agreed.

"Give her a break, meeting people for the first time is hard!" Amie spoke up, and then agreed with Barron, "I think she seemed nice enough."

"She passed the test, so I'm happy with her." Amie looked toward Scarlett, "what test?"

"Come on Amie, finger grips, the same as always." Scarlett rolled her eyes.

"Well, I never do it with them, do I?" Amie huffed, then smirked, "did she win?"

Scarlett averted her eyes and bit her tongue before responding, "that's neither here nor there, really."

"It's both here and there!" Amie threw her hands out wide, "Ouuh, that must be so embarrassing for my big sister."

"Oh, shut it."

Everyone around the table laughed at the sister's exchange, seemingly happy with their new recruit-to-be.

Meeting up early the following morning, Eve met with Scarlett at the entrance to the inn she was staying at. The latter was waiting with arms folded across her chest.

"Hey stranger, shall we get going?"

Patting herself down to ensure she had all she needed, Eve and Scarlett headed toward Ember Woods, making small talk along the way.

There was a crisp chill in the air as vendors were still in process of setting up the marketplace for the day. Once they passed, their footsteps sounded louder, clacking across the cobblestones, without the natural hustle and bustle of Thous as they neared the gates, where the only other people were the gatekeeper and two guards. Scarlett started explaining the mission as they were granted exit to the outside.

"Scarlett, what do you know about werewolves?" Eve questioned, wanting to see what her partner might have already known.

"The basics," Scarlett replied, "they're humans transformed into a beast, and their wild hunger causes them to be aggressive and unpredictable. I've never fought one before, but I'm confident that we can take it down."

"It would be nice if they could become human again, wouldn't it?"

"I agree," Scarlett trailed off, lost in thought, "it certainly is a nice thought, if nothing else."

The two walked in near silence for roughly an hour until they found themselves at the border of Ember Woods, with its tangled knots of branches, thorny bushes, and a looming darkness spared only by small rays of light breaking through the leaves of abundant trees.

With a small nod between them, Eve and Scarlett took a synchronised step into Ember Woods.

Despite the pair's thorough search, there was no trace of a werewolf's presence, only markings and trails left by other smaller creatures. In the darkness of the woods, it is hard to say how much of it they had covered. Only someone unprepared would neglect to leave a trail to avoid becoming lost. Tying a red thread around a number of tree trunks, Eve ensured that the two would be able to find their way out.

"Hmm, that reminds me of something," exclaimed Scarlett as she watched Eve finish tying her knot, "but I can't quite place it."

"It's just from a children's story," Eve responded, "it's something I used to read and pore over as a child. Who knew that such a simple childhood story could prove to be so useful as an adult."

Shortly after tying another thread around a tree, much deeper in the forest, the two finally started to notice bloodstained grass and smaller animal carcasses. Pressing her fingers to one of the animal's flanks, Scarlett noted, "it's still warm. These creatures were killed recently."

A brief rustling in the bushes nearby was all Eve needed to trust Scarlett's assessment, and she quickly unfolded her scythe. A harsh snarling sounds from the bush and is soon accompanied by a giant ball of gnashing teeth then fur and claws as the wolf collides with the pole of Eve's scythe, sending her tumbling back.

Scarlett jumped to Eve's assistance in the space of her next breath, shooting with her two dragon Pistols loaded with silver bullets. The wolf deflected the bullets with its claws, their shattered shells landing with dull impact into the dirt and bark behind.

"W-what?!" Scarlett was stunned. there could only be one explanation. All the people who have attempted to kill this werewolf never came back. The werewolf has been learning from its multiple battles, and adapted in its on-going fight for survival.

"This is going to be tougher than we thought..." With a grunt, Eve pushed the werewolf back with the shaft of her scythe and followed by a slash toward it.

She missed, the werewolf proving to be deftly swift, but it had given her some breathing room.

Scarlett holstered her dragon pistols and withdrew her sabre. "I guess we're going to be getting up close and personal with this one!"

She twirled to the werewolf's side and slashed, skimming the topmost layer of its skin and fur. With a growl, the werewolf quickly retaliated with its claws, and with them mere centimetres from Scarlett's face, she nimbly stepped back into range, and slashed again, this time scoring a deeper gash along its chest. The beast howled as blood stained its dark grey fur red.

Not one to allow this to become a solo job, Eve charged forth and hooked her scythe into the werewolf's shoulder. the werewolf lashed out against the person closest to it, which was Scarlett. Armed with a weapon not quite as sturdy as a scythe, Scarlett was quickly knocked down and forced to do all she could to defend herself from the snapping and snarling of the werewolf, her sabre raised above her face, unable to attack.

"E-Eve!" Scarlett cried out, panic in her voice.

Eve pulled back her scythe from the beast's shoulder, swung again and plunged it deep into its back. with a deeper push, she began heating up the scythe with her Presence, causing the werewolf to wail in agony.

Albeit weakened and in shock, Scarlett pushed the werewolf off of her and onto its back, where she quickly climbed on top and stabbed it repeatedly in the torso with heavy piercings of her sabre. Its resistance faltered as its body spasmed and convulsed, long limbs scraping large clumps of dirt from the floor before it dropped limp. Scarlett rolled away from its body and rested on the floor, panting. "That was far too close for my liking."

Taking a seat beside her, Eve observed the blood streaming from Scarlett's forearm where the werewolf managed to make contact during its merciless assault on her.

"You're bleeding. Hold on, I'll bandage this and we can get you proper treatment when we're back in Thous."

Scarlett sat up with the help of Eve, "thanks, Evie."

Eve's skin prickled and she looked away, "please don't call me that."

"Why not?"

"I just don't like it."

Without missing a beat, Scarlett apologised. "Okay, I'm sorry."

Following a brief silence as Eve focused on cleaning Scarlett's wound the best she could, she replied "It's okay."

Further silence followed as Eve finished wrapping and tightening a bandage dressing before Eve helped Scarlett to her feet.

"So, your Presence is Flame?"

"Yes, although it wouldn't be my first choice. I guess it's good for lighting campfires." Eve let out a single laugh.

Scarlett held up her good arm and electricity crackled around it. "I've always been fond of my Spark, although it makes armour a pain in the arse."

"Good thing leather is in fashion, huh?" Eve joked.

Scarlett smiled and shrugged, "let's head back, shall we, Eve?"

Using the threads from earlier, Eve led them both back to Thous, worrying about the intelligence that the werewolf had shown in battle.

Back at Thous, Scarlett visited a medical professional to have her wound properly treated. It would likely scar, but there would be no long-lasting damage. They then headed to Willkeep's Tavern to meet up with the rest of the Marauders of Light. Eve scrunched her nose. She still did not really like the team's name.

Amie, Drake, Clarissa, and Barron were already there, having finished their missions earlier. As Scarlett often had her forearms on show, it became obvious to the rest of the crew what had happened, and they were quick to say some less than pleasant things about the slain werewolf. Thankfully, their missions went off without a hitch, though Barron did hear something of interest.

"Sounds like former s still can't keep themselves to themselves," he said, stroking his beard, "a fire broke out in a little village in the South, leaving a fair few dead."

Eve felt her stomach drop, a chill running through her body, imagining how dense the bloodshed could be between former s.

"Yes," Amie's clear voice piped up,, "it's not unheard of, but it's not unusual either."

Barron watched her as she patted Eve on the back, his eyes narrowed as he patted his beard. "Hmm, I guess so. .."

"But do you know what isn't unusual, Barron?"

"Oh?" His suspicion vanished, replaced by a cocked eyebrow. "What is it?"

"That I'm darn hungry, so let's go get some food!" Amie pointed toward the counter. Barron followed her gaze and nodded.

"Now that's a battle I can get behind!"

Amie stepped away from Eve to make her way to the counter to place an order, Barron close behind her.

A murmur of agreement rippled across the group, and the rest followed to do the same.

With no missions planned the following day, Amie offered to show Eve around Thous. Seeing it as a good opportunity to learn more about the group and her new home, Eve gratefully accepted.

Having had a light snack of some meat skewers from the market, the two were making their way to a smaller, quieter tavern away from the city centre at Amie's recommendation. This tavern didn't appeal to those who want a heavy night of drinking, nor did it attract the attention of mercenary groups due to its position away from the main road, making it the perfect place to speak without distraction.

The tavern appeared normal on the outside – primarily brown, with slits of faded blue wood creating the walls – but on the inside it homed a cosy ambience, with an always burning fireplace, burgundy, brown and yellow furniture and cushions, flickering lanterns, and natural sunlight pouring in through the windows, spreading warmth throughout the tavern.

It was very cosy. Eve liked it.

A bell rang cheerfully as Amie led the way in, and the pair were cheerfully greeted by an older man behind the counter, sporting a toothy grin. "Morning! Make yourselves at home."

Eve was not one to "make herself at home" anywhere, but here, she was happy to sit at one of the tables closer to the fireplace, with its padded, wooden chairs and red velvet tablecloth. In the centre of the table sat a lit candle in a glass holder, casting playful shadows as the flame danced. Each table had a different colour tablecloth and design, but still managed to fit in with the homely feel of the tavern.

"So, Eve, this is Humbone's Tavern. It's a little quieter compared to Willkeep's Tavern, but that's why I like it!" Amie explained, with a smile on her face, taking a seat opposite Eve.

"It's nice. I can see why you like it," Eve agreed, "thanks for bringing me here."

"I just thought it would be good to, y'know, get to know each other a little bit."

They both ordered coffee. Eve noted that they both ordered the same kind. She was not a black coffee drinker? That made a nice change.

"It would," Eve admitted, "would you mind telling me more about the Marauders of Light? How did, uh, that name come about?"

Amie laughed, crossing one leg over the other and rested her elbow on the table "well, you see, we're not the biggest mercenary group out there. We're talented, but in numbers, we pale compared to the likes of countless other mercenary groups out there. They're so large and can tackle so many missions at once, but we wanted to keep it small. That's just personal preference between me and my sister, we view our group as something of a family. That's why we tend to go for smaller jobs, such as gathering items or slaying nearby monsters."

Eve nodded in understanding as Amie continued. The latter stirred her coffee again before taking a small sip. Her nose twitched slightly.

"So, we wanted to have a name that could inspire hope. It's not subtle, and it's not ordinary, but the Marauders of Light does more than what I mentioned earlier. We also help those in need, even if it isn't something we get paid for. We have to put some good out into this world, right?" Amie added some extra sugar and stirred her coffee before speaking again, "what's your reason for being in Thous, Eve?" She smacked her lips and sighed happily.

Eve chewed the inside of her cheek, absent-mindedly stirring a second spoonful of sugar in her own coffee while she mulled over her answer.

"It's complicated. I lived in Fallwood until recently, but having exhausted venues of work there, I decided to come here instead, to Thous." Eve gazed out of the window, hoping that explanation would be enough to satiate Amie's interest. She felt relieved that Amie didn't ask any follow-up questions.

"Well, it's good to have you aboard. I know you've been welcomed already, but allow me to welcome you once again to the Marauders of Light, Eve." She smiled again, softly, with her chin resting on her hand.

Eve returned the smile and thanked her.

Having bid farewell to Amie a few hours later after a brief tour of the necessities, such as the blacksmiths and chemists, Eve explored the city in search of something to eat. The sun was beginning to set as early evening rolled in, delicious scents unavoidable as cooks served hungry patrons looking to fill their bellies. Hoping that she could find something to take back to her room, Eve strolled to a quieter part of the street, aiming to avoid the growing throngs of people clamouring around the busier stalls. Eve was never too picky with food, and sometimes had to settle for less favourable meals when returning from a mission with a growling stomach.

The crowd thinned as Eve made her way down the street, and the aroma of roasting meats and earthy vegetables went with them. Here, she was greeted by a small smattering of stalls, all offering far fewer savoury options.

"Hey lady, looking for some good eats?" drawled a heavyset man from behind one of the closer stalls. Eve shrugged her shoulders in response, ambling over to see what he had to offer.

"Take a look," he waved a hand over various dishes, "I have roasted squirrel, a vegetable medley – don't mind the insects, they add flavour – and some salted chicken skewers."

Eve grimaced at the first two options, the vegetables in particular looked limp and shrivelled, but the chicken skewers, even if the only flavour they offered was salt, did not sound too bad. Right now, they looked downright delicious.

He asked for four aulins. There was a singular currency in Thous that took the shape of thin golden coins known as aulin. They were so thin that if you sat on one at the wrong angle, it would likely be bent beyond use and not accepted as valid currency any longer. Whilst most items in the world would cost more than one aulin, Eve noted that many food stalls from places she had visited would usually part with a generous amount of food for one just one aulin.

Eve held the money out and the man immediately pocketed the money with a grubby hand, "pleasure doing business with you, lady."

Eve grasped the brown paper bag with her food in it. "Yeah, thanks. Have a good evening."

With bag in hand, Eve briskly walked back the way she came, wanting only to return to her home for the night. She squeezed past the never-diminishing queues in danger of overlapping until something made her halt. Sure, she had brushed against countless people in her attempt to return to the inn, but she knew when someone was trying to pickpocket her. Careful not to harm anyone else around her, she grabbed the person's wrist, which was fingertips deep in her back pocket, and turned to face the culprit.

"What do you think you're doing?" She snarled.

The culprit stammered in response, trying fruitlessly to free themselves from Eve's grip. Eve let the woman's wrist go, but maintained eye contact. She made a run for it, muttering apologies to the people she bumped into as she scurried to put distance between herself and Eve.

With a sigh of frustration, Eve continued her journey back to the inn, unsure if she should pity the unsuccessful thief. Instead, she put it out of mind, chalking it down to something that is likely a common problem in Thous.

The following evening the Marauders of Light met again at Willkeep's Tavern to discuss their next mission.

"This one will involve the whole team," Scarlett began, "and it's a bit of a doozy."

"A doozy?" Barron asked, interest written across his face.

"Yep. A doozy. Our merry little band hasn't quite had anything like this before."

"Pray tell, what is 'this', exactly?" Clarissa asked, prompting Scarlett to forgo any further teasing.

"We've been asked to look into the muggings and shakedowns as of late," Scarlett took a swig from her tankard and continued, "this one is an official request from higher up due to the large number of reports made about this specific issue, and they want us to, well, "resolve this amicably."" Scarlett put on air quotes and pulled a funny face. "I mean, do they think the thieves will just peacefully turn themselves in?"

"A pickpocket tried it on with me just last night, but their efforts were fruitless," Eve chimed in.

"Exactly, Eve," Scarlett said, with a flourish of her hand, "and now it's up to us to get to the bottom of this."

There was little enthusiasm around the table for this mission, the rest of the team deep in thought as they drank, ate, or looked idly at their hands or jewellery. Scarlett looked around at them all, noticing their lack of interest. Eve thought it sounded like something that should not be left up on a mission board for someone else to take care of, and that it should fall to Thous' government instead.

"Look, I know this doesn't sound like the most exciting mission in the world, but it's all we have, and the pay is fair," Scarlett continued, looking at each of the team members one by one, "and we'll be doing good. Besides, we haven't had a team mission in a while. It would be nice to work as a full team again, don't you think?"

With this, the rest of the team started to agree, and excitement for the mission grew at the thought of a full Marauders of Light outing.

"Glad to see you're all on-board!" Scarlett exclaimed in relief, "so, let's get down to business."

With that, the Marauders of Light had a mission that suited them best – small, tidy, and close to home. Or, at least, that was what each of them hoped for that night.

Chapter Four

In advance of the evening's mission, Eve stocked up on vital essentials such as ammunition and first aid supplies and bought a whetstone to sharpen her weapons. It was cheap and made redundant after only one use, but did the job. Her scythe would become far less effective if the blade was allowed to dull, and Eve would feel more vulnerable without it up to scratch.

With no expectation of a lengthy or particularly difficult evening ahead, Eve had packed light.

She met with the rest of the team ahead of the dinner rush, just before pick-pocketing would be most likely to occur. Eve looked the group over and noted that they more or less looked the same, although they had also packed light. Clarissa was without her shawl, and Barron looked much smaller without the giant axe strapped to his back. Scarlett, Amie and Drake looked generally the same, given that they usually equipped light anyway.

"So, what's the plan?" Barron asked, his large axe left at home in favour of two, easily-hidden, hand axes.

"We split up and keep an eye out for any pickpockets," Scarlett replied, "and if you're able to catch one and bring them back to us, maybe we can get some information from them."

With everyone clued in, they headed into the growing crowd as if they were examining stalls or queuing for food. As he disappeared into the crowd, Drake laughed to himself, "I bet Clarissa wins this one!"

"Why must you make everything a game, Drake?" Clarissa sounded unimpressed before she was out of earshot.

Alone, Eve returned to where she was almost pick-pocketed the night prior, and feigned interest in the nearby stalls.

Just as she was stretching her neck to look at a wooden menu with small text carved into it, she felt someone brush against her elbow. When she turned, at a speed not many could hope to match, the culprit was gone. She patted at her side. They had made off with her dragon pistol.

She spun around on the spot, looking each and every way, but she could not detect anyone out of the ordinary. Whoever the thief was, they were successful this time. She grunted loudly, gaining herself a few odd looks. She clenched her fists and bit the inside of her cheek. She seethed. How could a pickpocket get the better of her?

Frustrated at both herself and the pickpocket, Eve breathed deep to steady herself before walking back to where the group originally dispersed, now only hoping anybody else was successful.

Having been leaning against a nearby wall in wait for the better part of an hour, Eve's impatience grew until, one by one, the group reconvened. As predicted by Drake, Clarissa had brought someone back. A boy, but how? She didn't seem to be using any force, but surely he hadn't come of his own free will?

Looking the pickpocket up and down, Eve deduced that he could barely be older than twenty years old. He was gangly and thin, with grimy hands and an outfit that looked well-worn; he seemed to be struggling to draw breath, as if an invisible force had wrapped around his throat.

Clarissa stepped forward with the man and, with a wave of her hand, he began speaking quickly and desperately, gulping air as if he had never been able to before that very moment.

"I-I don't know much!" the man spluttered, his words fighting to escape from his mouth. Eve thought that he looked like he was in terrible pain. "But if you pro-promise not to hurt me, I'll t-tell you where the others hide out," he continued, a pleading note in his strained voice, "just p-please don't take me with you."

Suddenly, he buckled over and took several deep breaths, his hands gripping his knees.

"Bargaining?" asked Clarissa, her hands on her hips with an eyebrow raised, "really?"

The man looked up, his face flushed red and glistening from sweat, "lady, was that necessary?"

Clarissa looked down at him and shrugged, "who knows? but I wasn't going to take any chances."

It turned out that Clarissa, with her Wind Presence, had tightened the man's windpipes which forced him to tag along with her if he wanted to be freed. It was a clever move, and such a subtle Presence compared to Eve's Flame. She felt a tinge of bitterness towards her own Presence, something she felt was better fit for destruction than for aiding others.

The man, with their promise to not hurt him, revealed where he and the other pickpockets were hiding out, but insisted that he knew nothing more about any of the ongoing robberies. Satisfied that they had all the information they needed from him, the Marauders suggested that he retire for the night and look into a different profession, unless he wanted to get caught up in this any further. With a meek word of thanks, the man scampered into the night.

"As I called it, Clarissa came back as if it cost her no effort at all!" Drake chuckled loudly as Clarissa looked away from him. Eve spotted her lips tugging upwards, and thought that she looked rather proud of herself despite chiding Drake earlier for his jokes.

"Well, you know, what is it they say? Oh, right, the quickest way to a man's truth is through crushing his lungs."

The group solemnly nodded in agreement, Drake and Barron exchanged a nervous glance, before they all burst into laughter. Eve enjoyed watching, unsure if she should participate, and still angry at being robbed herself.

Once the laughter subsided, Eve filled them in on her own encounter.

"I'm missing my dragon pistol," she said through gritted teeth, " I was pick-pocketed, and I have no idea who did it. Whoever did it was long gone the moment they robbed me." Eve recounted this calmly, despite feeling foolish and ignoring the bubbling rage within her.

"We're going to their hideout now, so let's reclaim what's rightfully yours, okay?" Amie placed a warm hand on Eve's forearm.

"I, uh, yes, let's do this." Eve straightened, surprised by the display of comforting physical affection.

Eve had spent a long time alone. Something in the pit of her stomach gnawed away at her as she looked at Amie and the others. Maybe this time would be different.

The hideout was supposedly based on the outskirts of town, far from the security guards patrolling the streets of Thous at all hours of the day. After a thirty-five minute walk from the city gates, the Marauders of Light stood near the entrance of a cave filled with staggering darkness far as the eye could see.

"Eve, Barron, do you mind doing the honours?" Scarlett stood back so that they could each create light for the group with their Presence.

"I'll take point, and you follow up on the rear, Eve," Barron directed, leaving the rest of the group to take their places between them both.

The scenery seemed unchanging as they made their way slowly through the cave, careful not to trigger any potential alarms or bring attention to themselves – the thieves may not see their Flame just yet, but they would certainly hear the echo of any noise. Soon, they could hear the chatter of several voices ahead. Barron extinguished his Flame and Eve did the same.

"We'll have to hope for no nasty surprises waiting for us in the dark. but if there are voices, we should be able to use them to guide us," Barron explained, "be alert, and be careful." The group quietly murmured their agreement in unison. To ensure nobody would get lost, the group decided to each place a hand on the shoulder of the person in front of them. In front of Eve was Amie, and Eve placed her hand on Amie's shoulder. Eve felt her shoulder trembling beneath her hand and wondered if she did not like the dark.

Before long, the group spotted a wooden barricade ahead, illuminated by two rusty, flickering flames nestled within makeshift sconces. As they approached, they saw a door with a letterbox-sized slit a couple of feet behind the barricade. It seemed the thief that Clarissa found before had neglected to tell them they would need a password to get in.

"Hey, Scarlett, what's the plan?" Barron turned and asked the group's leader, who mulled it over, a fingertip scratching at her chin.

Scarlett grinned. Eve saw her profile from the side, and thought that Scarlett looked excited to get into the thick of it, and had a hunch at what she would say next. "Blow it open."

"Blow it open?" Barron asked, an equally excited grin spreading across his own face.

"Yes," Scarlett grinned and placed her hands together before mimicking an explosion with them, "blow it wide open."

"Aha, the element of surprise. I like it." Barron signalled Eve over, "here, Eve, help me with this. I can use Flame, but my true strength is in, well, my strength. Can I count on you?"

Eve nodded and grasped the hand axe which was being held out to her. After gripping it for a few seconds, the head of it bloomed into a bright orange, the steel wobbling in the onslaught of intense heat. The rest took a step back and Barron slammed the hand axe forward. Eve's infused Flame caused the barricade to explode inward, splintering in all directions. The once muffled, happy chattering heard behind the door turned into screams and shouts of surprise, followed by the clamouring of feet, scraping of tables, and the clanging of steel and creaking of leather as weapons were upholstered.

With a yell, Amie jumped forward and used her presence to freeze the floor ahead of them. Several people slid on the ice, their legs flapping wildly out of control. Behind them, dozens more fell to the ground out of sight.

Drake raised his hands in a show of innocence, "we're only here to ask a few questions about the rise in pickpocket activity. I suggest that you help us."

Those closest to Drake hesitated, looking at one another for direction, but an astonished shout of "what are you all doin', standing around gawking for?!" from further back whipped the thieves into action and the tips of several weapons were suddenly pointed at the mercenaries.

"Well, can't say we didn't give them the option for a peaceful resolution, eh?" Drake shrugged, completely ignoring those still attempting to scrabble to their feet, as he unsheathed his sword in preparation for a fight.

"Drake, no!" Amie moaned, "we can still settle this peace–" She was cut off as Drake leaped ahead of her, blocking a small knife that had just been thrown at her. She whipped around and her hair swirled around her, and she stamped her foot on the floor. He shrugged. "Fine then, I guess we can't!"

With no other options available, the Marauders of Light all jumped into action. Having not seen the entire team in action before, Eve lingered behind, wanting to see how they complement each other and not wanting to disrupt their flow or get in the way.

Amie's ice was melting in the face of several light sources placed ahead of the group. Several thieves seemed to be utilising Flame Presence, but nowhere near as strongly as Eve nor Barron. Mastering Presence took time, practice, and a little bit of natural talent. It was all too easy to be careless and cause a fatal accident. The worst case would be a Blowback, through overuse or inexperience, where one lost control of their Presence entirely.

Multiple small, wispy fireballs were tossed from further in the cavern, but their aim lacked accuracy. They extinguished as soon as they met the muddy walls, whether due to misfire or Clarissa blowing them away with Wind before they got too close.

"Don't worry – I'll keep them at bay," Clarissa assured the group, blowing further fireballs away and back toward the thieves that were still fighting, their weapons held in front of their faces as they tried to approach in the mayhem. Shrieks of confusion and horror rang out, and bodies of those remaining and those escaping stumbled over one another, all trying to escape Clarissa's onslaught. The thieves who simply wanted to escape were ignored by the group, who were hoping to find the leader behind them instead.

Scarlett and Drake charged ahead and fell foes with the hilts and flats of their blades, taking care to avoid inflicting any fatal injuries. It was as if they were dancing, moving in sync while ensuring that nobody crept up on the other.

"It gets even more impressive when Amie gets involved," mentioned Barron, who, like Eve, had remained on the back lines as the others led the attack, ensuring that none of the stragglers decide to change their mind during their escape. He pointed his chin toward Amie who had also stepped back behind the rest of the fighting group, "that sabre isn't just for show!"

With various Presences active and weapons clanging and scraping, Eve decided that it was now time for her to jump into the action, too. Unholstering her scythe, she imbued it with Flame and slammed it into the ground, a group of incoming thieves jumping out of harm's way as the Flame rose and soared past them. Seeing them scrambling back to their feet, Eve dashed over and punched the closest thief. They flew backward into the wall, their now unconscious body slowly slumping down to the ground, along with their dagger. The handful who remained were on their feet, looking toward one another for direction or using their own initiative to continue their attack. Eve took a nimble step back before propelling herself forward and ramming her shoulder into one thief, who then bumbled into two others.

"Do ya need a hand?" Barron appeared after having rendered the other two thieves' unconscious with the blunt ends of his axes.he deftly followed up with a short hop, headbutting another thief in the chin. The thief stumbled back, clutching his head, as he fell to the floor and kicked himself away toward the exit. Barron laughed, "look at him go!"

Barron's face was illuminated as another thief appeared, summoning Flame, and he snarled as he punched forward. Barron scarcely avoided the attack, ducking low as he felt the heat pass over his head. Eve jumped forward as she summoned a larger Flame of her own and raised it in challenge. The sight of Eve's Flame caused the thief to falter, and his own Flame suddenly exploded in his face. With a smirk, Eve extinguished her Flame too, but not before it could shed light on her dear stolen firearm, discarded in the dirt by one of the thieves. She would have rather they had actually used it, than having just tossed it in the dirt like this. She quickly picked it up, brushing the dirt off and placing it back in its holster, her hand lingering on it before she jumped back into the fray.

The thief with the Flame mishap was not the only one attempting to escape now, their weaponry and will to fight stamped out – many others were too, with several injured and flailing in a small radius around Scarlett and Drake, no longer attacking. Some claimed their injured while others simply chose to run or limp out as fast as they could.

"We've still got it, Scarlett," said Drake, admiring their handiwork, "but I'm not too impressed to have been singed a few times." He grunted, examining his arms and torso for other burn marks.

"We can sort that out," Scarlett replied, panting and eyeing the various burns on Drake's arms, "hey, Amie, can you help Drake out, please?" Amie walked over and sat Drake down by the wall. She took his arms into her own, one after the other, to cool down the agitated spots with icy fingertips.

"Sorry," She grimaced as Drake took several sharp intakes of breath at the press of her fingers into his skin, "don't worry, I'll be done in a moment."

Amie finished up despite how sore the burns still looked, Drake seemed to be in a better mood.

"Thanks Amie, I don't know what we'd do without you."

"It's what we'd do for any of us," Amie smiled in response.

Eve suddenly had the overwhelming feeling that she had not earned her place here, as she watched Amie working hard to help Drake. Watching the group interact, she felt as though she had barged in on an intimate family moment, and she had no idea what to do other than to look around the cavern for anything that might help them in their search, but before she could, Amie appeared before her.

"Don't worry Eve, I'd make you chilly too!" Amie exclaimed, giggling as she poked Eve in the shoulder with a now warm fingertip, seemingly having sensed Eve's awkwardness.

"Yeah, I know." Eve smiled, feeling relief that, for a little while at least, she was not alone.

Many mercenaries chose to fight in a team. It was easier to have someone watch your back and cover all the bases that one sole individual could not hope to do on their own. The Marauders of Light were in a perfect position to build on one anothers strengths. For a long time now, Eve had been alone, and forced to adapt to working solo. It could take a while for her to adapt to the various personalities and skills in this team, but she was nothing if not flexible.

The rest of the group had been chattering away now that the thieves had either cleared out or been rendered unconscious whilst Eve was lost in her thoughts, until Barron reminded them why they were all there in the first place.

"Did any of them seem like the leader to you?" He said, pointedly, as he looked around the cavern.

"Don't worry Barron, we haven't forgotten. What's the urgency?" Drake questioned, confident in the team's abilities to find the ringleader of the group of thieves.

"The urgency, Drake, is that no matter how competent we may be, there's very little to go on here," Clarissa cut in, "and I'd prefer that we all keep our wits about us."

Drake rolled his eyes but remained silent and Clarissa huffed. Tension had re-entered the atmosphere and Amie now looked uncomfortable, looking down as she shuffled her feet. Eve noticed this but kept her thoughts to herself, not wanting to weigh in, thinking that maybe Amie was chiding herself for not taking the situation seriously enough. She knew full well how misplaced confidence could lead to life-changing errors, and agreed with Barron and Clarissa, but it was Scarlett's responsibility to bring the team together.

"Alright all, game faces on – we have a job to finish," Scarlett commanded to the group, and they set about exploring the cavern surrounded them, despite it looking like a dead end.

Eve was not sure where to look, so she approached Barron to ask him something that had been on her mind since seeing him use Flame earlier. "Barron, why don't you use Flame in combat?"

He was crouched by a wall and was rapping his knuckles against it, but looked up as she directed her question at him. "Oh that, noticed, did ya?" He scratched at his chin, "I don't have a very strong Presence, to be honest about it."

Eve mulled his response over, and knew that Presence's came in all shapes and sizes, but every mercenary she had met before had been proficient in their own Presence.

"Does it make work difficult?" Eve enquired, "if you don't mind me asking?"

"Not at all, to both questions." Barron grinned at her, still crouched to the floor, "I haven't met a Presence better than my ultimate Presence, cold steel." He laughed as he tapped the hand axe at his side, and Eve could not help but laugh at his joke too.

He shook his head as he got to his feet, "there's nothing out of the ordinary here. I thought maybe one of the walls would be hollow, but there's a lot of cavern to knock against." he looked around the cavern with a sigh, and lit a Flame in his hand as he made his way around, tapping his knuckles against each wall. Eve decided to follow him, and did the same at a height he could not reach.

"Huh, hold on," he abruptly stopped and Eve almost bumped into him, "there's something funny about this one.

Eve leaned forward to inspect the wall that Barron was standing in front of, and watched as it slightly shimmered, viewable only by their Flames. Eve thought to herself, inching closer, wanting to be sure that the nearly unnoticeable shimmering was real.

"If I were to guess," Eve summoned a larger Flame, which she held closer to the wall "this isn't a wall at all."

As if speaking her suspicion out loud turned it into truth, the wall in front of them both slowly vanished, turning less solid until all that stood in place of the illusion was a young woman, looking entirely out of place in the cavern. She stared at Eve, her eyebrows knit together in what Eve thought was anger, a small pout on her face.

"And who are you?" Eve inquired, looking the woman up and down. She was short with too-neat-to-be-a-thief blonde, straight shoulder-length hair, bright green eyes that were staring daggers at the group. Her shining aqua earrings, and sleeveless, black dress with aqua trimmings that reached down to her calves, were too well-kept to belong to a thief. There was barely a scuff on her to be seen, but the aulins scattered around her feet told Eve that they had found the right person.

"I am Kerri, and you would be wise to remember it," the woman gave them a small, mocking curtsy and smirked at the group, looking up at them without even a stroke of fear on her face.

"Are you joking?" Drake's voice pitched higher than usual as he suddenly stomped forward, indignant at the newcomer's attitude, or so Eve had thought, "what are you doing here, Kerri?"

"Ah, Drake, just the man I wanted to see!" Kerri strode forward and took Drake's arm in hers. The group were stunned into silence. Drake's wide eyes and gaping mouth told Eve clearer than words that this was not pre-planned.

"Kerri, what are you doing here? This is no life for someone like you." Drake said, softly, looking down at

Kerri as she leaned against his arm. Drake looked comfortable with Kerri latched to his arm, but small beads of sweat had formed along his forehead. His eyes would dart anxiously from Kerri to Scarlett, and back again.

"Excuse me," Amie interjected, her finger rapidly pointing between them both, whereas her eyes would also be drawn to the aulins on the ground, "but how do you two know each other?"

Kerri ignored Amie entirely, and responded to Drake. "You are not my father. I can do what I want." Kerri pouted but tightened her grip on Drake.

"And why were you hiding from us?" Amie persisted, an edge to her voice, and her lip twitched, "poor leadership, don't you think?"

"Amie!" Drake groaned, but this time, Kerri did turn to look at Amie, a scowl on her face.

"Is it not obvious?" Kerri raised an eyebrow and smirked again, "why would I want to be caught?"

"Okay, okay, let's all calm down," Scarlett put an arm out in front of Amie, who had opened her mouth to retort, and looked at Drake, "Drake, can you tell us what's going on here?"

"I, uh, don't know?" Drake looked as confused as he sounded. Eve thought it would have been funny in a different situation.

Scarlett shook her head and raised her hands, "actually, I don't care. If she wants to latch on to your arm, then that'll make taking her back all the more easier. Look at all those aulins!" She gestured with her arm to the ground before pinching the bridge of her nose. "It looks like we've got our girl."

Kerri ignored Scarlett's comments completely, choosing to lock onto Drake's arm tighter. The man buckled slightly before regaining his posture. Eve felt her skin prickle in annoyance.

The group looked at one another as they shuffled or shrugged their shoulders. It was evident that none of them knew the best course of action to take. Eve felt that this situation was a little more personal than she had bargained for on what should be a simple mission. Before she could speak up, Scarlett continued, "our mission was to put a stop to the muggings, and now we'll have done just that. If you're too frightened, we can render you unconscious and take you back that way," Scarlett bared her teeth at Kerri, exasperated and irritated at this turn of events, "it's your choice, until it isn't."

Scarlett was angry. Eve could not blame her, the girl was getting under her skin too.

"I'm not sure if we should, Scarlett," Drake finally spoke up and tentatively reached his arm out, with his other arm still tightly trapped in Kerri's arms. "I know Kerri. She's a good person, I don't think she'd have done this without good reason."

Kerri smiled at Drake's words. Eve could not tell if it was genuine. As Eve was watching her, they locked eyes. Her smile fell before she looked away again.

"What?" Scarlett said curtly, sparks of electricity were crackling around her hands, "we need this, Drake. Unless you have a damn good reason not to, I will drag this girl back to town myself, kicking and screaming, with or without you."

"If it was any other girl I would, but not Kerri," Drake shook his head, defeat in his face, "she's kinda like family." There was a tone of pleading in his voice.

Scarlett huffed, taking notice, and stepped away from the group to gather herself, pinching her nose as she took deep breaths. With Kerri doting over Drake, Eve, Amie, Barron and Clarissa stepped away also to talk among themselves.

"I don't like her," Clarissa said with a shrug, "not one bit."

"I think that sentiment is echoed throughout the group, but Drake's clearly not willing to budge." Barron replied. "It's safe to assume that if we go forward with the mission, we could lose him." Amie pondered, a sad look on her face as she watched Kerri, looking slightly downcast as the light illuminated her eyes.

"We were issued a job. Whether or not Drake knows this girl, we owe results," Eve explained. The decision seemed clear to her, "we have to take her back, there's no hiding her guilt."

The group all turned to look at Eve. For a moment there was total silence, bar Kerri and Drake's whispering from a few feet away. A moment later, they each sighed, realising that Eve was correct. Only someone not so closely entwined with the group could have put it so clearly.

"If there are no objections, let's go back," Barron suggested, and the four walked back to where Drake and Kerri stood.

Scarlett, still angry but managing to stop her Presence sending sparks everywhere, stomped over and asked the group for their thoughts. "What do you all think?"

There was a moment of hesitation before Eve spoke up, "we have to take Kerri back. We have a mission, and we have to fulfil it." Eve spoke with confidence and clarity, but Drake looked hurt. Not missing a beat, Scarlett stormed over to Drake and Kerri and forcibly removed the girl from his arm. Kerri instantly barraged the group with insults and a scream of "you'll be sorry!" until Scarlett paralysed her with her Presence. Kerri instantly fell limp into Drake's arms.

"That's enough out of her," Scarlett said, her lip twitching, "let's get out of this damn cave, we'll let someone know where they can collect the aulins."

Clarissa used her Wind to lift Kerri and followed Scarlett as she led the way out.

Drake, last to leave, shuffled uncomfortably and bit his lower lip before following the group from a distance.

Chapter Five

Scarlett led the trek back to Thous with Clarissa, Barron, and Kerri in tow. Kerri walked ahead of Eve, Drake and Amie, so any attempt to escape would be easily thwarted. She would sometimes look back over her shoulder, her eyebrows drawn together in concern, at Drake, who would nod at her, and she would look forward again, seemingly satisfied.

Amie and Drake lagged together behind Eve, deep in conversation. Eve caught snippets of their conversation behind her and felt guilty for listening in, but also did not want to let Kerri out of her sight if they were preoccupied.

"—but if you don't talk to us, then we can't help you, you know?"

"It's not that simple, Amie," Drake sounded torn, his voice strained despite his whispering, "I want this for us just as much as anyone else does, but I need some time with Kerri," he paused for a short while, the pleading note inching back into his voice, "just for a little while."

Amie paused, then sighed, "and you really won't tell us why?"

"No," he hesitated, "not yet."

"Okay. Okay," Amie repeated, relenting to his wishes. Well, I'm here for you if you ever want to talk about it, okay?"

Drake's tone softened and he chuckled, "I know. Thanks, Amie."

The conversation ended, and Eve had kept a strict eye on Kerri until she felt Amie clutch her arm. She momentarily drew her eyes away to glance at Amie, but returned to keeping an eye on Kerri. She could have sworn that the woman in front's shoulders had twitched a little.

"I suppose you heard all that, huh?" She looked forward, walking in sync with Eve's arm still clasped in her grip.

Eve felt her face go slightly red, "oh, yes, well, some of it."

"Well, you want to help Drake too, don't you?" Amie asked, her tone level.

Eve felt as if she was being tested. She glanced toward Amie again, who was looking directly ahead, before responding. She already knew what she would say. "Yes, I do."

Amie pulled Eve down so that she could whisper in her ear, "okay, so, when we get back to Thous, here's the plan." Amie paused for dramatic effect, a wide grin on her face, "we're going to convince Scarlett to let us have Kerri for an evening!"

Eve waited, and waited some more. Silence. She realised that really might be all of it, the entire plan. She attempted to keep the disappointment out of her voice, "I really don't think she would be happy with that, Amie."

"Ah, but you don't know my sister," Amie said proudly, "she will want to march that little girl right down to

the Gaol, and she wouldn't think twice about throwing her behind bars herself."

"Alright, so how do you plan to convince her?"

"Well, I was thinking, if you appealed to her, she might be more likely to concede. You're the up-and-coming star of the group, right, Eve?" Amie smiled.

Eve tilted her head in confusion unsure what to make of Amie's words. "What do you mean by that?"

"Scarlett has taken a real liking to you, and so have I." Amie grinned, "but don't let her know I said that."

Eve was not sure how to respond, so she continued the conversation from before. "Fine, I'll ask her. I'm not going to make a song and dance of it, but I'll talk to her." She shrugged, weighed down by the redhead latched onto her.

"Thank you," Amie loosened her hold on Eve, "that's all I ask."

Unsure of how Amie always seemed to involve Eve in her plans, Eve resigned herself to the fact that she might have a slightly awkward conversation with her new boss coming up in the near future. Scarlett was not going to be pleased, but she had already made the promise to Amie. Eve had considered saying no to her, but felt any willpower to follow it through vanish when the redhead stared at her.

Scarlett had already stormed off with Kerri, Clarissa and Barron in tow, the latter running to keep up with her large strides. Drake walked next to Clarissa, his gaze steadfastly fixed to Kerri's bobbing form. Eve took a step forward and looked back at Amie, her eyes drawn to the floor as she bit her thumb, before she rapidly shook her head and joined Eve in catching up to the others.

"Scarlett." Eve approached Scarlett at the front of the group, and the latter finally slowed her pace.

"Eve?" She said it curtly, her nostrils flaring. She must have still been angry at Drake.

Eve felt a cold drip in her stomach. A familiar feeling she had not felt in a long time. "Does the mission need to be completed tonight?"

Scarlett stopped in her tracks, and Barron skidded to a stop in front of her, just inches away from bumping into her.

"Why are you asking this?"

Eve was about to respond but she threw a hand up to stop her.

"Not you." She pointed at Amie with her index finger. "You."

Amie pointed at herself in faux shock. "Me?!"

"Yes, you, who else? What does Eve care? This has you written all over it, however." Scarlett sounded frustrated and tired. She looked over her shoulder, the gates of Thous were close enough that only a few more minutes of walking would be needed to see them through.

Eve took a step back and glanced at Amie, who just shrugged at her with a smile. She stepped forward. "Thanks for trying, Eve." She patted Eve on the shoulder before looking at her sister.

"What's the harm in letting us have Amie for the night?" Amie flashed her teeth, putting on her most stunning smile.

Scarlett bared her teeth in return. "You have to be joking. You have to be." She pinched the bridge of her nose and turned on the spot, as if she was trying to spin the frustration from her bones. "My sister is not this stupid."

"Alright, let's not attack each other, okay?" Drake took a tentative step forward with his hands out, but one glare from Scarlett and he stepped back to where he stood again. Clarissa smiled at him pitifully, and Barron looked as if he was holding back a laugh, fighting to keep it within his rounded cheeks.

"Eve, Drake and I will look after her." Eve jolted, but Scarlett only gave her a passing glance.

"Why would I agree to this? We've literally done the job, Amie!"

"Because," Amie put emphasis on the word as she made a point to turn to Drake, "we're doing it for a member of the team."

Scarlett let out an exasperated sigh as she slapped a hand to her forehead. "That girl couldn't have stuffed any more aulin's in her thieving little hands, and you want to not turn her over?" There was a pleading note in her voice.

"Come on, please!" Amie pleaded harder as Drake uncomfortably shuffled behind her, "I don't ask for much, and I promise that we'll keep her in check." Amie closed the gap between herself and her sister, gently pulled her away from the group, then lowered her voice to a gentle whisper. "Drake needs this, sis, can you please do it," she paused, looking Scarlett directly in the eyes, "for him?" Her relentless pleas seemed to finally reach her older sister, who threw her hands up in frustration, relenting.

"Fine! I don't care what you do. but if she gets away, I will not be impressed. We're throwing away money right now, Amie."

"I know, this is important. I've never treated the mission as anything but that, but this is important, too. Whatever this is, he needs to work it out, otherwise it's really going to affect our teamwork." She reached out and took Scarlett's hand in her own, stroking the top of it with her thumb.

Scarlett pinched the bridge of her nose and sighed, "you have until tomorrow morning. Regardless of his feelings about it, we'll be taking her in then. Don't waste this time."

The pair returned to the group where Scarlett flicked her hand toward Drake, and Clarissa raised Kerri to Drake's chest. Drake held his arms out and Clarissa gently dropped Kerri into them.

"Scarlett, thank you." Relief broke out across his face. He looked as if a heavy weight had been removed from his shoulders.

"Don't mention it," Scarlett turned to walk away with Barron and Clarissa in tow, "seriously."

Drake laughed. "It never happened." He looked at Kerri in his arms and smiled.

Amie nudged Eve and grinned at her. Eve felt that she understood a little better the bonds between the Marauders of Light and she returned the smile with a small one of her own.

She hoped that they had done the right thing. By the look on Drake's face, it was hard to believe otherwise, and she found herself feeling a little guilty knowing that she almost took this away from him.

Drake carried Kerri through the gates of Thous, and Amie pulled Eve along by the hand as they hurried after them, pulling her from her thoughts.

Shortly after they entered Thous, Kerri roused from her sleep.

"Drake, is that you?" She peered through half-lidded eyes, groggily trying to make sense of her surroundings. She leaned over Drake's arms and looked at the buildings around her. Her face could not mask her feelings of confusion. "Where are we?"

"We're in Thous," Drake responded kindly. With this Kerri jumped to alert and began to protest, but was calmed down by Drake, "don't worry, you're safe. We're just going to Willkeep's Tavern. We can talk there, okay?"

"Okay..." Kerri briefly closed her eyes before shuffling, "you can put me down now, thank you."

"Oh, yes, of course," Drake flustered then returned Kerri to her feet and straightened out her dress.

"Hmph." She put on exaggerated airs, putting her hands on her hips and flicking her hair back, although she did not genuinely seem all that displeased.

"Well, after you then, Drake," she thrust her arms about in different directions, "you know full well I do not occupy taverns and have no idea where to go." She then thrust her arms toward Eve and Amie respectively, "also, who are these people?" Amie had been watching the interaction with glee, and looked excited to be acknowledged by Kerri.

Amie jumped forward, "I'm Amie, and this is Eve,"

Amie pulled Eve in closer, prompting Eve to give a quick "hello, Kerri", before stepping back, opting to pass the conversational reins back to Amie.

"It's a pleasure to meet you, Kerri." Amie offered out her hand. Kerri looked at it questioningly.

"Yes, I'm sure it is a pleasure, for you." She left Amie's hand hanging.

If Amie was irritated by this remark, then she did well not to show it. Instead, she heartily slapped Kerri on the shoulder. "Come on, Willkeep's Tavern is this way."

Amie linked arms with Kerri and took charge in directing her down the street to their destination. Drake, again, looked a little dumbfounded, but quickly followed after them. Kerri kicked up a scene as she tried to dislodge herself from Amie's unbothered grip.

Eve stared curiously for a moment at their retreating backs before shaking her head and following along herself.

As they neared the tavern they heard the muffled cheers and echoes of the lively night within as it spilled out onto the street. Eve caught up to see Drake and Kerri bickering.

"I am not going in there," Kerri stopped still several feet away from the tavern, "I am not."

"It's our regular haunt, it's okay," Drake explained, attempting to comfort Kerri, "it's a good place, I swear."

"Drake, I do not care,""I am simply not going in there." Kerri was adamant, not budging an inch.

"Kerri, plea—"

"Please don't make me." Desperation rang out in Kerri's shrill voice. She looked at Drake with wide eyes, frantically darting from him to the tavern, giving Drake reason to pause. The following silence was pierced only by the raucous chatter inside the tavern.

Drake scratched at his head, his shoulders slumped, "okay. We can go to mine. It's not far from here ."

"Thank you." Kerri, who was gripping the folds of her dress, relaxed slightly.

Drake began heading right, where houses lined both sides of the street, and Kerri met his pace. Eve and Amie followed after them.

"Do you know where Drake lives?" Eve asked.

"I do, we've been there a few times." Amie briefly paused before smiling, "it's nice."

"To be fair to Kerri, the tavern can be a little loud."

"It can, but I like that," Amie continued, "it's exciting to hear stories from other people."

"Yeah? Well, I hope their lives are a little less busy than ours, for their sake."

Amie laughed, "that's odd! Who are they to you?"

Eve was taken aback by the bluntness of the question and took a moment to mull over an answer. Before she could though, Amie jumped in, "oh, no, please don't take that the wrong way! It's just, you don't often see mercenaries with such a soft side often."

Eve shrugged away Amie's concern, "well, there's you, right?" Amie nodded but said nothing in response. "And no offence taken. It's just sad to know that there are so many more doing what we do, because they need to. It's not exactly a good life."

"You think so? If it wasn't for this, we wouldn't have met..." Amie looked a little hurt.

"Amie," Eve fumbled, looking for the right words. "I'm sorry, I didn't mean it like that. I'm happy to be with you all, but the reasons why we do this... I just wish it wasn't this way. Does that make sense? I don't think it's a life anybody should have been forced to live."

"I think that makes sense, but let's put a pin in this for now." Amie stopped and looked at a nearby house. She then skipped ahead, gesturing with both of her arms in front of one house in particular. "we're here!"

Drake opened the front door, his arm outstretched to allow Kerri inside first. He stood at the door where he beckoned Eve and Amie to hurry along. They walked up the steps and Drake closed the door behind them. Eve was hit with the warm scent of… cinnamon?

"Ah!" Amie exclaimed with a squeal of delight, "walking into your home always reminds me of Christmas! You have to share your cinnamon goodies with me Drake, please!"

Eve laughed, Amie's childish outburst took her by surprise after such a tense night, "it does smell good in here, Drake."

Drake looked bashful and scratched the back of his head. "Well, uh, thank you. Please come in and make yourselves at home."

They removed their boots at the door. Drake then led the duo into a room on the right, where Kerri was already kneeling by the fireplace, trying to ignite the logs eager to burn.

"Argh! I cannot get this stupid thing to work!" Frustrated, Kerri threw the matchbox to her side and took a deep breath. "I give up."

This sent a pang of pain through Eve's chest, and she knelt beside Kerri. She recalled a moment in the past where she also found herself frustrated when trying to start a fire.

"Eve," the girl in question raised her head, crouched over a book, "can you get the fire going?"

"Okay!" She tucked a thin strip of leather in the book to mark her page and closed it. She stood up, "where are the matches again?"

"The same place they always are, on top of the fireplace." A woman with straight long jet black hair peeked her head around the corner, "did you even look?"

"Yes, Adara, I looked!" Eve's voice came out bratty, and she instantly felt silly. "I could've maybe looked harder."

"Yes, maybe just a bit." Adara smiled at her. "Now get on with it."

Eve found the matches and turned the box over in her hands. It read 'KEEP AWAY FROM CHILDREN'. She shrugged. She was not a child, she was sixteen years old. That said, she had not lit any fires before. Eve removed a match from the box and stared at it. The box did not have much in the way of instructions. She thought about using her Presence, but with such a tiny pointy end, she worried she might miss and set something alight. The last thing she wanted was for Adara and the rest of the guild to be mad at her.

Eve scratched the centre of the darker end roughly against the box, but it only whittled down into nothing. She huffed. If she could light it with the way she felt inside right now, she was sure it would go up in flames.

She shook the box hard. The matches rattled but gave no answers. She heard the sound of vegetables being cut in the kitchen. She did not want to bother anyone over this. She felt stupid, and this incensed her further. She exhaled through her nose. Her jaw tensed.

"Is the fire on yet?"

"N-not yet!" She stuttered.

"What's taking so long?" There was the clang of tools, and Adara walked into the living area with her hands on her hips. "Do you need a hand?"

Eve's eyes dropped to the small matchbox in her hands. She gripped it tightly and bit her lip. She felt frustrated.

"C'mon, pass it here," Adara encouraged, "I'll show you how to do it."

Eve nodded and handed over the box. She felt too embarrassed to look her in the face.

"This is easy enough, although I guess it can seem a little confusing if you've never done it before," Adara explained, "you just take the match and rub it along here." She pointed at the rough textured strip on the side. "This is called a striking surface, and just as the name implies…" she scratched the match along it in one swift motion, and it caught aflame, "you strike it." She blew out the match and handed the box back to Eve. "Now you try."

"Okay." Eve responded in a small voice, still not meeting Adara's eyes. She took the box and did the same, but it did not work. She inhaled deeply, and Adara nodded at her to try again. So she did, and it caught alight. "Yes!" She looked up with wide eyes at Adara, who was gently smiling at her.

"Yes, you did it!" Adara reached forward and squeezed her shoulder. "Now just throw it at the logs and watch the magic happen."

Eve did as she was told, and they spent a few minutes watching the logs catch fire, before Adara returned to preparing some food for friends they were entertaining later that evening.

Eve smiled to herself. It was a memory that filled her with warmth, and she felt obliged to share it. She felt compelled to help the younger woman. "It's okay, look," Eve showed one side of the matchbox to Kerri, "this side has been used so much that it'll be hard to get a spark from it. The other side, however," Eve turned the box over, "might work. Give it a try." Eve held the box and a fresh match out to Kerri, who tentatively accepted it.

"Please, go on." Eve urged the young girl to try again, noting the apprehension and frustration written across her face.

Kerri grabbed the box and began swiping it across the opposing side of the box. After a few strikes it set alight.

"Ah!" Kerri exclaimed, wide-eyed. A wide smile broke out across her face, and she flicked the match into the fireplace where the flames rapidly spread out to engulf the wood. The heating instantly began to warm their bodies.

"Ah, that is much better," breathing a sigh of relief, Kerri stood up and offered her hand to Eve, "thank you,

I do not believe I have introduced myself." Eve accepted her hand and was helped to her feet. "I'm Kerri, Kerri Morgan. And you are?"

"Eve. Just Eve, please."

"Okay, just Eve, it is a pleasure to meet you." Kerri flashed a stunning smile. Eve groaned at the awful joke, but returned the pleasantries with a smile of her own. "Thank you for helping me just now. Come, let us sit."

Kerri dropped herself onto a dark, well-worn brown leather sofa by the fireplace. Eve sat next to her. On the opposite sofa was Drake. Amie had taken the lone armchair placed between them.

"So, what is this about, Drake?" Kerri asked. Eve noted that she seemed to be in a better mood.

"We've been tasked to catch whoever was behind the rise in theft in Thous recently, and—" Drake began, but he was cut off by Kerri.

"Do you think that I am behind this?"

Drake fidgeted before responding, "it did look that way, yeah," Drake gestured toward Kerri's attire, "you're not dressed like a common thief, and I know you're more than capable of leading a ragtag band of idiots like them, Kerri."

"You've known me for how long, Drake?" She huffed and crossed her arms, looking away from him.

Drake sighed. "I haven't forgotten."

"Excuse me," Amie leaned forward in her chair and wiggled a finger between the two of them, "how is it that you two know each other?"

"Through work." Drake grunted. He did not elaborate.

"Oh," Kerri's nostrils flared, "I'm just 'through work' to you?"

"Don't put it like that, they'll get the wrong idea." Drake jerked his head towards Eve and Amie. "I met Kerri a long time after I met you and Scarlett, actually." Drake looked at Amie with a smile. "Her father was worried after, uh…" he trailed off, his eyes drifting over to Kerri.

She did not look at him. "It's fine. Drake was hired to make sure that I wasn't getting into trouble after my mother's passing." Her eyes were illuminated by the fire. They were shining.

"Right," Drake continued, "and speaking of trouble, what are we going to do about those aulins, Kerri? Scarlett's going to have to report those as found."

Kerri opened her mouth as if to protest, but took a deep breath instead. "I promise you that it is not what it seems." When she spoke again, it lacked her usual confidence, "Drake, I'm in trouble." She clutched at her dress. Eve felt bad for her.

Drake leaned forward, his brow furrowed, "this isn't like you, Kerri. What's going on?"

Kerri took a deep breath. She did not look up from her hands. "Father has gotten himself into a spot of bother. You know he has a bit of a… gambling streak, shall we call it? Well, that foolish old man has racked up a debt with some unlikely sorts," she finally looked up at Drake, "and, okay, it is what it seems, and I- I mean I only did it because I really need the money! We need the money!" She went on frantically, "but I can't go to Gaol, Drake, not now!" Kerri looked small as she pleaded and clutched the fabric of her dress, her knuckles turning white as they shook, "he- my father, he still needs me."

Silence fell over the room, disturbed only by the crackling fire. As Eve watched Kerri, subdued, the elation of having helped the younger woman dissipated. Eve's thoughts were interrupted by Drake himself, who suddenly stood up. "Amie, Eve, can I talk to you for a sec over here, please?"

Eve and Amie did not hesitate to follow Drake to the hallway. Eve glanced over her shoulder. She noticed that Kerri was still grasping her dress, fidgeting restlessly.

"Eve?" Drake's voice brought her back to reality, "are you okay?"

Eve finally tore her eyes away from Kerri, shaking her head gently, "yeah, yeah, I'm okay, sorry."

Amie was staring at her, and Eve suddenly felt self-conscious and averted her eyes, instead looking at the wall next to her.

Drake's voice brought the conversation back to Kerri. "I'm sorry, but I can't turn her in. I won't."

"Drake, whatever you decide here, I'll have your back," Amie put a hand on his shoulder, "I don't want you to regret what you don't do, okay?"

Drake placed his hand on top of her own, "thank you, Ames." He smiled and looked towards Eve. "Eve, what do you think?"

Tired but sure, Eve agreed, albeit exasperated.

Relief broke out across Drake's face. Amie jumped in, "well, if we're all on the same page, let's go get the story from Kerri, yeah?"

"Thank you both," Drake looked between them both, "so much." He smiled gently. Eve felt reassured that this was the right thing to do.

They could make money another time, but offering Kerri this chance was something they could only do now. Resolved in their decision, Eve felt the knot in her chest loosen. She just hoped that Scarlett would understand.

They returned to the living room and sat. Kerri was staring into the fire, the flickering orange glow illuminating the side of her face as she thought.

"Kerri," Drake called out, knocking Kerri from her thoughts, "we're not going to turn you over. We'll explain it to Scarlett later."

Her relief was replaced by confusion, "Scarlett?"

"Do you remember the woman who knocked you out?"

"Ah, y-yes, I do, thank you." The realisation dawned upon her face. "She is a little frightening."

"She's the leader of our group, but don't worry, we'll handle her." Drake smiled softly.

Kerri turned, examining each person's face. "I don't know what to say." Her eyes darted around the room, searching the other's faces for any signs of deceit, but they simply smiled back at her. She was able to recognise that she truly was not going to be delivered to the guards. "Thank you. all of you." She stood up, curtsying to each in turn. Eve felt surprised, but thought that maybe this was just the way Kerri was raised.

"Ah, the bows aren't necessary, Kerri," Drake blushed but Kerri's back stiffened. She looked up from her pose, still slightly bent over.

"It's a curtsy, Drake, not a bow!"

Drake shrugged. "I don't know what the difference is. Does it really matter?"

Kerri scoffed, back to her standing position. "Does it really matter, he says." She rolled her eyes. "Really though, thank you so much."

"Besides, do we need a reason to help people?" Drake asked. "Not a single one of us here wants to turn you over. It wouldn't be right."

"Thank you, but I don't think we can get that sort of money so quickly," Kerri brought her hands together before she repeatedly ran them down to smooth out her dress.

"We don't have to," Amie leapt to her feet, "we just have to clear the debt, right? There are many ways of doing that outside of collecting money."

Kerri's eyes widened, "what are you saying, uh, sorry what was your name, again?"

"Amie. Amie Brantley. It's nice to meet you too," said Amie with a smile, and she offered her hand once again.

This time, Kerri took it.

"Yes, it is my pleasure indeed, "replied Kerri, "but what do you mean by "other ways"?"

"Well, if we can get whoever is behind this to clear the debt, then we don't need to actually get the money, right?"

Kerri's jaw slacked, her eyebrows knitted together in suspicion, "are you suggesting we kill this man?"

"No, no, no, well…" Amie paused for dramatic effect before she resumed her frantic dismissal of the idea, "no, not at all!" Maybe we can work the debt off? I mean, we're pretty good at what we do."

Kerri mulled the idea over, "yes, maybe that could work," she held a hand to her chin as she bit the inside of her cheek, "it is quite a lot of money, but this could be the solution, and my way has not exactly been fruitful."

"Who is this man, Kerri?" Eve asked.

"Edin Garret. He has a bit of a reputation."

Eve's lips parted, her eyes wide, "Edin Garret? Is that what you just said?"

"Yes?" Kerri, hand still resting on her face, looked confused as she looked at Eve.

"Okay. I'm in."

Drake and Amie exchanged confused glances, but they did not pry further.

"I'm in, too!"

"Yeah, me too."

Kerri looked at the three. "Again, thank you." She went to curtsy, but Drake stopped her with a hand on her shoulder. "A handshake works just as well, Kerri."

"I see. Well, in that case…" She offered her hand out to each in turn, "thank you, so much."

Eve smiled as she accepted Kerri's hand. Kerri returned the smile in kind.

The fireplace continued to crackle softly beside them, a new friendship blooming in its glow.

Chapter Six

Having woken up early the next morning, Eve decided to visit Scarlett and Amie at their home. If anyone was up and about this early, she was sure it would be those two. Kerri had spent the night at Drake's, having accepted that she would not be turned in. Amie returned home, and Eve returned to the inn, knowing that they'd have to tackle the issue of convincing Scarlett to spare Kerri in the morning.

She walked down the cobbled streets as the first rays of sunshine broke through the clouds, taking in the crisp, cool air and feeling revitalised. The early hours of the morning were her favourite. She took another deep breath and slowly let it out, feeling elated. The stalls were beginning to set up for the day, with tarps being stripped and stall owners replenishing stock so that they could earn another day's wages.

It was unsafe to leave them overnight, even with strict security – thieves found a way to commit crimes regardless, leaving business owners no choice but to take their goods home.

Scarlett had told Eve where she lived shortly after their first mission together, but this was the first time that she had ever visited. In truth, she had felt uncomfortable doing so.

The street eventually split into a fork. Both sides were only around four houses deep and Eve took the left street, finding Scarlett and Amie's home right at the very end.

Eve rapped the brass knocker a few times and stepped back from the door, hoping she had not disturbed them both.

A sleepy Amie opened the door, her eyes unfocused, but she instantly brightened when she realised it was Eve.

"Eve! Good morning," she stifled a yawn but was unable to stifle her excitement, a wide grin tugging at her lips, "come on in!"

Saying good morning in return, Eve walked into the shared home, taking in the sights and smells. As she had expected, there was a lot of red.

"I hope you like the hallway. If you don't, you might not like the rest of our home." Amie said sheepishly, chuckling as she stifled another yawn.

Thick wooden pillars held the house up in each corner of each room, all featuring a burgundy carpet and red walls with intricate black, floral, velvet patterns scrawled upon them. The soft light of the rising dawn basked everything in a warm glow and instantly Eve felt relaxed, as if she had drawn herself a long, hot bath to soak in.

"So, my sister isn't much of a morning person, but I can give you a tour of the downstairs." Amie offered, taking a few steps into the room closest to the front door. "This is the living room," Amie ushered Eve into the room which, as promised, featured a design identical to the main hallway. There was a round oak table in the centre which sat upon a bright red, fluffy circular rug. There was a fireplace behind it, the logs charred from use. Several chairs as well as sofas were placed around the room, by a bay window looking out onto the street outside. A handful of small paintings were gently floating, tied to the top of the bay window with string, disturbed by Eve's and Amie's movements.

Unable to hide her curiosity, Eve walked over to the paintings. Some of them depicted the two sisters together, whilst others showed them with their family – both the Marauders of Light, and who seemed to be their biological family. Eve wondered if they also lived in this house.

"Ah, those are our parents," Amie noticed the painting that Eve was holding, featuring the older red-headed male and female, along with a much younger Amie and Scarlett, "sadly, they aren't with us anymore."

Eve looked up to see Amie staring at the painting with a wistful look in her eyes, "but don't worry, it's okay. Look, maybe they're with us after all?" Amie took the painting from Eve and held it beside her own face, grinning toothily to match it.

"Yeah, maybe so..." Eve replied, with a small smile of her own, "the whole family has that red hair then, huh?"

"That's right," Amie perked up, "it's like tradition!"

They both shared a laugh but were interrupted by an even louder sound coming from upstairs.

"Amie!" Scarlett yelled down the stairs, "just what is going on down there?!"

The pair laughed even harder, causing Scarlett to stomp down the stairs. As she was about to shout once more, she spotted Eve, and did her best attempt to look untroubled. She flicked back her hair, and leaned her elbow against the banister at the bottom of the staircase.

"Eve, it's great of you to join us at..." She rubbed her eyes, yawned, and squinted at the clock in the hallway, "at just gone six in the morning?"

"It's okay, sis, Eve's just here for, uh," Amie faltered, realising that she had not asked why Eve had visited so early. "Actually," she said, another yawn breaking free, "why are you here so early, Eve?"

Eve shrugged, feeling slightly embarrassed that she had visited first thing. "Sorry, I'm a bit of an early riser and thought we could talk about Kerri?" Amie stared at her before rubbing her eyes. "I can come back later."

Eve went to move but Amie clasped her wrist, "no, no, it's okay. We're both up now. I'll put the kettle on, but let's save the Kerri talk for when we meet up with the others." Amie smiled. She stood and walked toward the kitchen, "you take your coffee with milk and two sugars, right?" She winked.

"Yes, I do. You remembered."

"How could I forget? It's what I have. It's sweet, just like you!" As she walked away, Eve could hear her say, "I knew she wasn't just ordering the same as me." Amie vanished through the doorway, and soon Eve could hear the rushing tap. Her? Sweet?

Scarlett came down with a change of clothes, "Amie already filled me in. but just so I'm sure, you don't want to turn over Kerri?"

"I don't."

She put her hands on her waist, "this could potentially put a dent in our reputation, you know."

"I know," Eve looked Scarlett in the eyes, "I'm sorry."

Scarlett looked away, focusing on the paintings hanging in the living room with a sigh. "It's okay. There's never a shortage of missions, anyway. We'll just say we couldn't find the ringleader, and the others scattered when we got too close," Scarlett smiled. Eve relaxed, now having noticed how worried she had been.

"Thanks, Scarlett."

Amie returned with two steaming mugs. "She wasn't quite so understanding last night, were you, sis?"

"Shut it, you."

Amie flashed a grin as she placed two of the mugs down on the table.

Eve grasped the mug with both hands, letting the warmth spread through her. Was that a smiley face drawn in the froth? She studied it longer before bringing it to her lips. "Ahh..."

"Is it good?" Amie sat between Eve and Scarlett on the sofa with her own mug in hand.

Eve took another sip. "It's great, thank you."

The three sat in silence, sipping at their coffees. Eve noticed that Scarlett took hers black, which didn't come as much of a surprise, though it made her wrinkle her nose.

"Don't worry, Eve, I'm in the milk and two sugars camp, too!" Amie said, grinning at Eve's reaction.

"Black coffee is too bitter, if you ask me."

Eve laughed, and Scarlett scoffed, rolling her eyes fondly.

The paintings in the back rotated slowly, and Eve saw the Brantley family painting smiling back at her, their smiles forever protected within it.

Once Amie had prepared for the day, the trio headed for the market stalls.

"Ahh," Amie breathed in deeply, taking in the delicious aromas, "did you know that meat skewers are part of a healthy and balanced breakfast, Eve?"

"I'm sure they are, Amie," Eve replied, rolling her eyes, "did you know that fruit is actually part of a healthy and balanced breakfast?"

"I don't believe you," Amie huffed playfully and crossed her arms.

"Cut it out, you two," Scarlett interjected, "get whatever you want, but let's not be late."

Despite her earlier statements, Amie joined Scarlett and Eve in picking up a few bananas. "We'll eat breakfast at the tavern anyway, right?"

Scarlett shrugged and headed toward Willkeep's Tavern where they were meeting Kerri and the other members of the Marauders.

Clarissa and Barron were already inside and Barron captured their attention with a booming, "we're over here!"

They made to approach the table but Amie fell short to order at the counter.

"I'm hungry, okay?!" she said in response to Eve and Scarlett's raised eyebrows.

"We've ordered already. Got tired of waiting for you slowpokes!" Barron guffawed as a plate piled with food is placed before him with sausages, bacon, eggs, beans, tomatoes, mushrooms, and toast in excess.

"You always overdo it, dear." Clarissa looked at Barron's plate but was soon distracted by her own food arriving, "porridge is quite enough."

"Sis, Eve, come order before it gets busy!" Amie beckoned the duo over to place their own orders. Eve and Scarlett joined Clarissa in opting for porridge, which they planned to cut their bananas into, while Amie joined Barron on the eyes to big for her stomach train.

"Amie," Scarlett pinched the bridge of her nose, exasperated, "you're literally never able to finish it. Ever. Why not just get a smaller breakfast?"

"Because I can and will finish it. You believe in me, Eve, don't you?" Amie looked at Eve with a joyful, toothy grin.

"I believe in you," Eve replied, cutting her banana into slices and dropping them into her porridge, "but you aren't finishing that."

Amie pulled a face of faux shock and put a hand to her forehead as if she was going to faint, "I cannot believe it."

"Woe is you, Amie," Eve said as she poured honey into her breakfast.

"Come on, let's go sit." Scarlett led the group back to the table. She took the empty seat beside Drake, with another two besides her where Amie and Eve sat. Further along the table were Barron and Clarissa.

"Have any of you seen Drake yet?" Barron asked through a mouthful of food.

"No, not since last night, but I'm sure they'll be here soon." Amie turned in her chair to look at the entrance. As if she had planned it, Drake and Kerri walked through the door. Amie had a smug grin plastered to her face.

"Hey guys, thanks for waiting," Drake approached the table with Kerri in tow, who he nudged forward, "this is Kerri." She looked fresh faced and a little bashful, but much gentler than the scowl that was plastered to her face the night before.

"Hello," Kerri stood to attention, "it is a pleasure to make your acquaintance on better terms and, um, I'm sorry for any trouble I caused last night." She slumped a little and grabbed at the hem of her dress, looking away sheepishly.

"Barron." Said the man himself, thrusting a large thumb at his chest. "Don't mention it, Kerri. It's great to meet you!" He somehow got out an understandable sentence while still shovelling food into his mouth.

"I'm Clarissa. It's lovely to meet you again, Kerri." Clarissa, having finished her meal, stood up to take Kerri's hand. This seemed to put Kerri at ease.

"Thank you both for your kindness." She curtsied

"Kerri, you don't have to do that."

"Oh, gosh, I'm sorry! I-it is a habit."

Drake and Kerri joined in on the conversation until Scarlett glared at her, her lips drawn into a scowl.

"You've cost us a lot of money, girl."

Kerri withdrew and looked down, her hair falling in front of her face.

"You're lucky that the others care a damn about you."

"I know. I am very thankful." Kerri said meekly.

"Good. Don't you forget it," Scarlett went to sit back down, but stopped with her hands on the head of her chair, "we're all here to help you, too. You're one of us now."

Kerri blushed, not quite yet used to someone with Scarlett's way of showing affection. "Again, I thank you." She curtseyed once again.

"Kerri" Drake groaned.

"I'm sorry!"

The Marauders of Light laughed heartily and continued their breakfast.

They reported on the status of their mission. They had received little more than a large red stamp that read 'INCOMPLETE'. They'd also received no money as they were unsuccessful, but managed to salvage their reputation for location and clearing out the thieves' hideout. They were free of the responsibility of discovering further about the thievery, and everybody else was none the wiser about Kerri.

"Good thing our reputation can't be blown away with one little failure now, isn't it?" Scarlett looked proud, and a little boastful. Eve could not help but admire the woman before her. The leader who had brought this ragtag group together, and still put both her reputation and her life on the line for them. Eve had a feeling she would do so even for Kerri.

"And speaking of the 'failure' in question…" Scarlett spun around and looked directly at Kerri, "where does your father live now?"

"He lives in Ilas, a little Westward from Thous—"

"Ilas? As in the same Ilas that is home to Ilas Arena? That Ilas?"

Kerri bit her lower lip, crumpled the hem of her dress, "y-yes, that Ilas…"

The group fell silent after Kerri's admission. Every mercenary worth their salt knew of Ilas and the secret arena it held. Ilas Arena was used to settle disputes among s, and among guilds, back in the days of the war. Enough blood was shed there that you could stain the surrounding rivers red for days after.

Eve happened to know the danger of Ilas firsthand and turned to the young girl. "Kerri, what exactly did your father do to get into debt?"

"He, um, bet on Warriors at the arena…"

Her brows furrowed. "No, that can't be right. Warriors aren't a thing anymore. What do you mean?"

71

Kerri shook her head. "Ilas Arena is still in use. It is a bit, um, below board."

"Below board?" Eve sighed, "get to the point, Kerri."

Kerri recoiled but continued, "well, you know how Ilas Arena was used back in the day, right? Well, it never stopped. Former s and other hopefuls enter the arena doors, even today, for a shot at fame and glory," she stopped as she kicked up dirt from the floor, mulling her words over, "and money..."

Eve was perplexed. What was wrong with the world for Ilas Arena to continue running even now?

A tense atmosphere hung over the group at this news and what it could mean for them. Whether she went alone or with the Marauders, Eve was returning to Ilas Arena.

"Well, we help our own," Scarlett spoke up, "so let's get prepared for another outing, shall we?"

At that, the group sprung to life, with not a single disagreement to be heard.

The Marauders of Light were due to set out for Ilas the very next day. Eve was alone, wandering Thous for anything that she might need for the journey.

Rubbing her eyes, Eve thought back to her own time at Ilas Arena. She was never the instigator, but it was nigh impossible to back down once challenged. If you did, you'd spend your days looking over your shoulder, expecting an ambush or another unfair trick. Enemies made in Ilas Arena were for life, or at least until one of them reigned victorious in battle. Ilas Arena was gross, it was wicked, and beyond cruelty. Ilas was a lawless arena where blood was shed over petty disagreements by Warriors with large egos.

Eve's reputation had existed prior to her winning streak at Ilas Arena. She had never lost a match in her time as a . The challenges had supposedly ceased once the war was over. Eve had assumed that with the war behind them, the arena simply closed without a steady stream of combatants. A knot formed in her stomach.

She still regretted all the blood spilled. The constant forcing of her hand to defend herself, knowing that backing down was the same as signing your own life away. Eve thought she had left this life behind her, but the past had a funny way of coming back, no matter how you tried to run from it.

Eve had no interest in getting new equipment, but she visited the local blacksmith to have her weaponry sharpened.

"Huh?" The Blacksmith looked up, taken aback by Eve's request, "you want to use the forge yourself?" The man lifted his face guard, revealing a face stained in sweat.

"Yes, if that isn't a problem. I'll still pay you your usual wage."

"Hmm," the blacksmith looked Eve over, eyeing up her equipment. His eyes lingered on her compact scythe, narrowing as he took it in. It was filthy and worn, a sign of its recent battles. "Don't see one of those very often, but with equipment like that, I guess I can make an exception."

"An unusual weapon, so I'm often told." Eve responded with a shrug.

Eric rubbed at his chin. "Don't they supposedly bring bad luck? You know, like black cats?"

Eve stared at him for a moment, then laughed. "That would explain a lot, but it's served me well."

"As long as it needs repairing and keeps me in business, then it could be a wooden spoon for all I care." Eric grinned, and he stepped aside, leaving room for Eve to approach the forge.

"You can borrow my equipment, of course," said the blacksmith, "I just ask that you take good care of it."

Eve nodded and, with the forge already heated, she set to work.

"People don't usually pay to do the work themselves, you know." The blacksmith watched as Eve worked, sweat beginning to drip down her face from the intense heat.

"I enjoy it," she replied, relishing the work, "I just don't have my own forge."

The blacksmith eyed Eve's scythe, "you don't see weapons like that often."

Eve stopped, mulling over the statement, "I know," she continued to sharpen the blade of her scythe with one of Eric's whetstones, "but a scythe has its advantages, and one of those is that nobody has any idea how to deal with one."

"Mmm, I see. I'll have to take your word for it!"

Silence rang out, punctuated only by the noise of Eve working away along with changing of tools. The unintelligible chattering of passersby would float in from outside before being dispelled by the clanging from inside the forge.

Eve let out a breath of satisfaction, wiping the sweat from her brow. "There, perfect." She admired her handywork. The renewed sharpness of her scythe shone in the glow of the fire.

"Nice work, lady."

"Thanks," Eve turned to face the blacksmith "did you learn anything?"

The blacksmith pointed at himself, laughter already escaping his lips as he spoke, "an old dog learning new tricks? I don't think we'll ever see the day!"

The two shared a laugh as Eve prepared payment. As she was about to hand it over, the blacksmith held his hand out to stop her.

"You keep it, I didn't do anything."

Eve contemplated pushing the issue, but noticed that the blacksmith looked so happy. "Okay. Thank you...?"

"Eric."

"Thank you, Eric. If I'm ever in need of a forge, I'll come back here."

"And you'll always be welcome, miss...?"

"Eve. Just Eve."

"So, make sure you come by again, Eve, you hear me?"

Eve smiled. "Loud and clear."

The next morning, Eve finished lacing up her boots and was ready to go.

The bags under her eyes betrayed her lack of sleep, due to the knot in her stomach throughout the night at the thought of having to revisit Ilas. It might be a beautiful town on the surface, but the arena was an abomination once you scratched deeper. She placed a hand to her chest and took a few deep breaths to calm herself before leaving her room.

The steps creaked as she made her way down, and as she entered the reception, she was greeted by two familiar faces.

"Mornin', Eve." Drake raised a hand in greeting.

"Good morning, Eve." Kerri appeared prim and proper, as always, and had somehow found time to pick out a new dress for the adventure.

Short-sleeved and raven black with a white collar, her dress bore minimal frills and came to rest just above her knees. Eve thought it suited her.

"Good morning to you both," Eve greeted the pair, "I didn't expect to see anybody here."

"I wasn't expecting to come either, but someone wanted to see you."

With a soft push from Drake, Kerri stepped forward.

"I just wanted to thank you for agreeing to help my father and I. We may be little more than strangers to you, and I appreciate your kindness, from the bottom of my heart." Kerri curtsied. Drake did not comment on it this time.

Eve placed a hand on the younger woman's shoulder, as she remained bowed, "it's okay, Kerri, I'm more than happy to help."

Kerri looked up as Eve smiled at her. She straightened, looking a little bashful, before clearing her throat. "Thank you."

Drake watched the two happily, not wanting to interrupt. It was not too long until Kerri came to him, beaming, and they took their leave.

After a quick breakfast, the Marauders of Light left the gates of Thous, coming together in a circle just outside.

"So, West, was it?" Clarissa asked, looking in that direction.

"Yes, it is only a short journey," Kerri replied, "we should be there in a little under two days."

"Good thing we've packed some good food then, eh?" Barron turned around to show off his bulging backpack.

"Does that mean you're on cooking duty, too?" Drake elbowed Barron playfully.

"Oh, no, I want a break away from cooking!"

Kerri appeared relaxed, looking in the direction of her home.

"I'll see you soon, dad."

*

Their first day on the road passed without issue and the group set up camp a little way from the main road, closer to a thicket of trees leading to the forest. The sun was setting, ushering in the dusk. Amie and Drake tended to the food which consisted primarily of pork and chicken and sizzled over a makeshift fire as Clarissa oversaw them. Kerri sat on a nearby log, smiling as the two chefs bantered with each other. Scarlett stood watching the main road for any activity. Barron was eager to eat, idly fidgeting with a hungry gleam in his eyes.

Eve walked over to Scarlett, looking up and down the road with her, "are we expecting trouble?"

"No, but I'm trying to make myself useful," Scarlett turned to face her, "there haven't been many people on this road all day."

"This road isn't known for its danger, outside of the odd theft, so we should be okay."

Scarlett nodded, "I've heard the same, but until we've left this road behind, I won't be leaving it up to chance."

A shout from Amie broke the two away from their conversation, and the group circled around the campfire as Amie and Drake dished out the food. Everyone was already eating by the time Barron had his own food. Drake had decided to serve him last for not helping them, "and here you are..."

Barron inhaled his food and was already preparing a second plate for himself before the rest had even finished their first helpings. Not even Drake was able to act quickly enough to stop him, leading to laughter from Amie and an eye-roll from Clarissa.

As she finished her meal, Kerri used a napkin to clean her face, and let it fall to her lap as she stared at the bonfire.

"What's up?" Drake asked.

"I'm sorry, I'm just thinking about my father. He was not always like this, you know", she shuffled uncomfortably, her aqua eyes twinkling by the glow of fire, "as a single parent, he has always put my best interests first. He lacked a social life, he never pursued another relationship, and he always ensured that he put a lot of time aside for me." She looked dejected as she continued staring at the dancing flames, lost in her thoughts.

"We'll help you and your father, don't worry," Eve said in a soft voice, "I know my way around Ilas."

"Oh, Eve!" Amie suddenly jumped up, "I actually need your help with something. If you're done, can you come along, please?"

"Um, sure." Eve, puzzled, put her plate aside and followed the younger redhead behind the tent the group had erected for the night.

Amie had her back to Eve, rocking to and fro on her heels. She stretched her arms in front of her and entangled her fingers, endlessly fidgeting.

Eve watched her. She worried that Amie might have regretted asking her for help. "Amie, what is it?"

"You're Eve, right?" Amie turned around to face her, "*the* Eve?"

Eve felt a chill run through her bones as her guard shuttered into place. "I'm Eve. Just Eve." She glanced away from Amie's face, away from those piercing blue eyes.

Amie stepped forward, only inches away from Eve. "I'd heard stories about a legendary named Eve who went unbeaten at Ilas Arena. Are those stories about you? She was also said to have snow white hair, just like yours."

"I—do I really seem that strong to you?" Eve attempted to laugh it off, but it was a weak attempt.

"You do, and it's okay, your secret is safe with me." Amie smiled and squeezed Eve's forearm before brushing past her and back to the others.

Her perfume lingered in the air, leaving Eve feeling dazed as to what just happened. Would this change things between them? Would she have to leave? Could she trust Amie and take her at her word? Her stomach twinged and her lips felt dry, but she wanted to believe Amie. She wanted to stay. She looked back toward the group and saw Amie waving her over, and so she decided to simply hope for the best.

Much of the journey the next day consisted of Kerri speaking about her father to herself, or to anybody listening. Nobody dared interrupt her after hearing the sadness in her voice. Her father apparently sacrificed everything for her. When her mother died, her father did all he could to keep their small family afloat and please his daughter. It wasn't shocking that she was a little spoiled, given her circumstances. Though Eve could see that Kerri was more than that. She was strong, especially for someone so young.

It became clear that her father took to gambling at Ilas Arena to ensure she could live a rich life, but his risks soon took their toll. Although he tried his best to keep it hidden, Kerri was able to piece together how he owed a ludicrous, unthinkable sum to Ilas Arena.

Kerri wanted to help, in any way she could, and that was why she had gotten involved in thievery.

"I did not enjoy it, but what else could I have done? What else should I have done?" Kerri's voice broke as she continued, "I saw the letters. So many of them tucked away between the pages of books and hidden in drawers. As I collected the post, I always wondered why some of the couriers looked so menacing. It makes sense now. They had been debt collectors. I did what I had to do, to help my father," her voice faltered once again, "so we could go back to our happy lives together."

The group grew quiet, unsure how best to respond to Kerri's admission of guilt and her palpable sadness. The silence stretched into the last leg of their journey, Kerri remained at the back of the group, shuffling her feet and grabbing at the skirt of her dress.

"I've heard that Ilas Arena is worse than before now, you know. You don't have to do this." Kerri stated.

"It's fine, we've already decided to do this." Scarlett replied.

"Yep," Amie agreed, pointing a thumb at herself, "the Marauders of Light have to stick together!"

Kerri looked around at each member as they nodded their consent and raised her head high. "Then let's go, we're not far off now."

Not long after, the peak of Ilas Castle arose on the horizon. Its single, aqua-hued tip pierced the clouds above. The castle shimmered grandly in the sunlight, like an ocean suspended in the sky, and stood at the centre of Ilas. The city itself almost seemed alive. It was full of buildings and stores of vibrant colour. Brick and cobblestones made primarily of differing hues of blue, yellow, white, and orange, giving it a pleasingly quaint feel. The smell of baked goods and soot reached Eve's nose, along with the clanging of blacksmith tools and yells of people peddling their wares. A city big or small, some things never change, Eve thought. Large throngs of people could be seen even from a distance. It was underneath the shining, sharp landmark where Ilas Arena was held, though you would never guess from the outside. Eve could not help but feel disgusted when she thought about all of this being built on the seedy underbelly beneath it.

As they entered the city, Ilas appeared even more normal, with nothing malicious or out of place. Crowds of people bustled around, checking out the shops, admiring the sights, and chattering cheerfully as their shoes clacked across the cobblestone roads. There was a large lake opposite the castle where people fed the ducks or enjoyed picnics. It was the perfect hotspot for couples, having been transformed into a tourist hotspot long after the age of Warriors passed. Everything looked idyllic, making the city the perfect spot for a trip away. It was a grim reality that dawned on Eve as she realised these people had no idea what lurked beneath their feet. "We've been travelling for two days," said Clarissa, "before we take care of business, shall we rest first?"

"Good, I didn't want to be the first one to say it!" Barron laughed, but the nervous energy humming amongst the group stopped him short.

"You're both right though, we should rest." Scarlett agreed and so they all headed for one of the local inns.

Eve felt a slight chill. She looked around as she stood at the entrance of the inn, sensing someone's eyes on her. She scanned the surrounding area for anything amiss, but found nothing.

"Are you okay?" Kerri's voice snapped her from her thoughts.

She gently shook her head, clearing her thoughts, "oh, no, it's nothing."

The inn door's bell finally fell silent once Eve entered behind the group.

Chapter Seven

The Marauders of Light approached a guard standing beside the entryway to Castle Ilas. Kerri reached her arm forward, but the man held his arm out and stopped her. "What business do you have here?" He asked sternly.

"I'm here to see my father." Kerri responded curtly, her brow creasing as she looked up at his face.

"Your father? And he is? Why should he be here?"

Eve felt the man was being annoying, but she supposed not anybody should be able to waltz through.

"William Morgan," Kerri stated. The man's eyes flickered. "I believe he's here. Downstairs?" She stared at the guard, raising her eyebrows slightly at him, her eyes darting to the floor.

"I see." He pushed open the door behind him, "go in, and someone will be with you shortly."

They walked through and the door closed behind them. The room was large and circular, the walls decorated in blue and yellow marble tiling. A plush yellow carpet was laid ahead, looking like a skinned canary.

"I guess that's him." Scarlett nodded her head forward, and they all turned their gaze to a smaller man with his hair slicked back. He wore a blue suit with an aqua button-up shirt, yellow handkerchief and matching tie. Eve's nose crumpled and her mouth twisted. She was growing tired of the colour scheme already. He greeted them plainly.

The group followed the man through various twisting hallways and down several flights of stairs, some concealed with Illusion Presence. They walked until the blue walls and yellow carpets gave way to stone, stone, and more stone.

Dim lights led the way, and soon the faint sound of cheering could be heard in the distance. However, they turned away from the noise and descended further down. It seemed as though the arena should have been in the other direction.

Eve did not voice her concern, but followed the man until they reached a corridor almost devoid of light. A few candles flickered feebly along the damp and narrow walls, reflecting off of the bars of cells.

"Head further down, and you'll see old William," he said as he gestured down the path, "I will be right behind you."

Eve took point with her Flame, the candles providing insufficient light on their own.

The prisoners reached out as they passed by the cells, pleading for help. The group either ignored them or uttered a small apology. One hand reached out where it caught the cuff of Eve's jacket. She turned to illuminate the frail face of an older woman, her sunken cheeks and eye bags making her look ghoulish. Eve stared at her as she coughed before shaking herself free. Her Flame flickered as she turned her attention away, guilt, frustration and pity forming within her stomach. Right now, their focus was on finding William.

More coughing could be heard just ahead, followed by a raspy, dry voice, "Kerri, is that you?"

A weary-looking man was sitting on a thin sheet in one of the cells. Eve caught the glimmer of his sunken eyes as he looked up, his cheekbones protruding sharply above hollow cheeks. She stepped on something so hard that she worried it might have pierced her boot, but it was just an extraordinarily stale crust of bread.

"Ah, yes, the guards sometimes like to tease us." The man said in a voice little louder than a whisper.

Eve frowned, but Kerri sped past her before she could respond.

"Father?" Kerri ran toward the cell and gripped the iron bars. "Father, it's so good to see you." She trailed off as she got a better look at her father in the light of Eve's Flamer, "My goodness. I'm sorry I didn't return sooner." Her voice hitched, and her grip tightened on the bars.

William placed a frail hand on Kerri's, "It's fine, dear daughter—", he paused to cough, "I'm relieved to see that you are okay."

"I am not okay," Kerri's voice took on a sharper and higher tone, "why on earth did you gamble here of all places?!" She slammed one of her fists against a beam, the clang echoing in the small space.

William smiled softly, "I'm sorry, Kerri, I just wanted what was best for you."

Kerri took a deep breath, "I know, but you don't get to put this on me. I just wanted you here with me, dad."

William squeezed Kerri's hand, his bony hand shaking with the effort, "I know. I love you, Kerri."

"I love you too, dad." Their foreheads met through the bars. Kerri's watery eyes betrayed how difficult this was for her.

"Look," she pulled away and gestured towards the others, "I brought friends."

"Friends?"

"Yes, dear friends," Kerri looked at them, and then at her father, "I tried my hand at pickpocketing, but it turns out that I'm quite a failure at that!" She laughed, but William's eyes grew wide.

"You what?!"

"Well, you left me no choice, Father!"

William had no response. He had to have known that Kerri would do anything for him, as he had done for her.

"But yes, that didn't quite work out as well as I had hoped." Kerri continued and gestured toward Drake, "because Drake and his friends caught me."

"Is that really you, Drake?" William's eyes lit up, squinting as he peered in the direction Kerri had pointed.

"Hey, old man," Drake placed a hand on Kerri's shoulder and stood tall, "we're gonna get you out of here."

"How?"

"Easy," replied Drake, "we fight."

The man with the slick-backed hair escorted Eve and the others from the dungeon.

"So, you wish to fight, do you?" he asked with glee, having overheard everything, "well, do keep in mind that you'll have to fight some very difficult battles if you wish to pay off that fool's debt."

"He is not a fool," Kerri bit back indignantly, "he is my father."

"Now, hold on, Kerri," Drake began in an attempt to calm the younger girl, "you're not a fighter. We'll handle this."

Kerri huffed and turned away, tapping her foot as she crossed her arms. Eve agreed with Drake. She would not last a minute in the arena.

Their decision made, the man took the group to a plush waiting room, decked out with sofas, grandiose paintings, with a comically large mahogany desk on the far side by an equally large set of heavy wooden doors. Classical music played softly from somewhere Eve couldn't identify. The ambience contrasted greatly with the dungeons not far below it.

"You can register over there." They were directed to a desk where a woman was sitting. The man turned on his heel and vanished back upstairs without another word.

The woman lifted her head from her papers as the group approached. "Hello, are you here to compete or to spectate?"

"We're competing." Scarlett responded.

"And which of you, exactly, will be competing?"

"I will." Drake put himself forward before anybody else had a chance to. He looked towards the others, his eyebrows furrowing in the centre. "I'm sorry, I have to do this."

Scarlett opened her mouth as if she was going to reprimand him, but decided to keep quiet and instead nodded her approval.

"Today we're hosting duo battles, so that leaves space for one more."

"One more?" Scarlett repeated, surprised. "Okay, in that case—" She went to step forward to volunteer, but was cut off as a head of white hair appeared ahead of her.

"I will be the second contestant." Eve confirmed.

"Eve! What do you think you're doing? Drake, I understand, but you?" Her hands were held out, as if waiting for Eve to physically place a reason for her actions into her palms.

Eve glanced away as she struggled to keep eye contact, "I'm sorry, but I've been here before. Nobody else should have to experience this if they don't have to." She felt guilty, but she was glad to be wearing her combat gear of choice. Her trusty dark green jacket, white t-shirt, black leather trousers and brown boots had never steered her wrong before.

"What?" Scarlett appeared stunned, her jaw slack, but said no more.

"It's okay, sis!" Amie jumped in, "Drake and Eve have this in the bag!" She gently prodded her sister below the jaw, "let's just put that back where it was..."

Scarlett grunted and jerked her head away, folding her arms as she turned away. Clarissa and Barron's eyes followed her. They looked at each other and nodded,, but Kerri was aghast as she watched the white-haired woman put her life on the line for her sake once again.

"Eve, it should be me." Kerri stared down at her feet, shuffling as she pulled at her fingers.

"But it's me, Kerri, and don't you worry," Eve crouched to meet Kerri at eye level, "there's no way I'd enter if I thought we'd have any chance of losing." She placed a comforting hand on Kerri's shoulder, gently squeezing it. Kerri continued to fidget. Eve wondered if lying to her was the best thing to do.

Chapter Eight

With Eve and Drake having officially registered for participation in the day's battles, the rest of the team wished them luck before they were escorted to front row seats in the arena's spectator stands. Kerri was looking back at them both, leaving only when Eve nodded at her.

Eve and Drake were left to wait in the corridor leading toward the arena. Eve watched as Drake took deep breaths with his eyes closed, his hand restlessly grasping at the hilt of his sword.

"Drake, I won't sugar-coat this," Eve fixed Drake with a serious look, "this is going to be rough."

"How do you know so much about Ilas Arena, Eve?" Drake asked, neither disregarding her warning, nor acknowledging it, either.

"I told you. I've been here before."

"You've competed here?"

Eve paused momentarily, but she decided there was no point in hiding the truth any longer, not now that they were about able to fight for their lives together.

She exhaled, "yes, more times than I'd care to remember."

"I see." After a moment's silence, Drake asked, "any advice?"

"Never underestimate your opponent, and never hold back. If you do, it's as good as lights out."

Another moment of silence followed Eve's words, before Drake filled it once more, "I'm sorry, Eve, for getting you involved in this." His face creased. He looked deeply apologetic, idly running a finger around the hilt of his sword.

"Don't. I chose to be here, and besides, I want to make it up to you and Kerri."

"Make it up to us?" Drake responded, looking confused, "what do you mean?"

"Back at the cave, when we first found Kerri. It was me who made the decision to return her, not knowing who she was, and not caring what she meant to you, so, I'm sorry, too."

"You have no reason to apologise, Eve," Drake spoke in a comforting tone, "it was you who helped us to convince Scarlett to not turn Kerri in, so I think you've more than made up for it already if you ask me."

Drake glanced up to see Eve smiling softly but any further possibility of conversation was drowned out by the wailing of a siren. Moments after, the doors to the waiting room opened again, and the two were escorted by a couple of guards down a corridor towards the arena entrance.

An announcer was yelling through the speakers, "and today we have two unlucky folks, looking to clear the debt of one William Morgan!" They broke into laughter and the audience followed along, with jeers as well as murmurs of how it would be an impossible task. Eve ignored them, deciding to not make eye contact.

"Due to the nature of his debt, and the reputation of one of our new contenders, we've decided to bring the big guns out early tonight. That's right, we have the reigning champions themselves here tonight, please welcome Holly and Leo!" The crowd went wild with an ear-splitting cacophony of noise, but it was nothing compared to what followed next.

"And you're wondering who they could be fighting, eh? Well, hold on to your seats, ladies and gentlemen, because their challengers tonight are..."

The doors swung open. Eve and Drake looked around to see themselves surrounded by rows upon rows of people reaching high into the air. Across the sandy arena, with no ceiling in sight, were their two opponents hungrily eyeing them up.

"Drake, of the Marauders of Light, and Eve, our old champion! Who could've guessed it?!"

If the crowd went wild before, they were now loud enough to send the ground rumbling. Shouts of awe and surprise rang around the arena, the palpable excitement of the audience acting as the arena's heartbeat.

Everyone had an opinion, and Eve did her best to ignore them. She located her friends in the stands, looking bewildered at the reception the announcement of her competing received. She found it hard to keep eye contact with them.

"Something of a legend here, eh, Eve?" Drake said this as he looked around, his eyes wide in astonishment.

"We'll talk about it later." Eve sighed.

As they reached the centre of the arena, Eve caught a good look at their opponents. Holly's shaggy dirty-blonde hair reached no longer than her chin, and black makeup splashed across her eyes making her look feral. Leo, too, had dirty-blonde hair but it was neatly cut in comparison. He looked unnaturally stiff, sporting a similar slim frame to his partner. Holly was armed with two lengthy daggers whilst Leo held a sword and shield.

"Wouldn't you look at that, Leo? Eve, in the flesh!"

"Hmm."

Eve knew her return would ruffle feathers, but the unwanted attention still made her skin prickle. She felt her jaw tense as so much of it was directed at her.

"I want her dead." Holly looked directly at Eve before spitting on the ground.

"Do what you will." Leo turned his attention onto Drake. "Will you be a worthy opponent, like her?" He jerked his chin toward Eve.

"Her name is Eve," spat Drake,, "and it doesn't matter—I don't need to be worthy; I just need to win."

Leo narrowed his eyes. "We'll see."

Eve's heart threatened to burst through her chest, and her throat threatened to close in on itself. Her palms were clammy, and she felt a touch light-headed. Here, there was no mercy for someone who lacked skill in combat – who could not battle to the death – so Eve focused on the match ahead, doing her best to set aside her worries. After all, she was not only fighting for herself tonight. Eve might have been a little rusty and out of practice, but her talent was just as great as it ever was. She unsheathed her scythe, kicking up sand as she prepared for battle.

"I won't take it easy on you."

Holly flashed a wide grin, her lips stretched wide. "Heh, good! Make it worth my while, Eeeeevie."

Eve's brows furrowed at the nickname. She grasped her scythe tightly across its snath.

The announcer was still whipping the crowd into a frenzy. She could not hear them, Eve could see her friends shouting support, hands cupped around mouths and arms raised high into the air. It made her feel grounded, helping her to mentally prepare for the brawl ahead.

"Let's see a good fight tonight!" The announcer's voice yelled in a jubilant and dramatic fashion, and the ringing of another siren set the combatants into motion.

The four fighters broke off into pairs with Eve and Holly facing each other, and Drake and Leo doing the same. Eve was a little worried about Drake, this being his first time at Ilas Arena, but—

"Your distraction will get you killed!" Holly leapt in quickly with her daggers brandished. Eve weaved away from one of her swings by a hairbreadth, and was kept on the defensive during her opponent's mad, furious flurry of attacks. Her scythe was too long to utilise its reach. Not wanting to be kept on the defensive for long, Eve evaded and used the blade of her scythe to throw herself backward, scorching the ground behind her which caused Holly to yell expletives. It did little to quench her inner fire.

"You could make a killing if you returned full-time to the arena. It's a shame you won't live to see the day." Holly swung her head back to sweep her hair from her face. Her voice was ecstatic.

Eve yelled in frustration. She hated people like Holly, those who relished in the bloodshed. Even more so when she was the one of the two champions of Ilas Arena, bringing death whenever she could without remorse.

Before she could lose momentum, Eve dashed forward. She used her Flame to propel herself and cover distance more quickly. She swung her scythe as she approached Holly, who blocked the blow with a grunt, both of her daggers crossed over her chest.

"You'll have to be faster than that, Evie!"

Eve felt her skin bristle and surge with heat, a flash of panic shot down her nerves as she struggled to keep her Presence under control. Over Holly's shoulder she spotted Scarlett, Amie, Clarissa, Barron, and Kerri in the stands. They stood in their seats, their faces contorted as they cupped their hands around their mouths, crying out for their teammates' victory. Even from the arena, Eve could see Kerri's face crumple.

"Don't you dare look away from me!" Holly pushed back with her daggers and Eve leapt backward, swinging her scythe across. "Ha, missed me!"

"You think?" Eve extended her polearm, and the blunt head of the scythe plunged into Holly's stomach.

She cried out in pain, clutching her stomach. Eve retracted the polearm, twirled to the side, and ensnared

Holly in the arm of her scythe. She avoided cutting her, instead using her momentum to swing Holly across the arena, where she skidded along the floor into the wall with a sickening thud.

As a heavy cloud of sand enveloped Holly, Eve dropped to her knee to catch her breath. Her arm tingled from fighting, the impact of heavy blows exhausting the strength in her body. Through heavy breaths, her eyes found Drake and Leo.

Drake was on the backfoot, each of his attempts to land an attack were parried and pushed away by Leo's shield. Eve willed herself to her feet and stomped over, sweat pouring down her face. As she approached, she caught Drake's eye, and he shook his head no. Instead, she continued to watch.

Drake found himself at a disadvantage, armed with only a sword and bracer for defence, not knowing if Leo possessed a Presence. Every time he lunged, he was either parried or knocked back by Leo's shield. He was good.

Drake stamped the ground with his foot, using his Presence to cause the floor between the two to shake. Unsettled sand flew around, but was little more than a nuisance to Leo.

"Is that quite all you've got, swordsman?" Leo jeered. "I need no Presence to defeat you."

"If only it were so easy!" Drake ducked low and swept Leo's legs, sending Leo tumbling "Hah!" With a swift jump, he thrust his sword into his opponent—or he would have, if Leo were not equally as nimble.

Back on his feet, Leo smirked, "if only it were so easy, right?"

Eve was watching the sand settle where Holly fell. She was clambering back to her feet. Her unkempt hair hung loose in front of her face. "You'll pay for that, you know!" She charged across the battlefield and with each furious slash, she flung a black kind of liquid at Eve.

Although Eve was fast, she was not able to dodge all of what was thrown at her. As the object connected with her, she realised that it was acid being thrown. Her green jacket took the brunt of the attack, but the acid sizzled as it continued to burn through the material. Eve quickly removed the garment to toss it at her enemy. The jacket landed with a thud in Holly's face, causing her to become unbalanced. Eve pulled out her dragon pistol and aimed a flame-infused pellet at her jacket. The acid was bubbling away, distorting the fabric. She fired, and the jacket was ignited in a bright, sweltering flame.

Her opponent's ear piercing scream punctured the arena.

"Holly!" Leo had turned, distracted, allowing Drake to tackle him to the ground. Leo dropped his sword as he raised his shield to defend against Drake's furious punches. Leo cursed his moment of distraction, but Drake did not cease in mercilessly punching the steel further and further toward his opponent's face.

Holly freed herself from the flaming jacket and rolled in the sand to extinguish the remnants of the fire. When she stood again, her clothes were torn and tattered. Parts of her skin and hair were singed. They smouldered, smoke fleeing from her wounds. The real fire remained underneath her appearance, in her eyes, roaring with life and refusing to be extinguished. She burst into a sprint toward Drake and Leo, who did not hear Holly approaching as she flew across the arena.

Eve realised what she was planning to do, but Holly was fast, and she was already closer to the other pair. Realising that she would not reach them in time if she gave chase, and that Drake could be quickly outmatched if they both teamed up on him, she did the only thing that she could—she aimed to kill.

Eve steadied her dragon pistol, took a deep breath, and aimed at the retreating figure. She likely would only have one shot.

Many emotions and thoughts ran through Eve's head at that moment. The thought that she would once again be dubbed a champion of Ilas Arena, and how much that truly disgusted her. How her former way of life had well and truly burst its way back into her world, despite her best attempts to be free from it. How her new friends might be revolted by the truth as her past came to light. How she truly did not want to kill this woman, but knowing that there was nothing else she could do if she wanted Drake to live. These thoughts ran through her head in a flurry, but she refused to let them become a distraction. Exhaling, she let go of those thoughts to deal with later. She fired. In the next few seconds, the fiery pellet found its target. Holly did not scream. She made no noise at all. She fell flat with a crunch. The sand kicked up around her. Blood pooled under her body.

The gunshot caused Drake to stop momentarily, and Leo kicked him away, searching for the source of the noise. He frantically glanced around before he spotted Holly, face down in the sand.

"Holly?" Leo crawled over to Holly's body and turned her over. Her nose was broken, and her jaw had been dislocated.. "She's already going cold." He looked up angrily and saw Eve still holding her gun. "You monster." His voice broke as he bared his teeth at her. Eve felt sick.

"That's our killer Eve, right folks?!" The announcer cut in. They cheered in admiration and excitement, sending a cold chill down Eve's spine.

Leo softly lowered Holly's body down, and forced himself to his feet with fresh determination, tossing aside his sword and shield. "You will die here, former champion. I promise you that." He held his fists up, "I want you to fight me, Eve."

Eve glanced at Drake, who was still kneeling in the position where he had been thrown. He looked lost at the current situation, but climbed to his feet and approached his opponent.

"You're mine, Leo. I won't let you turn your back to me."

Leo turned his head toward Drake, but did not tear his gaze from Eve, "I'll deal with you afterward."

Drake threw his arms out. "Afterward? There won't be an afterward, not once she's through with you, and you know that."

"Don't you dare stand in my way!" Leo shouted at Drake, who looked at Eve.

She nodded to Drake, and he relented, stepping back. "I'm jumping in if I need to, Eve."

Eve nodded, keeping her eyes trained on Leo.

"Oho, fisticuffs can still remedy any conflict, isn't that right, folks?!" The crowd roared in agreement with the announcer and Eve's stomach twisted further.

She placed her own sword and pistol aside and raised her fists. "Did you help to bring back Ilas Arena?"

The man smirked. "Of course. It's the only place we feel alive. We were once s too, you know." Leo replied.

"Why would I know that?" In fact, she was shocked that people who once had such great pride in themselves would stoop so low as to murder for entertainment. "You've lost your way, and I'll ensure you don't lose it again."

Eve glanced at the audience where she saw the other members of the Marauders of Light reacting to the ongoing events. Amie was wide-eyed and had her hands over her mouth, Scarlett silent but watching intently. Barron and Clarissa were looking away, both at Kerri's shoulders who had her head in her hands. Eve watched her shoulders heave with sobs, which renewed her resolve to free her father.

Eve focused on Leo again, and the two began their battle anew. It was a bloody brawl, one that lacked rhyme or reason. The two former s gave no inch, trying their best to make their murder as personal as possible. At least, that was how it was for Leo. Eve knew that this fight would only come to an end when Leo had given in. She at least wanted to grant him a death on his terms.

Leo was not as nimble as Eve, and he was still distraught by Holly's death. Eve was better focused, taking advantage of his openings and landing hit after hit after hit. Blood dripped and bruises blossomed. Ragged breaths as punches were thrown were all the two could hear. Soon, Leo was too exhausted to stand. He fell to his knees, his body and spirit unable to take much more.

Eve spat blood and wiped at her mouth, watching the man before her come to terms with his loss.

"Are we done?"

"You're clearly the victor." Leo sank further to the floor, as if his strings had been cut. "Finish it."

"No," Eve shook her head once. "I won't."

"Why not?" He pointed a tired finger toward Holly, blood dripping from its tip, "you had no problem killing her." He stared forlorn at Holly's body, his will to fight now completely shattered.

"You damn idiot. I never wanted to kill her, and I never wanted to be here." She raised her voice louder, "I can't believe that a former would condone bringing back Ilas Arena. You... you're the worst." She spat again, a splatter of blood disturbing the sand at her feet.

"It was good pay, and we weren't coming across that elsewhere." Leo looked up, searching Eve's face with his eyes, "surely even you understand the desire to be even a shadow of what we once were?"

Eve stared and bit back at him, "not like this. Never like this."

She walked away to join Drake when the announcer's voice boomed out again, "it looks like the battle is over!" The crowd roared "but we know the rules—if one side is still standing, then nobody leaves the arena!" The crowd cheered louder, chanting for one more death.

"Such pigs," Eve raised her arm. "I won't do it, he has already conceded!"

"I'm sorry, but I say when someone concedes." A new voice rang out, perfectly calm, and perfectly sinister.

"You will kill him."

Eve would recognise that voice anywhere. It was Edin Garret. "I won't."

"Then you will all die, and by all, I mean the friends you've brought with you, too."

Eve looked toward her teammates in the stands and saw that several guards had grabbed them, and were attempting to haul them away from their seats.

"Now, will you really not kill this man?"

Eve opened her mouth to speak, but was cut off by a squelching behind her. Drake had plunged his sword through Leo's chest. He caught the man's body as it slumped, and placed it beside Holly's.

"I'm sorry, Eve," he looked ashamed, "but I can't take the risk."

Eve managed to give a small nod. She understood that there was no hope it would end any other day.

"Good," the voice took on a more charismatic tone, "that wasn't so hard now, was it?"

Eve boiled at the words but had nothing to say in response. Instead, the crowd exploded in cheers. Cheers at the action, cheers at the unbending rules of the arena, cheers at the death tonight, and lastly cheers for the hollow victory of their two murderers.

Eve and Drake were back in the waiting room, when the Marauders of Light were brought back to them. The silence was deafening for a moment as they stared at each other, then Amie strode along, grabbed both of them from their seats, and threw her arms around them. "I'm so glad you're both okay..."

Eve trembled now that the adrenaline was wearing off, her heartbeat had begun to take on a normal pace once again. She hugged Amie back, and with the stress and pressure from the fight now removed, and Drake and her friends' safety assured, she rested her chin on Amie's shoulder. Drake removed himself from the hug, patted Amie on the arm, and headed over to Scarlett, Barron, Clarissa, and Kerri.

"I hope I made you proud, Scarlett." Drake wore an unsure smile.

Scarlett grinned and squeezed his arm, "you did, as you always do, Drake." Her wide smile faded, and she looked Drake in the eyes. "But are you okay?"

Drake hesitated, but answered truthfully, "I might need some time, but I will be okay."

Scarlett nodded and squeezed his forearm again.

Kerri's eyes were puffy, her face red. She was unable to look at Drake or Eve, although she kept stealing glances. Drake approached and knelt down to be eye level with her. "Kerri, are you doin' okay?"

Kerri threw herself into Drake's arms and began to cry. Barron and Clarissa stood unsure, but both shared brief nods with Drake and Scarlett before retreating to the corridor to talk amongst themselves.

Eve watched with Amie as Drake rubbed Kerri's back. The younger woman's sobs wracked her body, and her hands grasped at his tattered shirt. As he moved her head up, her watery red eyes momentarily found Eve's, before Drake pulled her into his chest. Eve felt her eyes suddenly grow warm and turned away from them both. She wiped at her eyes and felt Amie's hand on her back. She turned to look at her, and was pulled into another hug.

"It's okay, Eve, it's okay." Amie stroked Eve's hair, and Eve sniffed once. She wiped at her face as the evening caught up with her.

"Thank you, Amie." She looked up at Amie.

"It's okay to be sad, but let's not do the whole arena thing again, okay, Eve?" Amie smiled, softer than her usual radiant grin.

"I'd love that." Amie held onto Eve's shoulders for a little while longer, watching Eve wipe her eyes, before letting her go properly.

Seeing the pair separate, Scarlett came over. "Doing okay, Eve?" When Eve nodded in response, Scarlett went on, "thanks for fighting today. It couldn't have been easy to go through that."

"It wasn't, but I'd do it again in a heartbeat, if it meant none of you ever had to."

"You aren't doing it again, so get that idea out of your head. I'm proud to have you in the Marauders of Light." Scarlett clasped Eve's shoulder before leaving to join Clarissa and Barron in the corridor.

Amie guided Eve to a sofa where they sat next to each other. Drake and Kerri join them on the opposite sofa, the latter wiping her tears with a small napkin. "T-thank you, Eve," Kerri hiccuped, "I'll be able to live with my dad again." She smiled a small, crumbly smile. A genuine one. Eve suddenly felt stronger, seeing this younger girl so fragile. All she wanted to do was simply live with her father.

"Anytime, Kerri," she smiled back, "but let's keep your dad debt-free from now on, okay?" Kerri laughed and nodded her head frantically, plastering a toothy grin on her face.

A guard summoned Eve and Drake to confirm their winnings. There were no riches, but William Morgan was currently being escorted from the dungeon. It was then that another guard appeared once more, asking them to follow him back to the upper levels of Ilas Castle.

Chapter Nine

Outside Ilas Castle away from the arena, everyone had returned to the inn to clean up, and met up again in Scarlett and Amie's room. Kerri was with her father, catching up on lost time. Drake and Eve were exhausted, they heard their beds calling them—but this had to come first.

"Firstly," Scarlett began, "good job today, you two," she smiled briefly, raising her hands to her chest, before lowering them again with a frown, "but you," she pointed a steady finger at Eve, "what else are you hiding from us?" Scarlett approached Eve who stood her ground.

"Nothing, I swear." Eve was surprised to see Scarlett looking at her with a gentle smile and a warmth behind her eyes. A softer expression than she had expected.

"I didn't think you were, but I just wanted to be sure," the leader grinned, "but you can tell us anything, you know, we're family now." She waved her arm to the room, "never forget that this, right here, is your family, Eve."

Eve looked around, the word "family" felt almost foreign to her after so long alone. A warmth blossomed in her chest.

"But I do want to talk about it. Your past, I mean." Scarlett looked at Eve, whose brow furrowed. "Will you?"

Eve bit her lip, and Amie tentatively began to get up from the bed, "it's okay if you don't want to, Eve."

"No, Scarlett is right. you're family. You deserve to know." Eve closed her eyes and took a couple of deep breaths, before looking at everyone again. "I used to be a champion of Ilas Arena. Years and years ago, when it was still being used to settle arguments between Warriors, or even warring nations. Back then, it didn't have to end in death, unless those rules were agreed upon by both parties beforehand," Eve felt a lump form in her throat with what she had to say next, "but they often did. I did. I killed. I murdered. I'm a murderer, a murderer over petty squabbles, none that I can even call my own."

The intense silence threatened to suffocate the room as Eve's audience listened with rapt attention.

"Never once did I challenge someone. Time and time again, every time I entered that arena, I fought for my life. Was fighting in the war not enough bloodshed already?"

Amie made to raise her hand, but quickly pulled it back down, shifting awkwardly in her seat. This made Eve muster an imperceptible smile, distracting her from her growing anger. "What is it, Amie?"

"Well, we all know of the war, but what did you do in it, exactly? I mean, you're, like, the Eve, right?

"The Eve?" Barron raised an eyebrow.

Clarissa huffed. "Oh, come on, Barron, you can't say that you didn't realise it by now? Eve here is the Eve of legend, the one who slayed countless soldiers and beasts. You could say she is among the most infamous former Warriors of our time."

"Hm, really? I think we should have a one-on-one duel sometime, what d'ya think?" He smiled, wide and toothy, at Eve.

Eve chuckled, "sure, when we have the time, Barron."

"But," Scarlett interjected, "back to the story, what were you fighting for?"

"I was angry. So damn angry, at everything that the war took from me." Eve clenched her fists, struggling to keep her rage in check, baring her teeth as she remembered days long gone. She took another breath and continued, "it didn't matter what side people fought on; they were equally as guilty, equally as inhuman." She looked up. She felt that the faces staring back at her were boring a hole through her, so she looked away. "Now the war is over, but I'm still here."

"Why is it so wrong that you're still here?" Drake asked, "we all did our part in the war."

Eve's eye twitched. "That was what was expected of us. We had to, but we weren't supposed to be remembered for it." She pinched the bridge of her nose and closed her eyes tightly. "I wish I didn't remember it at all."

"I know how you feel." Drake sympathised, "but we're fortunate to still be here." He gripped Kerri's shoulders, who was sitting in a chair in front of him, "to be there for those still with us."

Eve knew he meant well, but his words only incensed her. "Do you know how horrible it is to be known as a murderer?" She balled her hands up into fists. "A murderer, in a war? We would have all been murderers, but an example was made out of me!" The pit of lava in her stomach exploded, "and I'm so tired of it! I'm so tired of carrying this guilt!"

"Ouch!" A loud thud rang out. "I'm sorry!" Kerri leaned down to massage her ankle. A glass of water on the table in front of her had spilled. "That startled me. I'm sorry."

"Stop apologising!" Eve was not sure why this bothered her so strongly, but the anger continued to rise from deep within.

Kerri froze. Drake placed a hand on her back.

"Damn it." Eve stormed out of the room.

"Eve!" Amie called out but Eve slammed the door behind her. Stomping down the corridor, she bumped into Kerri, who was peeking out through her own door. She had been watching over her father who rested on the bed behind her.

"Eve, what is—are you okay?" Eve ignored her and bristled past. "Eve...?"

Eve reached her room and as she grabbed the door handle, Kerri came running to her, looking anxious. "Is everything okay?"

"Kerri, please." Eve inhaled sharply, her hand turning white as it clenched the doorknob. "I don't want to talk about it."

"I just—dad always said that talking about things helps." She tugged on her fingers, shifting uncomfortably.

Eve felt her anger boil over, a wave of heat that flowed from her head to her toes. "Well, I killed for your father today! What has he said about that, Kerri?" Kerri withdrew, taking a step back from Eve. "Well? A fool and their money are easily parted, isn't that right?"

Kerri stared with wide eyes at Eve a moment longer, before she scowled. "That is not fair, and you know it!"

Eve huffed and looked toward the door, her hand still clenched tightly around the doorknob, "I just want to go in my room."

Kerri's door opened again. William's head appeared in a gap, his eyes groggy as he wiped at them. "Is something the matter, Kerri?"

Kerri looked at Eve, her eyebrows furrowed in anger, as she responded between clenched teeth. "No. I was just coming right back." She turned on her heel and walked briskly back into her room, nudging her father back inside, and slammed the door behind her.

Eve did the same, the door rattling in its frame as the others peeked their heads out. Amie frowned and bit her lip, but Scarlett guided her back into their room.

Eve sat with her back against the door, her head in her hands. She took deep breaths in an attempt to recentre herself, but she was unable to ignore the guilt gnawing at her from the inside. The guilt of being angry, the guilt of taking it out on Kerri, the guilt at upsetting her friends—her family. the anger did not subside, she was trembling with the rage she had carried with her for a long, long time. She bit her lip hard and dug her nails into her shoulders, shaking with rage and hurt.

A moment later, there was a gentle rap at her door, and a soft whisper travelled through, "Eve, can I come in?" It was Amie. Eve sank her head further into her chest and did not respond. "Eve, please?"

Eve grunted and opened the door but blocked Amie's passage in. Amie walked directly into her arm with a small "oof!"

"Eve, really?!"

"I didn't say you could come in."

"But you opened the door!"

Eve pinched the bridge of her nose. "What do you want?"

"You look like you need a friend."

"Right now, I just need to be alone."

Amie frowned. "Alone? We're a family."

Eve did not respond.

"Please let me in." Amie reached out to Eve's hand on the door frame, but Eve pulled back. She saw Amie's face fall before she did her best to smile again.

"I understand." Her voice had lost its energy, and her shoulders slumped. "I'll go, but I'll be here if you need me, okay?" She looked again at the door frame where Eve's hand was before leaving without a response from Eve.

Eve watched after her for a beat longer before she closed the door again.

Eve tossed and turned before looking at the clock on her bedside table. Two-fifteen a.m. Was it really still that early? She groaned and stared at the ceiling before deciding that she was not going to be able to sleep any longer.

Pushing herself up from her bed, she pulled on her white t-shirt and brown trousers before leaving and heading downstairs. The inn was open at all hours so she decided to get a decaf coffee. Just as she was about to order, she heard a voice behind her, "milk and two sugars, right?"

Eve turned and saw Amie, looking exhausted, but awake all the same. "Yeah. thanks." Amie ordered two of the same coffee and, with both mugs in hand, walked over to an empty table. At this hour, they had the luxury of sitting wherever they wanted.

"Don't worry, I'm not going to ask you about it," Amie smiled, having pre-empted Eve's worry, "but the offer is always there if you ever wish to take it." She took a sip from her coffee, looking at Eve over the rim of her mug, before she suddenly jerked away with a sharp intake of breath. "Dang, that's hot!"

Eve took a sip. "I have to disagree. I think it's the perfect temperature." She grasped the mug tightly, enjoying the heat soaking in through her fingers. "I'm sorry for earlier."

"It's okay. It's been a long day, especially for you." Eve met Amie's eyes before looking away. "I wish I was down there with you today, Eve."

Eve gripped the mug tighter. "No, never. Don't dare set foot in that place." Eve felt her hands begin to shake, so she placed the mug down. She watched as the rippling coffee came to a stop. "One thing I don't regret today was my choice to fight in place of someone else."

"Eve, do you think Ilas Arena will end one day?"

"Any collective of people can fall when its leader does," Eve replied, "so possibly, yeah. In this case, it would be Edin Garret."

Amie's eyes widened, "the man Kerri's father was in debt to?"

"Yes." Eve sipped her coffee, "He is the one who spoke at the end. How could he be pulling this off?"

"I hate it too, you know, Ilas Arena." Amie looked deep in thought, tapping a fingernail against the wooden table. "Nobody should fight, or die, for entertainment." She went silent, then let out a sigh. "It's disgusting."

"That's the sort of man Edin is, "but he'll pay for it, one day, I'm sure of it."

"He will." Amie confirmed, taking Eve by surprise, "but in the meantime, I just wanted to say that I'm glad you're here."

"Yeah, me too."

They fell into silence as they finished their coffees, both grateful not to be alone.

The next day, the Marauders of Light, sans Eve, were found in the inn's café talking to William Morgan. Drake had gotten him some new clothes rather than the rags he had been wearing when in confinement. He had shaved, making him look younger and cleaner, although his thin face became more evident for it. He sat next to Kerri and would often reach out to grab, touch, and hold her hands, sometimes these actions would spill into each other in a fast flurry, as if he was unsure what he wanted to do. Kerri smiled, just as eager as he was to not let go.

He confirmed what they had already expected–that he had gotten himself into debt in his efforts to give Kerri a luxurious life, hoping that it would distract her from the loss of her mother. He swore to have had no further dealings with Ilas Arena and mentioned that he and Kerri would be leaving to find a new home, far away from Ilas, where they could start anew.

"W-what? You did not mention this to me yesterday, father." Kerri's eyes widened. Feeling shocked and appalled, she could only spit out in frustration, "do you not think that you have made enough decisions on my behalf?!"

William batted his daughter's anger aside. "I'm still your father, and you're still young. A mercenary guild is no place for a young girl like you."

"A young girl like me?" Kerri's temper flared, "I am doing perfectly fine for myself, thank you. I might not have fought in the arena yesterday, but I worked just as hard doing all I could for you." Kerri stared her father down. She felt her stomach twist, aggravated at the thought of her efforts being dismissed due to her age, and fear of being torn away from pursuing a new life.

"I haven't forgotten." William averted his eyes and pursed his lips. "In that case, what is it that you want to do, then?"

"I-" Kerri looked around the group and met Scarlett's eyes, who nodded. "I want to stay here," she gestured with her arm to the others, "with them."

Footsteps echoed down the staircase, grabbing the attention of the others. As Eve reached the table, she placed a hand on Kerri's shoulder. "And then you should. We'd never let anything happen to you." Eve directed her next words to William, "I promise you that. I'd protect Kerri with my life."

At these words, Kerri laid her hand upon Eve's and grasped it softly. The rest of the team burst out into their own words of support.

"And you, Drake? How do you feel about it?" William noticed that Drake had not spoken up, deep in thought with his hand on his chin.

"Kerri has proven herself. It is dangerous, and she isn't trained in combat... but yes, I, too, would protect Kerri, with my life. We'll see to it that she's properly trained in combat, too."

William took the time to mull over the words of the group before he cupped Kerri's face in his hands. His fingers were bony and his veins were prevalent, malnourished from his time in the Ilas Arena dungeon, as they stroked Kerri's cheeks. "I'll miss you, my daughter."

"I love you, dad." She nestled her head into William's chest, holding him tightly.

"I'm going to be heading to Argol's Creek, the fishing town. Their crime rate is wonderfully low, don't you know?"

"That sounds wonderful!" Kerri's delight was real as she pulled away. She hoped that even her father would not be able to get himself into trouble in such a peaceful town. "And don't worry dad, I'll visit! Thanks for understanding. I'm going to be an incredible Marauder of Light, you know!" She pumped a fist against her chest, beaming brightly. She felt a warmth blossom in her chest, and a giddy joy that threatened to pour out from her mouth. She pumped her arms again.

William chuckled, "I know Kerri, you'll make me proud. You always have done." He pulled her back in for another quick hug before letting her go. "I've already been back home to get my stuff in order, and well, I think you might like to hold on to this."

He removed a tiny painting from his wallet. It looked yellow from age, and it was frayed around the edges. When Kerri saw it, she put a hand to her mouth as she gasped. "My mother."

"You look a lot like her."

"I really do, don't I?"

Kerri beamed, staring at the photo of the woman who looked as if she could be her twin.

They said their farewells to William, who boarded a carriage to take him on his way to Argol's Creek. Waving him off at the edge of town, Kerri looked around, a little teary-eyed, and asked, "so, what's next?"

Eve was not sure. She really did not expect Kerri to stay with them, or for William to allow it. She had taken a liking to Kerri, and believed that she had a lot of potential. A part of her was excited to see how much Kerri could grow, but anxious that she was in their care now. They were all much older than she was, would she be comfortable with them? Eve did not think she would be able to help much outside of combat-based education, so this nagged at her mind. Her eyes shifted towards Amie. Perhaps Amie would be a good friend to her, as the second youngest in the group? She did not want to be the bearer of bad news to William if something were to happen, as the man had already been through and sacrificed enough.

The team turned to Scarlett, "hmm, that is the question, isn't it? We don't currently have a mission, so what say you to us making our way back to Thous? I don't know about you lot, but I'm ready to say goodbye to Ilas." She regarded the town, its aqua tower shining bright in the sunlight, glimmering so strongly that it seemed as if a strong gust of wind could free it from its watery prison and drown the city. Eve shook her head. She disliked Ilas and its secrets. Is that why she could not appreciate the building and associated it with death?

Everyone murmured in agreement, and they took one last lap around the market to ensure that they had everything they needed. It was still a two-day trip to get home, so they loaded up on food, drink, and medicines.

Eve rubbed her eyes. She was tired. She felt something warm touching her other hand, and looked to her side to see Amie smiling at her. She swallowed hard, her senses and emotions felt dulled due to exhaustion, but as Amie tugged her forward, she felt relieved. Amie guided her without a word, and Eve wished that life could always be so straightforward.

Chapter Ten

The journey back to Thous was uneventful, with light banter shared around the campfire each night, and nobody talking specifically about Ilas Arena. Nobody brought up the events from the evening before, and Eve was grateful for it. Amie was often by her side when they ate, or spoke as a group. She thought maybe Amie wanted her to feel comfortable, but was not sure if she had turned the others away. When Eve's thoughts drifted, Amie would usually distract her with a question, or by pointing out something around them. It made her happy.

Eve, along with the others, all agreed on one thing. They were looking forward to resuming a more normal life, and taking on missions which provided more breathing room.

Whether it was collecting herbs for remedies from the local forests, doing some busywork in Thous, or even taking turns manning the stall throughout the day, the Marauders of Light were looking forward to something that did not involve high stakes life-or-death combat. As Eve was thinking of other things they could do, she remembered her jacket going up in flames. She hugged herself. It felt strange to be without the weight of the leather.

Arriving in Thous as the sun beat down on them, the Marauders were welcomed by the familiar scents of the morning market.

"Nothing like home sweet home!" Amie exclaimed happily, stretching her arms above her head.

A murmur of agreement rumbled across the group, along with a few stifled yawns, with the team all looking like they could use a good night's sleep.

"Hey, Eve, where are you staying at the moment?", Clarissa asked.

"I'm staying at an inn, but well," she thought about her dwindling funds, "I could definitely do with some paying work. I'm going to go check out the job board before heading back."

"The rent around here isn't that bad if you're thinking about sticking around for a while." Clarissa, who did not often smile, granted Eve a small one.

"Yeah, I think that could be a good idea." Eve felt a warmth spread within her chest, realising the implication behind Clarissa's words.

"C'mon, I'll come with you." Scarlett offered and Amie joined too. Drake took Kerri back to his home to rest, while Barron and Clarissa went off to do some food shopping together to restock the stand.

At Willkeep's Tavern there were only a small handful of people enjoying their morning coffee and breakfasts, leisurely enjoying their time alone as they read a newspaper or a book. The opening of the door disturbed dust in the air, causing Amie to sneeze.

She sniffed loudly, "actually, maybe I need to rest, too. I'll see you at home, sis. Good luck with the search, Eve!" Amie rubbed her eyes and yawned sneezing again as she headed back home.

Scarlett shrugged. "Well, shall we?"

The marketboard in the inn had several new job listings, seemingly recently posted, giving them the pick of the crop.

"Cullings, collecting materials and herbs, even one for returning a lost kitten... I don't think we should take that mission, but if we find it, let's return it anyway." Scarlett spoke aloud as she flicked through the options, looking for one that would pay well and wouldn't be too dangerous. "We'll split stall duties between us—all proceeds go towards a shared fund for equipment and items—but if you want to make a little extra income, then well," Scarlett removed a slip and presented it to Eve, "you can't go wrong with a friendly challenge, right?" The mission was posted by another guild, one looking to train its members. "Sometimes guilds will work together on missions, or even just for training. I can't see why they would object to sparring with us, and well, they're paying quite well for this."

Seeing another team would make for a nice change of pace and act as a good opportunity to improve as a team. Who knew, if they ever go to war again, maybe these will be the people they fought alongside. "Okay, let's do it."

They took the slip for themselves. They still had to go to the person responsible for posting it to officially accept the mission, but they could do that once the whole team was together. Eve felt that they could really do with the training though, especially as a unit. Drake was a competent fighter, but Eve worried about how things could have gone down with Leo, had things not gone down the way that they did.

"Whilst we're here, shall we grab a bite to eat?" Asked Scarlett.

As if on cue, Eve's stomach grumbled. "I think I'm spoken for."

Scarlett laughed and browsed the menu.

Eve's mind was already made up, a choice made with her hunger in mind. "I'm going to get the big breakfast."

Scarlett sighed, "et tu, Eve?"

"The heart wants what the heart wants, captain."

"Yeah, right, the heart." Scarlett ordered a smaller version of the breakfast and watched in horror as Eve devoured the entire dish in record time, not breaking a sweat. "Amie is going to be proud... I think? I mean, maybe you'll see Amie angry!" Scarlett pondered how her sister would react, knowing full well how passionate she was about this breakfast.

Their plates soon replaced by two cups of steaming coffee, Scarlett took the opportunity to broach a sensitive subject. "Eve, I apologise if this is unwelcome advice, but if you ever need a break, you can take one, you know?"

Eve narrowed her eyes and stared at the froth in her mug, feeling guilty for worrying her friend. "I'm okay, but thank you."

"Did you want to talk about it?"

Eve stirred her coffee, not looking up.

"It's okay if you don't want to, but take care of yourself, okay? Promise me."

"I promise."

"Good." Eve saw Scarlett break out into a toothy grin, reflected in her silver spoon.

"You what?!"

The following day, Eve informed Amie of her victory, leaving the younger sister shocked to her core. Appalled. Betrayed. "There's no way..." Amie turned and covered her face, playing the damsel of distress. Eve finishing the breakfast had clearly sent her into the deepest pits of despair. "However," she made a show of twirling back around, hands on her waist, this time with a look of determination on her face, "I will do it!" she declared, resulting in odd looks from people passing them by on the street.

"That's the spirit, Amie!" Barron joined in, adding to the ruckus.

"Will you two shut up?!" Scarlett shouted at the two over her shoulder, her face blushing. "I'm so sorry, I promise you that they'll make good training partners."

The man she was talking to was Marcus, leader of Rising Dawn, who had put out the training mission request.

He watched the situation behind Scarlett with amusement. "That's okay. As long as they can spar, it's fine if they laugh, even if very loudly." He winced slightly at the renewed laughter from Amie and Barron, who were intent on further embarrassing their leader.

"My God, just shut up!" This caused the members of Rising Dawn to laugh also, and Scarlett put her hand to her face.

"Listen up, everyone!" Marcus addressed both guilds with Scarlett at his side. The members of Rising Dawn snapped to attention, although like the Marauders of Light, they huddled together as a group rather than formally lining up. Eve wondered if this is what her guild looked like to others. Small. Disorderly. Maybe not all that capable? She frowned at herself for forming an opinion before even talking to them, especially as most of them certainly maintained their bodies.

"Today is a friendly training exercise, and so we'll be using wooden equipment." He pointed two fingers toward multiple racks of weaponry and defensive gear, stacked with wooden replicas of all sorts of melee weapons and firearms. "For firearms, please find replica guns which fire plastic shells - but do be wary of each other's faces. I promise you; they do sting!"

"Yep, I'm all good on the scars I've already got, thanks." Drake rubbed his face, tracing the large scar running down along it. A younger, scrawny man from Rising Dawn turned his gaze away from the scar, looking uncomfortable. Eve thought it was fortunate for the group that none had seemingly suffered any noticeable scarring.

"Exactly. A scar might make for a cool-looking battle memento, but getting one is gonna sting like hell." Marcus absentmindedly rubbed his arm before continuing, "this training exercise has been put together to help our members grow accustomed to fighting

115

enemies with different weapons and abilities. If battle comes along, it won't be enough to be comfortable—you need to be prepared for any potential match-up." Eve watched as the others nodded with confidence. She noted that two members of Rising Dawn looked excited. One was a tall muscular woman, while one was a slightly shorter, sturdy looking man who Eve felt did not look all that dissimilar to Drake. She knew Marcus was right. Not everyone here had seen war. They were hardly prepared to fight every battle like their last.

"With that said, we're going to split you into pairs. As we have two less members in our guild than yourselves, two of you will be on standby."

"Eve," interjected Scarlett, "you'll watch with us—you're already well-trained, so it'll be good to have your eyes focused on the battles to see where people can improve." Eve nodded, looking forward to a chance to watch the other's fight. "Kerri, you too, we don't expect you to fight today." Kerri softly sighed, her hand to her chest, a mix of relief and disappointment written on her face.

"Amie, you'll pair with Ellen." Sabre against lance? That match-up would be to Amie's disadvantage.

"Gordon, you'll be squaring off with Drake." Sword against axe. That was anybody's win.

"Clarissa, Arthur give it your best!" Eve had not yet seen Clarissa draw her daggers, but against another sword user? She was interested to see how that would go.

"And finally, Kyrie, you'll face off with Barron." Barron was slower due to his axe, but Kyrie had gauntlets. Was she fast enough to get in close and to make up for her lack of range? She had such a large frame, and much of that was muscle.

"As leaders, we'll give you a little taste of what we're expecting," Marcus collected a wooden sword and shield, getting into battle position, "are you ready, Scarlett?"

Scarlett smirked and readied her own wooden sabre. "Always."

The two squared off, and Marcus addresses his audience as he and Scarlett circled each other, "as you can see, Scarlett wields a sabre, which isn't too far removed from my own sword and shield. Equipment-wise, I have the advantage due to my extra defence, but in terms of mobility, that would be Scarlett, as she doesn't have a shield weighing her down. "

"Ah," Scarlett interjected, having just remembered something, "what's the rule on Presence?"

"If you have one, you can use it. Battle with an enemy in any real-world application isn't going to give you the option, after all."

"Go on, sis, get him!" Amie's cheer egged on the others to begin cheering, and soon a friendly competitive spirit surged throughout the training field.

Their wooden blades clashed, and Marcus' assumptions were proven correct as Scarlett danced around him at a pace that he struggled to keep up with. She displayed quick footwork as she slashed and parried, giving Marcus little time to react. On the defensive, Marcus switched tactics. Instead of attempting to outmanoeuvre Scarlett, he charged in, his shield raised. Scarlett sidestepped, but Marcus thrust his shield to his side, landing a clean hit on Scarlett to her ribs. She grunted in pain.

"That's one!" Ellen declared. It was first to three hits across all matches, meaning that Scarlett was only two hits away from a loss.

"Nice one, Marcus." Scarlett grinned, "don't expect that to work a second time."

Scarlett stood with one hand behind her back, and with the other she wiggled her sabre, inviting Marcus to attack her. Although wary of her play, he took the bait as his sword met her sabre, she returned with a riposte, jabbing his hand so quickly that he was unable to raise his shield in the hopes of blocking it.

"That's one! You each have two hits left!"

"I guess it's time I got serious." Marcus smiled and furrowed his eyebrows. In the next instant, he vanished.

"What?" Scarlett spun in a circle, head darting around as she searched for her opponent, when she was suddenly struck on the back of the head by the hilt of Marcus' sword. "Gah!"

"That's two!"

"Ah, damn it!" Scarlett turned with unmatched speed, but Marcus was still nowhere to be seen.

"Marcus' Presence allows him to turn invisible, but only as long as he isn't hit." Ellen explained, clearing up the confusion among the Marauders of Light.

"An impressive Presence, but if that's the case, Scarlett should manage just fine." Barron nodded and smiled, his unwavering trust in his leader's capabilities not shaken one bit.

One hit away from a loss, in front of her own team no less, Scarlett thrust her sabre into the floor, using Spark to shoot electricity out in a wide circle.

"Ah!" Marcus reappeared, thrown off-guard by Scarlett's Presence. Not allowing the opportunity to pass her, she leapt in with a slash, followed quickly by a second slash. Marcus was not quick enough to dodge or block, so both hits cleanly landed.

"That's two and three! The victory goes to Scarlett!"

The Rising Dawn groaned whilst the Marauders of Light erupted in cheers, and Scarlett shook hands with Marcus.

"That was really well fought. Your team is lucky to have such a competent leader." Scarlett praised, acknowledging how close the battle had been.

"You too, good fight." Marcus returned the handshake with a grin, "next time, I'll be the one to claim that third hit."

"I'd like to see you try." The two agreed to the future challenge before addressing their teammates again.

"If there are no questions, then we want to see Gordon and Drake up here next."

The two men approached the centre and readied their gear. "Damn, it feels so strange not using the real thing." Gordon stated. He was tall and muscular, with thick hair like a lion's mane. Compared to Drake's clean cut style, Gordon looked menacing. Being slightly shorter than Drake did not dampen his intimidating stature.

"It doesn't quite have the same feel, does it?" Drake agreed. The two finished preparations and assumed their battle stances.

"If you're both ready—begin!"

The two men were in motion and mirrored each other as they both stepped back, having anticipated that the other would jump forward. Both grunted before leaping into the fray and due to Gordon's larger, slower weapon, Drake ducked in with a quick jab, landing the first hit.

"That's one!" Ellen called, keeping track again.

"Ooh, nice one, but—" Gordon swung his axe in a semi-circle, forcing Drake to jump back, but he was unable to dodge the follow-up attack. "Ah, damn!" Gordon used his Presence to blow a gust of wind at Drake, successfully toppling him, before rushing over to land a clean hit to his stomach. Drake clambered to his feet and put some distance between them before he was able to follow up with another attack.

"That's one!"

"Two can play at that game!" Drake slammed a foot into the ground and created a small set of rising steps which he bound across. As he jumped from the last one, he used the momentum to topple it backwards, causing a domino effect. Using the dirt and dust to his advantage, he rolled and jabbed Gordon again, before rolling back out of range of any counterattacks.

Gordon was heard coughing in the cloud of dirt, followed by a yell of frustration.

"T-that's two!" Ellen, like the others, coughed due to the sudden swirling dust.

"In a situation like this, I guess I need to adapt!" shouted Gordon, swinging his axe at him. Drake went to defend but Gordon shifted his weight, instead ramming his shoulder into his opponent. Drake was pushed back by the charge, his feet skidding along the floor.

"That's two!

"You thought I'd be easy, huh?!" Gordon removed a small wooden knife from a strap around his calf which he swung madly at Drake.

Drake stamped the ground again, causing it to shake. Gordon lost his balance, and as he thrust with the axe, Drake pivoted aside, and gently tapped him on the shoulder with the tip of his sword.

"That's three! The victory goes to Drake!"

Eve shook her head, having foreseen this conclusion. Gordon had surrendered his chance at victory as soon as his emotions got the better of him.

Gordon was on the floor, panting heavily, as Drake approached, his hand held out. "Good fight, Gordon."

"Don't!" Gordon slapped his hand away as he pulled himself to his feet. "Next time, I'll win."

With his teeth clenched, Drake responded, "if this were a real fight, you'd be dead. It's best you learn that here today, rather than out there tomorrow. With that attitude, nobody is going to be saving your sorry arse on the battlefield."

Gordon went to argue, but was cut off by Scarlett and Marcus. "That's enough of that, you two!" "Don't embarrass me, Drake."

The two men left the centre and stood on opposite sides of the circle, quietly seething.

"This is all friendly training, is that clear?" Marcus raised his voice, "if you cannot respect each other, then you're free to go."

Eve watched silently. Gordon stomped off to his guild, where Kyrie slapped him on the back with a hearty guffaw. He yelled at her, his jaw jutted forward and his lips curled inwards. Drake was talking to Barron and Clarissa, as if being scolded rolled right off his back. Eve agreed with Drake. Ego had no place on the battlefield, and in a real world setting, Gordon would be dead. Everybody had been friendly until this battle, so she hoped that this would be the exception.

"Okay, good. Ellen, Amie, you're up! Let's see a nice fight."

Amie and Ellen took to the circle. Ellen was decked out in light, silver armour with a light blue lining. She was bright eyed, youthful and slightly gangly. She had a thin frame, and Eve wondered if a shorter, faster weapon would have been ideal for her. Her hands gripped the lance, one by the point and one by the heel. The lance had what looked like a heavy butt. Eve knew this is often used to act as a weight to give the lance a weight comfortable to the wielder. She wondered how heavy it was.

Amie only had a bracer and a chest guard for defence in today's battle. Eve thought she looked small, but knew that Amie had deceptive appearances.

Amie could get a hit counted from simply hitting Ellen's armour, but if this were a real battle, Ellen would only need one good hit to take Amie out of the fight.

"Begin!"

Using the range of her lance to her advantage, Ellen jabbed it forward to its full reach, but Amie evaded it and used her sabre to slam the head of the lance into the ground. Ellen swept left, but Amie deftly hopped over the lance and jabbed Ellen in the chest in the next breath. "Gah! Darn it, nice hit, Amie."

"That's one!" Marcus shouted, having taken over Ellen's announcer duties.

Ellen swung her lance up, creating distance between herself and Amie, forcing the latter to retreat. The younger redhead was even more swift on her feet than her sister, but the disadvantage of range hindered her ability to get close as Ellen focused on defence. Ellen forced Amie toward the edge of the circle, leaving Amie with no choice but to take the offence. She parried one hit of the lance, but Ellen was too quick on the second thrust, and Amie took a direct hit to the stomach.

She gasped, putting a hand to her stomach, "okay, ouch, I felt that."

"That's one!"

Still near the edge of the circle, Amie unleashed her Presence and created an icy floor ahead of her. This surprised Ellen, and she struggled to keep her footing in her steel boots. Already familiar with and adept at traversing on ice, Amie skid forward and slashed at Ellen with her wooden rapier as she skated by. She showed off a little, skating along and highfiving Drake as she went by, before she came to a halt.

"That's two!"

"You're pretty good!" Ellen grinned as her hand set alight. She tossed a small fireball at the ice Amie left behind, melting it entirely. Eve knew that this spelt bad news for Amie, but she was curious to see what else Ellen could do with Flame.

"Oh, shit." Amie furrowed her eyebrows and frowned. Eve knew that she was a capable fighter. All she had to do to win was to rely on her natural abilities.

Ellen leapt around as she hurled fireballs at Amie. She was dodging all of them spectacularly—bar one, which hit her cuff. Amie whimpered as she patted out the small flame blooming on her cuff. Ellen followed up with a jab of her lance, catching Amie on her chest. Ellen exhaled and wiped sweat from her forehead.

"That's two!"

The next move was unexpected. Ellen fired a larger wave of fire toward Amie, who hurriedly summoned a thick wall of ice in response. Eve watched Ellen. She looked as if Amie had poured ice water down her. She was absolutely dripping in sweat to a degree that Eve was concerned. Ellen grabbed at her head with her face scrunched, before letting out a roar. She lurched forward with her lance to break through the remaining icy barrier weakened by her flame, before using it as a make-shift javelin to propel herself forward and kick Amie in her chest plate and out of the circle.

"That's three! The victory goes to Ellen!"

Amie was still on the ground when Ellen approached her. Both were sweating due to the intensity of the battle and using their Presence so often. "Even though you were at a disadvantage, you put up an incredible fight. I'd love to spar with you again someday."

Amie grabbed Ellen's hand and the two shook on it. "I hate losing, but you won, fair and square. How will I deal with your Flame next time?" She tapped a finger idly against her chin as she thought. "Maybe I can ask Eve for a tip or two." They returned to the outer circle, continuing their conversation with smiles on their faces.

Eve was sad Amie had lost, but she really did put up a good fight.

Marcus nodded his approval. Scarlett clapped Amie on the shoulder and told her that she did well.

Ellen returned to her group where Arthur gave her a towel and a bottle of water. She sat down and took in deep breaths. She looked positively exhausted. Eve could hazard a guess as to why this was, and it was likely that Ellen was not too used to using her Presence.

Marcus clapped his hands to get everyone's attention. "Barron, Kyrie, you can begin when ready."

Kyrie was muscular. That was about Eve's only thought. That she was muscular, and she was huge. She had short hair that was thick on top and shaved on the sides. Her fringe bounced as she busied herself warming up. Kyrie banged her wooden gauntlets together, which were custom-made with flexibility which allowed her to wield them more naturally. Barron entered the battle with his large axe and two hand-axes. Barron's Flame was not very strong, so he could be at a disadvantage as he would be reliant on getting close to Kyrie.

"You ready?" Kyrie asked, grinning.

"Yep. Give it everything you've got!"

Kyrie grinned, "I plan to!"

She lunged forward with a punch, which collided with the flat side of Barron's axe, the impact reverberating outward. Eve could feel it from where she stood observing.

Kyrie did not let up and continued pummelling Barron's axe, leaving him with little chance to react.

As she threw another punch, Barron tilted his weight slightly with the flat of his axe held in front of him, causing Kyrie to slide from the axe's surface and stumble past him. With one swift movement, he swung his axe in an arc, aiming directly for Kyrie's back. Kyrie ducked and responded with a rising punch to Barron's stomach.

"That's one!"

Barron grunted, "those muscles aren't just for show, eh? Swift and strong, I can see when I'm at a disadvantage."

"Flattery will get you nowhere, but feel free to pile on the praise anyway!" Kyrie laughed, and Barron smiled before placing his axe on his back.

"Hand-axes might be the better choice here!" With that roar, Barron and Kyrie traded furious blows, hand-axe meeting gauntlet, with both wooden instruments beginning to splinter, unable to keep up with the fierce blows of their wielders. Deciding that this had gone on long enough, Kyrie pushed forward with her shoulder and sent Barron tumbling several feet, his axe braced in front of him. He rolled nimbly into a defensive position, "is that some sort of wind Presence?"

"Ah, close, but not quite. My Presence is called Shockwave. I can blow people away with great force." She thought briefly, then added," you might want to keep your eye on the edge of the circle."

"Hmm..." Barron eyed the edge of the circle, only a foot from where he stood, "point taken."

Unless he could throw his hand-axe, Barron had little range to work with. He could imbue his weapons with Flame, but he wasn't quite so proficient with it to use it as a projectile. Eve wondered what his next move would be.

"That's enough mercy!" Kyrie charged forward, rapidly closing the gap between the two, but instead of

punching, she leapt and drop-kicked Barron before artfully jumping from the hand-axes he raised to defend himself, landing at a safe distance away from him.

"That's two!" Barron had been kicked from the circle, leaving him with only one hit left.

"Desperate times call for desperate measures." He imbued one of his hand-axes with Flame, where it all but crumbled in his hand. His face went a deep red. "I forget these are made of wood."

Kyrie's laugh was so boisterous and loud that had Barron acted sooner, he could have taken her down right there and then. Barron flustered, and he followed up with his second hand-axe which collided with Kyrie's shoulder.

"That's one!"

"That's one, but at what cost? You're back to your axe." Kyrie was wiping tears from her eyes.

"I prefer my axe, anyway."

"It's a bad match-up."

Barron shrugged. "I know."

"Well, as long as you know." Kyrie charged in once more, and Barron swung his axe down, but Kyrie was too quick. She skirted to the side and used her momentum to knee Barron in the face, causing him to lose his footing and fall

"That's three! The victory goes to Kyrie!" Marcus was back on announcer duty.

"I like your attitude, old man, let's do this again sometime." Kyrie pulled Barron to his feet.

"Nicely fought, Kyrie, I have a lot to learn, it would seem, so I'll take you up on that!" They shook hands and returned to the outer circle.

"So that leaves Clarissa and Arthur. Take your places, both." Marcus declared the final battle of the day.

This was the match-up that interested Eve the most. She did not know what to expect from Arthur, but he was much smaller than the others, so she assumed he would mostly attack with his Presence. She knew what Clarissa was capable of when it came to her Presence, but hoped to see more from her today to get a better understanding of what she can do.

"Tell me, Arthur, what's your Presence?" Clarissa asked.

"That would ruin the surprise now, wouldn't it?" Arthur teased.

"Well," Clarissa smiled self-assuredly, "you'll have to tell me afterwards, then. When you've lost."

Arthur withdrew at Clarissa's confidence. "I-I won't go down without a fight!"

In the next moment, Arthur dropped his sword and grasped at his throat. Clarissa walked up and tapped him on the shoulder three times with a wooden dagger. As soon as the final tap landed, Arthur fell onto all fours, gasping for breath. "W-what was that?!"

"Uh, that's three?" Ellen announced.

Eve groaned. She was afraid that this would happen.

"Ah, I have a masterful control over Wind Presence, so I can squeeze the air out of someone's body with ease."

A rumble of comments round out across the audience.

"Damn, that's frightening."

"Yep, gotta feel sorry for Arthur."

"Glad that wasn't my match-up."

"If it's any consolation," said Clarissa, "you may very well have won a straight duel."

"I don't know about that," Arthur responded, dusting himself off, "my ego is pretty bruised."

Clarissa patted him on the back. "You'll get over it."

Arthur looked dejected but took it on the chin, addressing the rest of his team, "any of you think you'd do better?" Everyone else turned away or shook their heads. "Well, that does make me feel a little better!"

The two guilds talked among themselves whilst Eve spoke to Scarlett and Marcus about ways their respective team members could improve.

"Marcus, you have a strong team, and you seem to be a good leader. In regard to Kyrie, I have nothing to say. She's a remarkable fighter."

Marcus grinned, "Yep, she has no fear, and I haven't seen her lose a duel yet. Sometimes I wonder why she's hanging around with us!" He laughed.

"As for Ellen, she's also a competent fighter, and although she won today, she'll need to find a way to deal with close-up combatants more efficiently. Her Presence is incredible. I could see the drain it was having on her, and had the fight gone on much longer, she might have lost. Maybe a firearm or a dagger would be a good back-up weapon for her, or a customisable lance that can adapt to different scenarios."

"Interesting." He looked over at her with a finger on his chin. "I think she'd be receptive to that."

"I'm not sure what to say about Arthur. I wish Clarissa saved her trump card for last, but well, I haven't seen her wield those daggers yet. Let's mix up the pairings next time and give him another go."

"Yeah, that was sad to see. that Clarissa is quite a frightening woman, isn't she?" Marcus glanced over to Clarissa, who was happily conversing with Barron, Arthur,and Kyrie.

"The real issue is Gordon." Marcus winced, having expected this. "He can clearly hold his own, yet that won't be enough. I wouldn't trust him to have my back, and that lack of trust can harm more than just himself. His attitude needs working on, urgently."

"Point taken. I'm not best pleased with him either. Rest assured I'll speak with him."

"Good. Now you, Marcus." He stood straight and gave Scarlett his full attention. "You almost won, and your Presence would be a terrific tool against any fighter without the appropriate counter Presence. Today, it was your reliance on your Presence that lost you the fight. As a training match you did well, but you want to bait your opponent's Presence out, or confirm that they don't have one, before relying on your own defensive Presence so heavily."

He scratched his head. "I agree. I may have underestimated my opponent. I apologise, Scarlett." He bowed his head to Scarlett, who brushed it off.

"Don't worry, you almost had me beat, after all."

Eve directed her attention to her redheaded leader, who was waiting to hear what Eve made of her own crew. "Amie fought wonderfully. She lost, unfortunately the Presence match-up wasn't in her favour. As the two are now, if they fought without Presences, Amie may have won. They both have Presences, although so will most opponents Amie may find herself up against. We need to work on what she can do with her Ice, in the case that her sabre alone won't be enough."

"Sis made me proud today, nevertheless, I know she's capable of more." Scarlett glanced at her sister, who was deep in conversation with Ellen.

"Drake's performance had improved since the, uh, last time I saw it, although I assume that might be down to a clearer mind." She almost mentioned Ilas Arena but caught herself. "He utilised his Presence cleverly, blinding his opponent. He's a good swordsman too. I have little to say other than he just needs to keep at it, and to ensure that he has good control over his emotions."

Scarlett nodded and looked over at Drake, a smile blooming on her face.

Eve continued, "Clarissa? Well, I'd love to see her use her daggers, although I can't really fault her approach. One day, there will be a Presence which will deflect or overwhelm her own, and I worry she's too confident in herself. I need to know if she can fight without her Presence."

"I've seen it, and you can rest assured she certainly knows how to use them. I worry for anyone who manages to push her that far." Scarlett said with confidence. They watched Clarissa as she floated her two daggers using her Presence, the two bobbing in a small circle.

"Barron had a tough match-up, especially against such a powerful and swift opponent. I think the outcome may have been drawn before they battled, and we need to focus on improving Barron's Flame, as well as his weapon options."

"Sounds good to me, but what about me, Eve?" Scarlett asked, welcoming any feedback.

"You know damn well you're good. You used your Presence to your advantage and are highly skilled with your sabre. I often see you use your Presence defensively though when it's perfect for offence, too. Don't shy away from your Presence's full potential."

"Thanks, Eve, duly noted. Do you think today was a success?"

"I do. Everyone got along, with the exception of Drake and Gordon."

"Yeah, we'll have to work on Gord's attitude, sorry, both of you." Marcus sighed.

"I thought everyone was amazing." Kerri spoke in wide-eyed wonder as she approached from the sidelines, not used to seeing so many talented fighters come together. "Eve, do you think I could be like that one day?" The younger girl looked up, eyes shining.

"If you're inspired, then we can begin training you soon. I'll happily train you myself."

"Eve!" Kerri shouted in awe, "really?!"

"Of course." Eve smiled, feeling inspired by Kerri's enthusiasm.

Marcus clapped his hands together to grab everyone's attention, the setting sun reflected in his eyes. "Let's finish there! We hope you've all learned something from today because, if the Marauders of Light are willing, then I'd like to do this again sometime."

"No arguments here!" Scarlett gave her blessing.

All in agreement, everyone shook hands—including Drake and Gordon—before Rising Dawn took their leave.

"So," Scarlett turned to them and put her hands together, "how do we think that went?"

"I'm already itching for another bout with Kyrie." Barron exclaimed, his eyes sparkling.

"I wish I felt quite as energised." Amie said dejectedly, her eyes downcast.

"You did well," Eve placed a hand on her shoulder, "it was a rough match-up, and you should be proud of how you performed."

Amie looked up, a small smile on her face. "Thanks."

"I agree with Amie. I don't really fancy another round with ol' moody." Drake rolled his eyes and scowled, thrusting his wooden sword into the dirt.

"Oh, Drake, don't be like that." Scarlett chided, "I didn't take you to be such a sore winner."

"Can you blame me?" Drake retorted, "if we're going to be fighting together, then I know he has to have my back." He looked around at the group. "All of our backs."

"He's right. Gordon didn't instil me with confidence." Clarissa shook her head.

"You two are bringing the mood down!" Barron huffed. Eve watched him frown. He really did seem to enjoy the thrill of his fight with Kyrie.

"Don't worry about that. I'm sure Marcus will be having a chat with him tonight." Scarlett looked toward the direction that Rising Dawn had left, before turning to Eve. "What do you think, Eve? Can we work with them?"

Eve nodded. "Looks like a few of the pairings have hit it off already, so I don't see why not."

"Can I join in next time?" Kerri asked, her voice soft. She was tugging at her dress.

"We'll get training underway and see where you are then." Eve smiled at her, and Kerri returned it with a smile of her own.

"Right!" Scarlett clapped her hands together. "Time for food and drinks, don't you think?"

"Finally!" Barron shouted in joy, already walking away from the training field.

"Doesn't miss a chance to eat, does he?" Drake watched after him with a grin on his face. "Let's get after him because I'm not half hungry either!"

With rumbling stomachs, they headed to Willkeep's Tavern.

Chapter Eleven

Over the next couple of days, Eve decided to look for her own place to stay as opposed to paying each and every night to stay at an inn. So far though, she was not sure if she could afford single living, and would not ask for help from the others.

"—do you think?"

"Yeah, I don't have the extra room, so it would make sense."

Eve overheard Drake and Kerri, as both were heading her way. Drake spotted her first. "Hey Eve, how's it going?"

"Good afternoon, Eve!"

"Hey, both of you. Looking to move?" She jerked her head toward the home listings. She knew that Drake's place was only big enough for one person, and that he had been giving Kerri a place to stay since she arrived in Thous.

"Not quite." Drake shook his head. "Actually, we've been looking for you. Found a place yet?"

Eve sighed, "No, not just yet. It's not cheap living alone, is it?"

"We—the rest of the guild—bought our homes here towards the end of the war," Drake explained, "homes were cheaper, and cities were desperately trying to fill homes that had been permanently abandoned for," he paused and glanced over to Kerri, "for whatever reason.

We got pretty lucky with our homes, but Thous has been thriving again for a while now."

"Darn it." Eve was slightly disgruntled, and her shoulders drooped in disappointment.

"But that's what we wanted to talk to you about. Kerri and I were discussing what we should do, and we wondered, well, what about if you two got a place together?"

Kerri nervously smoothed out her dress. "I thought it might be nice, especially if we're training together."

"Huh? Oh! No, no, no, I have no issue with it." Eve panicked slightly. "It's just new for me." She furrowed her brow and bit her inner cheek, cursing herself for her awkwardness.

"Sometimes a change is nice!" Kerri grinned and Eve laughed, feeling relief flush through her.

"Yeah, sometimes a change is needed." Kerri certainly did not seem like she would be difficult to live with.

"Okay, let's do it."

Kerri's face lit up at Eve's words.

"Well, if you don't mind, Eve, I'll leave Kerri with you." As Drake began to walk away, he shouted over his shoulder, "she does snore though!"

"I do not snore!" Kerri indignantly stamped her foot, her face immediately going red.

Eve put a finger to her chin and looked towards the sky. "Can't tell you if I snore."

"Eve, noooo, Drake was bad enough!" Kerri scrunched her face and threw her hands up.

Eve shrugged. She tried to hide the smile on her face as she teased her friend. "You'll have to let me know if I do or not."

Kerri sighed in relief. "What sort of home do you want, Eve?"

"Nothing fancy, really. Most of my experience with homes has been inns or run-down housing, so as long as it's clean and warm, I'll be happy."

"That sounds nice. Do you think we could get Drake to share his, um, "cinnamon goodies", as Amie called them?"

With a smile, Eve replied, "It never hurts to ask!"

The two shortlisted a few potential homes over the following days that had grabbed their interest, factoring in budget, location, and sizing, before requesting that they were shown around to get a feel for them in person.

Out of the seven homes that they shortlisted; it was only as far as the fourth one when Kerri had her heart set.

Eve was easygoing, and was only searching for the necessary amenities for her house, but Kerri proved to be much pickier. Not that Eve could blame her, she understood her way of living was not what worked for everyone else. She learned that Kerri could be a gut-based person, in that she wanted things to feel right, not just tick the boxes. The first home she did not react much, but Eve watched as they looked around the house, and Kerri did not show much emotion toward it at all. When asked afterwards if she liked it, Kerri responded, "I don't think that's the one."

Eve had thought that maybe the second house had fared better. The younger woman's eyes lit up at the entry hallway and living room, but the kitchen and bathroom both were grotty. Even Eve with her easygoing nature felt that she would not want to deal with the mould that lined the walls and corners.

For all intents and purposes, Eve thought the third house was fine. Kerri seemed to agree, but when pushed further, she said "It just doesn't feel right."

Then along came house number four, already unoccupied, and Kerri was fully invested.

Eve was not sure what that meant, and Kerri could not provide an answer to it.

"Do you not want to check out the others?" inquired Eve, "we still have more that might be a good fit."

"Do you not feel it?" Kerri was standing in the hallway, their tour of this home finished, when she voiced her thoughts. "Eve, doesn't this just feel like the one?"

Eve looked at the younger girl, twirling in the hallway, darting her head into each room once more, her face glowing. The living room featured white walls with blue furniture, reminding Eve of the sky. Of course, it came with a fireplace, which was among the very short list of things that she had wanted. The kitchen matched the living room, but with a blue carpet, white walls, and silver appliances. Kerri was planning to paint her bedroom lilac, and Eve was considering painting hers brown. Perhaps green? All in all, they were both happy. Seeing how happy it made Kerri, and the house matching Eve's minimum requirements in what she would like in a home, she turned to the salesman. "We'll take it."

"Really?!" his eyes turned wide in shock.

"Why not? It's close to a few people we know, and it's a pretty nice home."

After signing several documents and making arrangements for further payments, the pair paid what was agreed upon for the deposit there and then with a stack of gleaming aulins. Kerri could not contribute much, but Drake helped her, whilst Eve pulled from her now meagre savings. The salesman left Eve with the key to their new home.

"We'll have to get a second key made." Eve held the key in front of her face and Kerri prodded it, causing it to jingle.

"Sounds like home!" She beamed a wide, toothy grin.

Kerri could barely contain herself and it was not long until the two of them were informing the others in the Marauders of Light about their new lodgings. When they reached Barron, he suggested, enthusiastically, that they celebrate with "lots of food", and so everyone met up at Willkeep's Tavern, and were finishing a toast to celebrate.

"Cheers!" Glasses and tankards clinked and, after some bantering, Scarlett had her own announcement to make.

"Sorry that we didn't run this by the two of you before, but we're going to be away for a few days."

This took Eve and Kerri by surprise. They looked at each other. Kerri frowned and shook her head, so Eve asked, "is something the matter?"

"No, no, we've just taken on a quest to cull some forests, but not just the one. It means we'll be camping out for a few nights as we clear them all out."

Following on from Scarlett, Amie explained, "we were going to ask you to join us, but we thought you'd want to settle in. I'm sorry." Amie winced and put her hands together in apology.

"Eve said she's going to train me!" Kerri piped up, slightly flushed from the alcohol she had consumed. "How about we surprise them when they get back, Eve, huh?"

Eve did not mind that they took on a quest without her. They were mercenaries, it was what they did, after all. This would be a good opportunity to make good on her promise to Kerri.

"Sure but know I won't go easy on you." Eve gently nudged Kerri, who swayed all too easily.

"I want—" Kerri stopped and placed a hand over her mouth, the alcohol having taken its hold with alarming quickness, "I wanna... I wanna be like you... strong, a-and r-reliable." The young woman stared into her glass, her eyelids drooped and her entire body swayed as if it was being perturbed by a gentle breeze. Her face was incredibly flushed.

"She won't be up long!" Barron laughed, getting an unconvincing scowl from Kerri. This motion seemed to be too much for her as she closed her eyes and slumped in her chair, breathing softly.

Laughter rippled around the table and Drake removed the drink from her still clenched hand. "I was worried that she would crumble, but she's doing okay, isn't she?"

"She's strong, and she's still so young.", said Clarissa, "with the right training, she would be formidable."

"Indeed," Scarlett agreed, "I'm unsure how it happened, but we've somehow added two more to our ranks in a short period of time, after having been a five-person unit for so long." Scarlett flashed a grin at Eve, "you're a bit of a troublemaker though, aren't ya, Eve?"

"A troublemaker, am I?" Eve stood from her seat, downed her drink, and slammed the tankard on the table. "That sounds like another round, then!" She headed to the bar to place another order for the group, raucous laughter following behind her.

Ensuring that Eve was out of earshot, Scarlett leaned in towards the group remaining at the table. "How do you think Eve's doing? Ilas Arena can't have been easy." She eyed Eve from behind, waiting to be served at the counter.

"I worry about her," Drake admitted, "what happened there is only a little of the pressure we've seen her put under, and I'd never wish that on anyone."

"Do you think she would have done it," asked Barron, "do you think she would have killed Leo?"

"Had I not acted, I think…" Drake paused in thought, "I have faith that she would have done the same thing." He remembered the moment he saw Eve struggling with Edin's demands, "but I'm happy that I was able to do it in her place."

"She must be what, twenty-seven? Twenty-eight?" Clarissa wondered aloud, "that's younger than most of us, bar Amie and Kerri."

"Indeed, she seems experienced beyond her years, but. .." Barron trailed off, looking uncharacteristically awkward as he shuffled, unsure how to put his feelings into words.

"But she's still so young, underneath all of that. I feel sorry for her." Clarissa finished Barron's sentence,

knowing how he felt, whilst watching Eve as she bantered with the staff, bearing a carefree smile.

"I think she's great." Amie interjected, her face beginning to match her hair.

"No one's doubting she's great," replied Scarlett, softly laughing, "if anything, it's maybe that she's too great. She'll never be able to escape who she is."

Eve was laughing with the man behind the counter as he finished preparing the final drink.

"I hope she isn't overdoing it." Eyes half-closed, Amie watched Eve as she balanced the drinks, but she fell asleep before Eve reached the table.

A couple of hours later the Marauders of Light all headed home, with everyone pitching in to make sure Amie and Kerri were accompanied home safely. With Kerri's arm slung over his shoulder, Drake walked with Eve to their new home.

"When you're all settled in, I'd like to see it."

"Sure thing. Maybe this one will be up, too." Eve lightly ruffled Kerri's hair, and Kerri moaned and shook her head slightly in response.

Eve helped Drake carry Kerri up the stairs before Kerri was passed along to her. "Thanks, Drake."

"Anytime." He grinned, and lowered his voice to a whisper, "hey, are you okay, Eve?"

Although she was slightly unfocused from the alcohol, she responded honestly with a nod. "I'm getting there."

"Okay, well, I'm here—we're here—whenever you need us." Drake departed with a wave, closing the door behind him.

Eve carried Kerri to her room and gently laid her on her bed. She placed a blanket on top of her, and noted how peaceful she looked, before walking across the room to leave.

Kerri whimpered behind her, "don't go." She rolled over, her eyes half-open, wet with fresh tears.

Eve felt her stomach drop. "Kerri?"

The young girl put a hand outside of the blanket and stretched toward Eve, "just for a little while, stay with me? Please?"

A sad twinge shot through Eve's heart as she saw Kerri's tear-streaked face. She sat by Kerri's bed and held her hand. "Like this?"

"Mhm. just like that..." Kerri's breathing began to slow again, with Eve's breathing matching rhythm shortly afterwards as she too fell asleep.

*

Eve and Kerri worked on furnishing their home over the next couple of days, and Eve started work on creating a training schedule for Kerri. Cardio, muscle-building, and sword and shield—her weapon of choice—training were included, with the intention that she would be able to make up for lost time so she would soon be able to join the Marauders of Light on their missions. It would be hard work, but Eve knew that Kerri was more than up to the task.

Having said their farewells to the rest of the team, who departed a couple of days after the night at Willkeep's Tavern, Eve put Kerri to work. Using the same field that they used when training with Rising Dawn, Eve watched as Kerri pushed herself to her limits, her motivation making up for her lack of training and exercise until now.

Eve took note as Kerri ran and hurdled, her stamina seemingly above average, until she failed to muster the strength to manage another jump and tripped over one of the obstacles.

"Ouch." Kerri went to push herself from the floor but stumbled, her arms too exhausted to properly support her.

"It's okay, let me help you up." Eve grabbed Kerri by her hands and pulled her to her feet. Sweat was streaming down Kerri's flushed face, and her shoulders were slumped as she focused on catching her breath. Eve handed her a towel and Kerri buried her face in it, but the sweat came back almost instantly.

Eve watched proudly. "We can stop for today."

"Huh?" Kerri looked up, her unfocused eyes struggling to maintain steady eye contact.

"You've been running and jumping for around five hours now—you've done enough today." Eve attempted to sound encouraging, wanting Kerri to know that she had worked harder than most would have at this stage.

"I want to do more, though" Regardless, Kerri sounded dejected.

"You'll have your chance. Rest is just as important as exercise, Kerri. It's all about knowing your limits and breaking through them the next time." Eve patted her on the shoulder.

Kerri nodded and dropped to the ground with a thud and lay down, still catching her breath. "Okay. I won't let you down."

Eve sat beside her and smiled warmly, "you haven't, and I know you won't."

"When will we get to sword training?"

"Once you're physically fit enough. It's one thing to know how to use a sword, but your body needs to be able to keep up with the weight and motion of it."

"Oooh."

"Don't worry, you'll get there soon enough."

Kerri attempted to laugh, but winced, her breathing ragged. "Can we... stay here... for a little longer?"

Eve handed Kerri a fresh water bottle, the liquid having grown warm in the Sun. "Sure. It's nice out, anyway."

Thanks to her natural stamina and boundless enthusiasm, Kerri was able to improve each and every day. Seeing the clear improvement, Eve decided that it was time to test her further.

"Before we give you a sword, did you want to try something interesting?"

"Whatever it is, I'm ready for it."

Eve thrust out an open palm and Kerri dodged it with a yelp.

"D-did you just try to hit me?!" Kerri's eyes were wide and her mouth hung open.

Eve grinned. "I'd have stopped before I did, but it seems like you've got it covered."

"All I did was react, as anyone would!" She still looked bewildered.

Eve crossed her arms. "Not just anyone would dodge one of my hits in time, Kerri. That was impressive."

"If you say so, then thanks."

"Take five and we'll pick this back up in a few."

As Kerri went to sit down, Eve rustled through the bag she brought, removing a sword and shield from within.

"These," Eve handed the two items out to Kerri, "are for you."

Kerri stared at the sword and shield, rotating them around as they gleamed in the sunlight, before looking up in awe. "These are truly for me?"

"Take another look."

Kerri held the two items up to the sunlight, admiring them. Like her hometown, Ilas, both items were a pearly blue, looking as if they were made of water. They had little furnishing on them, but Kerri's name was etched into them in gold, on the handle and back of the shield respectively.

"They're so pretty. I might have mixed feelings about Ilas, but it's still been home to me and father for as long as I've known." With a smile that could thaw even the coldest of hearts, she thanked Eve, before getting to her feet, ready to continue training.

"Now, I'm sure you're eager to use your new equipment, but let's continue using wooden replicas for now." Eve handed a wooden sword and shield to Kerri, before choosing a sword for herself. They did not have a wooden scythe and Eve, who was also well-trained in swordplay, figured that using a sword herself would be best for Kerri to learn. It was unlikely she'd encounter many other opponents with a scythe.

"First, I want you to try and hit me. Do whatever you think will work but see if you can land your sword on me, just once."

"O-okay." Kerri held her sword in front of her, and strapped her shield to her right arm. "Here I come!

Kerri did not slash furiously or without thought, but she was unable to land a hit on Eve, no matter how she approached. After being parried for the umpteenth time, she cried out, exasperated, "I can't do it."

Eve stood up straight, relaxing from her battle pose. "You can't do it?"

With a look of determination written on her face, Kerri responded, "not yet, no, but I will."

"That's what I like to hear. Keep it up, Kerri." Eve resumed her fighting stance, "would you like to try again, anyway?"

Kerri shrugged and straightened up. "If I succeed, dinner is on you tonight!" With that battle roar, Kerri lunged in again and again, and the two continued training until the sun began to set.

*

"Damn it!"

Many miles from Thous, the Marauders of Light were nearing the end of their mission when they were ambushed by bandits on the outskirts of the final forest they were tasked with clearing out, their escape blocked by their opponent's larger numbers. They outnumbered the Marauders, but their skill sorely lacked in comparison.

"Amie, fall back!" Scarlett ordered, looking for a quick way to put an end to the on-going skirmish.

"You got it, sis!"

Amie parried the bandit she was fighting and kicked them back. Dashing behind her sister, Scarlett swung her sword in a wide arc, throwing small flashes of Spark toward the bandits. They leapt backwards and out of the way, tumbling over one another.

"Way to go, sis!"

The two redheads nodded to each other and went to assist their friends, with Scarlett heading to Drake who was being singled out by a handful of bandits. "This is unfair, even for bandits, don't you think?!" Drake attempted to scorn the bandit's sense of honour, but of course, they did not have any.

"What are you on about? Get 'im!"

Drake parried the first two bandits, causing them to stumble to the ground, but was left wide open for the third one. As he began to draw his sword back in front of him to defend himself, Scarlett appeared and slashed the approaching opponent. The bandit fell with a scream, blood blooming under his shirt. One of his friends rushed to his aid while the others regrouped for another attack.

"Scarlett!"

"Yeah!"

The two fought side by side, turning in a circle, quickly dealing with any bandit who dared to attack. With Scarlett and Drake watching each other's backs, no mere bandit could get a successful hit in. As they defeated the rest of the bandits, another wave approached, with one utilising their Shockwave Presence to send Scarlet and Drake flying backwards. They skidded along the floor near the others, rattled. Clarissa threw two enemies towards them with Wind, knocking them backwards and buying Scarlett and Drake time to recover.

"Scarlett? Drake?! Are you okay?!" Amie darted to help them, having just pushed back a group of attackers with

Barron. As she approached, Barron cut across her, intercepting another Shockwave blast. He grunted, managing to bear the brunt of it with his axe, with the impact only pushing him slightly back along the floor.

"Amie, give us a wall!"

"Got it!" Amie slammed her foot down, erecting a large wall of ice between them and the enemy. "That should buy us some time." Amie, winded, put her hand against a nearby tree, panting as she worked to catch her breath. Sweat poured down her face. Her cheeks were flushed. The tree in front of her looked blurry.

"I don't think I have much more left in me, guys." Amie's breath came out ragged. When she spoke or coughed, the cold hung visibly in the air. She had pushed herself and her Presence to the limit. Her body was screaming against it.

Shouting could be heard on the other side of the ice wall, muffled, as the bandits tried to smash through it. Scarlett, Drake and Clarissa prepared for battle, whilst Barron attempted to help warm Amie via Flame.

"Is she going to be okay, Barron?"

"She will be, as long as we finish this quickly."

Amie coughed, each one producing a small cloud of cold. "Go get 'em, guys."

A powerful Shockwave blast blew through the ice wall. Ice splintered in all directions as the remaining bandits charged through what was left of it.

"Those idiots. Thanks for the idea!" Clarissa stopped the flying icicles in their tracks and propelled them backward.

They impaled the bandits to differing degrees, causing some to drop to the floor or scatter in every direction to dodge the icicles. One of them slumped completely, her blood slowly melting the icicles sticking out of her body. The bandits began to retreat, but not before one pointed at Amie and shouted, "look, there's one we can finish off!"

"You won't touch a hair on her head, not on my damn life!" Scarlett Sparked with rage. She brandished her sabre and dove head-on into the fray. Mercilessly the bandits were sliced down with speed that they could not hope to react to. Blood spurted, screams echoed around the woods, and the trees in Scarlett's vicinity started to catch fire. Soon smoke billowed, thick and heavy, and everyone in the forest coughed and spluttered, trying to find their way out, the fight forgotten.

"D-damn it, sis." Amie coughed profusely, feeling her throat and lungs tear. Barron frowned, but Amie placed a hand on his shoulder, "thanks, Barron, I think I'll be okay now. Go help the others."

"Don't worry about them, they'll be fine." Barron replied, looking over his shoulder to see Drake fanning smoke away, looking for Scarlett.

"Please? I'm worried about Scarlett." Amie watched as Drake fought with the smoke, desperate to clear it out.

"Fine. Stay right there." Barron headed to Drake, using a small Flame to better light the area.

Amie coughed again, feeling her chest cry out, as she used the smoke as cover and inched forward. She placed both of her palms on the floor, took a deep breath, and summoned ice in all directions. The fire was extinguished, smoke replaced by fog, and the woods were frozen a frosty white-blue as far as the eye can see—including the remaining bandits who were attempting to escape.

"Shit, Amie, I'm sorry." Scarlett spluttered as she leant on Drake's shoulder, arms out to wave the fog away, but she did not hear the familiar voice of her sister calling out to her. Instead, she found Amie collapsed on the ground, unconscious. Patches of blue had bloomed across her face and arms.

Clarissa knelt down beside her and reached a hand to her forehead, but snapped back with a grunt. "She's absolutely freezing."

Barron knelt down on Amie's other side and lit a small fire. It wildly flickered, forcing him to stop trying in case the flames spread toward the surrounding forest. He closed his eyes and clenched his jaw.

Scarlett had been watching quietly but she now fell with a thud. "Amie, come on. Get up." Her voice trembled. She reached out to hold Amie's hands, but despite her best efforts, she could not bear the intensity of the cold. "I'm such a fool." Her lip trembled and her eyes watered as she watched Amie's chest shallowly rise and fall. She got to her feet. "Clarissa, can you help, please?"

"Of course." She used Wind to gently raise Amie. They left the frozen forest to head back to Thous.

Chapter Twelve

"No, no, like this!" Eve demonstrated the technique again and stepped back to watch Kerri attempt to replicate it.

Kerri stepped forward and performed the three-hit technique, which consisted of two jabs and a slash, and could quickly dispatch most opponents effortlessly in a pinch.

"I need to be faster." Kerri acknowledged that she was too slow, frustrated at the feeling that she could not move her body any faster. "I just can't seem to move my arm fast enough."

"Don't worry, you'll get it." Eve placed a hand on Kerri's shoulder. "You've made incredible progress in just a small handful of days. Before long, you'll be knocking me on my arse." She winked at her apprentice, hoping to keep her motivated.

"Hmm, I'm not so sure about that, but dang, I'd love to be able to do that." Kerri, with her hands on her waist, did not crumble after an intense training session now. Instead, she stood up straight, drenched in sweat, as she made eye contact with Eve. "I really, really would." She laughed and dabbed at her face with a towel.

"Well, we'll see how aggressive it is once you try it, eh?" Eve teased with a grin.

Kerri knelt down and wiped at her face again with a towel, and picked up her sword and shield once more. "Again."

"Go for it."

Kerri performed the same three attacks, time and time again, picking up speed as she found the rhythm of it.

She was able to execute it perfectly, but not consistently.

"Kerri," Eve interrupted as Kerri prepared to do the movements again, "try it on me now."

Eve readied into a defensive pose and Kerri followed, getting into position. After a deep breath, she rushed into action, barely giving Eve time to react. Had Eve not been so well-trained, and her reaction speed so firmly ingrained in her, she might have been taken by surprise. Instead, she deflected the first blow, knocking Kerri from her rhythm with ease.

"B-but I was so fast!" Kerri's eyes were wide, and Eve could see that Kerri truly thought she might have been able to best Eve today.

"You were. If I were someone else, you might've succeeded." Kerri looked downward, frustrated at herself. Eve lowered herself to Kerri's eye level and gently poked her on her chest plate. "Kerri, I mean it."

"Hmph." Kerri pouted, then smiled, "I can't wait to show the others what I've learnt!"

"Who knows, maybe they'll be able to teach you some tricks, too."

As they made their way back to Thous, they saw a throng of excited and panicked people on the main street.

"That poor girl really didn't look well, did she?"

"Presence isn't for playing around."

"Do you think she's gonna make it?"

"What a waste..."

"What's going on?" Eve questioned one of the nearby gossipers, eager for more information.

"A group of people just carried a girl in, a young thing, whose face was almost entirely blue." The person shivered as if she was cold herself. "I didn't even touch her, but just being so close made me wish I'd dressed warmer."

Eve felt her stomach drop. "This girl, did she have red hair?"

An older lady overheard and chimed in, "yes, she was a real pretty girl, too, it would be a sh—" Eve did not hear the rest of her sentence as she raced down to the local clinic, Kerri in tow. She prayed to whatever higher being was out there that it was not who she thought it might be.

They charged through the doors of the clinic, ignoring the protests of the receptionist—Kerri hurried to apologise for the trouble—and rushed down corridors until they found a familiar group of people huddled outside of a door. Drake, Clarissa, and Barron were outside, looking ragged, speaking with a nurse. Varying degrees of worry and anger were written across their faces.

Eve wordlessly approached the others who turned to look at her, and their faces confirmed her worst worry. Kerri glanced at Eve and squeezed her hand before talking to the others, "what's happened?"

They were met with silence from their friends, each of them uncomfortably shifting around, thinking over their responses.

Kerri, wanting to help Eve, spoke with confidence. "We were told a redheaded girl looked unwell. Is it Scarlett or Amie?"

"It's Amie..." Barron responded, a lack of strength in his voice that was very unlike him.

"We were ambushed by bandits, and the forest was set alight," Clarissa began to explain the events of the previous night, "Amie had been forced to use her Presence multiple times. We pushed her too hard..."

Clarissa trailed off and looked away, biting her thumb, her brows knit together.

Eve's eyes went wide. Concluding Amie's state based on what the others have told her, she rapidly shook her head, but the fuzziness that had set in did not disappear. "I need to see her."

She pushed her way past the nurse, despite her protests, and saw Scarlett sitting by a bed, the body in the bed hidden from view. A doctor was talking to her, but she did not respond. She was stable at least.

Scarlett did not turn around when Eve entered and instead put her head in her hands, sitting motionlessly. Eve regretted her rashness. Despite every fibre of her body screaming at her to stay, Eve stepped back out through the door, glancing once more at Scarlett before closing it behind her.

Eve apologised to the nurse, and gave a quick glance to her friends, not wanting to talk to any of them.

"I'm going home. If there's any change, please come tell me immediately."

Eve walked briskly down the corridor, her head down. Kerri watched her go, worried about her friend and teacher. Drake put a hand on her shoulder and squeezed tightly.

At home, in her bedroom, Eve sat on the edge of her bed, her hands clasped together as she leaned her forehead on them. She focused on her breathing but the intrusive thoughts relentlessly clambered into her mind, endlessly aggressive. They barrelled down on her like an avalanche, threatening to break her down from the inside. Eve grabbed her head before screaming. It felt as if it was being stretched apart, fruitlessly trying to put an end to the thoughts in her head. It howled, telling her that it was too late to do anything.

Her anger brought on frustrated tears. Her anger that she was not there to help her friends, believing her presence would have made a difference. Had she been there, perhaps her skills could have put an end to things before it got out of hand. Instead she was here, thinking that if she saw her friend, unconscious and cold, she would not have been able to stop herself from thinking of her as a corpse, lying motionless without the joy she always possessed.

Eve pounded at her pillow, unsure what to do with her emotions. She had only ever felt this hopeless once before.

Unable to stop the memories from streaming in, Eve recalled the early days of the war, years before it ended, when she was with her first guild, and the only one she had ever been with prior to the Marauders of Light.

*

"Eve, get out of here, that's an order!" The leader, Megara, screamed one final order at her ally before her bracer was pierced and shattered, and she was swiftly beheaded by the enemy. Her head lopped to the floor unceremoniously, panic and desperation plastered on her face.

The rest of her guild were either strewn across the battlefield, their limbs entangled, impossible to tell what belonged to who, or desperately doing their best to fight against overwhelming odds.

Being the youngest of the group, the team all came together to protect Eve, and to ensure that she was able to escape. They knew she would die here otherwise.

"C'mon, you heard her!" Ashe jumped in front of her, defending her from a swinging axe. "Get going, right now, damn it!" Eve's ally leapt in front of another axe, the heavy weapon plunging into her collarbone, as she tried to push it back with her free hand. Eve watched as it slowly sank deeper, fear rooting her to the spot.

Before Ashe could do any more to defend herself, the attacker drew a smaller blade and rammed it through her temple.

Eve watched in horror as Ashe instantly collapsed, as if her strings had been cut, and crumpled over as the axe was removed from her torso.

"Damn it!" Eve heard Oliver's roar over the clash of weapons and saw him kick back an enemy. Only a handful of the guild remained, and, as they rushed to Eve's side, she realised the horrible truth for herself—she had to go. She had to run, and she had to become strong enough to be able to get revenge. Tears in her eyes, and unable to find the words to say goodbye, she started running, her friends and allies all falling to keep her safe as the enemy attempted to give chase. She desperately wanted to look back, but knew that in doing so she might not find the strength to get moving again.

She stumbled, her vision blurry and her chest tight, but picked herself back up, and she was pumping her arms and legs for everything they had, she was hit with the cold realisation that nobody would be there for her anymore. She sprinted harder, lungs burning, desperate for this to have been a dream. As Eve distanced herself further and further away from the battle, she heard the forest grow deadly silent. The battle was over.

*

Kerri really hoped Eve was doing okay.

She opened the door to their home and made herself known with a "I'm home!", but nobody greeted her. As she closed the door and removed her shoes, she was overcome with a sense of dread that felt like lead in her stomach. A chill trickled down her spine. "Eve?" she said aloud, "are you here?"

There was no response.

Kerri bit her lip, her heart thrashing in her chest as she climbed the stairs, her mouth growing dry. "Eve?"

Eve's door was shut. She held her breath and strained her ears for any noise coming from within, but heard nothing other than the deafening silence. A cold chill ran through her. She struggled to swallow with a dry mouth. Her stomach felt as if it had dropped to her feet, making her legs feel like lead. "Eve, are you in there?" She softly knocked on the door but again received no response. Kerri took a deep breath. "I'm coming in, okay?"

She heard a faint shuffling but nothing more.

Anxious, Kerri opened the door and peeked in. Maybe Eve was simply sleeping. However, what she saw did not remind her of Eve at all. Her strong role model looked like an empty shell of herself, her head in her hands. Her skin looked deathly pale. Kerri glanced around the room and saw several scorch marks, some still producing a thin layer of smoke, where small fires had been started and put out before they could spread. Kerri momentarily stared at Eve, seeing that some of her skin and hair was singed. Had she lost control?

Kerri threw the door open and rushed over to hug Eve, and Eve held Kerri tightly, as if she was the last thing anchoring her to this world.

*

The team, with the exception of Scarlett and Eve, met up every day, but they did not go on any missions.

Frankly, they did not do much of anything. Scarlett refused to leave Amie's side, and Eve had become despondent and isolated herself to her bedroom. Kerri had not seen her since that day, though she assumed that Eve may be leaving the room when Kerri was either out or occupied. The plates of food and water Kerri left outside her door were sometimes cleared, giving Kerri some relief that Eve would be okay if she was still able to eat and drink. She knew that Eve would bounce back eventually, she just needed rest for now.

The group did not talk much at all. About anything. They all shared pleasantries, asked how everyone was doing and exchanged small talk, but not wanting to talk much about Eve, Amie and Scarlett meant that the conversation would peter out, leading to them all sitting together in stifling and mournful silence. They were the gloomiest table at Willkeep's Tavern, casting a dismal air that nobody wanted to approach.

Soon, Kerri stopped heading to the tavern entirely, and decided to put time into training alone. She wanted the group to be proud of what she'd achieved once things returned to normal.

She still had a copy of the schedule that Eve created for her, and would spend days rerunning the same drills, altering them to her comfort as she steadily improved. With no teacher to rely on to learn new techniques, she worked on perfecting what Eve had already begun teaching her, and soon began exploring her own unique style of fighting that felt more natural to her. Something that was unexpected and beautiful, something that she could truly call her own.

Day after day she practised, incorporating her speed into her fighting style. She lacked the build and strength of her allies, but she was fast-footed and nimble, and so she focused on quick slashes and jabs rather than heavy swings. She placed an emphasis on finishing things quickly rather than prolonging them, which suited Kerri to a tee as fighting was not something she could see herself taking enjoyment in.

Several days later, Kerri slammed a slip of paper onto the table at Willkeep's Tavern, shocking Drake, Barron, and Clarissa, who looked up with a jolt to face her. "Here, we've got a mission."

They stared blankly at her, and Drake feebly protested. "I'm not sure that's a good idea right now."

"You're right, it's not a good idea—it's a great idea." Kerri responded firmly, not open to the idea of not moving forward any longer.

"What is it?" Clarissa asked, a faint spark of interest taking hold of her.

"It's a simple one, and it's not far from home, don't worry, I have thought about it, all we have to do is look after our stall."

"Huh, the stall?" Barron sounded confused. Kerri did not know why. She loved Barron, but it irked her that he was their best cook and she was having to convince them to care for their own stall.

The others looked down at the slip between them. On it read: *To whom it may concern, we have dire need of help at our food stall. Please speak to Kerri if interested.*

"We can sit around drinking all day, or we can make some money whilst we wait for Amie to recover," Kerri left them with the slip before walking to the doorway, "either way, you know where to find me."

The doors swung behind her as the others looked again at Kerri's note. They nodded at each other, an unspoken agreement between them.

Outside, Kerri set up the stall and served a limited selection, unable to forage and hunt as much on her own as she could in a group. She'd had to hunt smaller animals on the outskirts of Thous, and harvest vegetables - some of which she had to purchase instead- to be able to provide a small handful of options for customers. Tying an apron around her waist, she called out enthusiastically to potential customers as they walked by, a large smile on her face. her determination to do right by her friends burned deep inside of her. She would not have Eve, Amie and Scarlett to return to see they'd done nothing.

"Ohoy, it's the Marauders of Light!" An older man approached and squinted at Kerri over his chunky glasses. "I don't think I've met you before. Who might you be?"

"I'm Kerri, and it is a pleasure to meet you!" Kerri smiled broadly and explained that she was the newest member of the Marauders of Light, and that she was handling stall duty for the time being.

"Well, it's always wonderful to see a new face." The old man softly laughed before ordering two vegetable skewers. As Kerri bagged his food, he said, "give my best to the rest of the team, please, will you?" He bowed his head before he walked off, blending into the crowd.

Taking a deep breath, Kerri yelled to be overheard by the competing neighbouring stalls, attracting customers who might otherwise have passed her by.

As the sun began its descent, Kerri, exhausted, started to throw the tarps over the stall, securing it for the night. She felt her eyelids growing heavy, as she fastened the final knot before she stood up and stretched, multiple bones popping as she did. She sighed in relief, a hard day's work put behind her. It felt good. She hoped the others would come by to help out soon.

The night breeze wafted over her, cooling her down, as she made her way back home. As she gazed at the stars, her mind drifted to her father and she wondered how he was doing in Argol's Creek.

The door shut quietly, but it was enough to rouse Eve from her disturbed sleep. Her emotional wounds felt fresh again, and try as she might, she struggled to muster the motivation in herself to leave her home. She stared at the glass of water on her bedside table overcome by stale bubbles, before reaching out and taking a sip. Swallowing hurt, and she realised how dry her lips and throat were. She had neglected to take care of herself the past couple of weeks, and she had not spoken to anyone since the day she found out about Amie. She would hear Kerri leave early every morning, and return late every evening, but she didn't know what the younger woman was up to. Kerri left food for Eve outside of her door before leaving for the morning, and then again shortly after she got back, along with water and juice. It was all Eve could manage to eat, let alone keep down.

She told herself that no news was good news, as it meant that the worst had not come. However the memories of her old guild, and the thoughts of her current one being torn apart, chewed at Eve deep inside. A bottomless pit of torment tortured her thoughts. It sucked at her strength and her will, and intrusive thoughts attacked her, telling her that she would never get revenge. That she had failed yet again to protect her friends. Nightmares riddled her sleep, featuring the blank faces of her friends lying in distorted positions at her feet, but she had no more to give. She felt empty, that spark of life extinguished. She rattled herself with no avail to snap out of it.

Her attention was drawn to a rustling outside of her door, along with Kerri's soft voice. "I'm leaving food here. please eat, Eve." She heard the soft shuffling of feet moving away and the door next to hers close for the evening.

Eve rolled over and buried her face in her pillow, hoping that she could drift off to sleep again.

Kerri's alarm rang at 6am, the sunlight breaking through her window. Desperate to maintain her early morning routine, Kerri slept with her curtains open so that the sun would encourage her to wake up each day. The alarm alone was not enough to stir Kerri from her exhausted slumber.

She put on her training gear, ate a hearty breakfast, and set out for training. As she went to close the door, she whispered, "see you later, Eve," and closed the door gently behind her, hoping not to disturb her, same as she did every other morning.

She greeted the early risers at the market, all of whom cheerily greeted her back as she walked to the training field.

Although she had not been there long, Kerri had made herself a much-adored fixture of Thous, and the townspeople enjoyed seeing such a young face working so hard.

As she was training alone, she used the sword and shield that Eve gifted her, wanting to get used to the weight of them. After all, she would not be fighting real people or monsters with wooden equipment. After stretching and doing some light cardio, Kerri began again to hone her own fighting style in earnest.

She picked up some books with the money earned from working at the stall, being sure to put some aside for the rest of the team, and had spent her nights and downtime at work studying them. She had poured over stories about famous swordsmen and swordswomen, diagrams of how to perform certain techniques, and had learned many training exercises, implementing the parts that she liked into her daily regime.

"Hey!"

Kerri stopped mid-thrust, turning to face the incoming figure. It was Ellen, who she had not crossed paths with since they trained before.

"Fancy seeing you here." Ellen had a joyful grin on her face as she approached.

"Good morning, Ellen. I didn't think anybody else would be here so early." Kerri returned the smile as she wiped sweat from her forehead.

"Me neither! I'm early, but I'm guessing you've been here a while already?"

Kerri tilted her head quizzically. "What makes you say that?"

Ellen laughed. "Look at you. You're sweating enough to make me sweat."

Kerri could not help but laugh either, as she again patted at her forehead with a cloth. "What about you? Are you alone?"

"Yeah, none of the others would get up this early. We usually train a little later in the day, but I wanted to get in some extra training on our rest day." Ellen clapped her hands together, "well, this is a good chance for us to catch up, don't you think?"

The thought gave Kerri a slight twinge of anxiety. She had not spoken to anybody about recent events outside of her guild, and even then, the communication had been limited. If it wasn't a variation of "What can I get for you?" and "Have a nice day!", then she had not done much talking at all. Had she really grown so rusty at making simple conversation? She frowned at herself a little but quickly wiped it away, not wanting Ellen to think she was rejecting her offer.

"Sure, but I have to open up shop soon, so sorry if I have to cut this short." She gave a small smile.

"Open up shop? Oh! The stall?"

"Yes, we run it as a guild. You should come by after. Maybe I'll throw in a little extra." This caused Ellen to laugh, although it quickly turned into a small frown of her own.

"I hope you aren't running yourself ragged."

Kerri flashed a smile, but it was not enough to hide the bags that had taken near-permanent residence under her eyes. "Don't worry, I'm not."

"I have some free time if you need a hand—free of charge."

"I'll keep that in mind, thank you." If Ellen did decide to help, Kerri would certainly pay her for it.

Ellen removed her lance from the strap along her back and started her own training regime. She practised large, spiralling twirls, using her lance to fend off enemies from any direction, and would switch to several quick thrusts, each with great force behind them, before she ended with an underhand swing. "Phew!"

Kerri watched, amazed, before going back to her own training. "Ellen, did you train yourself?"

"I did. Nobody else in my guild uses a lance, but I like them." She looked down at her own lance. The long white weapon was decorated with gold embellishments and designs. Kerri thought it looked like something royalty would wield.

"Why a lance?"

"I like the control that holding a weapon with both hands gives me. It's great for defence, and it keeps enemies at bay. I don't know, it just spoke to me, you know?"

Kerri looked at her own sword and shield, feeling at home with her own weapons. "I know what you mean." She slashed forward again before stopping to catch her breath. "Any advice for a fellow self-trainee?"

"You're training yourself?" Ellen stabbed her lance into the floor, turning toward Kerri with a small frown on her face. "But why? There are many sword users in your guild."

Kerri felt her stomach drop.

"Oh, um, Eve has been training me, but I've wanted to develop my own style, you know, before hers became

too ingrained." She shrugged, feeling awkward.

"Ah," Ellen smiled an all-knowingly, "I see. Well, I don't have any experience with a sword and shield, but I'm sure Marcus would lend you a hand, if you like. Did you want me to mention it to him?"

Kerri mulled over the idea but declined it, not wanting to be a burden, especially as she had hardly exchanged two words with Marcus. "I'll keep it in mind though, so thank you for the idea."

The two continued training, side by side, until Kerri had to leave to prepare for work at the stall once again.

*

Drake was the only other member of the Marauders of Light to have a key to the Brantley household, and today he had decided that he felt ready to check up on their home to ensure everything was okay. Scarlett had not been home in weeks and, feeling useless, Drake wanted to at least see if the home needed any care.

As he let himself in through the front door, he felt as if the stifling silence could overwhelm him. The notable lack of the two sisters welcoming him made the home feel foreign. It didn't feel right.

He removed his shoes and checked the house over, avoiding Scarlett and Amie's bedrooms. Amie's door had a whiteboard on it, and in pink marker was written, 'if you dare, then you're square!' with a little heart and a winking face in the corner. Drake let out a single laugh and placed a hand on the door, before heading downstairs.

He approached the paintings in the living room, examining each one. Scarlett and Amie both had large smiles as children, sat besides their parents in what looked like a grassy field. In another, two teenage daughters stood with their parents in a happy family photo at home. In the next photo, Scarlett and Amie posed together, their smiles smaller, perhaps shortly before the Marauders of Light was founded.

A strong sense of shame and sorrow overtook Drake as he started at the last painting, feeling guilty for neglecting those who meant most to him for so long.

It reminded him of how he first met the sisters, and he could not help but laugh to find himself welcome in the house of two women who were little more than a thorn in his side.In a life long since left to the past, Drake could be found scouring the streets for his next target. Someone to shake down of all their valuables, to line his own pockets with a fat stack of aulins hard-earned by someone else. As he stalked one man down a narrow alleyway, a blue flash from ahead blinded him, and he saw his target knocked unconscious by a young redheaded girl.

"Easy, as always." The girl said, a toothy grin on her face.

"Oi!" Drake yelled as he rubbed his eyes, "that was my mark!"

The girl turned toward him, still grinning, jingling the small sack in her palm. "Finders keepers, right? Should've been faster."

Drake scowled. "C'mon, just hand it over."

The girl laughed. "Try and take it from me."

Drake examined her as she stood there. She was small in stature, but she could not have been much different in age to himself. He needed that money if he was going to eat tonight. He snarled. "You're on." Loose bricks littered the alleyway. He grabbed one and, using his Presence, he threw it towards her with incredible strength, but she ducked it. It flew over her head, where it smashed into a cloud of dust and debris. She coughed and waved in front of her, trying to dispel it, and Drake used the distraction to run up and charge her with his shoulder. She tumbled backwards, but deftly got back to her feet. A smile was on her face.

"Not bad, not bad." She said, but Drake felt his skin prickle. She was teasing him. "But you forgot the first thing about being a thief.

"Huh?"

"You should never work alone." As she said this, Drake felt a sudden cold take over him. How could it be this cold in the middle of Summer? Ice had taken hold of his feet, locking him into place. He went to throw his fist down, but more ice appeared, trapping him as he crouched.

"Yay, sis, we did it!" A far smaller girl appeared, with equally red hair, jumping towards the other girl in glee.

"Good job." The older sister ruffled the other one's hair, "we'll be able to eat well tonight with this."

She loosened the drawstring on the sack, revealing a hefty pile of aulins. Drake stared at them and felt his lip tremble. His stomach was grumbling something fierce.

The older sister looked his way. "Better luck next time, huh?" She turned on her heel with her sister in tow.

"No, please!" Drake's voice broke as he desperately shouted, still unable to move, "please just one aulin!" He looked up and saw the younger sister tugging on the other's arm, and shouted again. "Just one, please!" Tears and dribble pooled on the ground beneath him, and he felt his heart racing. It felt irregular. It panicked him further. The walls felt like they were closing in on him, trapping him forever in this dingy alleyway, where nobody would collect his body.

He heard a small clatter near his feet. In front of him were five aulins. If he was savvy enough, that could last him three days.

The younger sister appeared in front of him and patted him on the head. She melted the ice. Drake fell to his knees and scrabbled forward to collect the aulins. He looked up at her and sobbed. He could not formulate any words for her, but he hoped she understood how grateful she was to him.

The older sister called her over. "Come on, Amie, we need to go."

Amie ran back a few steps, and looked over her shoulder at Drake. Their eyes met, and she smiled. He felt a little warm.

That day changed him, and he became a mercenary. A person who wanted to help others, rather than to send them into despair. To make up for all of the bad he had done.

It would be a while until they met again, fighting together in the war that changed Evergaune, but they were inseparable since.

He loved them. He would do anything to bring Amie back.

He held the last painting of the Brantley family seen all together and apologised to their parents for failing to protect Amie. He wiped at his tears. A fire in him began to burn again.

He closed the door behind him as he left, locking the door, and walked down the street with purpose for the first time in what felt like a long time.

*

As Kerri closed shop on another working day and busied herself with tidying away, she struggled to stifle a large yawn. She rubbed her eyes, which began to water in fatigue, as she finished securing the stall. She yawned again, looking at the stars. "Gosh, I'm exhausted." As she locked up, her thoughts travelled to her father again. She wished he was there to tell her what to do.

Kerri had sent a letter to her father a few days ago but had not yet received a reply. She mulled over the contents of her letter again.

Dear father,

I trust that you are doing well. I would love to say the same for myself, but things have been difficult recently. So, so difficult, dad. Amie is currently receiving care from a doctor, but she has been unconscious for three weeks now. I was not there, but the team said that she pushed herself too hard when they were ambushed by bandits, and she suffered a Blowback. I have been so worried about her, but since then, the whole team has been in disarray. I had not realised it, but Amie seemed to be the force keeping the team going forward.

Eve is struggling, beyond belief, and I do not know how to help her. She will not talk to me about it. I prepare food for her every day, but I have not seen her since that day three weeks ago. I had been meeting up with Drake, Clarissa, and Barron, but I just had to do something with myself. I have been training with a sword and shield, which are a beautiful set that Eve gifted me, and they remind me of home. They are a clear blue, just like Ilas. Sometimes, I miss it, and I miss you, but I do love being here, too.

Eve had been training me, so I have been following the schedule she created for me, and I have bought some study books to learn from. I have re-opened our stall too, to earn some money, but I do have to admit that I am exhausted. I feel in over my head. I need to slow down, but I could really do with the help from my friends. Dad, what do you think I should do? I do not know what to do anymore, and I could really do with the help, so please, please tell me you have advice for me.

I'm scared things will never be the same again.

I love you, always,
Kerri

When she arrived home, she exclaimed, as always, "I'm home!" and, as always, received no response. Of course, she was not expecting one, but she lived in hope that she would hear from Eve again, even if it was just Eve unintentionally reacting to her call. Kerri stopped at the door, waiting a little while longer than usual, but the silence simply rang out with no regard for her or her feelings. She sighed deeply and sat on the stairs to remove her boots. As she yawned once more, she closed her eyes, and fell asleep without making it to her bed.

Chapter Thirteen

A knock at the door awoke Kerri. She jolted upright and went to look out of her bedroom window as she did every morning, but only saw a wall. "Huh?" She rubbed her eyes and realised that she'd never even made it up the stairs. "I could've sworn that I only closed my eyes for a moment." Feeling heavy and unrested, Kerri trudged over to the front door, yawning, and looked through the peephole. She saw Drake standing there, a nervous grin on his face, patiently waiting. He was fidgeting with the neckline of his shirt.

"Good morning, Drake." Kerri failed to stifle another yawn as she opened the door and greeted her friend.

"Mornin' Kerri, you doin' okay?" Drake's brow was furrowed, and he tentatively reached his hand toward her own, before pulling it back. Kerri did not notice, for she was yawning again, unable to hide how exhausted she was.

"Yeah, I'd invite you in, but do you mind if we talk outside instead?"

"Sure."

Kerri cracked the door ajar as the cold morning air nipped at her. "So, how are you feeling, Drake? Better?"

"Yeah, yeah, I am. Sorry for leaving you to shoulder this on your own for the last few weeks."

Kerri could not help but look down at the floor, the pressure from the recent weeks momentarily threatened to overwhelm her. She gulped before responding. "I've missed you."

"I've missed you too." Drake put a heavy hand on Kerri's shoulder, then ruffled her hair. "Seeing you working so hard inspired me to do better. Thanks, Kerri."

"I'm glad," her smile was interrupted by another yawn, intent on not letting her get her words out. "I'm about to get ready to train, if you want to come along?"

"You what?" Drake was dumbstruck, "you're not training in this state. Look at you, you can barely stand straight!"

As if on cue, Kerri's knee buckled and she quickly straightened herself up again, rapidly blinking."You're just scared I'm better with a sword than you are now." She attempted to laugh but it quickly turned into yet another yawn. Perhaps the longest one yet.

"I'm more than willing to put you to the test, but not today." Drake took her by the shoulders and gently guided her back through the front door. "Rest today, before you collapse on us, okay? It's been a while, but we're ready to do our share now, too."

Kerri groaned, but relented, "okay, but what about the stall?"

"Don't worry 'bout that, Barron is there now, and Clarissa will be joining him soon. We've got it handled for today, so don't worry about a thing."

Kerri gave a sleepy smile in response, "I've really missed Barron's cooking."

Drake grinned, "that would make two of us. I'll ask him to bring something to ya later on today."

Kerri managed a hearty laugh this time, feeling lighter than she had in weeks. "Thanks, Drake. I'll be sure to catch up with you later."

They said their farewells and, barely remembering even walking up the stairs, sleep claimed Kerri the moment she dropped down onto her bed. For the first time in a long time, she slept peacefully.

Kerri stirred in the early evening, and the first thought that came to her was that she had forgotten to care for Eve today. Jumping from her bed, Kerri raced down the stairs to begin preparing something for the two of them to eat. As she passed the front door, she spotted a solitary envelope on the floor, with her name on it, waiting to be collected.

"I'd recognise that handwriting anywhere..." She skimmed the top of the envelope with her hand before opening it, taking in her father's words.

My darling daughter,

I'm very sorry to hear about Amie. Blowbacks are uncommon these days, but they're not always fatal. Trust in your friend, trust in Amie, that she'll bounce back. Have you seen Scarlett recently?

I wouldn't worry too much about Drake, Clarissa, and Barron. I bet by the time this letter reaches you, they'll
already have picked themselves up from their slump. If you give Drake time, he'll become sick of his own company, so don't expect him to stay away for too long. When you need them most, they'll be there. I'm sure of it.

As for Eve? I don't know much about her, or her past, but I know that she fought to save me, and that it must have taken a toll on her. She's still so young, as are you, and it's important that you stay by her side. Eve won't abandon you. When she's ready to talk, be there for her, my daughter.

I'll come to Thous, if you need me to.

I love you too, always,
Your father

Teardrops ran down Kerri's face. She quickly moved the letter to one side, taking care not to stain it as it shook in her hand. She wished that she could give him a big hug. Seeing that her dad's words had already begun coming true, Kerri wiped her eyes and began preparing dinner in earnest. This time, she was cooking for three.

After leaving a plate outside Eve's door, and eating her own food, Kerri wrapped up the final dish and left home with it. The sun was setting, but the streets were still bustling with people shopping before heading home for the evening.

Dodging the crowd, Kerri made her way to the clinic to meet the friends that she had been too afraid to see. Kerri was still within visiting hours, so she was able to go visit Scarlett and Amie, with nothing more than a warning to keep the noise down.

As the nurse quietly opened the door to Amie's room and ushered Kerri inside, she saw Scarlett sleeping softly in a chair beside Amie's bed. Kerri felt a knot in her throat and goosebumps ripple across her skin. She wrapped her free arm around herself as she shivered. "It's cold."

She gently placed the food down on Amie's bedside table and willed herself to look at her friend. Amie was lying there, her skin was an icy blue and a soft smoky mist billowed up from her skin. Her chest rose and fell slowly, evidence that she was still fighting to be among the living. Other than the movement of her breathing, it was as if she was frozen in time. Kerri touched her forehead with the back of her hand and winced. She was so cold.

"She's freezing, isn't she?" Scarlett spoke, causing Kerri to jump a little. "It's good to see you, Kerri." Her smile did not reach her eyes, staved off by the dark circles that had grown under them. Her hair was unkempt but she did not seem to care as she turned back to her sister.

"I-it's good to see you too," Kerri plopped down in an open seat by Scarlett, "I brought some food for you. Sorry I haven't visited sooner."

"Thank you." Scarlett smiled softly at the younger girl, "you look different."

"I do?" Kerri suddenly felt self-conscious as she tugged at her hair.

"You look stronger." Scarlett nodded, examining Kerri.

"Well, I've been training! Eve bought me a sword and shield, and I've bought some books to study from–" She trailed off, feeling as if she was being inconsiderate to the Brantley sisters by talking about herself.

"It's good to see. Never be ashamed of your growth." Scarlett looked back to Amie, holding her sister's hand over the covers. "Sorry that I haven't been of much use." Kerri began to protest Scarlett's words but she was cut off, "I'm going to be leaving Amie here soon. I just hope I'm here when she wakes up." She squeezed her sister's hand, a bittersweet smile on her lips. "Amie would be disappointed in me if I let the guild fall apart, but one look at you, Kerri, and it seems like it's in safe hands."

Kerri blushed at these words, "I just did what I could."

"That's perhaps more than what the rest of us were doing. Speaking of them, how are the others?"

"I haven't seen them all recently, but Drake stopped by today. He, Clarissa, and Barron are tending to the stall and gathering food today. We're just waiting on our favourite redheads, now."

"That's good to hear. What about Eve?"

Kerri bit her lip and broke eye contact. "Eve isn't doing so well. I haven't seen her since the night you brought Amie back." Kerri faltered as she saw Scarlett's face fall, and hurried to add "but she is eating!"

Scarlett smiled at her, and under her fatigue Kerri could still feel the warmth coming from her. Kerri was shocked when Scarlett laid her hand on top of her own.

"I knew she'd be okay in your hands. Amie would be disappointed in me, she would be heartbroken hearing about Eve. Before Amie returns to us, we need to make sure that Eve is back to her usual self." Scarlett watched her sister, who was still as a statue. "She'd hate knowing Eve is struggling."

"I know. I miss them both, but I don't know what to do for them."

Scarlett squeezed Kerri's hand with her free one, "you've done wonderfully, Kerri. Us adults have let you down." Scarlett leaned in to hug Kerri, and Kerri, still so young and raw to this lifestyle, began to feel her lips tremble.

"It's been so hard."

"I know, but I'm here now. Tomorrow, I'm going to come visit, okay?" Scarlett stroked Kerri's hair, speaking soothingly to her. Kerri felt a little as if she was with her mother again. She nodded, sniffling.

"I like the new look, by the way."

"Oh, thank you," Kerri touched the tips of her hair, now reaching only as far as her chin.

In silence, they both watched Amie. Her chest slowly rose and fell. They both hoped that she would wake up any minute now.

Having said her goodbyes to Scarlett and Amie, Kerri left the clinic. It was getting dark, but she could take a guess where she might find the others.

When she arrived at Willkeep's Tavern, she spotted Drake, Clarissa, and Barron around a table, looking more cheerful than the last time she had seen them. She pulled up a seat and was met with loud greetings as they all welcomed her to the table.

"It's good to see you again!" Kerri felt a warmth spread across her at Barron's smile being back where it belonged.

She told them about her training, but did not mention Eve. She could see the curiosity written on their faces, but they did not ask either. Instead, she told Drake that she would see him early tomorrow morning by the training field, much to his horror, and bid the others good night.

Her mind turned to Eve, and how Scarlett might be able to draw her out of her shell. She hoped that tomorrow would be the day that she finally saw her dear friend again.

Continuing her routine of greeting Eve as she took her shoes off, Kerri knocked on her door to tell her that Scarlett is visiting tomorrow. "I just didn't want it to come as a surprise to you. She wants to see you, and I do too, but we understand if you need more time. Good night, Eve."

*

As Kerri was making coffee for herself the following morning, she heard a rapt knock at the door. She placed the kettle down and opened the front door to see Scarlett looking radiant as the morning sun beamed down on her, every bit the leader that Kerri recognised her as. Her smile did not quite meet her eyes just yet, but she was still a sight for sore eyes. In Kerri's case, incredibly sore and tired eyes.

"Good morning, Kerri!"

"Good morning, Scarlett," Kerri stepped back to let Scarlett in, "oh, and welcome to our home!"

As Kerri welcomed Scarlett, she was struck by a feeling of guilt, which did not go unnoticed by her perceptive friend. She shuffled her feet and bit at the nail on her thumb. She wished that Eve was here for the first time they welcomed their friends home.

Scarlett placed a hand on her shoulder. "Is Eve upstairs?"

"Yes, I'm not sure if she's awake yet, though."

Scarlett tilted her head to the side, only for a very brief second, before exclaiming "well, she's about to be."

172

Scarlett charged up the stairs—after removing her shoes at Kerri's insistence—and slammed her fist against Eve's bedroom door. Kerri winced but did not stop her. "Eve, it's Scarlett. I'm not leaving 'til I've seen you with my own eyes."

Her declaration was met by silence, so Scarlett tried a different tact. "Please, Eve, we miss you. I could really do with your company, you know." Scarlett rested her forehead against the door, and almost fell forward when Eve suddenly opened it.

Kerri's heart ached as she laid eyes on Eve. She looked thinner, her hair was greasy, the bags under her eyes looked as if they might never vanish, and stale air choked Kerri and Scarlett as it blew into the corridor. Seeing Eve for the first time in weeks, Kerri is overcome by emotion, but the fact that the leading emotion was anger surprised her, and she pushed her way past the two women and into Eve's room. She threw Eve's curtains and window open, and turned to shout at her, but stammered as she saw Eve staring at the ground, her shoulders slumped, looking as if the force of Kerri's words could cause her to crumple like paper. Instead, she took a deep breath and began tidying Eve's room. She removed her bedsheets, collected some laundry and disappeared downstairs with as much as she could carry in her arms.

"Kerri's really gotten strong, you know, in more ways than one." Scarlett smiled at Eve, but Eve just stood there listlessly. "Hey, she's going to be okay, you know?" This grabbed Eve's attention, and she slowly looked up. "Come on, let's get you washed and fed." Scarlett took Eve by the hand and guided her gently from the room. Eve did not protest or resist. She allowed Scarlett to take her to the bathroom, and she momentarily disappeared to collect Eve a fresh set of clothes. Eve glanced at herself in the mirror, but looked away seconds later, pain and disgust on her face. She winced and squinted, as if someone had shone a bright light in her face, and turned

173

her back to the mirror. Scarlett returned with her clothing, along with a towel. "Here, wash, we'll be downstairs with a hot breakfast for you, once you're ready." Eve nodded, and Scarlett closed the bathroom door behind her as she left.

Scarlett made her way downstairs to the appetising scent of meat sizzling, as she turned the corner into the kitchen to see Kerri turning bacon over in a frying pan. "Smells good!"

"I've become a pretty okay cook, if I do say so myself."

"C'mon, let me help you with the vegetables." Scarlett focused on the vegetables whilst Kerri cooked the meat, and as they were serving the third and final plate, they heard soft footsteps coming down the stairs.

Eve stood in the hallway and looked down at herself self-consciously, before shuffling into the kitchen.

"Sit!" Scarlett pulled up a seat as Eve entered, and Kerri placed the last plate of food in front of her.

"Only the freshest plate for my Eve!" Kerri posed with her spatula before removing her apron and taking a seat for herself.

"Thank you." Eve poked at the food, slowly making her way through it then picking up speed as her appetite grew. As she ate, she commented on Kerri's new hair, "your hair looks like mine. I like it."

Kerri smiled and played with the tips of her hair as she watched Eve finish her food, and Scarlett made a round of coffee for everyone.

"Milk and two sugars, right, Eve? As sweet as you are, if I remember right!"

Eve managed the tiniest of smiles as Amie's face briefly appeared in her mind, "yeah, that's right."

"We won't force you to do anything today, but if you're able, I'd like you to go visit Amie."

Eve looked up, "she's still...?"

Scarlett paused as she was scooping another spoonful of sugar into Eve's mug, "yeah, she's still sleeping. A real sleeping beauty, just waiting for her prince to come. Or should I say princess?" Scarlett laughed softly before warning Eve, "do be prepared if you go there, though, Eve."

Eve nodded, "I'm going, now." She rushed upstairs to get changed, and only moments after she was on the doorstep, putting on her boots and preparing to leave.

"Hey, Eve, before you go," Kerri disappeared into her room, reappearing with a jacket draped over her arm. "This is for you."

Eve looked at the jacket. It was similar to her old one that had been destroyed in Ilas Arena, but this time it was in a breathtaking deep red. She accepted the jacket and hugged it to her chest as she admired Kerri. "Kerri, I love it. thank you." She put it on with care and bounded down the street, a flicker of hope growing within her chest.

Scarlett leant against the doorframe as they watched Eve make her way down the street. "Wouldn't it be nice if the princess got to be the hero sometimes?"

"Yeah, it sure would be." The two women watched until Eve vanished into the crowd of people before going back inside.

*

Eve slowed as she approached the clinic. It looked intimidating to her. There was nothing menacing about the building at all, but inside was the home to her greatest fear. She did not want to return and face the truth that she had no idea what she could do to help Amie. The tightness in her chest and throat threatened to stop her in her tracks entirely. The lethargy and self-doubt still clung to her. She still felt as if a part of her was missing, but for now she was done hiding. She took a deep breath, steadied herself, and entered.

The receptionist bowed to a customer who was leaving, and she looked back up to see Eve. "Oh, hello!"

"Oh, um, hi," Eve felt embarrassed, but powered through, "could you please tell me where Amie Brantley is?"

The receptionist asked Eve a few questions about who she was and why she was here, then happily directed her to where Amie was resting. The cold persisted throughout the corridor, and she wrapped her arms around herself to keep some warmth within her. Her breath hung in front of her face. another nurse quickly walked by in a large coat, her teeth chattering. Eve found the room, and could barely peek in through the window due to the cold fog. She placed her hand on the steel doorknob which almost burned her with its fierce cold, and pulled her hand back. Shame and guilt poured from somewhere deep within and into every area of her body, an inky black mess that felt capable of physically choking her. She stood in front of the door for ten, maybe fifteen minutes, when a nurse approached and draped a blanket over her shoulders. "It's okay, you can go in, dear."

"R-right, yeah." Feeling foolish, and thanking the nurse for her kindness, Eve opened the door and let herself in. Nobody else was currently in the room. The cold chill hit her in full blast. She instinctively lit a small fire from her hand using her Presence, but quickly snuffed it out as she remembered where she was. She shook her head roughly and scolded herself. "Stop being such an idiot!"

After another deep breath, Eve looked toward the only bed in the room but could not bring herself to pull back the curtain. Instead, she sat in a chair on the other side, only seeing the soft movement of the bed sheets as Amie breathed.

"This is stupid. I'm being stupid." Eve thought that saying it aloud would make her stronger, or that Amie might laugh and comfort her, but she remained glued to her seat, and Amie remained glued to her bed, unable to draw the comfort she longed for from the woman behind the curtain. "I'm so sorry, Amie." Her apology lingered in the air. On the slow road to recovery, this was the one thing that could send her plummeting back down, and right now, her friends needed her. She needed them.

Eve was not sure how long she sat there, but when she moved to stand up, she almost buckled forward. Her legs were numb and weak, and she had to grab the nearby table to support herself. She let out a breath and laughed, almost hoping that Amie would comment on how clumsy she could be. Nevertheless, the room remained as silent as it was when she got there. As she went to leave, she looked back at the curtain one more time, not knowing what to say, and so she went with the one thing that was on her mind. "I love you."

The door gently closed behind her, and as Eve left the clinic, she felt colder than she had just moments before.

With the sun still high and feeling the need to clear her head, Eve walked towards main street where she hoped the barrage of aromas and noise would distract her. one noise in particular did.

"Hey, Eve! What's got you looking so glum?" Eve turned to see Eric, idly re-arranging his sale display of weaponry.

"Hi, Eric. Just stuff, but it'll be okay."

Eric raised an eyebrow questioningly but did not push for details."How is Kerri finding her new sword and shield?"

"She loves them, she's been training most days, so I've heard." Eve rubbed her arm, feeling the muscle definition waning due to her self-imposed isolation. "Maybe I don't need to watch out for her anymore."

"If she's anything like you, then I feel sorry for anyone who crosses either of you!" Eric laughed loudly. "I've seen her, you know, training in the early hours of the morning. It's only when I'm on my way here, but damn, I get here early, and she's already there, working up a sweat."

"She's a hard worker," Eve laughed too, and remembered what Kerri said to her the last time they trained, "she wants to be able to knock me on my arse sometime."

Eric chuckled, a toothy grin on his face, "it sounds like you best be ready then!"

Eve smiled warmly at Eric, "yeah, I really should be. She had not seemed to notice Eve's presence yet. "Thanks, Eric."

"Anytime, Eve." With a wink, he headed into the back of his shop, and Eve heard him hammering away as she walked down the street.

The sound comforted her, knowing that life would go on as normal, no matter how bad it got, and knowing that it would work itself out for the better eventually.

As the training field came into sight, Eve saw Kerri, using the sword and shield that she gave to her. She hadn't seemed to notice Eve's presence just yet.

Sneaking behind the younger woman, Eve collected one of the wooden swords and went to tap her on the shoulder, but Kerri performed a swirling slash that knocked the sword clean from her hand.

Kerri's eyes glinted as she glanced up, a broad grin on her face. "Bet you didn't expect that now, did you?"

Eve could not help but have the shock evident on her face. "No, but maybe I should have. You've come a long way in only three weeks." She collected her sword from the ground and held it in front of her, "let's see if you can do it again."

Kerri replaced her sword and shield for wooden ones and remarked, "these feel so light now." She swung them around, getting used to the difference in weight.

As soon as Kerri confirmed that she was ready, Eve dashed in, her sword colliding with Kerri's shield. "Nice block."

"Wow, you're so fast!" Eve might have been rusty, but it would take a lot longer than three weeks to ruin all of her hard work throughout life.

Eve side-stepped to Kerri's left, away from her sword arm, and pushed her away with her forearm. Kerri quickly recovered, using the momentum from the push to re-centre herself and put distance between them.

Eve pointed her wooden sword at Kerri. "You've improved."

"I can do better!" Kerri dashed in, covering the distance with inhuman speed. It was as if she had teleported faster than Eve could blink. "I can be better!" Eve heard a voice behind as the image of Kerri in front of her vanished into smoke, and Kerri appeared behind her instead and tapped Eve on the shoulder with her sword. Eve turned, leaving the smoke behind her to look at the very real Kerri in front of her. Eve realised what had happened.

"You've found a way to use your Illusion in battle? Very clever."

"I never thought my Presence would be good for anything other than magic tricks, but I want to hold my own in battle, too." Kerri's smile was replaced by a look of pure determination, her desire to contribute to the team almost had its own physical sensation.

"Then let's resume training. I want to see all you've learned."

"I hope you're ready then, teach!"

Eve adapted to Kerri as she revealed more of her new techniques and Illusion abilities, forcing Kerri to work hard to find new ways to approach the seasoned ex-. After a few minutes, Eve parried another swing, slower than the last, and Kerri fell backward to the floor.

Eve looked down at her, sweat dripping down her face, as she gulped for air. Her face, hair and clothes were dirty, but she never once complained. Instead, she tried and tried again, doing her best to beat Eve. She could only feel admiration and respect for Kerri's progress, thinking back to the girl they rescued from the cave that she had assumed would be nothing more than a spoiled brat of a child.

"There are a lot of great fighters out there, Kerri," the younger woman looked up, her face flushed, "and whilst you still have a ways to go, know that you've come very far already. Be proud."

"T-thanks, Eve."

"Come on, have some water." Eve tapped a lukewarm water bottle to Kerri's forehead, which she gratefully accepted.

"I'm exhausted. Training with you is much more tiring than training alone."

"We're back to it now. Hope you can keep up." Eve grinned at Kerri, who grinned back.

"Is that a challenge? Don't worry, I will knock you on your arse one day! I will!" The two laughed, and Eve felt as if an invisible weight lifted from her shoulders, if only a little bit.

Chapter Fourteen

Life began to feel normal again in the following days, but the looming cloud of Amie's condition weighed heavily on everyone. The clinic informed Scarlett that all they could do now was let her rest, and hope that she recovered naturally. Due to Ice being her Presence, she was able to withstand colder temperatures than most people but having used it so often and having generated so much Ice in a short period of time, meant that this was a battle that only she could fight now. The risk of over-generating Presence was a fear that any Presence-wielder had, with each having differing effects.

Not wanting Amie to return to a dour group with no funds, they decided to take turns working the stall and accepting missions which were neither close to home nor too daring. With Kerri eager to prove herself, Eve, Scarlett, and Drake accompanied her on a mission to collect plants and herbs for a local apothecary. Although it could be entirely uneventful, there was a chance that they could run into aggressive wildlife in the forest, hence why a guild had been hired to carry out the job. This mission was hand-picked by Eve. It seemed like the perfect way to see how Kerri could handle herself in a real, threatening situation before she took on the likes of bandits and rogue guilds. She shuddered as she imagined the werewolf she and Scarlett fought, hoping that nothing quite as gruelling would await them.

Using some of the money earned through the stall, especially as Kerri manned it alone for so long, the group allowed her to use a large chunk of it to buy battle-ready gear. Matching her weapons, and inspired by her hometown, Ilas, Kerri wore aqua-coloured light armour, complete with chest piece, armguards, waistguard and steel boots, with dark brown leather covering every other inch of her. She was dressed fairly bright, but pulled it off well.

The sun reflected brilliantly from her armour, making it hard to look at directly.

"It's hard to imagine you wearing a different colour." Eve said, admiring Eric's handiwork.

"Some of my best work, if I do say so myself!" Eric looked Kerri up and down, "you look like you're all ready to go."

"Thanks, Eric."

"Yes, thank you so much, Eric—I love it!" Kerri twisted and turned, looking at herself with a wide smile on her face. "With this, I can finally help you all in battle!"

The rest of the team had sparred with Kerri, giving her the opportunity to show what she could do. It was time for her first mission. Scarlett's one request was "nothing human", but fortunately there was never any shortage of missions to choose from.

Saying their farewells to Eric, the group of four headed toward Theid's Forest, where they had been informed by the apothecary that they would have the best chance of collecting what they needed.

"So…" Scarlett trailed off, running her finger along the list of ingredients they had been given, "we need handfuls of poison ivy, witch hazel, hawthorn and elderberry." She pocketed the list and grinned, "that shouldn't be too hard."

"Don't jinx us." Drake joked, but his nervous laughter had a ring of honesty to it. "The last thing we want is for Kerri to have a bad first mission, isn't that right, Kerri?"

Kerri pumped her arms and exhaled harshly, "I'm ready for anything and everything! Poison ivy won't claim me today!"

"Yeah, Drake, what's your deal with poison ivy, eh?" Scarlett joined in, inspired by Kerri's enthusiasm.

"Nothing! I have no issues with poison ivy, well, except for when I fell into a bush full of it when I was around Kerri's age. That stung something awful." Drake grimaced, recalling the presumably long forgotten memory.

"Again, no poison ivy is claiming me today! I shall be the victor!" Kerri's enthusiasm slowly spread across the group, her cheer encouraging smiles on all faces, each unable to contain their laughter as the youngest of the group threw away any attempt of quelling her excitement.

"Alright, alright, let's get there before this one bursts!" Drake tilted his head towards Kerri, and they quickened their pace to reach Theid's Forest.

As they took their first steps among its many trees, Eve asked for them to stop. "I want to tie this around a few of these, so we don't get lost," she explained as she finished tying a piece of red thread into a knot near the entrance. She gave it a final tug and stepped away looking satisfied. "Okay, let's go."

As they walked deeper into the brush, the sunlight dimmed, their armour losing their shine. "Anyone have any idea where to look?" Drake asked.

A short silence followed.

"Not too sure, guess we'll just have to keep an eye out. I'm not certain on what it looks like, exactly." Scarlett responded.

"If you're not sure about something, feel free to ask me, and I'll verify it." Eve jumped in. "Someone taught me about flora a long time ago." She thought back to

Megara; how she would teach her about plants and herbs, what was dangerous to consume, what could be mixed together to create certain potions, and more.

"That's good, it wouldn't do us well to return with the wrong ingredients, and I won't have us come back when it's dark." Scarlett declared, wanting to play it safe with a smaller group.

"Don't worry, we'll get—" Drake was cut off by Scarlett, her arm blocking his path.

"Quiet!"

Each member slowed their breathing and strained their hearing. They heard a moist, squelching sound not far from where they stood. A chomping sound that could not be mistaken for anything other than of a beast, and the growling and snapping of jaws put them on guard. Eve gripped her scythe, still stored away, ready to wield it at a moment's notice.

"Kerri?" Eve looked at her apprentice, the younger woman's smile gone and her face pale, "you can do this. You can do this today, you can do this tomorrow, and you can do this any day of the week."

Kerri nodded, her sword and shield steady in front of her. "You're right. I can do this."

Scarlett slowly inched forward, leaves and twigs snapping and crunching underneath her feet. One particularly loud snap rang out. Everyone held their breath. The forest in its entirety turned deathly silent. A low rumbling noise reverberated around the group, and two wolves jumped from a gap in-between the trees, lunging straight at Scarlett.

Scarlett performed a wide slash, her rapier just inches away from drawing blood, and the two wolves dodged to the sides. Drake followed with a stab of his own, but the wolf he aimed for was too quick and had jumped backwards with its teeth bared, its eyes set on Drake.

"Fine!" he yelled, "let's see how you like this!" Drake stamped the floor, and the ground cracked open ahead of him, clamping down like teeth on the wolf's legs. It whimpered, struggling to free itself, and Eve took the opportunity to put it down with one swift motion of her scythe. One down.

Eve looked up as four more wolves joined the fray, appearing from the thick woods like shadows. The group primarily focused on Eve, Scarlett, and Drake, who were closest, but one split from the pack, running towards Kerri.

"A-ah!" Kerri yelped, taken by surprise in her very first life-or-death battle.

"Kerri!" Eve shouted, kicking one of the wolves into a nearby tree. it squealed as a flurry of leaves rained down, "don't forget, you can do this!"

Kerri dashed backwards as the wolf leapt at her, activating her Presence, and narrowly avoided its snapping jaws. Confused as its target vanished from thin air, the wolf tumbled into the ground and skidded as it attempted to climb back to its feet. Before it could find its footing, Kerri reappeared and plunged her sword deep into its chest. Blood spurt out, the red splatting across her armour. Kerri felt her throat tighten, bile burning it.

"Good work!" Kerri turned toward the others at Eve's praise, deciding to deal with those new feelings later.

Seeing that Scarlett was contending with two wolves alone, she charged forth and knocked one aside with her shield. It whimpered as it hit the floor, kicking at the dirt as it panicked from its shocking blow. Scarlett dashed forward in the next moment, cutting the wolf along its belly. Only halfway to its feet, it fell, unable to fight back, and bled out as Scarlett turned her attention to another battle.

Kerri watched the light fade from the wolf's eyes, a pang of guilt searing through her heart, and mumbled an apology under her breath before she, too, turned her attention elsewhere.

The wolves, now outnumbered, were becoming more aggressive in their attacks, darting around as they hunted for an opening.

"There aren't many left. Keep going!" Scarlett yelled.

Drake slashed at a wolf jumping toward him. It skidded along the floor at Eve's feet. She pushed its head into the ground with her hand, its legs kicking wildly, as she summoned a strong flame from within its skull. It ceased resisting almost instantly. Eve removed her hand and looked away from the wolf's body. Her face twisted in disgust. She wiped her hand along the floor to remove the drooping flesh and fur as best as she could.

The two remaining wolves snarled and gnashed their teeth, retreating slowly into the trees. As Drake took a menacing step forward, they turned around, running away deep into the forest. "Let's hope they haven't gone to find friends." Scarlett panted and wiped the sweat from her brow then cleaned the blood marks from her face.

As Scarlett and Drake cleaned themselves the best they could, Eve walked over to Kerri and patted her on the back, "you did well."

"I- I didn't like that."

Eve smiles knowingly at her. She was all too aware herself that this was not fun, enjoyable, or pleasurable in any way.

"I would say it gets easier, but it doesn't. You'll feel guilty, and sometimes that guilt will eat away at you, but we didn't pick this fight, the same way that we don't pick many others. Sometimes, we have to do bad things, things we hate, but we," she looked at Scarlett and Drake, watching Scarlett clean a bit of dirt from Drake's cheek, "we have each other." Eve pat Kerri on the back again, and helped clean her armour.

"Thanks, Eve. Just so you know, I want to keep going forward, so don't worry about me." Kerri pumped her arms again, with a little less gusto, but her meaning was clear all the same.this made Eve smile.

"Hey, look," Drake pointed through the clearing where the wolves had appeared, "is that...?"

"Yeah, it is." The four stepped through the clearing where they saw a mangled body, torn open, their features damaged beyond recognition. "Poor bastard." Scarlett clicked her tongue, disgusted and annoyed.

Kerri averted her gaze away from the body with a small whimper and spied a bag lying on the floor, various berries and herbs strewn across the ground before it.

"Look! Are these any of what we're looking for, Eve?"

Eve tore her eyes away from the body, joining Kerri as she looked at the items on the floor. "It's some of it. This should be enough hawthorn and elderberry, and we'll just have to continue searching for the others." She plucked the berries and tucked them away inside of her satchel. "Good catch, Kerri."

Eve glanced at Kerri, noting the colour returning to her face, but paler still than she was before the fight. "Let's get the rest and go. I don't like this forest."

"Agreed. What do we still need?"

"Poison ivy and witch hazel."

"Okay, at least we've got the berries sorted."

Eve nodded, but the hairs on her neck and arms were raised, thinking back to the wolves from earlier. She wished they had finished them off.

The group resumed their search for the rest of the ingredients, examining the bushes and branches nearby for what they needed. Eve continued to tie red thread across trees, making their path back home clear to them.

"Ouch!"

Eve jogged over to Drake, who is sucking on the tip of his finger. "I see you've found the poison ivy!" She scooped a handful of poison ivy, and brought Drake's attention to her glove, "this is why we have gloves!"

Drakes sighed and looked at his finger, the tip of it sore and red, then laughed, "note taken."

"Shit, I'm not sure which way we came from." Scarlett spun on the spot, looking for the tree with the red thread.

Eve did the same. She found the tree she had tied it to, but the red thread had disappeared. "I put it here, though, just a moment ago." Eve rubbed her hand on the tree, searching for anything suspicious, but did not see anything. "I—maybe I didn't?" She tied another red thread to the trees, beginning to doubt herself, the tight knot in her stomach growing.

"C'mon, let's look for the witch hazel on our way out of here." Scarlett led the group through the trees, following Eve's red thread, until it stopped once again. "Eve?" Scarlett looked back toward Eve, worry creeping into her voice.

"No. I put it there. I-I know I did. I know I did." Eve examined the tree and the flooring. She spotted some red thread on the floor, the end of it vanishing into a bush. As she looked up, she also saw the last ingredient. "Here's the witch hazel, but how...?" She walked forward and reached out to collect some, when a large, furred hand grabbed her arm and threw her effortlessly into a thicket of trees as she screamed.

"Eve!" Kerri dove into the trees after her, but Scarlett and Drake were cut off by a small pack of wolves.

"More of them?"

"Kerri, please find Eve!" The wolves formed a line in front of the two, refusing to let them pass. "Fine," said Scarlett, furious, "this time, none of you are getting out alive."

Sprawled across the dirt, Eve pulled herself to her feet, dazed.

"What in the hell was that?" She stumbled, putting her hand to her head, and removed it to see blood smearing her hand. "Damn it."

"Eve! Eve! Where are you?!" Kerri's voice echoed around the forest.

"I'm here."

"Eve?!"

Weak and groggy, Eve summoned a small flame to illuminate herself in the darkness, hoping the light would be strong enough for Kerri to see.

"Eve! There you are!" Kerri appeared from behind a tree and ran over to Eve, shock wrinkling her features.

"No." Kerri lifted Eve's chin to get a better look at her. Her brows knit together and she frowned, "don't worry, I have some bandages, but we need to get you out of here, now." Kerri searched her satchel, hidden beneath her waistguard, and pulled out some bandages which she then used to wrap around Eve's wound. The white quickly turned to red, but there was not much else she could do in this forest.

"Can you walk?"

"Yes"

Kerri pulled Eve to her feet, and Eve felt her stomach churn as dizziness hit her, her footing unsteady

and her surroundings blurry. She shook her head and stopped before she retched.

Kerri grabbed her by the cheeks and looked into her eyes, worried. "Eve, I'm sorry, but we need to help Drake and Scarlett."

A cold chill ran through Eve. "Yeah, of course. Let's go, we'll get them, then we'll get out, no problem." Kerri nodded and supported Eve as they went back to where the other two were.

"Take that!" Drake stabbed one wolf through the chest and threw its body at another approaching, knocking it off of its feet. Another wolf lay dead in the bushes, its fur singed. Slamming the floor once again with his fist, Drake summoned a small wall of dirt and crushed the wolf he'd just knocked over. The last wolf snarled and yapped, fiercely fighting its corner, but Scarlett reached out her hand and shot Spark from her fingertips. It yelped and growled, but darted away into the bushes.

"Little bastards." Drake spat.

"Don't worry about them now, we need to find the other two." Scarlett tried to find the direction that Kerri had run off in but suddenly stopped in her tracks, her face going pale and her heart feeling as if it had fallen like lead into her stomach. "That's a big wolf!"

As if on cue, the werewolf howled and stood up straight, its frame reaching larger than any ordinary human could hope to be.

"Shit!" Eve rasped, fresh sweat breaking out across her forehead.

"What was that?" Kerri asked, fear creeping into her voice.

"That's a werewolf. They're in trouble. We need to get there, now!" As soon as the words left her mouth, Eve felt herself growing increasingly light-headed; her head was still bleeding relentlessly. She could try and cauterise it herself with her Presence, but she couldn't chance it. Not when she could not even see the wound.

Kerri trudged along as fast as she could, slowed down by Eve, huffing as she tried to get them there as soon as possible.

The werewolf loomed over the two mercenaries. It was at least a foot and a half taller than Drake, with arms that could reach them with little effort. As drool made its way down the beast's chin and onto the floor, Drake felt a shiver run down his spine.

"This bastard's much bigger than the last one!"

Drake's eyes darted toward Scarlett as she spoke, his leader ready to defend herself and Drake at a moment's notice. "How did you take that one down?"

"With Eve. It almost killed us, and she's damn good, but we got lucky."

Drake scrutinised the werewolf and shrugged. "Not the most convincing pep talk, but we don't have any other choice but to win."

He charged at the beast, but stopped short as its arm moved fast towards him in a foul swipe, its claws glinting as they narrowly missed his face. Drake swung with his sword but the arm was already back at the werewolf's side, its speed truly frightening.

"Scarlett, can you distract it?"

At his question Scarlett leapt, and she and the beast began their vicious attack, both too fast to land a decisive hit. Drake took a step back, not fast enough to keep up with either of them with his sword.

"Okay, here I go!" He summoned a large wall of dirt; wood, rock, and berries caught up in the flurry, towering higher than the werewolf, and with a swing of his arm he threw it towards the werewolf. "Scarlett, fall back!"

She did, instantly appearing at Drake's side as the wall enveloped the werewolf with a deafening roar. The beast attempted to escape but the sheer mass of the wall forced it to the ground and buried it beneath its rubble.

Drake fell to his knees, exhausted.

"Drake! Are you okay?" Scarlett knelt down, looking into his eyes.

"Yeah, I'll be fine, just a little tired, is all. Let's find the others and get out of this shithole."

"Sounds like a good plan to me." Scarlett helped him to his feet, just in time to see Kerri approaching with Eve weakly clinging to her shoulder.

"You look like shit."

"Thanks, so do you." Drake and Eve shared the joke, both leaning on their friends.

"The red thread was last tied to that tree, so we should be able to get out that way." A few small fibres of red thread poked out beneath the dirt by the foot of the tree Eve was pointing at.

A few feet into their escape, they felt the ground rumbling behind them, and looked to see the pile of dirt lifting, the large grey figure inside rising to its feet, its lean body resembling more of a hulking beast as it flung the rubble from itself.

"Shit! Kerri, put Eve down!"

Kerri nodded and helped Eve to the ground, as Scarlett placed Drake beside her. He looked pale and clammy, his sweat sticking to his forehead. His head lulled, his eyebrows pulling together as if in pain.

"We've got this! Just rest!" Scarlett yelled over her shoulder. As she turned her attention back to the werewolf, Eve felt another wave of dizziness wash over her and her head lolled.

Scarlett and Kerri prepared for battle. the red eyes of the werewolf glinted eerily in the darkened wood, and it stalked toward them menacingly, its feet thumping against the ground. Each thump felt like a knock on death's door, and Kerri's heart raced, her chest tightening as all of her senses screamed at her that she would die here. To dispel her fears, she slammed her sword against her shield and charged in with a yell, not allowing the werewolf to get too close to her wounded allies.

It swung, its claws skidding across Kerri's shield as sher orolled and slashed at the back of its legs. A small spray of blood spurt out.

The werewolf stumbled back, the light graze not seeming to hurt it too greatly, but it howled, a great, piercing howl which threatened to bring its opposition to their knees with intimidation alone. It swiped the floor, throwing dirt into Kerri's face. Scarlett tried to attack whilst it was focused on Kerri, but as she closed the space between them, it got on all fours, tackling Kerri with incredible speed. Howling again, it dragged Kerri along the floor and picked her up by her shield, pulling her to eye level. It snarled in her face, opening its mouth wide, as Kerri tried to unstrap her shield from her arm. Her sword lay helpless on the ground

"Don't you dare!" Eve screamed as the werewolf turned to face her, she punched it with a fist full of Flame, causing it to stumble several feet and drop Kerri. Without a glance at Kerri, Eve jumped on the werewolf.

She delivered a series of furious punches to its skull, every hit thrown with the intent to kill, until the werewolf smacked her away. Eve, too exhausted to maintain her Presence and strength, spat and wiped her mouth of fresh blood, as she watched the werewolf stand. Several spots of it were blackened and smoking, its jaw slack and broken from Eve's fierce barrage.

Eve scrambled to her feet, but Scarlett stood in her way. "No, you need to rest. We've got this."

Kerri stood by her side, ready to continue fighting.

"I've got an idea." Kerri said, tightening the straps on her shield.

"Yeah?" Scarlett replied curiously, "what is it?"

"I'm going to create an opening, and when I do, hit it. Something it simply cannot recover from."

Scarlett grinned, "sure, consider it done."

The werewolf was on all fours again. Kerri split from Scarlett, running along the outer trees, shouting at the werewolf to grab its attention. "Come on, finish the job, beast!"

The werewolf halted to a stop, searching for Kerri. As soon as they made eye contact, he leapt from where he stood, but Kerri used a tree behind her to boost herself up and over its body, not wasting any momentum in her escape. the werewolf collided with the trunk with a sickening crunch. As Kerri landed, she slashed its back legs again, a much deeper gouge than before.

It howled in pain, turning around as it lashed out with its claws, but Kerri had already created distance between the two and positioned herself in Scarlett's way.

She banged her shield and the werewolf began running on all fours before climbing to its hind legs, running as if it were human.

Kerri raised her sword and shield, creating her strongest defence, and the werewolf swung its claws downwards meeting the dirt with a thud. The illusion of Kerri vanished into a thin smoke.

"Now!"

Scarlett jumped into action, her sabre imbued with Spark, and plunged it in the beast's shoulder. It screamed, endlessly as Scarlett's electricity coursed throughout its body, causing it to convulse. Scarlett removed her sabre and kicked the werewolf to the floor, watching as it struggled to regain control of its body, unable to support itself as its muscles spasmed with aggressive irregularity.

She took aim with one of her pistols, pointing directly at its head. As she went to pull the trigger, it suddenly lashed out, slapping the gun from her hand. It grabbed Scarlett by the leg and she collapsed to the floor as it began pulling her closer towards itself. It got a better grip on her body, and it threw her up and slammed her down, one hand firmly keeping her in place as she tried fruitlessly to push back against it.

"G-get off me!"

The werewolf kept Kerri at bay with its other hand, swiping widely whenever she attempted to approach. It tightened its hold on Scarlett's upper body, squeezing on her ribs. Choking, Scarlett scratched at the hand, her lungs screaming for air and her Spark diminishing as her consciousness began to fade.

Kerri tried to get in closer, but the werewolf took advantage of a mis-swing, and grabbed her by the head, slamming her into the ground. It tossed her body aside, limp.

Eve watched as the scene unfolded, mouth agape as the werewolf single-handedly tore her guild apart. Fear turning into anger, she picked up Scarlett's sabre and charged, deftly dodging the werewolf's swing, and slashing at its forearm. It screamed and lashed out in a panic, throwing Scarlett between the trees. Eve glanced over but could not see her.

The werewolf made to grab Eve with both arms, and she stepped into its grasp, grabbing tightly onto its upper arms. It closed its hold on her and crushed her to its chest.

"You better kill me quick, because I'm about to end your miserable existence!"

Eve ignited her hands, singing its fur, and began to burn through its skin and muscle. She cried out as sweat ran down her face. The werewolf was trying to crush her, but she set her arms alight in an effort to deter it in its effort. She squeezed as hard as she could, screaming with exertion as stars clouded her vision until she successfully sank her hands through its arm to its very bones, and it staggered backwards. It fell with its legs kicking wildly in panic, unable to get back up as blood trickled from its partly cauterised wounds. Eve raised Scarlett's sabre again and stabbed it through the head. She glared down at the body as it spasmed its last, her rage slowly subsided, before her adrenaline returned as she remembered Kerri's unconscious form. She spun around wildly, looking for her, until she saw the girl lying face down, her hair covering her face from view. She skidded to Kerri's side and moved her hair. Once it was confirmed that she was still breathing, although a shallow gouge across her face was seeping blood, and a bruise was blooming across her right cheekbone and jaw, Eve felt relief flush through her.

"Oh, thank God."

Drake came to her aid, his strength beginning to return, although he was still shaky on his feet. "It's the least I can do." His words were bitter as he looked down, a mixture of frustration and upset written on his face.

"We couldn't have the same happen to you, Drake." Scarlett rubbed his arm, smiling gently at him. "C'mon, let's get out of here."

Eve picked up Kerri's sword and shield and remembered something else.

"Hold on," she searched the bush by the werewolf's body, pulling free a clump of witch hazel. "After all that, this apothecary better be damn well happy."

Chapter Fifteen

Eve dropped the bag of ingredients on the desk of the apothecary, whose eyes fell on Kerri. She stared at the still wet wound with squinting eyes, and rested her chin on her interlaced fingers. Kerri averted her eyes and shuffled her feet, grabbing again at her dress. Finally the apothecary turned away and approached a curtain behind her. "Bring her back here." She waved her hand and beckoned them over to the curtain, and disappeared behind it.

Everyone followed silently. No one had the energy to do much else.

"Place her here, on this table." Drake did as he was told. "I'm going to tend to her wound and rouse her back to consciousness."

Drake mumbled something that sounded like worry, but stepped aside to let the apothecary work.

She examined the wound and ran one finger along it. She stepped away briefly with a small pot in her hand, and she opened it to reveal a white cream in it. With a gentle touch, she massaged this cream along the length of Kerri's wound. "She'll be scarred, but this will at least allow the wound to heal much faster." Eve looked over and saw the wound healing before her very eyes, looking as if it had been there for weeks now rather than having happened the very same day. She nodded her approval. Impressive.

"And this scent," she opened a small, round glass bottle, and put it to Kerri's nose, "should wake her up."

As promised, Kerri woke up, coughing, and instantly rose to attention, looking around in a panic. "Lay down!" The apothecary forced Kerri back down, and it quickly dawned on Kerri that they were not in Theid's Forest anymore. "What happened?" She felt her face, her finger lining the thin line that spread from her right eyebrow, across the bridge of her nose, and ended just past her lips. A permanent scar, and her first earned in battle. Her brows knitted together in worry as she looked toward the group.

"We beat the werewolf," Scarlett spoke up as Eve was next to have her wound treated, "but only barely." She grimaced, rubbed her eyelids, and sighed, "that was so much worse than the last one."

"But how did we win?" Kerri questioned.

"Brutally, that's how." Scarlett recapped the events from the moment that the werewolf gained the upper hand on them both. Kerri's jaw dropped and her eyes widened. She stared at Eve as if it was her first time looking at her.

"But that's insane! You were in no condition to fight!"

Instead of answering Kerri, Eve directed a question to her apothecary. "How's my wound looking?" The apothecary was dabbing the same cream she used on Kerri into Eve's scalp, causing the wound to furiously tingle.

"You'll be fine, but any deeper and we might not be having this discussion right now." She rubbed some more cream in before applying new bandages. "Theid's Forest sounds like a hoot."

"Hmm, you could say that again." Having watched the apothecary finishing attending to the two with major wounds, Scarlett approached her with an eyebrow raised, "did you know there would be a werewolf there?

"No, no idea." She crossed her arms and scowled. "They're not exactly common, are they?"

Scarlett took a moment to think before responding. "Hmm, I guess not." Putting her suspicions aside, she apologised to the older woman, "sorry, just wanted to be sure. Thanks for dealing with these two."

"It's the least I could do. And here," she produced a heavy-looking pouch from her desk, jingling as she lifted it, "your payment."

"Thanks, lady. Send us to a different forest next time if you could."

She laughed, "I'll consider it."

They headed to the stall to report to Clarissa and Barron, who had been watching over it in their absence. Barron was the first to notice them.

"What's happened? You look like you've all seen a ghost!" He was busily wiping down a wooden chopping board in front of him.

"A ghost? Try a werewolf!" Kerri boasted this as she stood in a victory pose, her hands on her waist and her head held high. "Look, I've even got a scar!"

This caught Clarissa's attention and both of them crowded around the counter, wanting to get a better look.

"Well, would you look at that, Clarissa?" Barron sounded awed, and Clarissa slapped his hand.

"It's nothing to be amazed at." She came out from around the counter and rounded on Kerri. "That scar isn't a sign of victory. It's a reminder of what could've been."

Kerri's face fell and she stammered. "What do you mean?"

"A scar like that? You're lucky to be alive. So very lucky." Clarissa frowned as she tugged at her hair. "Don't forget how fortunate you are to be here today."

Eve thought that Clarissa was being a little harsh, but also agreed with what she said. They had all been at the foot of death's door and were incredibly lucky to not have rang the doorbell. She looked around at the others. Scarlett was nodding, and Drake was watching Kerri anxiously.

Kerri looked as if she could cry. She looked down at her feet and shuffled uncomfortably. "I know. I'm sorry."

Clarissa sighed. "There's nothing to apologise for, dear." She stared for a moment longer before asking, "would you be against a hug?"

Kerri shook her head and Clarissa stepped forward to hug her. She pulled her in and patted her head. "I'm sure you did great, but don't forget the girl who almost died today as you get stronger."

Kerri nodded as she leant her head against Clarissa's chest. Eve was surprised to see that Kerri was not crying.

"Now, let's set you all up with some food and go home, okay?"

After cooking the group some meat and vegetables, the two shooed the group away, insisting that they rest. The pair's Flame and Wind Presence worked wonderfully together in preparing food and wafting smells over to attract customers. They watched as Eve and the others walked away, their shoulders sagged and their pace slower than usual.

"They looked like right shit, didn't they?"

"I'm not sure I would put it that way, but yes, Barron, they did look worse for wear." She sighed again. "Can you be a dear and put a notice up on the job board about werewolf sightings?"

"No problem. I'll throw them up once we're done here for the night."

Their attention was pulled away from watching their friend's retreating backs as a man approached and made a request for two chicken skewers.

*

"I wonder what dad will think." Kerri looked at herself in the mirror, unable to look away from her scar.

"I'm sure all he'll be thinking about is how you're okay, and how it could've been much worse." Eve spoke over the whistling of the kettle, preparing herbal tea for the both of them. She hoped that maybe it would bring a sense of calm to Kerri.

"I'm still pretty, right?"

"Hmm..." Eve stared at Kerri, putting on a show of scrutinising her face before answering, "of course. You didn't even need to ask."

Kerri pulled herself away from the mirror as Eve told her that her tea was ready, but she could not get the werewolf's claws out of her mind.

"That was pretty scary, huh?"

"Yeah. It really was. It was much worse than when Scarlett and I fought one." Kerri appeared astonished. She had known that Eve and Scarlett had fought a werewolf, but did not know much more about it other than this small snippet of information.

Eve thought back to her early days with the Marauders of Light, "we hadn't met you then. On a mission, not much different to the one we went on today, we ran into a werewolf. It was much smaller, less stubborn, and younger. It didn't strike me as someone who had been a werewolf for too long."

Kerri visibly shivered. "I hope we don't come across any more of them."

Eve tilted her head and scratched her neck. "Me neither. I've seen enough of those bastards to last me a lifetime, to be perfectly honest."

Kerri lowered her voice to a whisper, "I really thought I was going to die today, Eve."

Eve watched Kerri as she fidgeted and squeezed the tips of her fingers, "I'd never allow it, but it is okay if you want to reconsider."

Confusion contorted Kerri's face, "reconsider? Reconsider what?"

"Being a mercenary."

The worry that had gripped her features was replaced with flared nostrils and watery eyes. She pointed a finger at Eve. "I will not. I will have you know that leaving the Marauders of Light never crossed my mind, not even after today. It was scary, and I cannot say that I liked it, but this is what I want to do, and I want to do it with all of you."

Eve hesitated before replying, and opted to push her point further, "I understand, but your father has a place for you, if you need it. Nobody here would blame you."

"I know, but you're family now, and, well, I proved myself today, right?" Kerri suddenly looked down, unsure of herself, her finger tracing her scar once again.

Eve smiled, "we might have been screwed without you today, so hold your head up high."

Kerri looked up and smiled back, looking a little bashful, before changing subject. "I want to visit Amie later."

Eve felt a cold chill, as if a droplet of ice was rolling down her back. In the same moment she felt her head grow light and her vision wavered. It was as if any weight she had in her head had dropped into her stomach, making her feel unwell. "Why today?"

"Oh, um, I just wanted to tell her about today." Kerri fidgeted. "It's okay if you don't want to come."

"I see." Eve tapped her mug in thought, her tea untouched. She had been avoiding thinking about it, and was not prepared for Kerri to simply ask her to come along for a visit. The thought of running away irked her, and maybe seeing Amie with Kerri would make it a little easier.

"No, it's okay. If you don't mind, I'll take you up on that." She knew could not run from this forever.

*

It was just as cold as it was before.

"Chilly." Kerri hugged herself, shivering slightly as she closed the door behind them.

Eve and Kerri's breath turned to mist before their eyes, and Eve placed the flowers for Amie in a nearby vase. Roses, tulips, sunflowers, and hydrangeas. She brought them together in a bunch before letting them go, watching them fall neatly into position. She thought that Amie would love them.

As before, Amie was partially hidden behind a curtain, her face obscured from sight. Kerri immediately went over to strike up a one-sided conversation with her.

"Hello, Amie! I almost died today!" Kerri pulled an exaggerated face of surprise, and it was like watching a one-woman theatre troupe perform. "We—myself, Eve, Drake, and Scarlett—fought a wretched werewolf today. It was huge! I mean it, it must have been at least seven feet tall. Can you believe my luck on my very first mission with the team? That said, it was no match for us!" She pumped an arm, showing off her bicep. "I mean, we did almost all die, but we didn't, so that's a win, right? Clarissa did scold me for talking about it so freely, so maybe I shouldn't be boasting…" She slowed down, her façade losing steam, "maybe, if you were there, you could've frozen it in place and we could've smashed it, or maybe have escaped," Kerri took a deep, shaky breath, "we miss you, Amie. Come back to us soon, okay? Please?" She took a hold of Amie's hand, but only managed to keep her grip for a handful of seconds before she was forced to let go. She rubbed her hands together. "Gah, she really is so cold."

Eve only glanced, not wanting to look directly at Amie. She knew that Kerri is trying her best, and she almost envied the younger girl for being able to be so brave. With her arms crossed, leaning against a wall, and looking at the exit, Eve was the very picture of someone who did not want to be there.

"Eve, come over."

Eve narrowed her eyes at Kerri, feeling slight animosity. She internally scolded herself for feeling this way and relented. "Okay." She wanted to move, but her legs would not listen to her. She closed her eyes and internally chided herself. Kerri walked over to Eve and took her by the hand, guiding her over to Amie, before letting her go and taking a step back. "It's okay. She's still-she's still Amie. I'll be outside if you need me."

Eve's eyes were still tightly closed. She built up the courage to open them, before losing it at the last second. She repeated this routine several times, and her breathing had turned irregular while she tried to convince herself, searing across her chest. Feeling flushed, light-headed, and frustrated with herself, she threw all caution to the wind and opened her eyes.

She looked at Amie. Her red hair flowed down and across the pillows. Her face was entirely blue. Her soft breathing caused small clouds of mist to form. She looked as if she was an ice statue incapable of melting, forced to remain the same as the seasons changed, unable to return to the living world.

Eve tried to talk to her, but as she tried to keep a straight face, her lips quivered and her vision blurred. She could not get a word out. Her entire body shook and she bit her lip hard, not wanting to cry. When she felt that she finally had a handle on herself, she glanced at Amie again, and the frail string holding her emotions together snapped. Grief racked her body, to her very core, and she sobbed loudly. She grasped the bed's railing for support. She cried deeply into Amie's bedsheets. Her tears flowed thick and heavy as she cried out all that she had been through, in front of the very person who made her feel everything. She paced the room, clenching her fists and taking deep breaths. Her thoughts were a jumble in her mind. She found the strength to approach the bed once more and sat down, willing herself to look.

Several minutes passed as she watched over Amie. With a weak voice, she finally spoke to her. "I miss you." Eve held Amie's hand, lightly stroking it with her thumb. The natural warmth of her Presence helped her to cope with the freezing cold of Amie's own. In her hand, Amie's hand almost felt normal. The two Presences worked together as if they had become one and the same. "I'll—" Eve was not sure what she wanted to say, she just knew that she wanted to keep talking to Amie. "I'll, um, try to visit more often, and I promise,"she squeezed Amie's hand tighter, "I'll bring you back to us. Whatever it takes, whatever I have to do, I'll bring you back to us."

Eve stood up to leave, but as she glanced back, she realised that she wanted to spend a little more time with her. She sat again by Amie's bed, not quite watching her but not quite doing anything else, until Kerri knocked on the door.

"Eve, are you okay?"

"Yeah." with one final look at Amie, she felt her resolve strengthen, "I'm coming out now."

Eve closed the door behind her. The warmth of the corridor quickly swept over her, washing away the icy chill which had begun to feel something like comfort. She felt a little sad at the loss of the chill.

"Come on, Eve, let's go home." Her eyes were red and watery, and her eyebrows knit together in a way that made Eve feel bad for worrying her. Kerri grabbed her hand and gave it a soft squeeze.

"Sure, that sounds good."

Eve glanced over her shoulder one more time, just catching Amie's door as she turned a corner in the hallway, and then it was gone.

*

That evening, Eve sat at the desk in her room, tapping her pen against her new journal. Kerri had recommended that she keep a diary to write her feelings into, although Eve was not sure how much it would help. She felt a little foolish, but began to write;

I'm not sure how long I'll write in this for, but I owe it to Kerri to at least try it. The worst that can happen is that I burn this book. Or I could tear this page out and give it to Kerri.

I visited Amie today. Seeing her lying so still was difficult. I cried. No one deserves to suffer a Blowback, but Amie, of all people? The whole thing angers me. I thought I was stronger than this. I might've never had much pride in my strength, but I've acknowledged it. So why was I weak today? I've fought damn werewolves that not many could hope to come back to their families from, but I can't bear to see Amie like that. It's so much worse. Sometimes, I regret coming to Thous, but then I hate myself for feeling that way. Despite everything, this is the happiest I've been in a long time. Do I deserve this?

I've racked my brain for a way to help Amie, but I'm not sure if a healing Presence that strong even exists. Could it?

Is there medicine, or do we really just have to sit and wait? I hate it. I hate feeling so useless, and I damn well hate feeling so damn passionate about it.

Why do I feel so strongly about this? Okay, maybe I know why I feel this way, but I'm not ready to write it down just yet. It's meaningless until Amie returns.

Eve closed the journal and placed it on her bookshelf. She stared at it, and felt her stomach turn. Instead of leaving it in the open, she tucked it between a few of her larger books, where it hid in the shadows instead. She did feel a little lighter for having written something, but she did not want to dwell on it more than she needed to.

The following days passed by slowly as each of the Marauders of Light manned the stall, took on missions exclusively within the walls of Thous, and trained. Sometimes they were joined by members of Rising Dawn, with Eve, Scarlett, Kerri, and Ellen often training together. Drake and Gordon had gotten to a point where their competitiveness was now considered a friendly rivalry. Eve noted they shook hands without being told to, anyway.

Members from each guild would sometimes spar with Clarissa, but nobody had managed to force her to use her daggers yet. On request, she had restrained from using her Presence, and still proved to be a force to be reckoned with. With quick, relentless flurries and a keen intellect, Clarissa had yet to lose a match.

Today, every member from the Marauders of Light, minus Amie, and Rising Dawn had come together to watch Eve and Clarissa battle for the first time.

"The rules today are simple!" Marcus announced, "no Presence, and first to three hits."

Eve and Clarissa stood ready for battle, wooden replacement weapons in hand.

"Ready? Fight!"

The atmosphere was cheerful, both guilds still reeling from an energetic training session, all excited to see if someone could finally best Clarissa in battle. Their names were cheered, skewered slightly in favour of Eve, as some scorned mercenaries on Rising Dawn's guild were rooting to see Clarissa lose.

Clarissa swooped in, her dress fluttering behind her as she went for a direct hit to Eve's stomach. Eve dodged backward, preparing to parry, but did not expect the dagger Clarissa had thrown She parried it successfully, but Clarissa had already thrown another at the ground. As the hilt connected with the dirt, it bounced directly at her. As she twirled to the side, Clarissa caught the other dagger and landed a hit across Eve's back.

"That's one!"

The audience groaned, watching history repeat itself.

Eve grinned, "you're very hard to predict."

Clarissa tossed a dagger upward, catching it as it fell, and returned the smile with a wink, "you're damn right I am."

Eve knew that Clarissa was swift and had great control over her weaponry. She hoped to outmanoeuvre Clarissa instead, using her years of experience to try and predict her next movements. She bent backward onto all fours as Clarissa threw a dagger at her. It soared overhead, and she used the momentum as she got back into a standing position to cartwheel forward. She propelled herself into a flying kick which sent Clarissa tumbling to the floor.

"That's one!" Marcus confirmed.

Clarissa got up, wiping dirt from her cheek, "you're not so predictable yourself."

Eve huffed, beads of sweat rolling down her face, "it's a lot more tiring!"

Clarissa performed an aggressive flurry of slashes and swings, her daggers coming down fast and relentless, and Eve parried them each time, slightly changing the angles of her sword as she saw each dagger swipe. Unable to go on the offensive, they kept clashing, until a shaky voice from the side-lines brought them both to a stop.

"Eve!" The two stopped fighting instantly as Kerri ran over, worry written across her face, "you'll want to see this." She held out a slip of paper, and Eve and Clarissa both leaned in to read it.

Eve,

We're holding another Ilas Arena competition in seven days, but our reigning champion isn't here. A pity, to be sure, so please do come back.

If you win, maybe it'll be worth your while. I'm sure that there is something that even you could possibly want, am I right?

Perhaps, if you lay your life on the line, even the most wilted rose can bloom back to life.

I will not offer you this kindness again.

Sincerely yours,
Edin Garret

"Bastard," Eve growled through gritted teeth, her good mood ruined. "Where did you get this?"

"Um, a little kid brought it over, and said to give it to the woman with the white hair."

"A kid?" Eve huffed, frustrated. "You swine, Edin"

Scarlett, Drake and Barron walked over, and Clarissa recapped the contents of the letter to them. Scarlett leaned in to read the letter for herself. "What are you going to do?" She asked.

"I'm going. He's right. There is something I want." This could be her only chance to bring Amie back.

"And that is?" Scarlett probed.

"Edin must know about Amie. If he really does have something that can help her, then I'm going to see it through. The clinic won't look after her forever. We may not have long."

"Good. Then I'm going with you."

"Of course, we all are."

"I'll be with you, Eve!"

"Anything for Amie."

"I agree."

Eve listened to each of her friends. None of them hesitated to revisit one of the most dangerous places known to them in Evergaune, and with one of the most dangerous people leading it. She nodded, assuming Edin was only likely truly interested in having her fight once again in the arena, anyway.

"What's going on?" Marcus walked over, brows furrowed in confusion.

"Sorry, Marcus, we have to cut this short today. We'll be out of town for a while."

"Oh? I won't pry, but it doesn't seem like particularly good news. Why not have us come along, too?"

"No, no, that won't be necessary, but—"

Eve went to reject the offer, but Scarlett cut across her, "hold on, is it not? I don't think we should take any risks, not if it could help Amie."

Eve bit the inside of her cheek, mentally clashing between putting another guild at risk, and wanting to help Amie. "You're right, but we should tell them everything, and if they still wish to help, then so be it."

Scarlett agreed and so began to recap everything so far, beginning from meeting Kerri, up until Amie's blowback. As she got to the part about how Eve and Edin knew each other, she stumbled, realising that she did not know the particulars. "Eve, why does Edin have it out for you, exactly?"

"He's angry I'm not dead." Eve gritted her teeth and exhaled.

"Meaning?" Scarlett tilted her head curiously.

"He killed my guild, and I escaped. The sole survivor having escaped his attack on Irone, where we went to meet his forces, alongside many others, as they travelled through a forest. Irone fell that day, and Corrind won the war, but never once had someone given him the slip. He must've been angry someone who was barely eighteen could manage it." Eve seethed, remembering how much she truly hated Edin. "I became who I am now partially because of him. I've killed. I've killed so many, many from Corrind, trying to find him, but nobody would ever talk, and I'd long since given up. It was only at Ilas Arena that I had any proof he was still alive, but he never has been one for the limelight, so I guess I'm not surprised.

You've never seen him in newspapers following Corrind's victory, have you, despite how many he killed to make it happen?"

Both groups' shook their heads. The Marauders had only learnt about him when Kerri mentioned that he was the man her father was indebted to, while Rising Dawn had no idea who he was.

"If any of you want to come, know that if it gets out of hand, your lives will be on the line. He won't hesitate to kill you, not a single one of you." Eve looked at each person in turn, but they kept their eyes focused on her, not shying away from her warning.

"We became Rising Dawn to put a stop to people like that. We'll fight alongside you if it comes to that." Marcus declared.

"Never leave a marauder behind, or something like that!" Kerri added cheerfully.

"Good," Eve responded gratefully. "I suggest that you all prepare everything you'll need for a stay in Ilas, then. We'll be leaving in no more than three days."

The two groups split off to prepare.

Eve raised her voice as she watched them walk away, "and thank you!"

Some of them looked back to wave and smile, but only Marcus verbally responded with a "finish that fight with Clarissa when we get back, yeah?!"

"Consider it done." Eve grinned. She could not help but feel a spark of excitement at the prospect of finally being able to do something to help Amie.

Chapter Sixteen

In three days we leave for Ilas.

We spent last night at Willkeep's, talking about Amie, Edin, Ilas Arena and sharing whatever I thought would be helpful. Maybe I wouldn't admit this to the others, but I'm anxious. Not about the fighting, I doubt there's much that Edin could throw at me that would spell my end, but there's more pressure this time. This time, I'm responsible for people other than myself.

I feel it in the group, that they're counting on me. If Amie were with us, I could have simply told Edin to find someone else to bother, but she isn't, and so I can't. I don't dread what he'll put me through when I get there, but I have no way of knowing if what he promises is real. If I'm not marching to potential death for nothing. Hopefully he'll face me himself so I can put him out of his misery, and out of mine. I imagine I'm about to find out.

I let my old guild down once already, and I won't do it again. Meg? Ada? Ashe? Oliver? I miss all of you, but I'm not ready to join you just yet.

I think you'd have liked Amie.

*

"Good as new!" Eric placed their equipment on the counter, now looking as if the werewolf had never touched it.

"What's this?" Eve picked up an unfamiliar dagger among her gear.

"Consider it a gift. That scythe can't be the easiest thing to use at close range."

Eve studied the blade. Pure white, with red gems on both sides of the handle. She ran her hand along it, taking care to feel all of its etchings and carvings. She was too taken with it to worry about the fact that she was beaming. "Thank you. It's beautiful." She said in a mixture of awe and gratitude.

"Wow, favouritism much, Eric?" Kerri jokingly stuck her tongue out at the blacksmith before thanking him for mending her armour. "I hope I don't make a habit of getting my armour repaired."

"You could always use your Illusion to pretend otherwise, if it gets too much for you!" Eric laughed, and Kerri started bartering with him for future discounts. Eve enjoyed watching them both get along.

"I still have to make a living, but don't worry, I'd never let either of you set out with armour in disrepair."

Kerri put a finger to her chin, "free at the risk of our lives is an odd discount."

"It's not a discount, Kerri, don't take up dangerous missions for free repairs!"

"You said they weren't free!"

Eric took a deep breath, "fine, they are free," Kerri's face lit up, "an increase of three-hundred percent more than usual for you." He pointed at Kerri and her face fell.

"Whyyyyyyyy?"

Eve watched them both as she examined Eric's handiwork. A small smile bloomed across her face. "Come on, Kerri, your arse isn't going to kick itself."

Kerri turned with her mouth agape. "Et tu, Eve?!"

Eric laughed loudly. "Yeah yeah, et tu, Eve," she waved her hand lazily, her betrayal of Kerri's on-going plight not bothering her in the slightest.

"Come on." Eve put her gear on, making sure it fit as well as it did before, "you can come back in a couple hours once your armour's damaged again."

"I can't believe this," Kerri huffed as she strapped her armour on, "if anyone has to get their armour repaired again today, it's going to be you!"

"Sure. Catch you later, Eric."

He waved them off, his laughter chasing them down the street.

*

"You've certainly gotten better," Eve looked down at Kerri, sitting on the floor, her forehead resting against her knee, "but I'm still standing."

Kerri groaned, "I'll just have to get you next time."

Eve helped Kerri to her feet, "are you okay training alone for a while?"

"Sure, I think some of the others might drop by soon anyway. Can I ask why?"

Eve shrugged, fidgeting, "I want to tell Amie that we'll be leaving soon." She put a hand to her cheek, feeling self-conscious, "she'll be alone for the first time in a while."

Kerri smiled, "sure, she will be alone, but we'll be back for when it truly matters!"

Eve smiled weakly in return, "yeah, I like to think so."

"She has you working to bring her back. She's not going to get better care than that anywhere else. Now, get going. She's waiting." Kerri pushed Eve gently in the back, and Eve collected her belongings and left, greeting a few of the others as they reached the training field.

*

As always, the room was cold. "Hey, Amie, are you, uh, doing okay?" Eve felt her face grow warm. She looked

213

at the door over her shoulder, but it remained closed. She sighed in relief.

"The flowers are doing well." She cupped them close and they sprang outwards as she let them go. "I think you would like them. I really do."

She watched Amie, desperately hoping that she would stir. She did not. With a sigh, Eve continued to talk.

"We're heading to Ilas Arena in three days, and I know, I'll be careful." she gazed at Amie again, frozen in time, "I'll do whatever I have to to bring you back to us."

Amie's breath hovered above her lips, eternally frosty.

Eve idly ran her hand along the bed's railing. "Everyone is coming, including Rising Dawn. You still have some payback to get against Ellen, right?" Eve hated the silence. "Kerri's working hard to be a great fighter. You'll have to try her out once you're back with us. Her Illusion is becoming a pain to plan against. I'm glad she's on our side. I just—" Eve was cut off by the sound of the door opening behind her. She turned in her seat to see Scarlett.

"Sorry, I didn't think anyone was in here." Scarlett stood awkwardly in the doorway, looking unsure as to what to do.

"No, it's fine, I was just getting ready to leave." Eve rose and gestured towards the seat.

"Really? Well, I know that Amie would have been happy to know you've been visiting."

"Yeah." Eve tore her eyes away from Amie and brushed past Scarlett.

"Eve?" Scarlett turned in her seat with furrowed eyebrows.

"Yes?" Eve averted her eyes and hugged herself. She found it difficult to return Scarlett's gaze with Amie behind them.

"I know it must be hard for you, but I need to know, you've got this, right?"

The strength came back to her, and she met Scarlett's gaze. "I do. If Edin truly wanted to hurt me, he never should've reached out at all."

Eve closed the door behind her, leaving the Brantley sisters together.

*

Eve thought about what she should do next. She was itching to train with the others but she decided against it. She needed to rest and ensure she was in top shape when she reached Ilas. Instead, she decided to check up on the stall.

The smell reached her nostrils before the stall was in sight. Seeing Barron flipping bacon in a pan was nearly enough to make her drool. That was, at least, until one of the pieces almost fell out and he scooped it back in with his bare hand. Her jaw dropped.

"No, no, you have to throw that away, Barron," Clarissa scolded him, "nobody wants to eat food that's been in your grubby hands."

"I'd take offence to that, but well," he grabbed the bacon and popped it in his mouth, "guess it's a win for me!"

Clarissa groaned before greeting Eve. "See what I have to put up with, Eve? Hmm, you're not scheduled to work today." She said this as she tapped a piece of paper stuck up on the inner side of the stall, listing who was working each day.

"I haven't really had any time on the stall and I'm feeling restless." She tapped her foot. She had energy to spare, and she could only expend so much of it biting the inside of her cheek.

Clarissa shrugged. "It's good up here, you get to see a lot of faces. Talk to people, you know?"

"Sounds good. What do you want me to do?" Eve stepped behind the stall and put an apron on, "other than not grab the bacon?"

Barron laughed. "But that's how you get the bacon!"

"Ignore him," Clarissa turned Barron away with a gentle push of her hand, "you can fry vegetables, right?"

"Of course."

"Then here," she gave Eve a frying pan of her own whilst lighting another fire, "don't let it burn."

"I mean, I'll try, but this does look pretty good, and I'm prone to burning things. It's in my Presence, you know?" Barron laughed, and Clarissa sighed.

"Oh God, Eve, not you too." Clarissa sighed again, and Eve chuckled as she threw some chopped mushrooms, onion and garlic into the mix. It sizzled satisfyingly.

"If I'm no longer needed," Barron clapped his hands together, "I owe Kyrie a rematch."

"Of course. Good luck with that, dear." She waved him off, watching him dashing down the road with reckless abandon.

"Yeah, yeah, it must be nice having such a strong Presence." Barron grumbled, nabbing some food before Clarissa could stop him. He laughed as he ran away, before turning on the spot and wiggling his fingers back at her. He dangled the leg of chicken above his mouth before inserting it whole, removing it with barely any meat intact. Eve was impressed, although it was a skill that she could live without learning.

"That man, honestly," Clarissa hopelessly looked after him before turning her attention to Eve, "so, how's it going?"

"It's going. You know how it is." Eve shrugged. She knew things were not going particularly well, but did not want to talk about them when she was trying to busy herself instead.

"Yeah, but it'll be over soon." Clarissa replied.

Eve prodded the food around, keeping it from sticking to the pan.

"Do you think that Edin really has something that could cure Amie?"

Eve looked out towards the passersby, the pan in her hand almost forgotten. "I have to believe it."

"I see. And if he doesn't?" Clarissa tilted her head as she asked this casually.

Eve felt a pang of anger shoot through her, mixed with a crushing dread, "that'll be his mistake."

"Ah, watch the food!" The oil had begun sizzling more violently, visibly spitting from the pan.

Eve recoiled as a drop of oil burned her hand. She shook it instinctively and blew on it. "Damn it. Sorry."

"I won't ask any more about Edin, but for the record, he better not be lying as I wouldn't be quite happy with that, either."

"I dread to think of the man that crosses you, Clarissa." They both laughed, although Clarissa's Wind was no joke to be on the receiving end of.

Two men approached them, drawn in by the smells of various vegetables and meats. "Mmm, that smells wonderful!"

"What are you making?" One leaned in forward closely to the stall where Eve was cooking.

"Oh!" Eve flustered, but Clarissa came to her rescue, "we're frying some vegetables for skewers. Peppers, mushrooms, garlic, and onion. Want some? We might even add a little chicken in if you're lucky!"

"Ahh, it's the garlic I could smell! Well, you couldn't convince me to leave without some, so make that four, please."

"Four vegetable skewers, coming right up!"

Eve began to dish them out and Clarissa poked through each of them with a stick. She held one up, the steam rising from the scorching medley of colours.

"Would you like them wrapped?"

"No, I think we'll have them whilst they're hot."

Clarissa accepted payment of four aulins and handed the skewers over. The two men eagerly ate them as they left. Eve and Clarissa watched as one pointed out the chicken on his skewer in delight.

"Makes you feel good, right?"

"Yeah, it does." Clarissa observed as Eve smiled, watching her food being eaten with joy.

"One customer tends to spur on another, so let's prepare some more."

Eve added more oil as Clarissa chopped vegetables and slid them onto the pan. Eve was slightly surprised when another customer really did appear only a short moment later.

"What did I tell you?" Clarissa winked at Eve before turning to the customer, and the next couple of hours passed by in a flash as they continued to serve a steady stream of customers. As the sun casted an orange glow over the market, Eve's stomach rumbled.

Clarissa chuckled. "Come on, I'll make you something. What do you want?"

"Do we have anything that needs to be eaten today?"

"Hmm..." Clarissa cast an eye over their stock, "it would be good if we could get rid of some of this bacon, and we have eggs spare due to more arriving tomorrow. Fancy a bacon roll with eggs?"

"That sounds good, thanks. Can you do scrambled, please?"

"Can you do scrambled, please?"", mimicked Clarissa with a grin, "Just who do you think I am, Eve? These will be the best scrambled eggs you've ever had."

Eve responded with a "I'll hold you to it" and sat, closing her eyes. She was exhausted from having to interact with so many people. Cooking for others was not something that she was accustomed to.

"Tired?" Clarissa asked as she emptied out the remaining pack of bacon.

"Urgh, how do you do this so often?"

"You get used to it. Besides, I like talking to people."

"I'll take your word for it. It was fun."

Clarissa cracked an eggshell on the rim of the pan, and the egg began sizzling the moment it hit its surface. "How do you like your bacon?"

"Crispy, that way I can't taste the fat so much."

"Oh? I love the fat!"

"You can have it if you want it."

"Hmm no, I can make some for myself after."

Clarissa placed the scrambled egg on to a dish and scooped the bacon onto a thick slice of buttered bread. "Enjoy."

"Did you do something to these eggs?" Eve asked after her first bite.

She raised an eyebrow, looking a little confused. "Other than cooking them?"

"It's just, it tastes so good."

"Oh yes, that's my other Presence. Keep it a secret between us, dear."

Eve choked on her food, "what?" This reveal shocked her. She never knew anyone to have two Presence, and it was not something she had read in any history books.

Clarissa laughed, loudly, as Eve patted herself on the chest. "Oh Eve, you can be so gullible. If I had two Presence, I'd like to hope one was for more than simply cooking eggs. I think you're just hungry."

Eve finished the food, her eyes feeling heavy. "Thanks, Clarissa."

"No problem. you look done for the night. Go on ahead, I can close the stall."

"I can help, it's fine."

"Ah no, actually, watch this." After they packed the valuables and stored everything else away, Clarissa held both of her palms out over a large piece of tarp. She made a swishing motion, and it lifted into the air, and she guided it over the stall. "See? It's easy when you're me." She placed her hands on her hips, looking smug.

"I wish Flame was as useful." Eve looked solemnly down at the faint scars on her arms, as she remembered losing control of her Presence.

"Flame is a good compliment to Ice though, don't you think that's nice?" She put emphasis on the last word, looking very proud of herself.

"God damn it, Clarissa." It was now Eve's chance to groan, as she pinched the bridge of her nose. "I'm going to write that off because I'm tired. Night, Clarissa, and thanks for the meal."

Clarissa had a wide smile as she waved Eve off. "Night, Eve!"

As Eve opened the door to her home, she heard several voices coming from inside.

"—gotten so good!"

"I've had a good teacher!"

"I'm home!"

"Eve!" Kerri jumped from her seat and ran to greet Eve, "I sparred with Ellen today. I wish you could have seen it!"

"Oh yeah?" Eve saw Ellen sitting on one couch with Drake sat opposite her, "who won?"

"I did!"

"Hey!" Ellen shouted from her seat, "you did the second time! I won the first!"

"First one doesn't count. It's a warm-up!"

"What?! Honestly, Kerri, next time I'm bringing the heat."

Kerri laughed, "best of three tomorrow?"

"You're on." Ellen smiled broadly. Eve could not help but admire the respect that they had for one another. Kerri had such an incredible way at making people want to improve themselves.

"I might drop by to watch. Did Marcus talk to you?"

"Indeed, he did, and I've found a way to cover my weaknesses," Ellen grinned, looking proud, "but I'll keep it secret until we spar."

"Does that mean you're not going to use it against me?" Kerri asked, curious.

"I don't need it for you." Ellen shrugged.

220

"What?!" Indignant, Kerri rose to Ellen's provocation. "We'll see if you're saying that when you're zero and three tomorrow."

"Three to me, right?"

"Oh, ha ha." Kerri stuck her tongue out. "You know what I mean."

"They've been like this all day, Eve," Drake looked at a loss as he looked up at Eve, "I don't know where they get the energy from." He slumped back into the sofa, groaning.

Eve stood beside his chair, watching the two women. "To be young again, eh?"

The two laughed, watching as Kerri and Ellen continued bickering.

"Right, this old man wants to get some sleep." He yawned as if on cue, and slapped his hands against his thighs. "What time are we meeting tomorrow?"

"Shall we say early morning, around eight?"

"Sure, well, if I'm up." Drake stifled a yawn.

"We don't know what's waiting for us in Ilas, so make sure to take a break before we leave," Eve urged, looking at the group, "I need you at your best."

"We won't be training past tomorrow afternoon, which is about enough time for Ellen to hole up in her room all day, wondering where she went wrong." Kerri tilted her head towards Ellen, a playful smile reaching her eyes.

"Excuse you? It'll take more than magic tricks to get one over on me!"

"Alright, alright, you two." Drake broke up the jestful bickering before it kicked off again. "C'mon Ellen, I'll walk you home."

The two women hugged and said goodbye to each other. Ellen then shook Eve's hands before she followed Drake through the front door. "Don't be late, Kerri!"

As the door slammed shut, Eve turned to Kerri. "I see you've made pretty good friends with Ellen."

"We've been training. She trains harder than the others in Rising Dawn, so we're both at the training field from early morning," Kerri explained how they became close. She imitated thrusting forward with a spear, and blushed a little. "So we've been helping each other improve. It's been nice." She smiled warmly as she gazed up at Eve.

"Good. It's good to have another guild to train with. In future, we could team up on missions."

"We can do that?"

"Sure, if the mission is big enough. We're both small guilds compared to most others. My old guild was fairly small too."

"Would you ever want to be leader of a guild, Eve?" Kerri asked, idly pulling on her fingers.

Eve shook her head. Until recently, she did not think she would ever want to join a guild again, let alone consider leading one. It was not something she felt suited for or wanted to do. "No, I prefer supporting a leader. Even if something were to happen to Scarlett, Drake would assume the role of leader. The way he handled your case way back when was impressive, even if Scarlett was furious at the time."

"Oh yeah," Kerri's face crumpled as she recalled their first meeting, "I forgot how scary Scarlett can be."

"They'd be different leaders, but they've both displayed the qualities important to being one. Thoughtful, caring, strong, and decisive. It's not something just anybody can be."

"Well, I'd follow you to the ends of the world, teach."

"We'll need a bigger guild if we're going that far," Eve yawned, "but for now, I'm going to bed."

"Don't forget to write!"

"I won't!"

*

Eve was writing at her desk as the Sun began to set.

Kerri is a far cry from the girl we found a few months ago. it's hard to believe that this is the same girl that we almost put in prison. I hate to think of what would have become of her or William if we did that but, thankfully, Drake convinced us to let her stay, and I'm thankful that he did.

It's getting a little easier seeing Amie, although it still feels as if my chest is being stretched slowly outward every time I do. Despite it being so cold in that clinic room, it's impossible to feel numb.

The stall is fun to work and working with Clarissa solidifies that I really want to spar with her again. She's incredible, but I've barely seen her in action. How do you win against someone with such masterful control over her Presence? There must be something more that I can do with Flame.

Two more days until Ilas. Kerri is competent, but I wish that we could keep her here. She's still so young.

Chapter Seventeen

The Marauders met up for breakfast at Humbone's Tavern. Drake was absent as it was his turn to man the stall. Kerri would be joining him after her sparring session with Ellen.

"Will Drake be okay on his own?"

"He's fine," Scarlett waved Eve's worries away, "the morning rush has passed, so he'll mostly be dealing with the stragglers and late risers."

Clarissa stretched and took in the softer scenery around her. Instead of the rowdy clientele that usually inhabited the place, the early hours saw a lot of customers enjoying their favourite drink over a book, or in pairs speaking softly to one another. It was as if a curtain was raised when the sun set, masking the calm of the day. "We should come here more often. It's nice and quiet."

"Their coffee is to die for," Eve praised as she mixed another spoonful of sugar into her coffee and took a sip. She needed both hands to lift it due to how large it was.

"How'd you find this place, Eve?" Barron asked, trying to keep his voice low in this new, quaint place. He looked somewhat uncomfortable, but Eve thought it was endearing to see him making such an effort to quiet his booming voice.

Eve looked down into her coffee, idly stirring it, before responding. "Amie brought me here. Said it was a nice change of pace from Willkeep's Tavern and, well, I can't say I disagree."

"I wonder what it's like here in the evening." He scanned around and shook his head. "I can't imagine it's much noisier then, either."

Eve nodded. "Humbone's closes earlier, so nobody really comes here to drink. It's more of a morning and afternoon place. Barron, try the cinnamon bun." Eve split her own cinnamon bun in half, and placed one half onto Barron's empty plate.

"Hah, a cinnamon goodie." Scarlett looked forlorn, but quickly bounced back, "I think I'll have one too, and I can try coffee the way she loves so much."

As they ate, drank, and commented on how delicious everything was, Scarlett leaned in close to Eve and glanced around. She whispered quietly, but Eve picked up on her straight tone. "Are you worried about Rising Dawn joining us?"

"Hmm, not really, but I haven't seen much of them since the first time we trained together. Kerri has though. She seems happy enough, and they put up a good fight against us. I'm happy they're joining us."

"I feel sorry for anyone that has to deal with Kyrie." Barron mentioned.

"I think we're going to need all the hands we can get if things go to shit. If less of us could go, though, I'd have loved that." Eve poked at the remains of her cinnamon bun, guilt festering in her stomach.

"Don't worry about it," Scarlett waved her hand, "we're all professionals, and we all know Ilas Arena is a cesspit. We can only work toward the best outcome, and prepare for the worst."

"We all want Amie back with us, after all, dear." Clarissa placed a hand on Eve's, giving it a soft squeeze. It felt warm and comforting, and so she did not rush to remove her hand. She could feel how much Clarissa cared for Amie.

"Yeah, let's make sure this isn't for nothing."

"Her absence is really noticeable, isn't it?" Barron spoke, sounding more solemn compared to his usual self.

The group fell silent, all thinking the same thing.

Eve wanted to rest before they left for Ilas, but achieving it felt unattainable. How could she rest? With so little time left, she wanted to train night and day, and have the others do the same too. She did what she could. She woke up early to train, she met up with the others to see if there was anything they needed to do to prepare, and she walked past the clinic more times than she could count. She would have spent every day at Amie's bedside if she could, but she worried that if she spent too much time there then she would never leave. Instead, she helped out at the stall, feeling useful if she was helping the guild to earn money. She thought of what they might do with it when they returned. Her first thought was that it would go towards new gear, but that thought made her feel strange. Did she want new gear when Amie woke up? Maybe it was the stress talking, but she felt that maybe there really was a future that did not include fighting, and that all it would take was one more victory.

After wrapping up at the stall, Eve and Drake met up with the others for dinner at Willkeep's Tavern that evening. She was slightly surprised to see that Rising Dawn had joined them too.

Scarlett waved them both over and subtly pointed towards the others, mouthing a "sorry" from behind a cupped hand. Eve shook her head with a small smile in response. Scarlett smiled back.

"Busy here tonight, eh?" Eve clapped her hands upon Kerri's and Ellen's shoulders, prompting them both to jump in their seats. They screamed in unison, both rapidly turning in their seats to see Eve already making her way to a seat between Scarlett and Arthur.

"Good to see you, Eve!" Scarlett threw her arm around Eve's shoulder.

Eve couldn't help but note that everyone seemed in high spirits. Maybe it was because they knew that they might not all come back in a few days. She shook her head, she did not dare to think that way.

She leaned into Scarlett's arm and stole a hearty swig from her drink. "Hm, not bad."

"Come on, I'll buy you one." They left the table together,

Scarlett leant against the counter, facing Eve while they waited for their drinks. "You're probably wondering why Rising Dawn is with us tonight?"

"I am, but I can't say it's unpleasant, honestly. Might be what we all need before we leave for Ilas." Eve felt a twinge shoot through her chest, forcing her to shake it off again before the guilt and anxiety grew too strong. Scarlett simply closed her eyes and nodded in agreement.

"Well, it turns out that they'd never been here before, and Kerri invited them to come after training." Scarlett laughed, "how can you live in Thous and never have visited Willkeep's Tavern? It's madness to think about!"

Eve nodded her head but presented a counterpoint, "there must be loads of other taverns here too, right?"

Scarlett thought about it briefly, "well, yeah, but this is the best one, you know?"

Eve shrugged in response. "I'll have to take your word for it, Scarlett." She smiled.

The barman placed their tankards in front of them with a slam. The foam threatened to spill over as they carried the drinks back to their table. "Oh, bollocks." Scarlett swore, and Eve looked over her shoulder to see that she had spilt some of the foam down her sleeve. "Well, it'll come out overnight anyway!" She regained her good spirit, sipping from the tankard before taking her seat.

Returning to her original seat, Eve noticed that Arthur beside her was shuffling uncomfortably. As Scarlett handed out the drinks, Eve turned to him. "Arthur, are you okay?"

Arthur twitched, the question seemingly taking him off-guard, "y-yes, of course. Why wouldn't I be?"

"Well," Eve looked him up and down, "you look pale, you're fidgeting a lot, and you aren't talking to anyone."

"Thanks for noticing." He shuffled again, looking away from her.

Eve grimaced. She hadn't meant to make him uncomfortable. "No, I'm sorry, I didn't mean to be careless with my words. It's just- I get it. It's as if your stomach is replaced by the world's most lively snake, right? Is it your first time going on a mission like this?"

He took a moment to answer. "Yes, it is. I've been to forests and killed many beasts, but I've never killed another person."

Eve raised an eyebrow and squinted at him. "Not even when you've fought bandits, or as part of another mission?"

"Not personally. I've helped, but I've never been the one to land a finishing blow." Arthur shuffled again, a red tinge spreading across his face. "I can't say I like the idea of it."

"I see. Well, it certainly isn't a bad thing to not have killed another person, but if push comes to shove and you have to, which you might, then you can't hesitate." He was still endlessly fidgeting in his seat while his fingers twiddled with a wet coaster. "I mean it. They'll kill you without a second thought. Nobody will think less of you if you decide not to come."

Arthur stared at her, his eyes wide. "No, I want to support our guilds."

"Are you sure?"

"If it comes down to it, I'll do whatever it takes."

Eve studied him, seeing a fire in his eyes that was not there previously. "Good. I haven't seen much of what you can do, but if Marcus vouches for you, then I trust you to know your way around a battle."

"Yes, well, I think I need to get a hot drink or something." Arthur, looking slightly more composed, left to order a drink for himself.

Eve looked around the table to see Drake and Gordon getting along, their fiery rivalry now gladly a far cry from their first meeting. Kerri and Ellen were in the middle of a conversation, both of their mouths flapping animatedly. Scarlett and Marcus seemed deep in conversation, and their eyes would dart over to the others. Eve noticed that her gaze kept falling on her. Clarissa was resting her head on her hand as she waited for Barron to finish studying the menu and decide what he wanted to order next. Eve felt her good mood plunge. She wished Amie was here.

The sorrow must have shown on Eve's face as a shadow loomed behind her. Scarlett plopped herself down in Arthur's vacated seat and slapped her across the back, causing some of the drink in her hand to launch itself across the table. "What's got you so down, Eve?"

She sighed and looked at her. "I think you know."

"Yeah." Scarlet's lower lip jutted out and her brows knitted together, "I think I do."

"But not too long to go now!" Kerri came over and threw an arm around each woman. She leaned forward, her toothy grin appearing between their faces. "When we return, we can have a party." She looked at Eve and Scarlett in turn, "all of us."

*

We have one more day until we leave for Ilas. I'd be lying if I said I wasn't anxious. I wish that we had more opportunities to train with Rising Dawn first, but they're coming with us now regardless, with or without my full confidence in them. I have every faith in the Marauders of Light, but when we get there, I'm not sure how much I'll be able to do for everyone. I can only place my faith in them and hope that Scarlett and Marcus do their best to keep them all safe. It's been so long that I can't help but feel uneasy. What would you do, Meg?

*

It was the last day before both guilds were set to leave for Ilas, and so everybody was prioritising rest. The stall was closed, nobody was training, and everybody's gear was prepared for battle.

Eve sat at her desk, tapping her pen against her chin, before closing her journal.

"Beautiful day." She looked outside her open window to a clear blue sky. The crisp air made her feel refreshed.

Throughout the day, Eve had bumped into others from each guild. She had visited Eric and grabbed lunch at Humbone's Tavern with Kerri. It was now one of Eve's favourite places to truly relax, and she found herself there more often.

"Did you want to visit Amie before we leave?" Kerri asked as they sipped at their coffees.

Eve recoiled for a moment before she wrapped her arms around herself. "It doesn't get any easier, besides, I think I've said everything I've needed to." A voice in the back of her mind reminded her that she might not have the chance to see her again, so she hurriedly added on, "actually, yes, I'd like to see her."

"I'll see you at home, then!" Kerri grinned and finished her coffee, paying for both of their drinks before she left.

Eve watched her poke her head through the door again, waving at Eve. Kerri's enthusiasm was infectious, and she could not stop herself from heartily waving back.

Eve said little as she sat beside Amie's bed, stroking her hand. She felt her face flush, despite the cold of the room. It was as if time stopped when she was by Amie's side, and she felt as if she could stay there forever, just waiting for Amie to open her eyes again. She wanted to be there when she did. Eve remembered being cared for when she was unwell. How vulnerable it made her feel. She hated seeing someone so full of life, so eager to spread joy wherever she went, look so weak She kept telling herself that Amie would be okay, that she would do whatever it took, but she had no idea if anything could be done. This thought would intrude her mind, latching around her brain like an octopus, sucking out the air in her lungs. It twisted down deep within her gut, and she had to swallow it down before it spilled out. She took a deep breath, and focused on the features of Amie's hands. Her small fingernails. The smoothness of her skin. The creases on her palm. She looked at the clock. Unsure of how long she had been here already, Eve made a promise that she would be back soon. She kissed Amie on the forehead before leaving. The red lilies she left in the vase on the bedside table swayed in the breeze of the closing door.

That evening, Eve and Kerri were cooking dinner. They had invited the other members of the Marauders of Light to their home. Eve recalled when Scarlett was last in the house and shuddered. She realised just how much Kerri had been doing for her during her own self-imprisonment.

Kerri lightly nudged her to ask if she could please chop some cloves of garlic for their pasta. "If not, it's okay if you want to go talk with them. I can handle it here."

Eve kindly rejected her offer, and started cutting two cloves. She then continued to do the same to several slices of bacon that Kerri afterwards dropped into the sizzling pan. "Once you're done cutting everything, just drop them in and I'll mix it all together."

Eve did as directed and soon the aroma whetted every appetite in the house. Kerri added a homemade sauce containing tomatoes and a medley of herbs over the food once it was ready. "Go sit. I can dish and bring everything in."

"Okay, thanks. I'll take the cutlery in."

In the living room, Scarlett was sitting next to Clarissa and Barron on the larger sofa, and Drake was 'resting his eyes' on the armchair.

Kerri followed moments later. "Get up, old man!" She chuckled as she knocked Drake with her elbow before plopping a bowl in his lap.

"I'm up, I'm up." He yawned, blinking hard, "mmm, that smells good."

"And so it should! Eve and I worked ourselves to the bone to bring this meal to you, and here you sit, our work having bored you to sleep." She clasped a hand to her chest, closing her eyes as if wounded, hiding another pasta bowl behind her back.

"Yeah yeah, don't overdo it." Drake picked up a fork and began eating as Kerri served the others.

"Bon appétit! Is it good?" Everyone responded positively in their own way. Kerri beamed. "Not a bad team, are we, Eve?"

Eve returned with a gentle smile of her own. "Not bad at all. Pasta's one of my favourites, you know."

Kerri looked up in surprise, her pasta dangling from her fork. "Really?"

"It brings back good memories." She said it quietly, so that only Kerri beside her heard her. Kerri nodded before sparking a conversation with the others about their journey tomorrow, allowing Eve time with her thoughts. The conversation became background noise as she reminisced on her time with her previous guild.

*

"It's really not that hard, you just throw it in—" Meg poured a bunch of pasta into a boiling pot, "—and you stir it, so it doesn't stick. See?" She let the pasta sit for a bit, then stirred it with a wooden spoon, peeling it away from the surface of the steel pot.

"Oh, right. Sorry to bother you for this." Eve looked down, feeling her face grow hot with embarrassment.

The older woman stared at her, her features softening, "it's okay, I'd rather you ask than make a mess of dinner. You'll get the hang of it in no time!" She nudged Eve with her elbow, "my sister Ada had to ask me how to make pasta, too. Can you imagine that? Asking your younger sister how to essentially boil water? Wow!" She laughed and looked down at Eve, who was silent and looking down at the floor.

Eve fidgeted, playing with hair that reached midway down her back. "I just worry."

"You worry? About what?" Meg placed a hand on Eve's shoulder as she took over stirring the pasta with the other.

The water boiled and foamed, and Eve's fear came to the surface with it. "I don't think the rest of the team like me." She whispered, her voice wavering.

"Why do you think that?" Meg enquired.

"I, um," Eve stopped to think, not sure what to pinpoint specifically, "I'm just so young, you know? Inexperienced. I feel like a burden to you all."

"Do you feel like they make you feel like a burden, or is it you that believes you're a burden?"

Eve was not sure what to say. She bit her lip in silence and focused on stirring.

"You don't have to answer, but if we didn't want you here, then you wouldn't be here. It's as simple as that."

"What if only you wanted me here?"

"Hmm." Meg put a finger to her chin, tilted her head, "well, I guess it's my call, so screw them, right?"

Eve burst into laughter at Meg's response. She felt her tension slipping away. "Aye aye, captain!"

"That's more like it!" Meg leaned against the counter, watching Eve as she cooked. "But seriously, I don't know where you got the thought from, but to be clear, we do want you here. That goes for all of us, Eve."

Eve felt her face grow hot once more, a different kind of embarrassment taking over. She was not used to being told something like this so clearly. "I'm sorry."

"Don't apologise. You're young, you've never been part of a guild before. The doubt is not unreasonable, but you're earned your place here. One day, you might even outgrow our merry little guild, and set off on your own adventure, just like my sister did!" Meg thrust her arm out as if showcasing the wonders she would see, but all that laid ahead were wooden tables and chairs that made up most of the guild's home kitchen.

"I don't see that happening, Meg."

"And why not?"

Eve looked away shyly. "I like it here."

"You can't think everyone hates you but also want to stay here for the rest of your life. That's contradictory, my Evie!"

"Don't call me that!" Eve turned to Meg with a scowl, her eyebrows knit together tightly.

Meg ignored her annoyance and doubled down. "But you're my little Evie!"

"Meg, shut up!" Eve's annoyance came out as a childish whine, and Meg took the opportunity to ruffle her hair. Eve moved away and shook her hair.

"Oh, Evie, you're so wonderful."

"Whatever. Your sentimentality is going to ruin the pasta."

"Is that right? Are you a pasta connoisseur now then, hmm?" Meg poked her.

"Sh-shut up! I swear to God—"

"Okay, okay, it looks like the pasta is about ready anyway." Meg prepared the strainer and Eve carried the pot over. They strained the pasta and briefly ran it under hot water, then placed it into eight bowls. They finished the dishes with sauce, garlic, and bacon, but as Eve was preparing to lay the bowls on the table, Meg stopped her with a hug.

"We love having you here, Evie, and we love you. Remember that, okay?"

That was the last time the two of them had hugged.

Eve's eyes began to warm with tears. She tried to wash them away with a drink.

Kerri, ever observant, noticed and patted her hand. With a nod from Eve, Kerri smiled, and they returned to their food.

Chapter Eighteen

Early the next morning, the guilds clambered into two carriages and began their two-day journey to the capital of Ilas. This left them with a couple of days to prepare for Ilas Arena and whatever other horrors Edin may have in store for them.

"Are you nervous, Eve?" Kerri asked.

"Not really."

She instead turned to Drake. "What about you? Nervous?"

"Who, me? Never. Can't be worse than a werewolf, can it?"

"Hear hear," agreed Scarlett, "but let's not get ahead of ourselves." She was looking outside of the window. Her eyebrows creased, and she had a small frown on her face. Eve knew that, like on her own mind, Amie was on hers.

The carriage hit a bump and a deafening clash of weapons and armour followed it.

"We should've secured them more tightly." Barron muttered.

"Tell us more about Edin, if you could, please," Clarissa requested. "I'm still not quite sure what we're up against."

Eve pondered, trying to grasp the little information she knew of the illusive man, "honestly, I don't know too much about him. I saw him that one day, many years ago, and he led the group that killed my friends. He's certainly influential. I don't care to know much more about him."

"Let's hope that things won't be so bad there." Kerri said, but her furrowed eyebrows gave her lack of conviction away.

"Kerri, you know that's not possible." Eve turned away from the window to give Kerri a small smile. "I might've wanted to spare someone in Ilas Arena, but nobody other than the champion has ever left there alive. You've seen that for yourself. At this point, Edin must go. He won't use the same tactic twice to get what he wants, I'm sure of that."

"We won't be caught out by the same trick twice, either." Scarlett said through gritted teeth, still irritated that she let herself get held hostage so easily.

"Do we have to watch? Is there any benefit to us being in the stands?" Barron posed the question, idly stroking his beard.

"I'm watching," Kerri spoke up, her voice resolute this time, "if they try anything dirty, I won't allow it." She turned to Eve, fire burning in her eyes. "I'll cut my way down to you, if I must."

"I appreciate that, but I don't think it'll be necessary. still, thanks, Kerri." Eve returned Kerri's look with another smile.

"You gonna warn us all not to do the same?" Drake cocked his head to the side, smirking.

Eve sighed and changed tact, shrugging her arms and shaking her head, "none of you believe in me to get the job done, huh?"

"No, it's not that at all!" Drake threw his hands up in surrender, "but Kerri's right, if something untoward were to happen, we'd be there, right by your side, in an instant."

"I hope it won't come to that," Eve resumed watching the scenery as it blurred by the window, "but I appreciate it all the same."

They pulled over on the side of an open road by the edge of a forest for the night. Both guilds came together to pitch up enough tents for them all. The carriage drivers prepared to sleep in their carriages. Makeshift sleeping bags of all different colours and states of distress were laid out, it was clear at a glance that some members were more well-travelled than others. Some were adorned with knitted decorations that reminded Eve of a plush teddy bear. Eve spotted a teal coin-shaped keychain dangling from Ellen's sleeping bag as she placed it next to Kerri's.

Marcus saw Eve eyeing up the sleeping bags and tugged on his own keychain. "It gives me comfort, you know?"

The decoration in question was a piece of leather cut and coloured like a sunflower, matching his orange sleeping bag.

"No judgement from me. We don't choose what gives us comfort." Eve grabbed her jacket and pulled it closer to herself. She continued to watch Marcus as he looked down at the keychain, longing in his eyes, before she was pulled out of her reverie by a hand on her shoulder.

"I want to talk to you about something." Eve turned to see Scarlett, her face serious, and she allowed herself to be steered away from the others. "I want you to be real with me, Eve. Do you think our little guild is ready to deal with this?"

Eve did not think it mattered what she thought, not at this point. As far as she was concerned, they were all on the same boat now. "It's a bit late to ask now, isn't it?"

"Maybe, but I am asking now."

Eve remained silent, wondering how to respond.

"I'm going to take your silence as a no, unless you say otherwise."

"When I first joined, Amie made a point to mention how we're a guild that handles smaller problems—not necessarily one that would walk us into war or build a grudge against another guild."

"That doesn't mean we're not as competent."

"I never said that, and I never said we're not ready." Eve crossed her arms and averted her gaze. She looked at the others, a small frown on her face. She did not think they were fully ready, but they were here. What could she say?

"Your body language tells me otherwise." Scarlett put her hands on her hips, "look, I'm not going to be mad. We decided to come, regardless of whether or not you wanted us to, you know."

"I know, and I know I can't do this alone. I just wish that you all had more experience on the field." Eve stated the truth bluntly. She hoped that she would not upset Scarlett.

Scarlett grinned, "harsh, but fair." She turned to look at the others stoking the fire, cooking food, or talking with one another, "but we've come a damn long way, don't you think?"

"I don't think it, I know it, and that's why I think we'll be okay. If Edin underestimates you like I had done, then he'll be in for a sore surprise."

"For sure, he'll be sorry." Scarlett laughed, but quickly turned sombre as she watched over everyone. "Do you think he really has something for Amie?"

"I've tried not to think about it," Eve bit her lip, "but, either way, we've got to find out, haven't we?"

"Eve, listen to me," Scarlett grabbed Eve by the shoulders and looked directly into the younger woman's eyes. "Promise me that if things go south, you'll do whatever it takes to bring Amie back to us, okay?"

Eve was nonplussed. "What do you mean?"

"Promise me, Eve." Scarlett's gaze made Eve feel nervous, her eyes illuminated by the nearby campfire, and she nodded her head in response.

"I promise."

Scarlett removed her hands, "good, that's all I needed to know." Before she headed back to the camp, where they were being beckoned over for food, she paused and confided, "I really miss my little sis."

Eve pulled her jacket in on herself again, rubbing her upper arms, "I miss her, too."

It wasn't much longer until they reached Ilas, crossing through the entrance on foot. Many people bustled around, despite the setting sun bringing the day to a close, chattering and having fun. Eve thought of how they must be so blissfully unaware that Ilas Arena was seeing gratuitous bloodshed beneath their feet at this very moment, some contenders never setting foot to see the setting sun again. She was envious of them for not knowing, and angry at them for not being able to help.

"I'm going to get some food and call it night." Eve was the first to break the silence, grabbing the attention of the members of Rising Dawn who had been looking around in wonder.

The rest of the group nodded their heads in understanding. Some looked tired, some looked uncomfortable, shifting their weight as throngs of people walked past.

"Yeah, that sounds like a good plan." Marcus agreed, and they all set off to find a suitable tavern to fill their stomachs, before turning in at the inn they'd booked in advance for their large party. To save on costs, the rooms were booked in pairs. Eve and Kerri would be sharing a room.

After dinner, Kerri was sitting at the desk in their room, eyeing her scar in the mirror hanging on the wall. "I don't mind having this scar, you know."

Eve, who was looking out of the window, was taken by surprise by this comment. "Really? But you—"

Kerri cut her off. "I'm still pretty, I'll have you know."

"You are, but that's not the point I was trying to make."

"Then what is it?" Her brows knit together and her lips tugged downwards.

Eve's grip on the windowsill tightened, "you never would have gotten that, if I had protected you better."

"If you had protected me better?" Kerri's tone turned sharp. She stood and walked over to Eve. Her eyebrows knitted together as she thrust a finger at Eve. "I knew the risks, and although that mission went worse than expected, I still accepted that anything could happen. Even had I died that day, in no way would that have been your fault. All I have from it is this scar, and honestly, it's pretty cool looking, don't you think?"

"I mean, sure? Your marriage prospects certainly aren't hurt!" Eve joked and Kerri nudged her in the ribs.

"Yeah, right, I already have all the family I need."

"Have you told your father about all of this?"

Kerri scrunched her face, "well, no. I didn't want him to worry."

"After last time, I think that's fair, but—"

"I'll see him again, so don't say it."

"I was just going to say tha—"

"I think he would love to see you and Amie again, next time we see him. He was worried about you both." Kerri stared out of the window, her hair hanging in front of her face. Her knuckles turned white as they clutched the windowsill.

Eve decided not to push it any further. "Yeah, it would be nice to meet on better terms. Let's not leave it too long once we get home."

Kerri spun around, her hair swaying, "For sure, but should I tell him that a werewolf gave me this scar, or that I tripped?"

"Would he buy that you tripped?"

"He would probably suggest it before I can give a reason at all, to be perfectly honest. I was always a clumsy child."

Eve laughed before weighing in. "Own up to it. Not many people can face down a werewolf and live to tell the tale, so why choose not to share that story with him?"

"Yeah, you're right. All that matters is that we all got out relatively unscathed."

"Indeed."

They stood side by side, watching people as they walked by, absorbed in their conversations or eating steaming food as they took in the sights.

"I'm going to go to see Drake. Do you want to come with me?"

"No, that's okay, thanks, Kerri. Don't be too much of a nuisance, yeah?"

"Me, a nuisance?" She was already out of the door when she peeked her head back around it, sticking her tongue out at Eve. "Never!"

She closed the door behind her, leaving Eve to her thoughts.

The next morning arrived, and the anxiety growing in Eve's chest threatened to compress her to the mattress. She managed to summon the will to heave herself out of bed, but not without a heavy groan.

She heard voices outside of her room as she ran a hand along her shoulders, squeezing the stress out of them as she did so. She looked over to see Kerri's bed empty, her sheets astray, and realised that her voice was among those that she could hear. They were getting louder and more abrasive. Eve sprang to her feet in a panic.

"—it and go!"

"We must deliver it to her ourselves, personally."

"Get out of the way."

Eve threw the door open to see Kerri attempting to hold back two large men, both of who were attempting to pry her from the doorframe that she was desperately clutching on to. Her nails dug into the wood as she fought to keep her position.

"If you don't stop, I will hurt you." Eve snarled over Kerri's shoulder.

"Here," a burly arm appeared in front of her face, stretching past Kerri's head, "your summons."

Eve snatched the letter and stared incredulously at the man's face. "What do you think I'm doing here? Do you think I'm here for fun? I've already been summoned here, you idiot."

"Just doing our job." With that, the men made their leave, disappearing down the hallway in a matter of seconds. Kerri glared after them, standing her ground, until Eve ruffled her hair. "It's okay now. Sorry you had to deal with that."

"I-it's okay. Anytime." She tried to sound strong, but her shaky voice and the sweat trickling down her face betrayed her true feelings as to what had just transpired.

"Soon we won't have to deal with any shit like this." Eve huffed, angry.

Scarlett and Clarissa popped their heads out of their shared room. "What's going on?"

"Is everything okay?"

"Two men couldn't wait to hand this to me, at–at what time?" Eve looked over her shoulder, seeing a clock ticking away, getting ever closer to seven-thirty, "these people have no consideration whatsoever."

"What did they give to you?" Scarlett asked, rubbing her eyes.

"Let's see," Eve quickly read, "they want me at Ilas Arena at noon. Today." Eve spat out the words, disgust written across her face.

"Oh dear, well, the sooner we deal with him, the better, isn't that right?" Clarissa voiced her opinion, trying to twist the sudden events into something more appealing.

"You're right," Eve scrunched up the note in her hand, reducing it to a tiny smouldering mush with her Presence, "he won't even make it to sunset."

"Who has a last meal at breakfast time?" Barron grumbled, but his displeasure had not stopped him from stacking his plate ludicrously high.

"Planning on dying today, are we?" Clarissa smirked, and Barron rolled his eyes.

"Not planning on it, no, but I don't have a good feeling about it."

"You sure that's not the meat?" Drake jibed, eyeing Barron's meal, "it's not good to fight on an empty stomach, but you might be taking the saying a bit too literally, with all that you've got loaded on there."

Barron waved their worries away, a fork with a sausage pierced on it dancing around in front of their eyes, "hope for the best, prepare for the worst."

The table fell silent at his words. Everyone understood the implication. Kerri prodded at her food, her face pale. Eve placed a hand on her arm, and gently squeezed it.

"You don't have to come. Really, it's okay if you don't want to."

"I-I want to, though." Kerri's voice was soft, but even still she could not hide her voice faltering.

"You could even go to your dad's."

Kerri gently placed her fork down with a shaky hand, "I didn't train just to sit on the sidelines."

"I understand. If you're going to come, then, you should make sure you eat." Eve nudged Kerri's plate closer to her, "you're going to need the energy."

"Okay." Kerri took a small bite of her food, chewing it longer than usual, before swallowing.

Scarlett was sipping at orange juice, looking solemn. "Where's Amie when you need her? She would always know what to say to cheer everyone up, the idiot." She swirled her glass idly, watching the liquid spin. Eve was not sure what to say, she closed her eyes briefly and allowed herself a moment to think of happier times.

"Next time we see her, she'll be awake again. Let's focus on that, yeah?" Drake attempted to revitalise the group, reminding them of why they are here. "She's gonna hate that she's missed this." He chuckled.

Scarlett gave a soft laugh, "she will, and she'll be doubly annoyed to hear how close Eve and Kerri have grown." She winked at Eve. Kerri made a choking sound, pounding at her chest before rushing to swallow several gulps of water.

"What do you mean by that?!" She yelled, louder than intended, gaining a few glares from the handful of patrons at the café.

"I'm only kidding!" Scarlett raised her hands in mock surrender, "besides, it's Amie you have to worry about."

"What do you mean by *that*?!" Kerri's face grew red, and she dug into her food with renewed vigour, deciding to ignore the conversation entirely.

Eve smiled to herself, feeling slightly flushed. Did Amie talk about her at home? She felt a pang soar through her heart, wanting nothing more than to see Amie, but she also felt a warm joy spreading throughout her chest. The voices around her became background noise to her thoughts.

*

Eve was sitting in the waiting room of Ilas Arena, alone. She'd been separated from the others the moment they set foot in the downstairs reception, leaving her to assume that her friends would be taken to the stands to watch the proceedings.

Whilst Eve waited to be called to fight, the Marauders of Light and Rising Dawn found themselves somewhere entirely unexpected—Edin's office. The man himself presided at his desk, fingers entwined as he rested his chin on his hands.

"Take this," Edin presented a crystal bottle from within his jacket pocket, a sky-blue liquid sloshed inside, "and go home. I do not care for any of you—it is only Eve I want. She is here, so leave."

"What's this?" Scarlett walked over and took the bottle, examining it.

"Must I really explain it to you, Scarlett?" He raised an eyebrow before he sighed and continued, "this will cure your sister. It will wake her up from her eternal slumber. Without it, she has no hope of waking again. That is what you came here for, is it not?"

"How is it that you know my name? More importantly, haven't you got anything better to do than to spy on my sister?" She slammed her fist on his desk.

He was unfazed and simply looked up at her before responding. "I run Ilas Arena. A lot of people walk through these doors. Mercenaries, guilds, infobrokers, you name it, they've been here." He gestured nonchalantly with his hands, "information comes from Thous regularly, and who could ignore hearing about an Eve with such a bright white head of hair."

"I see." Scarlett's grip on the bottle tightened, "and if we wish to stay?"

Edin clapped his hands together, "oh, but of course! You can sit in the stands, just like everyone else. I fear it might be a tad more stressful for you, though, than our usual clientele."

Scarlett pondered before tucking the bottle safely away, "we'll take our chances."

Edin signalled the guards by the doorway and they grabbed Kerri and Ellen, forcibly removing them from the room, as they screamed and attempted to break free. As everyone else prepared to jump into action, Edin warned them against it. "Just a little collateral to ensure that you don't do anything stupid. Don't get involved, and they'll be able to return home safely with you."

The heavy-set doors to his office slammed closed, harshly cutting off the noise from the hallway. Scarlett, fuming, bit her tongue.

Edin smirked. "Good girl. Now go watch 'til your heart's content, and hers stops beating."

With another wave of his hand, the doors swung open, and four guards appeared to escort them to the audience stands.

*

"You absolute bastards!" Kerri screamed through the iron bars.

The guards snickered and left them to the damp, dark, stillness of the dungeon. Ellen swore under her breath, kicking at loose rocks scattered across the floor of their cell. Their weapons had been confiscated, leaving them with only their Presence available to them.

"I could burn these bars in a matter of seconds, but"

"I know. who knows what would happen if we did?"

The two fell silent. Kerri rattled the bars to see if any of them were loose. Once she had checked them all, she stepped back and sighed.

"What are we going to do?"

Chapter Nineteen

Eve walked out to thunderous roars and cheers. She was the only person on the arena's ground. She looked around and spotted her friends, giving them a firm nod, before realising that Kerri and Ellen were not there. She searched Scarlett's face, but she simply put a hand up. Eve took this to mean that things were okay, she couldn't worry about it any longer even if she wanted to. A booming voice reverberated through the entirety of the arena, greeting the attendees, and adding to Eve's festering anxiety.

"How many times are you going to come here, Eve? The only reigning champion who hates the glory, fame and money that comes with it! Pretty stupid if you ask me, right folks?"

The audience laughed in agreement, shouting taunts and criticisms at Eve. She paid them no attention, not wanting to give them the satisfaction of her anger. Instead, she wished that the announcer would get on with it. She wanted to know where Kerri and Ellen were. She swallowed hard and turned around to get a better look of her surroundings. The energy here was like nothing she had ever seen before. Cheers and yells mingled with the oppressive warmth of the arena, creating a blanket that Eve felt could wrap up its contestants and bundle them into a deep darkness. It felt as if she had stumbled somewhere and fell into an alternate reality, where the people were monsters in human skin.

"Alright, alright, keep it down! How else am I supposed to announce the first challenger of the night, eh?" The announcer's call did little to dampen the spirits of the bloodthirsty audience, but he continued anyway, his voice echoing out across the arena, "tonight's proceedings begin with a tidy and fair battle, and this is a group looking for a quick bit of cash!"

Eve froze. What did he mean by a group? Ilas Arena was historically one on one battles. Even if groups were involved, they had to nominate only one person to participate.

The announcer introduced a group of four bandits, two women and two men, who were armed with a variety of weapons. She glanced at them, noting a few things that stood out to her. There were two men, Eve assumed in their late twenties, one with shoulder-length shaggy blonde hair, and one with short brown hair and a steel sword. The latter had a dark splotch across his face. One of the women seemed to be a similar age to them. She was tall with long blonde hair, also bearing a sword. Eve's first thought was that her hair was way too long for combat. One of her eyes was pale, a faint scar running across it. Eve's eyes lingered a moment longer over the last woman. She was young. Maybe not even twenty years old. She had deep green eyes and brunette hair that reached down to her chin. She held a lance in both hands. She, like the others, looked towards Eve hungrily. They all looked like amateurs, too eager to throw their lives away. However, if Eve wanted to help Amie, then she could not hold back. She unsheathed her scythe and locked a steely gaze on her opponents.

"Ho ho, looks like someone's ready for battle! I suppose we should get this party started then." Eve briefly wondered if she could get away with throwing a fireball in the announcer's direction. "Fight!"

As soon as the signal was given, Eve charged forward with a burst of Flame and swung at the closest man, hooking him with her scythe before launching him to their nearest ally. He collided with her, and they were both thrown backward with a crunch. The younger woman dove to the side to avoid harm, coughing up sand as she looked back up from the floor. Eve followed up by shooting a fireball that set them in flames in an instant within seconds, however, they were doused with water. Eve glanced about to find out where it came from, and made eye contact with the other man. He smirked at her. The two who had been set alight turned to face Eve. Their hair was dripping and their clothes hung to them. Their brows furrowed deeply as they scowled, looking like drowned rats who just had their meal snatched from them.

The man with the shaggy blonde hair took a step back whilst the other three inched closer toward Eve with their lances and swords.

The youngest woman twirled her lance in her hand before swinging it back in an arc. She threw it with incredible speed toward Eve. Eve bent backward to dodge it, and felt the wind whip past her face as the lance flew narrowly past. Something felt off as she found her footing again. Why had the lance not made a noise when it landed? Eve's senses screamed at her to move, and she dropped flat to the floor. The lance flew past again and landed in her opponent's hand. Again, Eve was greeted by a smirk, and she felt a boiling sensation soar from her stomach to her throat as she climbed to her feet. She patted her side in a panic. Where had her pistol gone? The holster it was usually found in was split in half. She whipped around and spotted it several feet away, closer to the young woman with the lance than to herself. She gripped her scythe tightly, the white of her knuckles showing.

The man with the splotchy face raised his sword high above his head and charged. Eve swept wide with her scythe, causing him to cough and splutter as he was assailed by a gust of sand. Keeping momentum from the sweep, she leapt forward. Her foot found its home in his chest. He barrelled backwards and Eve parried a swing from the tall woman's sword. Her opponent bounced back, her foot unable to find a solid hold in the sand. Eve pulled out her new dagger and dashed forward, the tip directed at her neck. Before she was able to make contact, a lance flew forward and nicked her wrist. She sharply inhaled and lashed out with a roaring of Flame. She may have missed the woman with her dagger, but the Flame encompassed her entirely. Her hair wrapped around her like a cloak.

Her horrific screams shattered something in the arena. Eve had not realised how quiet the audience had been, but they hollered in excitement as the woman burned. Mercy was granted to her as the leader doused her in water. It did not matter. Eve was already on the move. The fire served as a distraction and she bridged the gap between her and the man with the splotchy face. She dug her dagger into his throat. He gripped her wrist tightly and tried to pry her grasp from his neck. A breath later, he went limp. Eve dropped him to the floor and wiped sweat from her forehead. Out of the corner of her eye she saw something hurtling her way. She barely reacted fast enough to evade the tip of a lance aimed at her head.

The aggressor snarled. "He was dead weight anyway!"

Eve studied the face of her opponent. Her teeth were bared, her hair was coming loose, and sweat trickled down her face. Eve knew that she could use this anger against her.

"What makes you so different? You'll be just like him." Her eyes darted to the corpse on the floor, blood still profusely streaming from the hole in its neck. The young woman with the lance glanced over too, only for a second, but Eve was ready for it. She punched the woman in the face, but she stopped herself from falling by digging her lance into the floor.

"I thought you said this would be an easy job, arsehole!" The woman with the lance shouted at the leader over her shoulder.

He shrugged her off. "It would be if you hurried up and got on with it, Jade." Jade looked as if she was about to argue back, but instead snarled at him.

Eve looked between them, flabbergasted. "Are you serious?"

Jade roared. Eve dodged a flurry of jabs, and felt a pang of sadness for the woman. She parried and knocked Jade off-centre, then saw her opportunity to end it. She pulled her scythe back and swung, but met with steel. The other woman had jumped in to save Jade. As scythe clashed against sword, Jade resorted to her tactic from earlier and jumped back to throw her lance at Eve from a safer distance.

Eve worked to keep the tall woman with the sword between her and Jade. "So, was this your idea to come here?"

The woman grunted with the effort of attempting to keep Eve in place, but said nothing in response. Her eyes shifted to the side, at the man with the aqua Presence. Splotches of her skin were steaming, the flesh red from Eve's Flame.

Eve glanced over at the blonde man standing back as his allies fiercely fought, feeling a mixture of anger and resentment boil within her. She looked back at the opponent in front of her. "I'm sorry."

A flash of confusion spread across the woman's face, followed by a flicker of understanding as her eyes opened wide and she gasped. Blood bloomed across her chest. Her sword fell to the floor. Eve supported the woman as she convulsed. She jerked as she removed the lance from her back, and Eve watched Jade look on in horror as she realised what Eve had done. Jade was acting too brashly, and it would not be too difficult to find the perfect moment to use it against her. The woman in her arms went slack, and Eve knelt down to lay her on the floor.

The audience erupted into cheers and yells, louder than the heartbeat that had made its way to Eve's ears. The lance next to Eve wobbled, and she grabbed it before it could find its way back to Jade. It shook in her hand, desperate to find its way back to its owner. The pull was strong, tugging Eve forward. Jade was sweating profusely with the effort of trying to reclaim it.

Feeling pity for her opponent, Eve set the lance on fire and let it go. Jade's eyes grew wide but the lance was already only inches away from her. It flew directly to her hand and she yelped. It turned into an ear-piercing scream. Although she dropped the lance quickly, the damage was done. Smoke raised from her palm, which she frantically rubbed into the sand to put out the remaining fire. As Eve expected, Jade was doused in water, but that man was no healer. With a bright red hand and skin peeling off, Jade tried to grasp the lance but could not maintain her grip on it. She tried again and again, a grimace on her face and tears in the corners of her eyes, but each time the lance would drop to the floor with a clatter. Her face contorted with frustration and hurt as the lance slipped from her hand one last time before she closed her eyes and sighed. "This isn't worth it. I can't beat you, not like this." Jade kicked her lance aside and raised her hands in surrender, "I forfeit."

The audience booed and Eve felt her skin prickle. "If you can do better, then come down here and see how you do." The boos only grew in intensity. Eve decided to try what she wanted to do earlier. She threw a fireball at the stands. It extinguished as soon as it hit the fence, which she expected based on her own experiences here, but seeing them scramble back in fear made her feel a little better.

"Now now, no more of that!" The announcer's voice rang out.

Eve approached Jade and held her hand out. "You fought well."

Jade slapped her outstretched palm aside with her good hand. "It doesn't matter, does it? Get on with it." Jade looked to the side. Eve took a closer look at her. She really could not have been much older than Kerri.

Before Eve could contemplate what to do, a bubble encapsulated Jade's head. Her eyes went wide as oxygen was cut off from her. Jade clawed at the bubble but could not pierce it, her hands simply slipped in through the water. Eve's gaze darted around, elated to find her dragon pistol not too far away. She sprinted over, snatched it up, and took aim at the final opponent.

His lips were twisted downwards, his brows lowered, and his nose scrunched. It was as if a rancid smell had taken control of his face. His eyes were locked on Jade. "You're a damned failure! I'll do it myself!"

Eve shot at him. The bullet pierced his skull and his body ungraciously collapsed to the floor with a thud.

Jade was freed and dropped to the floor, catching her breath. Her hair hung in clumps around her face, and her nails dug into the dirt. Eve aimed the pistol at Jade's head. Her gasps for air were punctuated by her coughing up copious amounts of water. Eve paused. It did not feel right. She closed her eyes tight. Despite her promises, her resolve had broken. She looked at Jade again, who had only avoided one miserable death to waltz straight into another.

Eve supported her wrist with her free hand and took several deep breaths. Jade looked up at her with bloodshot eyes. There was a small smile on her face, "you're not nearly as bad a person that they told me you were, Eve." Eve did not respond. A small lump formed in her throat. "Thanks to you, I can die a better person than I lived." Jade grasped the gun and squeezed Eve's hand. It happened so quickly. The bullet fired. It sounded louder than it ever had before. Jade collapsed, her soaked hair splayed out as the water mixed with fresh blood. The sliver of silence was interrupted as the announcer's voice boomed over the arena once again. She could hardly make out what he was saying over the ringing in her ears. Eve gritted her teeth and looked towards her friends. She found it difficult to be fighting alone again. She wished that they could have done this together, or better yet, not at all.

"Eve's penchant for wanting to see the good in people will get her killed one day," Scarlett said. She knew that the fight could have ended sooner had Eve willed it.

"You can't blame her," Drake replied, "that girl. She was so young."

"Young or not, I don't care. I want Eve to win, as quickly as she can." Scarlett was firm and Drake refrained from responding. Instead, he looked to the arena, watching as Eve sat by the wall waiting for her next opponents.

"Do you think anybody would notice if I used my Presence to help Eve out?" Clarissa mused, twirling her hair around her fingers.

"I wish," Barron responded, "but I don't think it's worth us chancing it." He exhaled as he looked at Eve with a small frown tugging at his lips.

"I won't interfere." She huffed, "but I really wish I could."

"Lighten up!" A grinning face jutted in between Clarissa and Barron, "excitement like this comes only once in a lifetime, y'know?"

Barron turned to face the man, his nostrils flaring. "Excitement? If it's so exciting, I can lob you down there myself."

The man put his hands up and backed away, "alright, alright, settle down, pal. Geez."

Barron shook his head and turned back to face the arena, just in time for the second fight.

The fight came and went with Eve standing victorious over a group of three. She felt winded. Her opponents might have just been searching to make some quick money, but they were not amateurs. Her muscles ached and she could hear her blood pumping in her ears. She glanced downwards. Another three bodies to add to the pile. None of the bodies were being removed. Instead, Eve pulled them aside herself before the next battle, wiping the sweat from her forehead as she ignored the jeers from the audience.

*

The ceiling shook. Dust and loose debris fell onto Kerri's and Ellen's heads as they were visited by the guard again.

"She's really something else, that Eve," said the guard, "I've never seen someone like her in the arena." He sounded almost wistful.

"Why do you work here?" Kerri posed the question at the guard, a hint of disgust in her voice. He shrugged.

"It pays the bills."

He walked off, leaving Kerri and Ellen to their dull, damp surroundings.

"I'm tired of this," Ellen complained, "how long do they intend to keep us here?"

"Next time that guard comes around, let's steal his keys and make a break for it," Kerri whispered.

Ellen's eyes lit up. "Do you have a plan?"

Kerri grinned. "You could say that."

Kerri's scream reverberated around the dungeon, followed by Ellen's cries for help. Two guards ran into the hallway, the clanking of their armour echoing loudly. They approached the gate to see Kerri's bleeding body slumped across it, and Ellen's hands clutching at her face in horror.

"W-what happened here?!"

"Did you kill her?!" One guard pointed an accusatory finger at Ellen.

Ellen frantically shook her head, not moving from the dark of the corner.

The first guard reached for his keys, when the other one stopped him.

"What do you think you're doing?"

"Huh? Well, I'm opening the gate to have a proper look, ain't I?"

The wary guard looked suspiciously at Ellen, who turned away in response, hoping that her show of fear would override any further probing and doubt.

After a moment the guard nodded his approval and his ally opened the gate. Kerri's slumped body vanished as he reached toward it, and Ellen lunged forward to steal his sword. She was successful and thrust it towards his neck.

Kerri left the shadow of the corner, unharmed, "not bad, huh?"

The other guard watched in confusion. He looked at his ally, his face covered in sweat, before running away in the opposite direction.

"Go!" Ellen encouraged. She sprinted and caught up quickly, with no heavy armour to weigh her down, tackling him around the waist. They tumbled to the floor.

Kerri's head hit the floor hard. She felt her throat constrict, and nausea bubble up from inside. Taking advantage of his dazed opponent, the guard flipped her onto her back and began to strangle her. His steeled fingertips firmly tightened around her throat. She was unable to pry his fingertips away, and unable to reach the hilt of the sword at his waist. She slammed her hands against the floor and the walls, hoping that Ellen would realise she was in trouble.

She caught a glint of something from behind the guard. He yelped as the blade of a key scraped along his face, and let go of Kerri. The guard leapt to his feet, unsheathing his sword as he did. Ellen wielded a sword she'd claimed from the other guard. Kerri felt her sight waver as she attempted to gather her bearings.

Ellen dodged each slash. The guard was not particularly skilled, but he had the range advantage. She surprised him by throwing the key at his face, before stepping in close to try and wrest his sword from him by force in his distraction.

"Get off, brat!" The guard spat, but she did not flinch.

With her back pushing into his front, she tried to force his arm outwards. She pushed down on his gauntlet, hoping to apply pressure to his wrist, when the other guard reappeared. He stormed forward, a crazed look in his eyes as he charged ahead with his arms outstretched.

The guard wrestling with Ellen threw her to the side in a panic. He held his arms up and tried to assure the guard that he was his ally, but his pleas went ignored. The other guard brought his sword down with a wide smile on his face, digging it deep into the other man's neck. Blood poured out from the wound, but he did not disappear. The guard's face fell as sombre realisation dawned upon him.

"What? No!" The guard grabbed the man's falling body as he bled out.He looked up to see Ellen helping Kerri to her feet, watching as Kerri placed her hand on the wall, her face down. Ellen held a sword in her free hand. He pointed at them with a shaky finger, his face drawn and white. "That was supposed to be you."

Ellen readied her sword. "Am I supposed to be sorry that you didn't kill us instead?" She gritted through her clenched jaw.

The guard rose to his feet but even Kerri, in her dazed state, could see that he was not prepared. Ellen disarmed him in seconds. She pointed the sword at his throat and kicked the other sword behind her toward Kerri. Her lips curled upward as she looked at the man in a mixture of disgust and pity. "If I didn't have to, I wouldn't."

The man swallowed. His eyes kept darting to his fallen comrade.

"That said, you deserve this, don't you?" Ellen thrust forward, slicing the man's throat.

She led Kerri away from the dungeons as he fell to the floor, twitching in near silence.

*

In the arena, Eve was drenched in blood and sweat. Her ragged form struggled to keep up with the pace of the on-going battles. Having now won six matches, she tirelessly moved the fallen bodies to the edge of the arena, creating a mountainous pile. Her muscles ached and it felt as if her bones had increased in density, weighing her down. She was tired in every imaginable way. She rested against the wall for what felt like only a second before the announcer's voice blared out once again, signalling the start of the next match.

*

"They can't have taken them too far," Kerri said to Ellen.

Searching for their possessions, Kerri and Ellen had fought against a handful of guards and so far managed to prevent word from spreading of their escape. They darted around from room to room, unsure of where to go.

"Come on, come on, come on…" Ellen pleaded.

As if on cue, Ellen stopped running and looked into what seemed to be a training room. Various weaponry lined the walls in their racks, with a number of training dummies and mats strewn across the room. Kerri's first thought was that it was incredibly grey and boring for a training room. A small group of guards were using their signature sword, shield and lance on training dummies.

"Very professional," she scoffed as Kerri appeared behind her. "Shall we?"

"Let's!"

They charged in, swords brandished.

*

"This is too much," Kyrie flinched as Eve beat down another opponent with her bare hands, her movements heavy and sluggish, "she won't last."

Scarlett gritted her teeth, her arms crossed, ignoring Kyrie's and the many other similar comments. She ran her fingers along the vial by her chest, vital to bringing her sister back to the world of the living. She wanted to shout out, to let Eve know that they had what would help Amie and that they could leave, but she was worried. Edin had already warned them against telling Eve, and doing so would put her at greater danger, along with the Marauders and Rising Dawn. She bit her lip and continued to watch.

*

Kerri grunted as she charged forward with her shield, knocking the guard she was fighting off her feet. As she landed on the floor, Kerri wrestled her shield back from her and put it on. "It feels so good to have this back!"

The woman snarled and jumped at her. There was a crunching sound as the shield made contact with her face. Blood now smeared the aqua-tinge of her shield. "Oh, come on!"

"Making a mess of things already, huh?" Ellen was at her back as she swiped her opponent from his feet with her lance. He fell backwards into a training dummy with a loud crash. She held her lance in front of her proudly. "I never did like swords much."

They fought and fought, unable to avoid reinforcements now that they had made so much noise.

Soon they were running up several staircases, getting closer and closer to the symphony of Ilas Arena.

*

"Ooh, and that's another one!" rang the announcer's voice at the end of another battle, "but it looks like our hero is struggling to stay on her feet."

Eve indeed struggled to stay steady as her next opponents were introduced in quick succession. She didn't have time to move the bodies from the prior fights anymore. Every muscle felt like lead, every breath felt as if it could be her last, and she finally collapsed to her knees. A mixture of roars, groans and insults burst out from every corner of the arena.

The floor rippled in front of her. She lacked the strength to lift her own head. Her eyes searched for her friends, to somehow tell them that she was sorry. She tried her hardest to focus on them, but it was as if someone had placed film over her eyes. She could see Scarlett, Drake, Clarissa and Barron together, gripping the wooden beam in front of them, leaning over it and shouting at her. She couldn't make out what they were saying, but she could see the spit. The scrunched faces. They were desperate for her to move. She could barely see the others, just a blurry mess of limbs being thrown into the air. She had let them down.

A memory appeared in her mind. It was of Kerri hugging her after Amie was rushed to the clinic. Of Eve losing control and almost setting her room – and their house – on fire. She felt her throat tighten. Because of her, Kerri could not even spectate. What would happen to her now?

Suddenly she was looking down at Amie, as if she was sitting by her bedside again. Would Amie be okay? Would she wake up to know that Eve had died for her? That she had loved her? She wanted nothing more than to feel her cool touch again.

"Well, I guess this is it for—" the announcer's voice cut off as one of the contestants collapsed to the floor. Confusion reigned as another contestant fell, accompanied by a clanging sound.

Eve felt the spark of adrenaline course through her, mixed with terror and pride. She knew of no one else that could use their Presence like this.

There was a sudden yelp as the third and final member of the opposing team quickly turned on the spot and grabbed the air in front of him. Kerri's Illusion dropped. "Got you, now, haven't I?" He snarled.

The next thing he uttered was a choking sound, for Kerri had rammed the side of her shield up against his chin. He stumbled backwards and fell arse first to the floor.

"Got me, have you?" Kerri grinned, the tip of her sword held to the man's face. He put his hands up in surrender. Eve felt her senses go haywire. Kerri looked back at her with a smile on her face, "we're done here!"

Blood splattered across her shield. The man in front of her crumpled to the floor, blood streaming from his head. Eve was resting on one knee. Her dragon pistol was smoking.

Kerri looked frozen in time, her face and stance unmoved.

"I had to, Kerri. Otherwise they would have killed us both. I'm sorry."

She dropped to the floor again, her adrenaline had exhausted itself. She heard the stomping of feet and two hands grabbed at her, forcing her onto her back.

"I'm sorry you had to do that." Kerri looked on the verge of tears. "I should've been the one–"

Eve reached out to cover Kerri's mouth, but in her exhaustion, she clumsily placed her entire bloody palm across Kerri's face. "No, I'd rather it had been me. Thanks for coming. To save me."

Kerri smiled in response. "I'm just glad I made it in time."

Eve could not help but smile too at the young woman who had saved her time and time again.

Chapter Twenty

"Edin won't just let us walk. Eve will need us. All of us, right now. Let's go." Scarlett stood and the group followed after her, but they were soon blocked by the guards assigned to escort them.

"Are you serious?" Barron shouted, "do you truly intend to stop us?"

The guards looked at each other for just a moment. Scarlett paralysed both and stepped over their twitching bodies. "We don't have time for this."

Scarlett led them as they all charged down to the arena. They arrived just in time to see that Edin Garrett himself had entered the arena, fury and indignation written across his face.

*

Ellen was closest to the entrance where Edin had entered. She raised her lance, but was thrown across the arena with an instantaneously summoned Spark. Her body became a blur until she hit the wall and slumped over into the pile of corpses Eve created. Eve's mind blanked as she laid eyes on Edin. He held his arms behind his back as he sneered at her. His piercing blue eyes were filled with contempt and pride. His lips curled upwards, looking as if he had caught a rat in a trap. For a moment, Eve felt as if she had frozen.

"Ellen!" Kerri's cry echoed across the arena, resounding over the uproar in the stands and bringing Eve back to her senses.

She lunged with her shield, deflecting the Spark aimed at her, fighting to get closer to Edin. Eve watched, willing her knees to stop shaking, willing herself to move.

Another bolt of Spark flew across the arena, from a different direction, but was negated by Edin's own Spark.

"Your fight's with me now," Scarlett entered the arena and threw the vial towards Eve, "catch!" Eve did so, and eyed the icy blue liquid inside. "That'll bring Amie back to us, so don't lose it, okay?"

She looked at the bottle again and clutched it close to her chest. Eve cried out as she forced herself to stand up straight. She unsheathed her scythe before locking eyes with the very person who had brought her immeasurable, indescribable pain.

"You just couldn't simply die, could you, Eve?" Edin barked, "but don't worry, you can all join each other in death." As if to give weight to his threat, he used Wind to summon one of the corpses with such ferocity that limbs tore off as it was twirled around with incredible speed. Blood sprayed in a whirlwind before he summoned a bolt of Spark that incinerated it entirely. Edin had two Presence. Eve's eyes opened wide and her jaw dropped.

"Interesting," Scarlett remarked, unfazed, "I don't think I've ever seen someone with two Presences before."

"Maybe I will keep you alive long enough to see exactly how painful the process of extracting another person's Presence can be." Edin cruelly smirked.

"Taking someone's Presence?" Eve said in disbelief, but her weak voice failed to carry over.

Scarlett grunted dismissively in the face of Edin's threat, "you should've stolen more for today then, eh?"

Edin's eye twitched as his attention shifted. "Funny. Speaking of taking things, I hope you know that you will die here today, with no hope of your sister making it back to the world of the living."

Scarlett's eyes narrowed and she jerked her chin towards the exit behind her, "Eve, Kerri, get going, I'll clean up here."

Eve did a double take. "It would be far safer if you went!"

"She's right," Kerri shouted as she approached them both with Ellen on her back, still unconscious. "It would be better if we fought together, right?"

"I'm your leader, and I ordered you to go!" Scarlett's eyes seared into Eve's green ones, and she faltered under a gaze so intense. She couldn't say no to her.

"Enough of this!" Edin used Wind to cast Eve and Kerri towards the back of the arena. They collided with the wall, knocking the air from their lungs. Kerri braced herself as she landed, but Eve fell unceremoniously to the floor.

"Ouch." Kerri grumbled as she pulled herself to her feet and rolled Eve over onto her back. Her head fell limply to the side, just like Ellen's had. Kerri clambered between them both to check for a pulse. Her face relaxed when she confirmed that both were still breathing. What was she going to do now?

She wiped sweat from her face and watched as Scarlett and Edin fought. She hadn't had the opportunity to see Scarlett fight against another person, and was in awe at the storm brewing in front of her.

"Kerri!" Kyrie was bending the arena's bars, slipping through them to join Kerri on the arena floor. "You okay?"

"I guess?" Kerri threw out her arms, highlighting the corpses surrounding her, Eve and Ellen's unconscious bodies, and the fight happening in the not-so-far distance.

"Good. You grab Eve," Kyrie said as she made to lift Ellen, who's hair was stained red with blood.

"O-okay!" Kerri huffed with the exertion of lifting Eve's dead weight. She spared a small thought of admiration and envy at Kyrie's athletic physique.

"The others are clearing the way out, all we need to do is get there," Kyrie began dragging Ellen around the outer rim of the arena, "trust in Scarlett. She won't let us get hurt."

Kerri nodded, and with Eve's arm slumped across her shoulder, she followed closely behind Kyrie.

*

Scarlett fought with everything she had, doing all she could to keep Edin's attention. Each time Edin tried to blow her off her feet, she dodged or interrupted his attack with Spark.

"I can keep this up all day!" Scarlett grunted, though her breathlessness gave her away.

"I'd rather not," said Edin, looking around and taking note of those attempting to escape. He raised his hand towards them and his fingers crackled. As he let loose bolts of electricity, Scarlett dashed in and blocked them with her sabre.

"Don't think I'm an easy target. I'm the leader of the best guild around, you know." Scarlett laughed. "Guess you won't be best pleased when they get away, will you?"

Edin turned his full attention to her. His eyes narrowed, his lips grew thin, and his nostrils flared. "Don't you dare deign to speak to me like you've won!" Every other word was punctuated with the clashing of swords.

Scarlett's sabre was knocked out of her hand. It arced up and away from her as Edin drew his sword back.

*

They watched as Scarlett's sabre was knocked away from her. Kyrie motioned to Kerri. "That's my cue. Take these two and leave!" Kyrie placed Ellen's weight onto Kerri and darted off towards Scarlett as the latter was put onto her back foot.

"W-wait!" Kerri's cry fell onto deaf ears as Kyrie reached Edin in seconds flat. She put a foot into his chest with thunderous force. Edin was propelled into the arena wall, where he disappeared into a thick cloud of sand.

"Damn, I wish I could kick half as hard as that," Scarlett complimented Kyrie as she straightened herself out. "I appreciate it."

"Don't mention it. You'd do the same for–" Kyrie stopped mid-sentence. Blood trickled from her mouth and along her jaw. Her eyes widened as she lurched forward and collapsed into Scarlett's arms. The blood flowed thicker and faster. Scarlett patted her back fruitlessly, trying to locate the source of the impact.

"Do not," chided Edin's cold voice, "think that you were ever going to get away with that."

Kyrie slumped deeper into Scarlett's arms. She struggled with her weight, bringing her to her knees.

"Kyrie, no. I'm so sorry." Scarlett held Kyrie's head close and winced from an unexpected blistering heat. Parting her thick hair the best she could, Scarlett saw a bright red burn which was black around the edges. Edin had sent a Spark directly through her head, bringing a swift but brutal end to Rising Dawn's fiercest team member.

*

Tearing her eyes away from Kyrie, Kerri made the decision to take Eve and Ellen away. If she could just get them both to the others, then she could come back to help Scarlett.

Struggling under the weight of the two women, Kerri forced her feet forward. She tightened her grip around them, when she felt the weight suddenly lessen. Eve had regained consciousness and was steadying herself on her feet.

"Just lean on me, okay, Eve? We're almost out now."

Eve nodded and grasped Kerri's shoulder tightly. They had only moved a few steps when Eve stopped. "What are you doing? We have to move!" Kerri re-arranged Ellen into a more comfortable position and looked at Eve, whose face was contorted as she watched a ragged Scarlett struggle to keep up with Edin, and at Kyrie, the pool of blood beneath her growing larger with each and every second.

"Eve, please, you're hurting me." Kerri's plea snapped Eve from her reverie, apparently having not realised that she had been subconsciously heating up Kerri's armour with her Presence.

"I'm sorry," she removed her hand, "take Ellen and get out of here."

"Don't be an idiot. We need to meet with the others, then some of us can come back to help Scarlett." Kerri looked into Eve's eyes, her eyes growing wet, and whispered, "please, don't do this."

Eve turned away from her gaze, "I'm sorry, but I can't just let her die."

Kerri conceded with a sigh. She gritted her teeth angrily, wanting nothing more than to escort Eve from the grounds of Ilas Arena forever.

"Okay. But I'm not delivering this vial to Amie without you, so make it quick."

Eve nodded again. "I promise." She said, and ran to join Scarlett in her furious fray against Edin.

Kerri moved with Ellen as fast as she possibly could.

Despite being injured and exhausted, Eve managed to keep up with the battle. Scarlett covered her weaknesses and was always there to deflect if needed. Eve did not know where her scythe was, though she had an idea it was probably hidden among the bodies from when she's been thrown. She instead fought with her body, imbuing her limbs with Flame when she felt like she could land a direct hit. Keeping it active constantly would tire her out long before she could bring the battle to an end. This was a thought that nagged away at the back of her mind as she battled with Edin.

Dodging furiously, Eve failed to land a hit with any meaningful impact. Edin was only slightly bruised and singed at her touch.

"Why would you do all of this, just for me?" Eve yelled, her anger finding no limit, "haven't you already taken enough from me?"

She threw a punch, but Edin deflected it with his forearm.

"You were all meant to die that day, don't flatter yourself into thinking you're important." Edin elbowed Eve in the chest, but she bounced back with a knee to his stomach. Catching his breath, he deflected a blow from Scarlett, who had lunged forward with her sabre. "This is just me finishing a job, and it comes with a second payday."

This caught Eve off-guard. She flustered, and Edin stepped back with a smug grin on his face.

"Everyone thought your entire group had died. You even made the effort to hide yourself from the world. Have you ever considered why you're here today? Have you ever even thought about it?"

Eve failed to see why else she would be here outside of Edin's own obsession. "Of course, it's because your damn ego can't let go! I was the one who lost that day. Not you."

"If only it were that simple, Evie."

"Don't call me that!" Eve feinted and followed with a direct punch to Edin's cheekbone, imbuing her fist with Flame that sent him skidding across the floor.

As the sand dispersed, Eve and Scarlett watched as Edin sat on his legs. His weapons were scattered away from his reach. "You are such a foolish woman, Eve, and stubborn as all hell to boot."

"Tell me then, if I'm wrong, why have you done all this? Was it worth it?" Eve gestured behind her at the scattered bodies in various states of dismemberment, blood staining multiple surfaces, and at Kyrie, laid to rest in the middle of an awful battlefield.

"It doesn't matter if I think it was worth it. As far as I'm concerned, I'm done with you. Maybe she has an answer for you instead." Edin motioned with his head behind the two women.

They twirled around to see a raven black-haired woman holding Kerri in her grip, a short knife brandished beside her temple. Ellen's body was crumpled behind them on the floor.

Eve bared her teeth. "Let her go."

The woman laughed. "You don't even want to know who I am?" She gestured with the knife, waving it with a flourish in front of her face.

"Sure, I do, once you've let her go."

"Come take her from me," the woman smiled thinly, her icy-blue eyes relishing the moment, "Evie."

"Watch him," Eve told Scarlett, nodding towards Edin, "and kill him if he tries anything."

"You've got it." Scarlett made her way to Edin, positioning herself behind him with her sabre, ready to slash at any moment. Edin simply sat still with a smirk on his face.

"Right." Eve locked eyes with this new threat as she approached.

"Eve, no, stay back!" Kerri pleaded, squirming as she tried to break away from her captor, "I'll be fine!"

Eve shook her head, her pace uninterrupted, "I can't do that. I'm taking you home, too."

"Not very obedient, are you?" The woman sneered. "I was led to believe you'd rush to any order given."

"What do you mean?" Eve desperately wanted to know more, but not at the risk of Kerri remaining in her grasp.

"You're such a fool. Don't I even bear the slightest resemblance to her?" With another flourish, she waved a hand over her face. Eve felt her stomach drop. She was heavily scarred, but she did bear a resemblance to someone.

"To who?"

The smile slipped from the woman's face as her answer came out in a hiss. "My sister."

"Your sister?"

Eve was bombarded with a rush of memories flooding her mind. A voice telling her to leave. A head soaring through the air as its body fell to the ground, its long black hair soon disappearing from view. She felt her stomach twist and her blood turn cold. It was as if she was a teenager again, feeling small and inadequate.

"Ada?" Eve's anger was momentarily forgotten in the face of Meg's older sister.

"Good to see you've remembered," she cocked an eyebrow, "also, that's Adara to you." She smiled thinly, "it's been a long time, hasn't it?"

"I thought you died in the war."

"You'd have liked that, wouldn't you?" Silence stilled the air as Eve was at a loss for words. "What, you thought I joined my dear younger sister already?" she sneered, "as if I'd be dead before killing you." Adara pushed the tip of the knife into Kerri's upper cheekbone, drawing blood. Kerri sharply inhaled through her teeth.

"So, with Meg out of the picture, this is your new friend now? Your replacement sister-figure?"

"It's not like that." Eve put a hand to her chest. "I loved Meg."

"Clearly. Loved seeing her die, I bet, when you left them to their lot."

"I coul-"

"You couldn't do anything. Right, right." Adara waved her free hand dismissively before returning to her iron grip on Kerri. "But you could've died, couldn't you?"

Eve stared, unsure of how to respond.

"You could die now."

Eve's hand found its way to the vial, relieved to find it still intact, and shook her head clear. Heat coursed through her body. Her jaw tensed. No matter who stood in her way, she could not let her family be taken away from her again. "I said let her go."

"Fine." Adara withdrew the knife and rendered Kerri unconscious with a swift chop to her neck before crudely tossing her body aside. "Will you save her, or will you let her die, too?"

"I'm sorry, but I'm going to make the most out of this life that Meg and the others protected."

"You will not!" Adara screamed, "her greatest failing was in rescuing your pathetic self, and I'll ensure that you join her, where you can repent in the eternity of the afterlife!"

"No, I'm done with this. I'm leaving, so get out of my way." Eve shouted to Scarlett, "knock him out and bring him with us. He isn't getting the easy way out."

Scarlett did as requested and propped Edin onto her shoulder, stowing her sabre away in the process.

"Oh, so you want him alive? I see." Adara pulled out a small dragon pistol and fired at Edin. The bullet went through his skull. "Tough luck."

Edin slipped from Scarlett's shoulder and landed on the floor with a moist thud face down in the sand, Edin Garret lay dead. Eve looked at the body in shock. She should have been happy, but she felt nothing toward him at all. She looked back at Adara with a shade of pity in her eyes.

"Meg would hate to see what you've become, Adara."

"Meg isn't here to see what I've become, thanks to you." Adara replied nonchalantly. She didn't remove her sight from Eve as she tucked her pistol away.

"And what? Her ideals, her values, her love just gets tossed aside because she's no longer with us?" Eve felt an overwhelming rage bubble up at the disrespect of everything Meg stood for.

"She was my sister, and you took her away from me!" Adara's eyes flew wide.

"I don't want to fight you," Eve stretched a hand out towards Adara, "she'd hate this."

"Again, you're using this argument on the wrong person." Adara shrugged, and this irked Eve. "Prepare yourself for death, Eve."

"So be it," Eve drew her proffered hand back and readied her fists. She was surprised to see Adara only wielding her short knife once again, "but I'm taking you back alive."

Chapter Twenty One

"Ellen? Ellen!"

Ellen woke to the muffled, but tremendous, noise of several pairs of feet clambering down the hallway. "W-what happened? Where's Kerri?" Ellen racked her brain, trying to remember what happened before she was knocked out. She looked around frantically. "Where is she?"

Marcus gently moved her hair away and checked her head for any severe damage. "You look okay, just a little, well a lot, bruised," he offered out his hand, "can you stand?"

With a small nod, Ellen took his hand and was pulled to her feet. She was assailed by a light-headed sensation at the sudden movement, but Marcus kept her grounded.

"I'm going to help the others. Arthur and the others will get you out of here," Marcus gently pushed her away from him, towards the others, "stay close to them. We'll be back soon."

With that, Marcus turned to join Eve and Scarlett but was stopped when Ellen grabbed onto his arm.

"Please, let me come with you! I need to help Kerri." She stumbled forward as she pleaded.

Gordon grabbed her shoulder firmly and shook his head. "Trust in Marcus. If he says he'll bring them back, he'll bring them back."

Ellen only stared at Gordon. With a single resolute nod, Marcus went to join the fray at last.

*

"Look at that, another has come," Adara noted as Marcus rushed into battle, "is he also with you?" She spoke with ease as she dodged Eve's strike, the latter feeling the effects of the day's persistent battles.

"It doesn't matter to you, does it?"

"Hmm, I guess you're right!" She deflected Eve's next attack and kicked her swiftly in the ribs, causing her to drop to her knees. "You'll want to watch this."

Adara summoned Flame in one hand and blew into it, as if she was blowing a kiss. It flitted forward, gliding past Marcus as he dived to the side. It collided with the entranceway he had just emerged from, destroying their only exit.

"Wow." Marcus muttered in awe.

Eve felt a sting of terror ripple through her when she saw how effortless Adara made it look, as if it was the simplest thing in the world. "How did you do that?"

"You didn't really think that your simple Flame was all that special, did you? One Presence pales in the presence of two. It's simple maths, Evie." Adara teased, smirking down at her.

Eve was taken back to the day Meg and her teammates all died for her. She could feel that same helplessness that sucked any and all pride from her. Her body screamed at her to run, to get as far away from here as her legs could carry her.

"Come on, Eve, get up and fight!" The shout came from behind her. Scarlett's voice was unyielding and angry, "I gave you an order, and you're going to follow it through!"

Eve felt her head begin to clear, and she felt for the vial. She could not falter here. She had to get back to Amie.

Scarlett charged ahead and Marcus followed behind. They attempted to disarm Adara, but she was faster than either of them. Eve watched them as she scrambled to her feet, the exertion of the action requiring more effort than slaying a werewolf. She swore she could hear her bones creaking.

"Damn it," shouted Marcus.

Adara ducked under Scarlett's sabre swing and pulled Marcus towards her, poking his neck with the tip of her knife. "It would be almost too easy." Content with her display of control, she pushed Marcus backwards "but you're getting in the way of what I came here for."

She bent forward and blew at her hand again. Eve saw embers drift forward until they exploded. Marcus was blown backwards.

"And what about you?" Adara asked Scarlett as she shifted in close, "such a pretty Flame would match your hair, wouldn't it?" Adara winked as she twirled one of Scarlett's locks around her finger before pushing her back like she did with Marcus.

"Oh, you're dead." Scarlett hissed as she regained her footing.

Their ongoing battle was similar to a dance. Adara laughed as she dodged Scarlett's attacks, peppering in a few taunting comments at the redhead.

"You might die in her presence too, you know," Adara tapped her chin and tilted her head to the side, "in fact, I've heard so much about you and your dying sister. Amie, was it?"

"You don't know shit about my sister!" Scarlett screamed as she lunged forward.

Adara ducked and grabbed Scarlett's hand at the hilt, inching close to her face. "Word of advice? Give up on that one." She gestured with her head towards Eve. "Do so, and you have my word that your sister will be fine." Scarlett's eyes widened, and Adara continued, "she'd be alive, healthy, and conscious."

Scarlett spluttered. "Don't think for–"

"I'm going to stop you right there, Scarlett, because I want you to choose your words more carefully than those you choose to fight with," Adara narrowed her eyes at Eve before returning them back to Scarlett, "so think hard, and give me your answer in five seconds."

"What?" Scarlett yelped as Adara burned her hand. The flame seared quickly throughout her arm, up her neck, and down her torso.

"Five."

Scarlett fruitlessly attempted to yank her arm back, "let me go!"

Suddenly, an explosion of Flame appeared as Adara threw her arm out. With no fanfare at all barring a muffled yelp, Marcus was released from his Invisibility, set alight as he'd been stealthily attempting to approach her. His charred body was tossed aside with Wind as if it never had life to begin with. Eve knew he was dead.

"Too easy," chided Adara, "but the clock still ticks." She raised a hand with four fingers up, slowly lowering her pinky finger.

Scarlett angrily reached out with Spark, but Adara grabbed her hand. She shrieked in agony as it burned black.

"Three. What a waste of time." Adara looked at Scarlett's injured hand, "don't worry, you won't have to worry about anything at all in a couple of seconds."

"No!" With incredible speed, Eve propelled herself forward and barrelled into Adara with reckless abandon. They tumbled several feet across the floor.

Scarlett stepped back, clutching her hand, watching it flicker with weak electricity. It failed to respond, injured beyond help. Her lips twisted downwards. A part of her would be forever lost.

"If your grief is with me, then leave them the hell alone!" Eve punched down, but Adara narrowly moved her head away just in time to avoid it.

"If you wanted a say, then you should have saved Meg!" Adara shouted back, her sinister playful nature disappearing as she tried to kick Eve off of her.

"Don't think it'll be so easy!" Eve used the momentum from Adara's kick and dropped down with a knee to Adara's stomach.

With an "oof!" Adara's eyes flew wide open, before she bared her teeth and spoke with a slightly more rattled voice. "You aren't winning this fight, no matter how hard you try, Evie."

"Shut up!" Eve grabbed her face in both hands. She grasped tightly, but her Flame struggled to generate enough heat. Her heart dropped. She was too tired to summon the heat needed to defend herself against Adara.

Adara laughed, "this is too good. Don't worry, I'll give you all the rest you need!" She grabbed Eve's face with both hands and lifted herself up closer so that they were only inches away from each other, "now die."

Eve tried to peel her hands away but Adara dug her nails in, gouging them deeper the more she tried to resist. She had an iron grip that Eve could not free herself from.

"Your eyes are growing bloodshot, Evie." Adara teased.

Eve squeezed her eyes shut, the pain overwhelming her. It felt as if her head would split open, if it did not melt first.

The heat suddenly came to a stop. Adara's grip had slackened. She fell backwards, and Eve fell too, exhausted, holding her head.

"Eve," Scarlett called out breathlessly without looking away from Adara, her good hand stretched out and crackling, "please tell me the vial's okay."

Eve rushed in a panic to locate the pocket where the vial was held. She sighed in relief after confirming its safety. "Yeah. Yeah it's okay."

The relief was visible on Scarlett's face and in her voice. "That Spark won't keep that one down for long, so take Kerri and go. If you lose that vial, then we have no chance of helping Amie. Don't forget why we came here."

"What will you do?" Eve asked as she began to pick up Kerri.

"I'll keep her down, for as long as it takes."

Eve's eyes met Scarlett's, and she nodded. She was far too exhausted to be much help in any battle now anyway. Her inability to summon Presence without pushing herself past her limit was proof of that. She hated to admit it, but she would only get in the way.

Eve walked past Scarlett who gave her a small smile. Eve was unable to support Kerri, and had to drag her away from the battlefield by holding her underneath her armpits. As she passed the blocked entryway, she heard muffled voices and the scraping and crumbling of rock.

"Drake? Is that you?" Eve took her best guess at the gruff voice as it heaved with effort.

She felt her heart soar at his response. "Yeah! Yeah, don't worry, we'll have you on this side in no time! Barron, can you just, you know, knock through this?"

"Yes yes, stand aside!"

"Wait!" Clarissa interjected. "The structural integrity has already suffered too much, and I don't wish to be buried down here. I can remove them much more safely with Wind."

"Hmm, okay, Eve?" Drake's voice called from across the debris, "can you wait a moment while we move this? Are you safe?"

"Yeah, we're—" Eve was cut off as the air around her suddenly changed.

She could hear a faint whooshing sound before her throat tightened as the oxygen was cut off from her. She grabbed at her throat as she felt her windpipes constrict, turning to see Adara reaching out from the floor, along with a knife barrelling towards her.

Scarlett charged over, shooting Spark at Adara, but it was blocked by a wall of Flame. The sand at her feet was unsettled and swirled around the floor as she turned on her heel, ready to intercept. She sliced the air in front of her the moment she was turned around, but with a wide smile Adara guided the knife across the top of Scarlett's sabre, flecks of light spitting as it glided along it before it slid up and into Scarlett's throat.

Eve mustered her remaining strength to look up and see the blood seeping through Scarlett's wound. Her eyes were wide in shock. Eve knew. She knew that Scarlett had really believed she was going to win. Adara smiled in the background, her breathing ragged and her face covered in fresh sweat. She stared directly at Eve, appearing to relish in her pain.

Scarlett removed the knife with her good hand, blood spurting out with it, and harnessed as much Spark as she could into it before throwing the imbued knife to the floor where Adara crawled. Adara attempted to block it with Flame, but the knife broke through and exploded on impact. In an instant, the surrounding structures began to give way. The hold on Eve was finally released, and she rushed to her feet, gasping for air. She rushed to Scarlett's side, attempting to compress the wound with her hands.

Behind them, Barron charged through the rock, his axe raised. He stopped in his tracks when he saw Scarlett covered in blood, attempting to tear Eve's hands from her throat.

Drake followed after Barron. When he saw Scarlett, his face crumpled and his shoulders sagged. It was almost as if his soul had been retrieved from his body. "Scarlett, no."

Scarlett stroked the top of Eve's hand. With little more than a guttural noise, she shocked Eve into letting go, and pushed her backwards into Barron's arms. She pointed at Kerri, who was lifted with Wind by Clarissa. "P-please go." Scarlett made eye contact with Eve, who was trying to tear herself away from Barron's firm grip.

She screamed herself hoarse as she was dragged away. If she was taken away now, this would be the final time she would see Scarlett.

Scarlett turned her tired gaze onto Drake, and smiled softly. The blood had turned her front red. She shot a tiny Spark at him. The last time she would make his heart flutter. With the last of her strength, Scarlett enveloped her body with light. She summoned a thunderbolt-sized Spark, which travelled through the ceiling and directly into herself, causing a rapturous explosion. The impact caused Ilas Arena to collapse in on itself.

Everyone was safely in one of the entrances Clarissa had blown them all out of harm's way moments before.

Drake scurried to his feet. He hardly knew what had happened. "Scarlett!" He pounded on the rock, which glowed slightly red with heat, "Scarlett, please! Please..." He fell to his knees and attempted to dig through the barricade with his hands.

Eve watched from the floor unable to form a proper sentence, her mouth hung open. Clarissa and Barron looked at each other sadly.

Barron pulled Eve to her feet and handed her his axe, "use this to help yourself walk."

Eve took it wordlessly, leaning onto it without almost all of her weight. She stared at the floor, unable to process all that had happened.

"Drake." Clarissa said softly, placing a hand on his shoulder, "we have to go."

"But Clarissa, Scarlett, s-she's still in there!" Drake looked up, his eyes filled with tears, as he clumsily grabbed Clarissa's arm and pointed at the rubble.

Clarissa knelt down and laid her hand over his, her eyes wet. "Drake, Amie's waiting for us."

Drake stared at Clarissa in silence before he broke down. His cries echoed throughout the corridor as Clarissa held him close.

After a few minutes, Drake stood up. He placed his hand on the largest rock, and said something that Eve did not catch before turning away.

"Let's go see Amie," he said, doing his best to put strength into his voice, "we've made her wait too long as it is."

*

On the surface, Ilas was in disarray. The crystal tower that housed Ilas Arena was severely damaged. Scarlett's last act had pierced a large hole through the ceiling and through each floor below it. The surrounding area was clustered with curious on-lookers, eyeing up the remaining members of the Marauders of Light and Rising Dawn as they left, bloodied, bruised, and broken.

Ellen, Gordon, and Arthur were all that was left of Rising Dawn.

"You might die in her presence too, you know." Adara's words echoed in Eve's head. The guilt threatened to crush her from within. It flipped her stomach over as a darkness grabbed at her chest. She vomited near a group of frightened bystanders. Although she had Barron's axe for support, it slipped from underneath her, and she collapsed onto the floor.

Before she lost consciousness, she hoped to wake up to this having been simply a terrible nightmare.

Chapter Twenty Two

Writing seemed to help Eve, so I figured it would be good to do it again for myself, considering all that has happened. It's been eleven days since we got back from Ilas. Thankfully, it was easy to leave with Edin's 'absence', and the authorities either didn't know about, or didn't want to admit to, Ilas Arena being a thing, so they weren't able to keep us.

They couldn't prove the damage to the tower was caused by us. we just pretended that we were caught in the blast, as innocent bystanders, so I guess we got lucky or something?

I thought that once this was over, everything would feel different. I don't know how. Maybe people would be happier. Maybe there would be less crime on the streets. That we'd all come home and celebrate. All of us together. I don't like thinking about how many of us died, how close to death I was myself. That I never would have even remembered my last conversation with my father, what he might have said to me. It's been so long since I've heard his voice, but I've not wanted to worry him. I'll make sure to visit him soon.

Drake's been visiting a lot. I know he wants to make sure that I'm okay, but I think that he's finding it difficult to be alone at the moment. He's manned the stall every day, with Clarissa and Barron helping out, just keeping himself busy.

I don't know what to feel, or what to think, but I do know something. I miss you, Eve. I miss you, Scarlett.

Kerri closed the book, placed the pen in its holder, and sighed. She was back home in Thous, although she had been living alone since returning. Eve had collapsed on the way home, and had been staying in the clinic since. Drake had been with Kerri most hours of the day. They were both doing okay, although she had a few new scars etched into her skin.

She approached her bedroom window and looked out onto the street below. It was busy, bustling with people going about their daily lives, laughing, talking, some looking exasperated; all blissfully unaware of what happened in Ilas.

Maybe, just maybe, something seemed a little bit dimmer now in Thous. To Kerri, she felt that Thous had lost someone irreplaceable, that helped to make the city what it was. She tore herself away from the windowsill just in time to hear the doorbell ring.

She peeked back through the windowsill, and with an audible gasp, rushed down the stairs and threw the door wide open. "Amie! You're back?!"

"Indeed I am!" Amie puffed out her chest, looking proud, but then tilted her head to the side and scratched her cheek. "Well, to me, it doesn't feel like I've been gone at all."

"I guess I wouldn't know what that must feel like" Kerri stood back and invited her in, "welcome to our home."

"I was told that you and Eve both lived here, together." She looked around the hallway, softly smiling, "you're quite the lucky lady."

Kerri felt embarrassed. "So when did you, uh, wake up?" She asked, uncertain of her choice of words. "Is that the way to put it?"

"I mean, I guess! I've been told that I was a real sleeping beauty!" Amie laughed, but she faltered when she saw that Kerri was not laughing along with her. "Look, I'm not exactly supposed to be here, you know." She intertwined her fingers in front of her chest. "I actually only woke up today. Maybe not even an hour ago."

Kerri felt herself freeze for a moment. "What? You should be resting!"

"I've rested enough!" Amie raised her voice, an almost imperceptible edge to it, "apparently, for way too long."

She breathed deeply, composing herself once more, "I'm sorry, I just don't know what's happened in the time I've been away. I came here because I had a note from Eve saying that when I 'wake up', this is the address I should go to." Amie glanced around, and poked her head "where is she?"

Kerri looked at Amie, feeling pity for the younger redhead, "can I make you a tea or coffee?"

"And, well, that brings us to now." Kerri trailed off. She had recapped everything from when Amie fell into her Presence-fuelled coma, all the way up to the events of Ilas Arena, and what they had been doing since. Which was, admittedly, very little.

Amie sat still, her eyes glazed over and her hand over her mouth, staring a hole through the floor. She would sometimes shake her head, but was otherwise despondent. Kerri worried about her, given that she was still recovering. Was it not right to share that information just yet?

"Amie?" She did not respond, and Kerri tentatively got to her feet. "Amie, I'm going to light a fire. It's a little cold now, don't you think?" She wrapped her arms around herself, and felt the air she was breathing agitate her nose.

She jolted when Amie spoke to her. "That won't work."

"W-what do you mean?" Kerri shivered as she turned back to look at her. Amie was staring intently at her. Her brows knitted together, and despite the cold, her nose and cheeks were red.

"It won't work because it's me." She grabbed the coffee cup in front of her, and it instantly froze over. "That's why you're cold, and I'm not."

Kerri shivered again. It was far colder inside than it could possibly be outside. Her breath hung in front of her, and a light layer of frost crept along the windows despite the sunlight beaming down. One person walked by wiping sweat from his forehead.

"Amie, are you okay?" Kerri attempted to grab her hand despite the cold, biting down on her lip in an attempt to bear her friend's far below sub-zero temperatures.

"Am I okay? Am I okay?" Amie repeated the words to herself before she turned to Kerri with tears in her eyes, "h-how could I be okay? My sister died over a week ago and I've only just found out!" She slammed her mug against the table. It shattered on impact, making Kerri jump. "It isn't fair!" Amie's tears were falling thick and fast, and she wailed in grief. "I-I didn't even get to say goodbye!" She sobbed loudly, grabbing Kerri tight, clutching at her clothes and arms. Her cold slightly dissipated as she cried.

They sat like that for a long while, with Kerri stroking Amie's hair, as Amie grieved the loss of her sister and her closest friend.

*

Amie stifled a yawn as she woke up. She looked up at a ceiling that was unfamiliar to her. She felt a little lightheaded, as if she had woken up from a restless nap.

"Wow, I know the cold doesn't bother me much, but it's a bit too chilly in here, isn't it?"

She wrapped her arms around herself, but nobody responded to her question. The endless silence chilled her more than any cold could. She squeezed her eyes shut and rubbed her head, trying to recall what happened. As she made an effort to get onto her feet, she stumbled, only preventing herself from falling by frantically grabbing at some nearby shelving. She glanced over an array of medicine bottles and paperwork. Her head throbbed.

Amie dropped herself back down on the edge of the bed and looked around. It was plain and sterile, entirely unlike her own room. A sharp pain split through her head again. "Of course, the forest fire."

Massaging her temples, she caught a glimpse of herself in the reflection of the window, a blue tinge still spread across her face and the tips of her hair. As she touched her face, the blue receded, revealing pale skin and red hair.

She wondered if Eve, Scarlett and the others had been visiting her, or if it had been long enough to require visitors at all. She half expected her sister to come into the room. She looked at the door, but it remained closed. She absent-mindedly kicked her feet as she waited, too small to reach the floor whilst sitting on the bed.

Looking at the table beside her, she noticed an empty vial and an envelope on the bedside table addressed with her name.

"To me, huh?"

She recognised Eve's scratchy handwriting immediately. A fluttering sensation tickled her chest.

Amie,

If you're reading this, then good. I'm happy because that means you're back with us.

If we're not with you right now, and if you've been told by the doctors that you're good to leave, then please come to the address written on the back. It's mine and Kerri's home. We'll be there waiting for you.

Eve.

Amie flipped the paper over and back again, but that was all that was written. As she peeked her head into the doorway, she figured that the doctors not knowing would not be that bad of an idea. She laughed as she re-read the letter again and headed off to Eve and Kerri's home to surprise them.

*

Kerri escorted Amie back to the clinic later that evening where Amie, wordlessly, allowed herself to be taken back to her room. Kerri was thanked for bringing her back by frantic staff, but as she went to ask about Eve, the receptionist shook her head, with a small "sorry". Each receptionist was used to Kerri asking about Eve now. She walked away disappointed each time.

"Hopefully we'll have better news for you tomorrow." The receptionist smiled kindly at Kerri.

"Yes, I hope so too." She gently rapped her knuckles on the desk dejectedly before leaving the clinic.

*

Unable to sleep, Amie stared at the ceiling of her room. She only now realised how cold it was due to the mist her breathing created. Generally, this did not bother her, but it made her feel isolated. Was this how her visitors had felt? Scattered across her bed and bedside table were several letters from Eve, Scarlett, and the others who had been wishing her well. She pulled one out and read it again. She had read it so many times that she did not even need to see the words to know them now, but ached to see that handwriting again.

Hey sis,

Yeah yeah, I know "sis" is your thing, but let me have it for once. You're my little sister, after all.

I wonder if you're mad at me. That, somewhere deep within your sleep, you hold my stupid actions against me.

You'd be right to do so. It's my fault you're in this position. What was I even thinking, using Spark so carelessly in a forest? I'm so, so sorry, Amie.

Amie's hand shook and crinkled the paper. This was the very last letter from Scarlett, and it was filled with her self-doubts and guilt.

I promise that I'll make this up to you one day, so I'll keep this short and sweet. I can tell you everything in person later.

There's a small smiley face drawn at the end of the line, winking at her.

We have a lead, so we'll be back soon. Next time I see you, you'll be with us again. I can't wait!

I love you,
Your sis, Scarlett.

Scarlett's scratchy signature was at the bottom, as familiar to Amie as her own.

"Of course, I don't blame you, sis." Amie smiled weakly and wiped a few stray tears from her eyes. With a sigh, she pushed herself up from her bed and dangled her legs off of the edge. She stared at the doorway to the corridor. What room was Eve in again? She had overheard Kerri mention it briefly to one of the staff that Eve was brought here after Ilas Arena. She made sure to repeat it in her head, not wanting to forget.

Unable to contain her curiosity, and unwilling to sleep any longer, Amie slipped into her clinic slippers and sneaked into the corridor. The hallway was dark and dimly lit. Amie took soft, slow steps as she looked through the circular windows inset into the doors, hoping to catch a glimpse of her neighbours. A small curtain was usually drawn over it outside of visiting hours, allowing the patients their privacy. If Amie remembered correctly, Eve was almost directly above her room.

Amie crept up the stairs, praying that they did not creak loudly. She peeked around the corners leading into each corridor, ensuring they were empty before she continued on. Her heart beat faster as she neared the room that she believed Eve to be in. She had no idea what she wanted to say to her. She only knew that she wanted to see Eve.

"Here we are." Amie peered at the number plate, but its gold sheen had no nearby light source strong enough to reflect off of it. It was roughly where she had worked out the room to be though, so she shrugged and gently pulled on the door handle. It did not budge. "Oh, darn it, I should've known it would be locked."

Instead of turning away, Amie scanned the hallway to ensure that the coast was clear, and fashioned a tiny lock pick made out of ice. After a few short moments, she heard a satisfying click, and opened the door with ease. Scarlett had taught her how to pick lock a long time ago, and Amie offered a silent thank you to her.

She entered the room and closed the door softly behind her, gulping several deep breaths to calm down. She felt frazzled, as if her emotions were going haywire. She clenched her eyes shut, focusing only on her breathing, until she felt that she could open them. Ahead of her was a room that looked remarkably similar to the one she was staying in. She approached the curtain drawn across Eve's bed and pulled it back with care so as to not disturb her.any trepidation or anxiety she had melted away upon seeing Eve's restful face.

Her bottom lip was slightly swollen. Several fading, but still noticeable, bruises lined her jaw, cheeks and eyebrows. Cuts and scars jutted across her face. Beyond all of this, she looked like she was sleeping soundly, and at peace.

Amie felt a rush of tears threaten to spill over. She sat down beside the bed and watched Eve as she slept, relishing in the feeling of normality that seeing Eve brought to her.Still feeling as alert as she did when she had decided to embark on her midnight rendezvous, Amie alternated between holding Eve's hand, pacing around the room, and creating objects with her Presence before melting them again. As she was creating a top hat for a miniature snowman, she looked over to see Eve watching her with sleepy eyes. The snowman's head rolled off, and Amie melted it in a hurry, feeling embarrassed at being watched.

"Ah," Eve's voice was weak, "I liked that one the most."

"How long have you been watching?" Amie questioned.

"Um," Eve looked toward the ceiling, squinting in thought. "Since the swan?"

"Welcome back, you." Amie put on a small smile.

"Yeah, you too." Eve grunted with exertion as she tried to sit up, only to collapse back into her pillow, "ouch."

"Take it easy, I'm sure you look worse than you feel."

"Well, after that comment, I'm not sure that's true."

Amie laughed softly. She glanced at Eve, a variety of emotions festering within her. Anger, disgust, and betrayal tainted feelings of love, care, and joy. She did not know which ones were prevailing. They mixed together in a concoction that she felt allergic to.

"I need to ask you some–"

"I'm so sorry!" Eve wailed from her pillow, slightly muffled without the strength to turn onto her back again, "I'm so, so sorry."

A sharp pain pierced Amie's chest. heartache not just for her sister, but for Eve, too. Any doubts towards Eve she was holding onto faded to nothing, replaced by a want to comfort her.

"Thank you for bringing the vial back. I almost feel as good as new!" Amie flexed her arms to show how healthy she was now, but stopped when she saw Eve's face. Raw grief and sorrow contorted her features, despite some of her face being sunken into her pillow. "Eve. It's okay. I don't blame you, not one bit," she stroked Eve's hair, which was now longer than she had ever seen it, "I know that Scarlett would have exhausted every possible avenue before doing what she did. At least she died doing what she did best."

"What's that?" Eve's weary eyes searched Amie's face for an answer.

"She died protecting those she loved."

The next few days flew by. Both Eve and Amie were visited by not only their teammates, but Eric, William, and Ellen and Arthur. Amie was usually found in Eve's room, as the latter was still recuperating, whereas Amie was as fit as a fiddle. Due to how severe her case was, she was being monitored for a few more days before being free to go.

One evening, the two were playing a simple game of Blackjack in Eve's room. Amie hit for another card, and bust, again, with a card total of twenty-six.

"Darn it, the deck hates me." Amie pouted.

Eve smiled, "sure, it's not you hitting when you've already got good cards."

"Well, I don't know what you have!"

They both laughed when Eve revealed her cards total to only be seventeen, two lower than Amie's original nineteen.

"Well, isn't that nice!" Amie slapped another card on top of Eve's, bringing the total to twenty-three, "now you're bust, too." She huffed playfully as she collected the cards.

Eve rolled her eyes and grinned, "let's play again."

Amie reshuffled the deck and began dealing the cards, leading to another two losses in Eve's favour.

"Argh, this is so frustrating!" Amie tugged at the curls in her hair, looking at her four cards. Another bust.

"Do you want to stop playing?"

"No, I want to win! J-just let me win already, Eve!" Amie pleaded, exasperated.

"Just stop hitting!"

"But my cards suck! It's frustrating!"

"Gah, you're frustrating!"

Amie sighed loudly as she collected the cards again, but smiled at Eve as she asked, "one more game?"

Eve looked at her softly. "Sure, one more game."

Praying for a victory, Amie shuffled and dealt the cards once more. She felt incredible relief when, finally, her two starting cards were an ace and a ten. A perfect twenty-one.

"Blackjack!"

Eve stared at her with wide eyes, her eyebrows creased and her mouth slightly open. "You don't have to actually say Blackjack, you know."

"Oh," feeling her face grow warm, Amie soldiered on, "well, it's fun, so boo you." She stuck her tongue out, and Eve laughed.

Amie was beginning to put the cards away when she suddenly stopped and looked up. "Hey, Eve?"

"Mhm?"

"I love you."

Eve's jaw went slack and she stared wordlessly at Amie. The candlelight flickered across her face.

Amie met her eyes, "I said I love you."

The clock ticked, counting each second. Eve looked as if her soul had left her body. Finally, her senses seemed to come back to her, and she responded. "I- I love you too."

Amie blushed, relief spreading through her chest. "I already knew that, you know."

"What? How?" Eve's jaw dropped. It was as if Amie had chilled her throughout her body.

"I guess 'know' is a strong word, but I feel like you've said it to me before? But I really think I'd remember that…"

Eve thought back too. A memory flashed across her mind, and she felt her face grow warm. "Ah, you're right, I did, but you weren't conscious, were you?"

"Oooh, that must have been hard for you!" Amie teased Eve, whose eyes narrowed as she looked away, her face growing red.

"Well, you seemed to say it with such ease." Eve pouted. Amie found it cute.

"I promised myself that if I won at Blackjack tonight, I would tell you." Amie thought, biting the tip of her thumb, "well, it did take longer than expected."

"Why Blackjack? You don't usually leave your fate to the cards, do you?" Eve teased.

"No, I don't." Amie blushed and she averted her eyes, "I just needed to give myself a little push."

"Well, I'm happy I let you win." Eve said, dropping back onto her pillow.

"You let me win?! I won on the deal!" Amie's voice became shrill, incredulous at Eve's claim.

One of the nurses walking by put her finger to her lips through the window. Eve laughed loudly and the two of them talked long, long into the night.

Chapter Twenty Three

"Home sweet home!" A little over a week later, Eve threw the door open to her shared home with Kerri, who ran down the stairs and leapt into her arms at the door.

"Welcome home!" She stepped back, beaming from ear to ear, giving room for Eve to walk inside, "your room is just as you left it."

"Well, I would hope so. I wasn't gone that long!" Eve grabbed Kerri by the shoulders, looking deep into her face, "but you look so different."

"I do?" Kerri tugged on her hair, one blonde curl bouncing back into place as she released it, "I'm not so sure about looks, but I'm sure I could kick your ass now." She grinned, a grin that Eve had sorely missed.

Eve stretched her arms. "Sure you could," she returned the smile, "I did want to talk to you, but I guess it can wait until I've laid you out flat."

Jogging up the stairs, Eve yelled at Kerri over her shoulder, telling her to prepare as if it was a real battle.

Kerri's armour, repaired by Eric, gleamed in the early sunlight, the lilac hues reminding Eve of lavender. "I like the new look."

"Thanks," Kerri pounded her fist against her chest plate, "I think I've had enough of aqua for a long time."

Eve nodded, sharing the sentiment. "This is an important test for you, Kerri," She readied her wooden practice sword, "give it all you've got!"

Kerri nodded, and with a "right!", she charged into battle with her wooden sword and shield.

Kerri darted to the side and summoned an Illusion, but Eve saw ahead and parried Kerri's true form. She followed up with a light tap to her stomach. "You shimmer lightly when you use Illusion. You'll want to keep an eye on that."

"I shimmer? I had no idea."

Taking advantage of Kerri's shock, Eve pushed her backwards, "I'm not your friend right now," Eve shouted, "I'm your enemy, looking to kill you!"

Eve summoned a tiny ball of Flame and tossed it at Kerri, who dived out of the way. It erupted a few metres past her, causing Kerri's hair to whoosh forward as she rooted herself to the ground and raised her shield in front of her face. That tiny ball packed a surprising amount of punch.

"Wow, you aren't playing around!" Kerri leaned back on to her heel and charged forward once more, her shield steadfast in front of her.

Eve rolled out of the way of Kerri's shield thrust, only to see the shield flying directly at her just as she'd steadied herself. Without the momentum to move out of the way quick enough, she allowed the shield to land a successful hit on her stomach. "Well, I do like that move a lot, but-" Eve tossed the shield far behind her, "now you're without your shield."

She parried Kerri's follow-up sword slash, causing her to become unbalanced, and kicked the younger woman in the back.

"Don't be discouraged, you've improved a hell of a lot."

"Yeah, I know that, but still, it's so frustrating." Kerri gritted her teeth, "why can't I have a Presence good for battle, too?"

"I don't know what Edin and Adara did to get their hands on two Presences, but whatever they did, it'sa abnormal. Be proud of your Presence. You don't see one like Illusion every day, and when you master it, you'll be terrifying for anyone to fight against."

"You're right," Kerri walked over to collect her shield, "can we go again?"

"Sure thing. You won't disappoint!"

The two fought another two rounds, with Kerri losing both, but she managed to get in successful hits each time, keeping Eve on her toes despite her wealth of experience.

"You really have improved. It's crazy to think that you had no fight experience at all only a year ago." Eve praised between ragged breaths.

"Thanks," Kerri plopped to the ground, her head swung back as sweat poured down her face and dampened her hair, "but I know I can do better."

"I agree, and you will, every day," the sunset soaked them both in orange, their sweat glistening, "with your own power, now."

"What do you mean?"

Eve watched the sunset for a moment before replying, "I'm leaving, Kerri," She met Kerri's eyes, watching the younger woman's aqua eyes widen in shock, "I never planned to stay here forever, and with everything that's happened. I think I just need to find a new home, away from Thous." Eve gestured towards the field and the setting sun, feeling a slight tinge of nostalgia for the place she was able to call home for a small time.

Kerri sighed deeply, looking towards the sky as she mulled over Eve's statement. "I don't want you to go."

"Sorry, kiddo, but I think I've had my fill of this life." Eve patted her on the shoulder, squeezing in comfort as she felt the younger woman shaking slightly.

"Scarlett's letter though, she wanted you to be leader if anything were to happen to her, Eve!"

"Scarlett would understand. She would want Amie and I to be happy," Eve searched Kerri's face and felt a warmth spread through her chest as she did, "we just want a normal life, away from all of this. I think that's all I've ever wanted."

Kerri frowned and stared at the ground again. She sniffed, and spoke up in a meek voice. "Promise you'll visit, okay?"

"Of course. Anytime." Kerri continued to stare at the floor, and Eve saw her struggle to smile, "and be a good co-leader to Drake, okay?"

"Huh?" Again, Kerri's eyes and mouth went wide with surprise.

"I've already spoken with him, but Drake has taken on the role of leader now, and with Amie also leaving, we thought it would be best that you take her position," Eve smiled, "will you do it?"

Kerri sniffed and wiped her eyes, determined to look Eve in the eyes. "If you think it's a good idea, then of course I will."

"Have more confidence in yourself."

Kerri took a deep breath and shouted, "of course I will!"

A bird that was roaming nearby, pecking at the ground, took flight after this startling shout.

Satisfied, Eve patted the ground then pulled herself up, "come on then, let's get some food, and you can then help me pack."

The two left for their usual hang-out spot, Humbone's Tavern, and saw Drake and Ellen waving at them at the entrance.

"Good to see you, good to see you!" Ellen's cheerful voice rang out. She grinned heartily and pulled the two women into a hug.

With a slap on the back, Drake greeted them with a "good to see ya," and then led them towards a table where everyone else already had a drink in hand, talking merrily among themselves.

"Both guilds have to make their numbers up with so many gone, and so many leaving…" Ellen drifted off, not needing to elaborate, and cast a bittersweet eye over Eve and Amie, "so we thought we'd come together just join as one big group instead!"

Eve looked around at the members of the newly formed guild of Rising Light, led by Drake, who was now supported by both Kerri and Ellen as his co-leaders. Clarissa, Barron, and Arthur made up the rest of the numbers. Ellen explained that Gordon had left after hearing their plans to form a new party. He apparently held a grudge against the Marauders of Light for the loss of Marcus and Kyrie.

"Well, I can't say I entirely fault him." Eve placed her drink down, watching it as it rippled, feeling a familiar sense of failure returning to her.

"No, no, it wasn't your fault," Ellen placed a sympathetic hand on Eve's forearm, "we all agreed to join you, and we all knew the risks. You kept no secrets from us, it was just…" she drew circles on the table with her finger, "it was a worst-case scenario come to life."

"She's right," chimed Arthur, "and neither of us blame a single one of you."

"Thank you for saying that," replied Eve, "it means a lot."

Arthur nodded, taking a sip from his stein.

"But you know, Arthur, there's one thing that's been bugging me."

"Oh? And that is?"

"What is your Presence?"

"Oh!" Arthur laughed loudly, "of course, you haven't been told," he waved his hand as if it was an unimportant question, "I don't have a Presence."

"What?" This claim stunned Eve, "there's no way you don't have a Presence. How is that possible?"

Arthur shrugged in response, "I have no idea. Perhaps I grew out of it." He chuckled, though a faint trace of frustration furrowed his eyebrows.

"I'm sorry for prying."

"Not at all. it just means I have to train even harder to prove my worth to Rising Dawn." He coughed and corrected himself, "I mean, the Rising Light."

"Hear, hear!" roared Barron, his stein held high in the air, "there will always be a home here for a fighter like you, Arthur."

The younger man blushed at Barron's straight-forward praise, and took a sip from his own stein to hide his embarrassment.

Barron shifted his gaze over to Eve and Amie, who were sitting side by side, smiling, "as there will always be a home for you both with us, too."

They smiled at each other before raising their own steins, "hear, hear!"

Epilogue

Sunlight beamed in through in-between the yellow curtains, bringing warmth into the small cottage. It dappled across the floors and walls, across a wooden chair with a red cushion resting upon it and a jacket neatly hung beside a cupboard. A painting on the wall was grinning, as if the two women inside were glowing. Dust particles radiated as they floated by, and the sound of pen on paper created a rhythmic, scratching sound. A gentle breeze made its way through the open window, jingling a blue wind chime as it travelled through. Greenery and a clear blue sky spread out as far as the eye could see. In their garden were meadow sweet, lavender, lilies, and other plants that they cared for together. Eve smiled. Her foot tapped against the small rug on the floor, the soft thudding accompanying her thoughts as she wrote.

It's been a while since I last saw them, but I hear about them often from passing travellers, or from my friends themselves. They seem to be achieving great things as Rising Light, and I'm so, so proud of them.

For me? I finally have what I've always wanted. A home. Someone to be there when I get back, and to be happy when I leave my things at the door. A real reason to see the next day instead of just going through the motions. Someone who accepts me for all that I am.

Things can sometimes be difficult, and the nightmares don't cease, but I don't have to face them alone anymore. I think I've realised this for a while now, but

A warm pair of thin arms crossed across Eve's chest, and she felt Amie's head rest on top of her own, red curls tickling her cheeks.

"Oh!" Amie exclaimed, quickly pulling away and covering her eyes with her hands, "I didn't see anything, sorry! I just wanted to check up on you."

"Oh no, don't worry about it. I'm just finishing now."

"Food's ready. Will I see you in a second?" Despite what she said, Amie still had her eyes covered as she mimed looking anywhere else other than in front of her.

Eve watched for a moment and laughed, "yes, you'll see me outside in a second."

Amie smiled widely, removed her hands, and bent over to kiss Eve. Her footsteps quietly padded away and she closed the door behind her. Eve's compact scythe hung behind it, bathed in sunlight. A layer of dust rested upon it.

I'm truly happy with this life I've been given.

Eve.

And finally, thanks to you all, too, for reading this far, and for picking up Eve in the first place.

Acknowledgements

I started writing The Forging of Eve (originally known as The Presence of Eve) roughly seven years ago. My life has changed a lot since then, and so has Eve. Kerri was never in my original draft, and large chunks of the book were removed and rewritten, but I feel like I've accomplished what I set out to do. I wanted to create a coming-of-age story for adults. The cast is primarily in their late 20s to late 30s, and this theme is almost exclusively reserved for teenagers and young adults. If you're reading this as an adult, you might still be finding your way in this world too, and that's okay. There are no guidelines or rulebooks on how to live, and I wanted to write something that would resonate with people who still aren't sure about what they want to do, or if they're doing everything they can be.

I also wanted to tackle mental health in a fantasy setting. I appreciate that the conversation around mental health has grown a lot in recent years, and I've suffered in many ways due to my own mental health. I wanted someone strong and independent like Eve to still be able to yearn for the contact of others, and to have her own personal issues, regardless of how incredible and awe-inspiring she is viewed as by others. Everyone's fighting their own battles, even if that isn't obvious at a glance.

Lastly, I've grown up around women, and reading books, watching shows, and playing games that feature strong women. I generally find myself identifying more with female characters more so than male characters, and I think this is because they're usually depicted as more empathetic, and their stories are often more grounded and personal. Cinderella, Princess Garnet, Aerith Gainsborough, Padmé Amidala, Samus Aran, and Sailor Moon are a few characters who I've grown up with and have been inspired by. I specifically wanted to work with women on The Forging of Eve, to ensure that it felt authentic and not like "men writing women", and honestly this is something that still greatly worries me even as I write this. I hope I've created engaging and relatable characters for everyone to enjoy, and I hope they simply entertain you or help you through tough times.

I am forever thankful to Zoe Heseltine for publishing this book (and I hope it acts as a great debut for Tiger Lily Publishing Co.) and Shannon Robinson for being a fantastic editor who has been crucial to shaping up Eve's and Kerri's stories. I dread to think how this book would have turned out if not for their help and expertise, but I'm sure you would not have made it this far into the book if it was in its original state. There are members of the team I've never met, but I know they've worked hard to bring this to life, and I'm incredibly grateful for their time and effort too.

I couldn't have done this without my better half, Fong, who has supported me every step of the way, not only in The Forging of Eve, but in everything I do. I'm a better person for knowing her, and my experiences with her have in turn allowed me to write better and to understand more. You've kept me going through the hardest times, and I'm glad that Eve has someone to bring sunshine into their life too.

I also thought of my nan, who passed away several years ago, a lot when writing this book. She loved reading, and although I think Eve wasn't something she would have usually read, I know she would have sung its highest praises to everyone she knew. She was one of the strongest role models I'll ever know. She and my grandad both always told me that I'd find my way, and they were right. I couldn't thank them enough.

I could never forget my friend, Amanda, who was the first person to read this back to front. She's never shied away from telling me how much she loved some bits and what parts needed more work, and I'm happy that these characters have stayed with her for so long. Her support was a huge motivator for me, and she would always be there to talk to when I needed her advice.

About The Author

Mitchell Lineham (he/they) lives in the United Kingdom where he has worked as a journalist and community manager in the video games and anime industries, before making the move to telecommunications, where he's still interested in all things community and DE&I. He posts short stories on his blog, and writes about video games and independent creators. He owns more mugs than he could possibly drink from. The Forging of Eve is his debut novel.

Printed in Great Britain
by Amazon

48416410R00179